D1107303

Mark Lawrence Requa

Both the scene and the subject matter of "Grubstake" are known at first hand by its author. Born in Virginia City, Nevada, he developed the Nevada Consolidated Copper Company, became a consulting engineer in the Bureau of Mines, built the Nevada Northern Railway, was assistant to Herbert Hoover when the former President was Food Administrator. He was the head of the oil division of the United States Fuel Administration, and later chairman of the government's committee on the standardization of petroleum specifications. He is a former vice-president of the American Institute of Mining and Metallurgical Engineers. He now lives at Santa Barbara.

GRUBSTAKE

GRUBSTAKE

A Story of Early Mining Days in Nevada Time—1874

By
Mark L. Requa

NEW YORK
CHARLES SCRIBNER'S SONS
1933

Printed in the United States of America

A

TO

HERBERT HOOVER

TO YOU I DEDICATE THIS BOOK WITH DEEPEST ADMIRATION FOR YOUR SERVICES TO YOUR COUNTRY AND TO MANKIND. IF THESE PAGES HAVE SERVED TO DIVERT, MOMENTARILY, YOUR MIND FROM THE CARES OF STATE, AND BRING BACK TO YOU MEMORIES OF THE DAYS WHEN YOU PACKED A TRANSIT AND RAN A PLANE-TABLE, I SHALL BE CONTENT

Introduction

As I look back over the years of an active career, I see dimly the climax and the decline of the great Comstock Lode, in Virginia City; of Eureka, Pioche, Candalaria, and in later years of Goldfield and Tonopah, together with innumerable smaller camps scattered over Nevada that are now but memories of more romantic days.

I see the fading of the frontier in Arizona; the replacement of the stagecoach by the railroad and the automobile. The frontier days of romance vanish. Great commonwealths, populated by millions of people, rise from the western wilderness.

Almost, but not quite, I see the prairie schooners wending their way toward the setting sun; the hordes of gold-mad fortune hunters seeking in the West the pot of gold at the end of the rainbow.

That West has vanished. Those who carved an empire out of the wilderness have played their parts. They live now only in pages of history, in story, and tradition. Some of their activities, I hope, will live again in these pages, in which most of the characters are faithful portrayals, many of the events actual occurrences.

GRUBSTAKE

Chapter I

ALMOST touching the western horizon, the moon illuminated the lonely camp. From the remnants of the campfire a flame now and then threw into relief a coffee-pot, black with smoke, a frying-pan, tin cups, and knives and forks, neatly arranged upon an old bit of canvas. Farther from the fire were a small water-keg and a few parcels of provisions, and still farther a shovel, a pick, hammers, and drills. Rolled in a blanket, feet to the fire, head resting on a pack-saddle, the prospector lay asleep. Sagebrush, rocks, sandy soil stretched away into the surrounding darkness. In the background, to the east, a mountain range outlined itself against the horizon.

The faint glow of dawn tinted the sky, broadened, and grew brighter. The darkness that followed the setting of the moon was replaced by gray. Soon the eastern sky was alight and distant objects became visible. A horned toad scuttled across the sand.

It was not until the sun was almost above the mountains that the prospector moved. Throwing back the blanket with a sweep of his arm, he rolled over and scrambled to his feet with much stretching and yawning.

He was not over five feet five inches in height, broad of shoulders and deep chested. His legs were short and stout. His big feet were made more pronounced by heavy hobnailed boots. Kindly brown eyes, set far apart, looked out from a tangle of scraggly hair and whiskers streaked with gray. This was Shorty Peterson, prospector and miner.

Grubstake

Shorty got to his feet and looked for his burro, tied the night before to a large sagebrush close by. The animal was gone. The sagebrush had been uprooted. Tracks in the sand indicated that the animal had started off in the direction of the mountains. Plain were the marks of hoofs and of the drag of the sagebrush at the end of the rope. Shorty stood for some moments meditatively pulling his whiskers and swearing softly to himself, as he surveyed the dreary landscape that stretched before him across the plain to the mountains, broken only by a few low hills some five or six miles away.

"What got into that damn critter, anyway?" he muttered, as he ruefully gazed in every direction. "No use to start hunting him on an empty stomach," he soliloquized. "Better get some grub first, and then pack up and go after him. He must be over on the other side of them hills, somewhere; there's water in that direction."

He began to stir the smouldering embers of his fire, throwing on some dead branches of sagebrush and vigorously fanning the fire with his hat. Soon the larger pieces of wood were ablaze, and the coffee-pot, propped up on two large rocks, was beginning to sing. It did not take him long to finish bacon, a potato, some hardtack from one of the packages, and coffee.

Carefully he filled the canteen from the keg. Grub and utensils were put into a canvas bag. With the canteen slung on one side, the bag on the other, and a prospecting pick in his hand, Shorty started off in the direction of the hills. He had taken perhaps a dozen steps when he heard the never-to-be-mistaken whir-r-r, the flat, dry sound that man and beast dread—the ominous whir-r-r of the rattlesnake. Stopping short, he gathered up some rocks, and, at a safe distance, began to bombard the snake. "Now I know," he said, between shots, "why my old burro skipped out. You, you ugly cuss, did the trick. Don't blame Mister Mule a durn bit, I'd light out under similar circumstances, pretty pronto, you bet." A rock struck the coiled snake. Another smashed its head as it writhed.

The low hills did not look more than a mile away, but Shorty was no novice to the desert and knew how deceptive distances were in that atmosphere. At the end of an hour the hills were still ahead of him, although closer than at first. In front of him the trail was plain. The general direction was toward the largest of the three low hills; if the course did not change, it would lead him close to the southern end of the middle one. He intended to prospect in the main range. Somewhere on one of the streams, flowing down from the melting snow high above, he would pitch his camp, and from there as a base he would prospect the surrounding country, moving camp as he worked farther and farther away from his first location.

Year after year in the summer months Shorty had scoured the hills with pack and burro. Grubstaked from expedition to expedition by the residents of some mining camp, he had come and gone on his quest, confident that sooner or later he would make his lucky strike. Sometimes it was a shift boss or a miner who put up the grub; again, some local merchant took a chance, or a saloon-keeper or gambler, and even the local minister once joined in. On one trip the residents of the redlight district had furnished the grubstake, with the understanding that if he found anything good enough to locate, the first claim should be called "Cleopatra," the second "Venus." Sometimes he gave a quarter-interest, sometimes a third, and sometimes a half.

Again, when times were hard, he took a job at mucking or pushing cars on top at some mine, and worked until he had accumulated a stake; then he would go off on a fresh expedition, financed in whole or in part by himself.

Shorty had been out on his "grubstake" now for more than a month. The intervening country between the Ruby Range and Sulphide had been prospected, without result, and now he was nearing the range itself, where he proposed to spend the summer, hoping to find his long-looked-for bonanza. He had two partners, Si Proctor, a cowboy, and Ralph Lee, surveyor and assayer at the Sulphide Consolidated. They were to furnish grub for four months. The interests were divided: Shorty one-half, Proctor one-fourth and Lee one-fourth.

In the present instance Shorty had agreed with Proctor and Lee to be back in Sulphide on the Fourth of July. Everybody would be in town then—freighters, miners, prospectors and the cowpunchers from the surrounding ranges—all bent on celebrating the day of days in one delirious revel of gunpowder and firewater. There would be a parade in the morning, led by the Marshal and his aides and headed by the band, followed by the G. A. R., then the orator of the day with an escort of several prominent citizens, then George Washington, impersonated by a small boy riding a shetland pony, led by two negroes, and followed by a float with the Goddess of Liberty, surrounded by Mose and Lize, the Fire Queen and a crowd of children dressed for the occasion. Behind the float would come the local fire company, resplendent in red shirts and shining helmets, then prominent citizens in decorated turnouts of one kind and another, some on horseback, and at the end of the parade the "Horribles"—boys and young men grotesquely masked and gowned. In the afternoon foot-races, horse races and other games, including rock-drilling contests for the miners, on the results of which much money would change hands and over which—and things in general—much whiskey would be consumed.

The mule's trail led straight toward the opening between the hills. "Follow that mule blindfolded, almost, now," soliloquized Shorty, as he tramped on. Soon he was at the base of the hill and had a full view of the country beyond. As he scanned the course of a small stream which flowed from the range out into the valley, he saw his burro grazing near the water.

"Had your belly full of water, eh, and now enjoyin' breakfast, I s'pose," he said. "Well, I don't blame you for stampedin' from that rattlesnake, but by jiminy, you needn't have run so durn far."

Shorty was not long in covering the distance to the stream. But as he approached, the burro looked up, kicked disdainfully and trotted off in the direction of the highest of the small hills, the sagebrush root dragging at the end of the stake-rope.

"If I can work that durn mule into them rocks, maybe the rope'll catch on one of 'em, and Mister Mule'll wind hisself up into a knot, and then I've got him." At last a large boulder, protruding above the ground, caught the rope as the burro dodged behind it. The root of the sagebrush held and the animal came to a halt, kicking and pawing the ground. Puffing and red in the face, Shorty grabbed the stake-rope and sat down. He waited patiently while the burro gave one or two final kicks before settling down with drooping head and closed eyes.

As he sat there, red in the face and short of breath, Shorty could plainly see the stream of water tumbling down in white cascades from the mountain heights. At the base of the mountain its course, before it lost itself in the desert, was marked here and there by patches of green. Trees dotted the sides of the mountain; the arid waste stretched away, north and south; overhead, the June sun, now high in the heavens, outlined in the clear atmosphere every roll of the plain, every spur and angle of the mountains. Somewhere in those hills, perhaps, he would find his bonanza! Unconsciously he began to pick up bits of rock and throw them at the projecting boulder under which the stake-rope had caught. One piece, larger than the rest, perhaps kicked there by the mule, he idly hammered with his small hand-pick. Breaking it up, he picked up a piece—the old instinct guiding him, as he turned it over negligently in his hand. He was about to throw it away, as he had thrown other pieces, when coming out of his abstracted mood, he looked at it.

"Quartz, by God! and damn good-looking quartz, too," he ejaculated, as he took a second look.

He picked up piece after piece of rock, broke them, looked them over carefully, threw them away—only to pick up other pieces and repeat the operation. For half an hour he examined and discarded piece after piece, walking meanwhile in both directions along the outcrop of what he soon recognized as a vein. Finally he paused, let out a yell, executed a jig-step, flung his arms around the burro's neck, and ecstatically kissed him.

"By gosh, old mule, we got a good prospect at last! Never in the world would have thought of prospectin' this little hill; would have kept to the main range and missed this entirely. Well, old beast of burden, you'll never have to pack another load, if this claim pans out. Outcrop must be five or six hundred feet long and six to ten feet wide. Quartz looks lively and has got mineral in it, too. How much, no one'll know till Hans Randt assays them samples I'm goin' to take in to him. S'pose they go sixty dollars a ton? She looks big enough to make plenty of tonnage. Open her up with a shaft an' some drifts, and sell out for $50,000. Whew!

"Golly! just to think you discovered this mine, you and that rattlesnake; goin' to give you the credit, though. Snake's dead; anyway, his intentions was hostile—yours wasn't."

Shorty felt hungry. The excitement had told on him; he was tired. "Nerves" were not a part of his make-up, but he wanted to sit down and rest. Funny, he thought, how tired he had become in the last hour. Gathering some dead sagebrush, he built a small fire, boiled some water in his big tin cup, poured in some coffee, and opened a tin of sardines.

Dinner over, he repacked his canvas bag and looked meditatively at the sun. "Guess we can't afford to take no chances with them claims; better stake 'em now." He produced from his pocket a pencil and some blank location notices and laboriously filled out nine of them. "Three claims long, that's 4500 feet; three claims wide, one on each side of the claim the vein runs through, that's 1800 feet wide. That ought to cover all the 'dips, spurs, and angles,' " he whispered to himself as he wrote. When finished, he carefully copied the notices, putting the duplicates in his pocket.

"We'll start by that boulder that stopped you, brother

mule. That's the centre of the 'Bucking Burro' claim, 750 feet north and 750 feet south from that boulder, and 300 feet east and 300 feet west. Got to pace it off, till I get my tapeline tomorrow, I guess, and set some piles of rock and dead sagebrush till I can cut some posts."

He folded the first notice, took the empty sardine can, put the notice inside it, and turned the can upside down under the boulder. Then he piled about it a rude mound of rocks and capped the pile with a branch of partly burned sagebrush that he took from the fire. This was his initial monument. Pacing off 750 feet, as nearly as he could, along the strike of the vein, he stopped and turned at a right angle up the hill, where, 300 feet away, he built another mound of rocks and stuck into it another burnt sagebrush root. So he went to each of the four corners, erecting monuments. That finished, he laid out the next two claims by erecting two monuments 1500 feet on the strike of the ledge from his north end line, and similar monuments 1500 feet from his south end line.

He had now laid out three claims, which he named "Bucking Burro," "June Bug," and "Fourth of July." In the centre of each claim he built his rock monument, and having no more tins, folded the location notices and tucked them carefully among the rock-piles.

It was getting late when he completed this work. His next task would be to bring up his supplies from yesterday's camp. That done, he must finish locating the other claims and do his sampling.

Leading the mule, he started toward the nearest water. He filled his canteen, gave the mule a drink, and struck out toward the dry camp of the night before.

As he walked on, the slanting rays of the setting sun crept

slowly up the side of the Ruby Range until only the snow-capped summits remained in the sunlight. It was almost dark when he reached the camp, thoroughly tired out. He gave the burro a drink of water from the keg, staked him, built a fire, and prepared his supper.

Before turning in, he got everything together, ready to load, carefully examined the stake-rope to satisfy himself that the burro was securely tied, rolled himself up in his blanket, and promptly dropped off to sleep.

Shorty woke with a start, sat up, and looked about. The moon was well on toward the western horizon. He rolled up his blanket, threw the pack saddle on the burro, loaded his supplies and tools, and covered the whole with the piece of canvas that served as tablecloth, mattress, pack cover and sample sheet. With a diamond hitch over the load, he coiled up the stake-rope, tied it to the pack and started the burro off in the direction of the mountains showing dimly in the moonlight.

In the moonlight and the silence of the desert he tramped on, lost in thought. He wondered if it was going to prove a real mine or whether he had simply turned up another false hope and found a vein that wouldn't stand close examination. He'd had several of that kind before—near mines, that just didn't pan out. His hopes had been dashed so often that he wasn't going to be disappointed this time if things didn't come his way. And if they did? Well, there were a lot of things he wanted to do. First, play square with his partners; make Ralph Lee superintendent, put Si Proctor in charge of the teaming that would have to be done. Some day he'd move down to the Bay (San Francisco) and find himself a nice, quiet place where he could spend his declining years. He was fifty years old now, but good for twenty miles on foot any day and every day. Life in the open, tramping the hills in summer, and mucking at the mines in winter had kept him in pretty fair physical shape. It was true he hadn't done much work the past winter; a fortunate turn in Burning Moscow had brought him over a thousand dollars. He had been mucking at the Wildcat, when the rumor of a big strike started, and had invested all his cash in stock at ten cents a share. He had sold out on the boom and had spent the rest of the winter in San Francisco.

It was shortly before four o'clock when he reached the spot he had picked for his camp. The moon had disappeared some time ago, the darkness before dawn had been intense, but he kept plodding along, now leading the burro by the stake-rope for fear of a stampede in the dark that might cost him another day's chase. It had begun to grow lighter before he arrived, and by the time he had unpacked and staked out the burro, it was daylight. After watering the burro and starting a fire, he prepared breakfast. The meal was soon over, and after leaving things in good order in the camp he shouldered his canteen, pick, shovel, hammers, sample sacks and canvas cloth and started to work.

Leaving his tools at the discovery monument, he unrolled his tapeline and began to measure off the distances between his stakes. By noon the monuments were corrected to correspond with the tapeline measurements, the notices of location carefully placed in the rock piles, and wooden corners of charred sagebrush set to make legal his possession.

He labored on during the afternoon completing the location of his group of claims, nine in number. When finished, the group on paper looked like this:

Grubstake

Stampede	Rattlesnake	High Hopes
Fourth of July	Bucking Burro (Discovery)	June Bug
Desert Queen	Moonlight	Rising Sun

The discovery was well protected, both on the strike and the dip; the ledge could be traced into both the "June Bug" and the "Fourth of July" claims; there were some indications of ore on the "Moonlight," "Rising Sun," and "Desert Queen"; anyway, float from the main ledge had rolled down the hill and lodged on these claims, and it would not take a great stretch of imagination to consider some of it, at least, as ore in place. He knew he had to have mineral in place to make a valid location, but he also knew that ore in place might be confused with "float" that had rolled down-hill from the ledge above. If it ever came to a mineral survey, U. S. Deputy Mineral surveyors were not too technical, and, anyway, his position was better than anybody else could hope for. Claim-jumping and horse-stealing were on a par, and the sympathy of the community would always be with the original locator.

It was growing dusk as he got back to his camp, tired and hungry. His supper was quickly prepared, and after looking over some specimens he had brought in with him, he made himself a "shake-down" and turned in. Tomorrow he would spend sampling the vein, and perhaps the next day too; then for Elko, and on to Sulphide.

Sunrise found him ready to start out again, but before starting he picked over the specimens he had brought in the night before, selected a lump of rock the size of a small apple, and placed it in the glowing coals of his camp fire. Carefully he watched it as it began to heat, and finally a few tiny blisters of metal showed on the surface.

"I knew it," he exclaimed excitedly. "It's horn silver, and she fries out like grease. Glory be, hallelujah! Hip, hip, hurray!! She's goin' to be a bonanza if there's much more of this kind of ore in the old claim; equal to anything the Comstock Lode at Virginia City has ever produced."

Leaving his burro quietly grazing by the water course, he walked over to the discovery point. Starting at the discovery monument, he chipped the quartz with hammer and moil across the entire width of the vein, as nearly as possible in equal quantities, collecting in this manner perhaps twenty-five pounds of rock. This he placed on his canvas cloth, and sitting down by the pile he picked the pieces up in turn, and laying them on a four-pound sledge hammer as an anvil, he broke them up until no piece was larger than a hazelnut. This pile of rock he then mixed thoroughly by rolling it over and over on the canvas, picking up a corner and rolling the pile to the other corner and then reversing the operation. Finally, he spread the pile after the manner of a pancake, cut it into four fairly equal parts, and scraped two of them off the canvas onto the ground. Again he rolled and mixed the sample, and again spread it out and rejected half of it. He now had perhaps five pounds left, which he again crushed until no piece was larger than a pea. This in turn was cut, quartered and halved. One half he poured into a small canvas sack, slipped in a piece of paper on which he had marked "No. 1," and tied up the sack. In a notebook he made an entry of number and location.

So all day he toiled, cutting samples across the ledge at

intervals of fifty feet; breaking them down, quartering and rejecting, until only a small quantity remained as the sample for the assayer. As sunset approached, he returned to his camp.

The evening meal was quickly prepared and disposed of; the burro needed no attention, being within reach of both feed and water. Shorty sat long by the fire, smoking his pipe and planning for the future. He had struck it rich.

It was the afternoon of the third day following the discovery before he completed the work to his satisfaction. Claims were staked, notices and monuments properly placed, duplicate location notices were written out for recording, samples gathered up. Everything was in readiness for an early morning start for Sulphide.

What time he had left before dark he put in looking over the surrounding country. He saw signs of mineralization in several places. Once or twice he was tempted to stop and make a location, but he figured he had enough for the crowd, if it was worth anything, and too much if it wasn't.

"Might be as big as Sulphide, or bigger," he soliloquized as he cooked his supper. "Maybe there'll be five hundred or a thousand people here, some day, maybe more. And then she'll boom, and finally she'll bust and go downhill till nobody's left 'cept the coyotes. All mining camps got to go that way, some day. Some'll last longer than others, but they all peter out sooner or later."

That night he dreamed of shafts, stopes, winzes, mills, and life in a new camp with all its romance, its comedy and its tragedy. In the morning he was up at daybreak, and shortly afterwards on the march behind his burro. He had ten days to make Sulphide, for the Fourth of July.

Mile after mile he tramped on, driving his burro ahead

of him, making a dry camp the first night, stopping at a cattle ranch the second night, and reaching Elko on the afternoon of the third day. He turned his burro into the corral, dumped his outfit down in a corner of the stable, greeted the boss and the hangers-on, and made himself at home. That night he unrolled his blankets and slept in the stable close to his outfit. No one would disturb it during the day, and probably no one would at night for that matter, but he would camp alongside the outfit, anyhow, just for the sake of his own peace of mind.

The next day he handed his location notices to the County Recorder. He paid the fee, and remarked: "Guess I won't be back here for some time, so you just keep them papers for me, and I'll come in and get 'em or send somebody to get 'em for me; and I'll give a written order, all right, in case I send for 'em."

The following day he loaded up again and was on his way to Sulphide. He had ample time. There were numerous places on the road where he could stop, or he could camp in the sagebrush if it suited him better. Equipped to meet any emergency, he started out carefree and light of heart. Whatever happened, he could reach Sulphide in time to have his assays made and get everything fixed up for the big celebration on the Fourth of July.

He had tramped too many miles over the Nevada hills prospecting for mineral not to realize the possibilities of his strike. He had been fooled once or twice before, but he had never been so sure of having made a real strike as now. The assays would tell the story, and only then would he know what it amounted to.

So day after day he tramped on, camping at night and driving his burro ahead of him by day, until at last he reached the summit of some low hills and saw before him, in the desert beyond, the town of Sulphide. It was the morning of July second, 1874.

Chapter II

The Miners Rest was the show place of eastern Nevada, with its bar of mahogany adorned with a shining brass rail, its brass spittoons, immaculately polished, and its plate-glass mirrors, reflecting not only those at the bar but also the faro, keno and roulette layouts at the rear of the room. At the end of the bar nearest the gambling games a closely fitting swinging door, covered on the inside with concealed boiler-plate, gave limited protection from stray bullets that on occasion had left more than one mark on various parts of the saloon. A large cabinet contained specimens of gold, silver, lead and other ores.

Bill Patrick, the owner, ran a thoroughly respectable place. He served the best whiskey he could buy and his other liquors were on a par with his whiskey. The games were straight. Drunkenness was frowned on. Now and then a drunk was thrown out. Now and then a coroner's jury viewed the remains of one who had run amuck with a gun and had been accommodated by some mild-mannered individual quick on the draw.

The customers of the Miners Rest could count on good "likker," a straight game, and protection from would-be bad men. What more could any one ask? No one did ask more, and so as a result the "Rest" came to be *the* institution of the town: a clearing-house, an information bureau, a private bank, the civic centre.

It wasn't much of a town, as towns go back east; 1500 or 2000 people, at most. One main street, a few side-streets and alleys, some scattered residences, lodging-houses and boarding houses, and the hoisting works of the mines up on the slope at the foot of the mountains. To the west the sagebrush desert stretched away to the distant mountain range. To the north the blue haze and the horizon marked the direction of the Idaho line. To the east, the hills rose sharply to meet the mountains that towered some 2000 feet above the valley. And to the south desert and mountain and valley, jumbled in inextricable confusion, stretched onward into Arizona and beyond, over the international boundary line into Mexico.

For five years the town had grown and prospered. Now three mines were producing and milling gold and silver ore; their stocks were listed on the Stock Exchange in San Francisco; numerous prospect holes, employing from two to a dozen men, were seeking the ledges of pay-ore that were, so the optimists believed, "just another round of shots" ahead. But, notwithstanding the seeming prosperity, Bill Patrick knew something had to be done to "raise the wind." Sulphide was starting on the down grade; there was no doubt about that, notwithstanding its outward signs of prosperity. The fate that sooner or later overtakes every mining camp was in plain view for those who were wise. Of course, things might pick up again; after all, the mines were only 500 or 600 feet deep, and while it was true that the bottom did look poor—rotten, in fact—it was always possible for a new ore shoot to open up in depth.

But the select circle that had its headquarters in the Miners Rest took no chances. Faro and keno were straight games that always showed a percentage to the house; poker was easy pickings; and all in all, there was no reason whatever for taking chances so long as the bottom of the mines looked good. But now unpleasant rumors, mostly confidential in character, were afloat. Nick Trevethan, shift boss at the Sulphide Consolidated (commonly called the "Con"), had been in with some samples he had taken in the face of the crosscut on the 700 level where it had just broken into the vein. Randt, the assayer for the crowd, had just given Patrick an assay certificate showing only five ounces in silver and a couple of dollars in gold—too low-grade to "pay." The shaft had been pushed down from the 600; the sump was finished; station pumps were set; the suction of the sump connected; the sinking pumps had been hoisted to the surface; the 700 station had been cut out; and the crosscut to the vein had been driven. Overhead, up to the 600, it was all virgin ground, not a pick in it anywhere; but the bottom seemed to have fallen out of things in that fatal hundred feet! The 600 had given them a few unhappy moments in times past, but nothing serious had happened until the crosscut was driven over to the foot-wall of the vein on the 700 level and cut—nothing.

The superintendent would know it, of course; he had been down soon after the round was fired that broke through, and had himself sampled the vein carefully. The foreman and a couple of shift bosses might know, but none of them would be likely to leak to the general public. Even the company assayer might not know; the "old man" had a way of mixing up his samples sometimes, sending in half a dozen at once with occasionally a sample or two of barren rock mixed in the bunch as a blind and with no location marks on any of them. The truth was bound to come out in time, of course, but for the present no one on the outside was supposed to know what the crosscut on the 700 level showed.

"But *we* know what's in that crosscut," remarked Patrick

ruefully, "and we got to know what's in the rest of that vein as they open it up on the strike; and if it's no better than what she's got in her now, it's goodbye to old Sulphide, unless somebody digs up another shoot of ore somewhere. The Desert Prince ain't producing a quarter as much as the 'Con,' and if the 'Con' peters out, the others just naturally are going to follow before long. As for the dozen cats and dogs living on assessments, why, they quit when the 'Con' does, because they got as much chance of striking ore as a snowball has in hell.

"The fact is," he went on, "that crosscut in the 'Con' is just as near smack in the centre of that shoot of ore as it could be put; 300 feet of pay, in either direction, vertically over it on the level above, ten to twelve feet wide, and good for from $60 to $80 a ton, every pound of it, from one end of the shoot to the other; some places higher in value than others, of course,—the best in the heart of the shoot—and this crosscut, directly under the best of it, shows nothing.

"Oh, hell!" Patrick continued, "why couldn't it have gone down another few hundred feet? Nice place for a camp, nice crowd, everybody settled and happy, and now maybe the bottom's going to fall out of it—just like it did over in Hamilton. No more funerals for me! I move on before the bats roost in the Miners Rest or the best house in town can be bought for $50. Tried it once myself; after the heavy winter of '69, saw Hamilton go from 15,000 to 200—doors hanging on one hinge, windows knocked out, everything falling to pieces; people mostly gone, and those still there good for nothing, some too old to move, just starving to death; some more or less *loco* in the top story, nobody left worth a damn.

"I stuck it out then, thinking the town would come

back, but it didn't, and I left the next spring, after two winters of it. The first wasn't so bad, but the second one was a fright! Everybody trying to borrow from everybody else; my saloon with about the only hot stove in town 'cept a few cookstoves; my likker a sort of community supply that everybody wanted to tap at my expense. Never again any old run-down mining camp for me! If the next six months don't show up a new ore body, I'm off for a new camp!"

Sitting around the table in the private room were Bill Patrick, Slim Wilson, Gus Anderson, and Hank Bartle. Patrick, the leader, was of medium height, spare in build, with black hair and blue-gray eyes—cold, steel-gray eyes, you might call them. They were set rather far apart. At times they stared, but mostly they roved from side to side without motion of the head.

Patrick had come to California in the '50's and had drifted into gambling in San Francisco and Sacramento. With the outbreak of the Comstock Lode in '61 he had crossed into Nevada, travelling from camp to camp, always quiet and undemonstrative, with a good name as a square sport, and known in almost every mining town of any prominence from Virginia City to Pioche. Bill owned the Miners Rest. It had long since repaid him the cost of construction. Whatever came to him now was all clear gain, and he was beginning to figure on the day when he would pull out for some new camp in Nevada or Arizona. He had the same vision most of those early Nevadans had: a home eventually in San Francisco.

Slim Wilson—thin, anemic, sharp-eyed, slender-fingered—didn't weight over 125 pounds, and had the reputation of being the slickest poker hand in eastern Nevada. Rumor had it that Slim could make the cards stand on their hind legs or do almost anything else. He seldom quit loser, and somehow he always managed at the critical moment to hold a hand just good enough to take the pot. Nobody ever caught him in a crooked deal, but it certainly was a wonder the way those cards did walk around for him. Ike Proctor, from the Circle R outfit, pulled a gun on him one day and went through the deck, under the table, and all over Slim, looking for phoney cards; but he found nothing, and Slim sat and took it with seeming indifference, though he suggested to Proctor when he got through that he apologize—which Ike did, handsomely and promptly. But Slim never played with him again.

"Never again, Proctor," he used to say. "Your gun might go off next time. One attack of heart failure is enough." And then he'd laugh a grim sort of a laugh—only his eyes didn't laugh—and Proctor never knew whether he was joshing or not.

Gus Anderson had started out in life as a steamboat clerk on the Mississippi; saw life on the river in the '50's; came to California and steamboated between Sacramento and San Francisco in the '60's for a spell; and little by little drifted into dealing faro. He didn't have the nerve or the skill to make a good poker player and he was too indolent to aspire to own a saloon. He drifted from camp to camp, dealing faro, good-natured, weak, and harmless. He was popular at the Miners Rest because of his complaisance and smiling acquiescence in almost every suggestion offered by the heterogeneous players surging about his faro table.

Hank Bartle came to California with the gold rush and drifted into his old job as barkeeper on the *Crisopolis* and the *New World*—river boats famous in their day on the run between San Francisco and Sacramento. An accidental meeting with Patrick on one of his trips to the Bay caused him to abandon the river steamers and become his head barkeeper. He was efficient in his work, diplomatic, soft-spoken, with morals fitted to the job, and with an eye to acquiring enough money to buy a saloon on Montgomery, or Pine or Leidsdorff Streets in San Francisco, near the Stock Exchange where his friends from Nevada could congregate, exchange stories, and feel at home.

One not actually on the inside could have little conception of the care with which incoming strangers were looked over by the natives in the smaller mining camps. The advent of a stranger was an occurrence of tremendous importance. He might come to buy somebody's claim, and if he bought that somebody must be so dealt with that he would pay what he owed the other residents. This was usually accomplished by filing with the escrowed deed instructions as to how the money should be distributed by whoever held the deed for delivery. On occasion, these assignments of payment fell thick as autumn leaves, but in the end the prospective purchaser usually failed to perform according to the hopes and expectations of the town. Sometimes the unexpected happened, and the payment was made. When Tom Rockhill sold the "Happy Day" for $50,000, he got just $7000 himself out of the deal; the town absorbed the balance for commissions, for money loaned, for interest accrued (3 to 5 per cent a month compounded), for legal advice, and for heaven knows what all.

"Nobody blew in with any new strike lately, has there?" asked Anderson, hopefully.

"Not a strike," replied Patrick, "and no particular prospect of any. Most of the boys that was working around these parts lit out for southern Nevada when that crazy Mexican brought in that fairy tale about veins of pure copper, sticking out of the ground as big as houses. Hell! the bunch grabbed him and cross-questioned him for an hour, and then stampeded hotfoot, the whole caboodle of them. That's two weeks ago now, and none of 'em are back yet; and the fellers that grubstaked 'em are getting sore and are willing to sell out cheap. Nothing in it, of course; just another of them damn lies that sets the town afire every once in so often and then dies down. Queer, people don't seem ever to learn anything; get bit over and over again, and always ready to grubstake some other prospector on the off-chance that he will turn up a bonanza. Done it myself, lots of times, but I'm getting kind of skittish. Still, you never can tell—they turn 'em up when you least expect it.

"From the looks of things, this camp has hit the high spot and now it's on the down-hill. It ain't going to take a hell of a long time for the bunch in San Francisco to find it out, either. Just keep your eye on the stock reports, and when you see 'Con' beginning to slide, make up your minds the insiders are unloading. It won't be right away, of course; they got to drift both ways on that level, and that'll take 'em several months. In the meantime, anybody who's got any stock better get ready to sell. Meanwhile, maybe we can rustle up something to keep us in pocket money."

Chapter III

THE four had agreed that the best way to make a stake was to find a prospect and sell it to some bunch of tenderfeet. Such things had been done. When Tom Rockhill sold out for $50,000, he threw in a bunch of six or eight claims more as part of the "group," insisting that it was no use trying to sell a single claim 1500 by 600 feet; that wasn't enough ground, especially when all you had to do was to drive a few stakes and post a few notices to make a group. "Selling scenery," one irreverent native had phrased it.

As Anderson wandered down the one main street of the town, along which were clustered hotel, stores, postoffice, express and telegraph office, a lawyer's office or two and a few nondescript establishments, he had not the faintest idea of where to turn or what to do to "scare up something." The board sidewalk, raised some eighteen inches above the level of the street, engaged his attention as he walked. It was worn smooth; here and there the knots had been kicked out of the boards, and nails were beginning to stick up with unpleasant frequency, but it was better than nothing. It ended at the corner below the postoffice, and beyond that was the dust of the desert with Simpson's Corral at the lower end of town to break the sweep of the horizon.

Disconsolately he surveyed the length of the main street. Nothing in sight to attract even momentary interest; a few people coming and going—a mixture of miners, cowboys, townspeople, Chinamen.

That afternoon and evening Anderson gave over to a

contemplative study of the problem that had been created by the assays from the 700-feet level of the Sulphide Consolidated. He lived at the Golden Eagle hotel, and he carried the problem to bed with him that night. The next morning after breakfast he sat listlessly in the office of the hotel with his feet on the iron railing that ran across the window. From where he sat he could see Simpson's Corral and the desert road winding beyond it into the distance, and even as he looked he noticed a speck on the horizon. Before long he could distinguish a single burro driven by a man on foot. He thought it must be a prospector coming into town; it would not be a charcoal-burner or a wood outfit, for they came in with a pack train loaded high with scrub pine or charcoal, and this was a single animal travelling light, pack flat and loosely tied. The man walking to one side and behind the burro was short and thick-set. He carried his hat in his hand. Shorty Peterson, of course, back from one of his perpetual prospecting trips.

There was nothing else to do, so he might as well watch Shorty, who was heading for Simpson's Corral, so Anderson lit a cigar and waited.

Simpson's Corral was the headquarters for prospecting outfits, freight teams and stage-coaches. Shorty Peterson stopped his burro near the buildings, which consisted of storehouses, barns, and a small dwelling and office, and unloaded his outfit, which he stored in one of the buildings, after an exchange of salutations with Simpson, who was seated in front of the small building that served as office and general headquarters. Taking a large canvas sack from the pack, he placed it to one side and turned his burro into the corral. Then he dropped down on the well-whittled bench that stood in front of the office door.

"Anything new?" he asked hopefully.

"Nary a thing, Shorty. Town's goin' along 'bout the same. What you got new?"

"Oh, nothin' much. Been out prospectin' an' got a few samples. Don't amount to much, I guess. Had to come in for some grub, an' wanted to take in the Fourth o' July show, too, so here I am."

"Reckon it'll be quite a time on the Fourth, from all accounts," remarked Simpson.

"Yeah, it usually is. 'Bout the greatest day of the year, in the minin' camps. Gives everybody a chance to turn loose an' blow off steam."

Shorty and Simpson both lapsed into silence.

"Well, I got to be movin'," said Shorty, as he rose and picked up the canvas sack containing his samples. This he slung over his shoulder, and started up the street.

Sulphide was in its prime. Bullion worth thousands of dollars was being shipped daily by Wells Fargo, consigned to the mining companies in San Francisco. Reports of new strikes came in rapid succession—most of them untrue, all grossly exaggerated—but what of it? The stocks moved up and down on the board in San Francisco. Everybody had money, or thought he had—which amounted to almost the same thing. Nobody lacked work, and if a man didn't make a fortune today, he would tomorrow.

It was toward the Miners Rest that Shorty was headed, as he wandered up the street. It was the surest source of information, and, after pausing to buy himself some tobacco at one of the general stores that carried everything from ladies' underwear to blasting powder, he walked on up the street and kicked through the swinging doors of the entrance to the Miners Rest.

Grubstake

Inside, Hank Bartle was wiping glasses and arranging them in neat rows on the shelf under the mirror behind the bar. "Hello, Hank, give us a drink," he said, as he dropped his sack by the case of specimens and walked up to the bar, where he deposited a half-dollar. Hank pushed a bottle of whiskey and a glass toward Shorty, who, helping himself to about all the glass would hold, gazed at it critically for a moment and then drained it at a gulp, heaved a sigh, drank a little water, wiped his mouth on the back of his hand, and rested his arms on the bar, with one foot on the rail.

"Say, Hank, seen anything of Si Proctor, last day or two?"

"No, he ain't back from the railroad yet. Went out swamping for Jim Langford 'bout ten days ago and the outfit ain't got back. What you want him for?"

"Aw, nothin' much; he was in on a grubstake with me, and I wanted to tell him I was out of grub."

"Find anything?"

"No, I guess not," replied Shorty, lighting his pipe. "Got a few samples, but I don't think they're much good. Guess I got to hunt some new country; don't seem to be much in this part of the State. Ain't seen nothin' nor nobody who has seen anything worth workin' on; lots of prospectors wanderin' 'round in the hills, but none of 'em ain't located no claims. Surface ain't hardly more'n scratched yet; you can't tell me there ain't more'n one Virginia City, or Eureka, or Pioche, or Austin, or Treasure Hill in Nevada. No one ain't fool enough to suppose all the bonanzas is found yet.

"Anybody in town struck a new lead, Hank?" asked Shorty. He referred to the numerous prospects scattered over the surrounding country for miles around, varying from a one-man windlass and a hole less than fifty feet deep, up to claims with steam hoists and shafts from one to several hundred feet in depth. Everybody lived in hopes of striking it and paid assessments levied with painful regularity by the "board of directors" in San Francisco. The assessments were paid with astonishing persistence, but sometimes the discouraged stockholders allowed them to go delinquent with resultant publication in the local papers of long lists of names, numbers of shares and amounts delinquent, preliminary to public sale. The game was kept up as long as any one would pay, and then, when it was played out, the delinquencies too great to be overcome, the work stopped; the shaft filled with water; the machinery was hauled away—often stolen—and another dream of bonanza days went to smash.

"Nary a strike, Shorty," replied Hank, "and not much doin', to tell the truth. Gettin' kind of slim pickin's for the boys, I guess; last delinquent assessment of the Burning Moscow covered almost a whole page of the paper. Fine for the newspaper outfit, but hell on the shareholders! Jim Barkley papered his cabin with certificates after the last sale. Said he guessed he might as well use 'em for that as for lightin' the fire with, and besides, it would keep his memory kind of fresh like and remind him that the fools ain't all dead yet."

"No, nor never will be," remarked Shorty sententiously. "But shucks, Hank, we can't afford to quit just because one or two prospects goes wrong. Just naturally have to keep everlastingly after it. Guess I'll go home and clean up and sort of get ready for Fourth of July," he remarked, as he picked up his sack.

He had decided he would give some of the samples to Hans Randt, just as a check, and turn a complete set over to Ralph Lee. He would take the whole lot over to his cabin, divide them into two portions, pick out those he wanted Randt to assay, and then await results.

Bartle made one last effort to extract some information. "Have a drink on the house before you go, Shorty."

But Shorty shook his head, and with a "No, thank you, Hank," pushed through the swinging doors and went on up the street.

Chapter IV

When Shorty emerged from the Miners Rest he turned and walked up the street in the direction of the hoisting works. He went past the stores, the more pretentious dwellings and the rows of miners' cabins and turned at length into a path that led to a nondescript cabin, half wood, half canvas. The style of construction was common enough in mining towns—a little better than a tent, less expensive than a house. Wind, rain, and snow might buffet it in vain; it stood, as many still stand in western mining camps, a symbol and survival of pioneer architecture.

Taking a key from his pocket, Shorty unlocked the door and entered. In one corner was a bunk, made of dressed lumber, and it had sheets—the upper one neatly folded back over the blankets, the whole covered with a piece of canvas. There were a chimney of stones, a fireplace used for cooking, an old, battered trunk, a homemade table, and a pile of odds and ends. In one corner were a mortar and pestle and a bookshelf covered with books and specimens of ores.

He started a fire on the hearth and swung a kettle of water over it. Then he took four small sacks from his canvas bag and, after carefully cleaning the mortar with some ashes and an old rag, he dumped into it the contents of one of the sacks and began to pulverize the ore. After reducing the rock in the mortar to pin-head size, he cut, quartered, rejected and re-cut the sample, on a piece of oilcloth, until he had left two piles, each of half a pound or less. These he placed in two small sacks; in each sack he enclosed a bit of paper on which he had written a number. In a small book, fished from an inside pocket, he made a notation and returned the book to his pocket. The second, third, and fourth samples he then treated in the same way. The larger sack he tied up, and, unlocking the trunk that stood in a corner, he took from it some clothes and dropped the sack into it.

He locked the trunk and put the key in his pocket, remarking to himself: "You can't be too careful with samples any time. Anyway, I got these four checks out, and they don't leave my possession till I give one lot to Lee and t'other to Randt."

After a liberal use of soap and water, he put on his "store clothes"; his "digging" clothes he kicked under the bunk.

The package for Lee he slipped into his pocket; the four sacks for Randt he took in his hands, and, locking the door behind him, retraced his steps in the direction of the main street.

He went along in the direction of the Miners Rest until he came to a sign nailed to the side of a small building—"ASSAYING—HANS RANDT." Here he entered. Inside, a wooden railing; behind the railing a desk, some books, a pile of old sample sacks, specimens, more or less covered with dust; in all, a space perhaps twelve by fifteen feet, and a partition with four half-sashes of window-glass giving view to the room beyond, chemicals and rock-crushing paraphernalia. Seated at the desk, entering some figures in a book, was Hans Randt, a chemist, who, forced by circumstances, had emigrated from Germany to New York and thence to San Francisco. Later, in Virginia City, he had become an assayer for several of the mines. But notoriety, having to do with the stealing of high-grade ores, led him to move to Sulphide, where for two years or more he had been carrying on the business of assaying. Incidentally, he picked up now and then, through one or two trusty scouts, some high-grade ore, stolen by miners working in the drifts or stopes where it was struck. Randt never dealt directly with these highgraders; he used some intermediary to avoid the risk of detection.

His position as assayer, too, gave him first-hand advance information as to what might be turned up by the ubiquitous prospector or found in the various "wildcats" scattered for several miles around the town. These small fry could not afford assayers of their own; in fact, they seldom had use for them.

As the only public assayer in the locality, he occupied a really strategic position, and, of course, there were those who cultivated his acquaintance. First among these were the little group who congregated in the back room of the Miners Rest. When the "Nevada Bell" shaft cut the "Queen" vein on its dip and strike beyond the end line of the "Queen," Randt had made the first assays from the strike, and had advised the crowd some three or four hours in advance. They had picked up some 26,000 shares of stock, on which they eventually made a clean-up of nearly $5 a share. There were six of them in on the deal. Bill Patrick, as banker and general boss, took for himself the largest cut and dictated the amounts of the others.

Shorty suspected that Randt was crooked, but he wanted to make sure. He thought that Randt was in league with Bill Patrick and that Patrick would try to euchre him. He wanted to make sure of this, too. But he took the samples to Randt mainly because of a spirit of adventure, a feeling of self-reliance that almost led him to court a conflict with Patrick.

"Got some samples I want assayed," remarked Shorty as he dumped the sacks down on the counter. "Gold and silver—and when can I have 'em?"

"Come in tomorrow morning aboud ten or elefen o'glock und I haf dem ready for you, Shordy."

Randt had been assaying samples for Peterson now for two years or more. Once or twice the results had come so close to the line of "pay ore" that Shorty had gone back with an outfit, camped near the discovery, and put in some weeks drilling, blasting and shovelling in the hope of finding something just a little better. He had even persuaded the superintendent of the "Con" to visit one of his prospect holes and sample the outcrop of the vein and the hole, some ten feet deep. However, it had all gone for nothing.

"How's times, Hans?"

"Oh, yust so-so. Noddings to brag aboud mooch. Some of der poys tought dey haf find somedings ofer py Sulphur Creek; got some goot assays, but ven dey goes pack dey digs him all oud in aboud a veek. Von of dem blowoudts in limestone dot makes you feel like you vas a prinz, und in aboud a veek you vonder vare you can find somebody vot gives you a square meal. Dem limestone debosits iss sure hell—dey iss rich as blazes but tam few of dem iss big enough to make a carload.

"Vot kind of a vormation you been chasing up dis drip, anyvay, Shordy?" he continued.

"Oh, no kind—every kind—any kind—wherever I think I can see a chance," Shorty replied. "I ain't so much stuck on these here geology ideas. The Bible says gold is where you find it. I heard a lot about them geology sharps, but I never seen one yet that had found a real mine. They lay back while us prospectors do the work, then along they come and look wise 'n' hand out a lot of talk, most o' which ain't so."

"Dot's yust de vay mit you tam brosbectors, Shordy. You dink you iss all zo smart ellicks mit your burros und grubstakes, but vat you do mitoudt me or some feller to assay your ore for you, eh? Zome day I go oudt myself mit a outfit und show you vat I can do my own self as a brosbector."

"You been saying that same thing for a year, Hans, and I ain't seen you behind no burro yet, and I don't ever expect to," said Shorty, as he kicked the door and went out on to the sidewalk, leaving Hans hefting the bags.

Meantime, Anderson had watched Shorty go to his cabin and had learned that Bartle had discovered nothing. He had seen Shorty reappear and enter the assay office. When Shorty came out and disappeared down the street, Anderson pushed through the door into the assay office, where Randt sat at his desk with the samples in front of him.

"Whatcher find out, Hans?" Anderson asked.

"Vell, vot I dond't find oud fills a hell of a lot of books, und vot I do find out is nix. Dot Shordy feller is vize alretty, und knows how to keep his moudt shut. I dond't get noddings oud of him. You has yust got to vait undil I gets dose sambles assayed; he's ground dem up in a mortar undil der devil himself cand't tell noddings aboudt vat der rock looks like. If us fellers iss going to bamboozle him ve yust got to ged up about der time der graveyard shift goes to vork, vich iss twelve o'glock in der night time.

"Ged oud of here," he went on, "und dis afternoon I vix up dose sambles und a lot more I got, und run 'em tomorrow morning, und if any iss vort a tam you shall know by nine o'glock. Dere is tree lots besides Shordy's, some from der Rattlesnake shaft north of town und two more bunches from some of doze vildcats vat iss called 'extension.' Neffer in my life iss I goin' to buy any stock in any of dose extension glaims! Yust because some feller finds a vein und strikes a ore shoot, der fool public tinks she iss goin' to continue from here ofer to Utah, und you find extensions tam near twenty miles away. If gold und silver was so common as dose extension glaims, der metal vould be vorth yust noddings."

Randt picked up the samples from his desk, entered the assay room in the rear and began the preparation of the various samples. There were some twenty, in all, and the pulverizing to the fineness of flour, the selecting of the small quantity to be assayed, the charging of the crucible with the chemicals and ore, and getting everything ready for the furnace would consume a good part of the remainder of the day. The fusing in the furnace, the pouring of the molten mass, the cupeling, the parting and weighing of the beads, would all be done in the morning.

Anderson slid down from the counter where he had been sitting and went toward the Miners Rest.

Meanwhile, the noon whistle had blown at the "Con" hoisting works. The top-men, carpenters, and trammers were going home to dinner, or finding comfortable seats about the works and opening their round dinner pails. To Shorty the whistle was a welcome sound; it meant he was no longer under the necessity of starting a fire of sagebrush and cooking the inevitable bacon and coffee plus some beans and hard-tack. He could sit down in front of Sam Hing's counter and order whatever his fancy dictated.

Hing greeted Shorty affably. A counter with high stools in front of it took up three sides of the room, leaving the rear open to the kitchen.

Shorty had scarcely finished giving his order when Ralph Lee entered. He had not known of Shorty's return and his welcome was therefore all the more cordial. They were alone; it was an opportune moment; and taking the package from his pocket, Shorty handed it quickly to Ralph, saying: "Put this in your pocket, son, and keep quiet. I got her, I think, this time, sure. Assay them samples this afternoon and come to my cabin after dark and tell me what they go."

"Sure, Shorty; but why all the mystery?"

"Well, Randt's got the four duplicates to them samples, and when he gets the results I think he's goin' right up in the air, and within an hour after that Bill Patrick'll be after me to buy me out or cheat me out of the claims. I don't want him to know you got any samples, or know anything about it.

Just then two or three customers came in and the conversation became general. The room filled quickly. It was the usual mining camp restaurant crowd—miners, shift bosses, a foreman or two, a sprinkling of townspeople, a cowboy or two, the editor of *The Sulphide Times;* in all, some fifteen or twenty men.

"Doesn't seem to be much doin' in the way of news," ventured Shorty to his neighbor opposite, a cowboy named Lacey.

"No, mighty little. Your side pardner, Si Proctor, was round inquirin' for you last time he was in town; saw him here in the rest'rant. Said there wan't anything new at the railroad, and not a thing on the road between here and there. That's a mighty fine sixteen-animal team that Si's swamping with; no flies on that outfit. And say, his boss is some artist when it comes to making 'em all get down and pull."

"They got a big load of machinery for the 'Con' this trip," said Lee. "A new sinking pump and some general hardware, a station pump for the 700 and a lot of powder; loaded down with our stuff, couldn't bring in another pound."

"Must be goin' to sink another lift or two, with all them pumps."

"Why, I guess maybe so. We wouldn't send for 'em if we weren't, but it may be some months before we use 'em. The old man is a great hand to have things on hand when he needs them."

And so the conversation ran on, as the customers came and went, until finally Shorty and Lee walked out together. Outside, and out of earshot, Shorty drew Lee over to the edge of the sidewalk, saying:

"Ralph, I think I got her this time. It's over on the edge of the Ruby Range, and she's a daisy if I don't miss my guess. Come over to my cabin after supper and bring that purp of yours to keep watch outside so nobody can sneak up and listen; and be sure to get them assays out. Nobody knows you're in on the grubstake, except Proctor, so you keep mum."

"I understand," said Lee, "and I got to be going now, as it's almost time for the whistle to blow." He started off up the street to the "Con" office.

The superintendent, generally known as "the old man," lived close by in a one-story cottage surrounded by a fence, within the boundaries of which the female members of the family made strenuous efforts to raise a few flowers and a patch of grass—about the only green things to be seen for miles around.

When the camp started, there had been no water closer than some springs on the mountain six miles away. It had been packed in on burro-back and later hauled in, in water-wagons, until the mines were opened up, when the flow from the springs had been piped in by gravity. Even now there was no water to spare, and there would not have been enough to go around had it not been for the fact that the mines had developed water in depth, which was used for battery water in the mills, for fire protection and similar purposes. The excess of mineral salts in it made it unfit for drinking, but it was invaluable for wet crushing of the ore in the battery of stamps that day in and day out, month in and month out maintained their ceaseless roar. The mine water was pumped to a large artificial pond some hundred feet higher than the mouth of the shaft, from whence it flowed by gravity to the mill. In an emergency the mine and spring supply could be joined by opening a valve, so that, so far as fire protection was concerned, the town was well supplied with water. It had never burned up yet, as do most mining camps, but the possibility was recognized, viewed with resignation by the inhabitants, and provided for by the provident ones with insurance policies—for which they had to pay a price that would have caused the residents of eastern towns to expire on the spot. However, to the citizens of those new western towns it was but part of the game.

Chapter V

In the afternoon Shorty visited the barber's, called on one or two old acquaintances who ran stores, and purchased a few papers and periodicals from the place where stationery was sold along with vegetables, candy, and groceries. He made the rounds, gossiping and thoroughly enjoying himself after being out of contact with his fellow men for weeks.

Of course, Shorty had had several drinks during the afternoon, but he did not permit himself to get full, notwithstanding pressing invitations at the Miners Rest. On his way to the cabin he was muttering to himself: "She's a daisy, and I ain't goin' to let no Bill Patrick and his gang do me out of what's mine. Of course, Ralph Lee'll boss the job; he can pick a good foreman and shift boss after we get to shippin' ore. There'll have to be some miners after we get out enough ore ourselves to pay wages, buy a hoist, build a bunkhouse, a boarding-house, and buy some grub, powder and things. Jiminy! it looks like money, when you stop to think of all the stuff you got to have to make even a small hole in the ground, to say nothing about such an outfit as there is on the 'Con' and the 'Desert Prince' and the 'Nevada Belle'! I just got to keep myself sober till we get them claims transferred and nail down the lid, and then won't we have a real celebration on the Fourth of July, me and some of the Patrick outfit! And that celebration ain't goin' to cost *me* much money for firewater, with that bunch standin' 'round tryin' to get me full and make a deal—for what? Why, for a bunch of claims I got, located off to the north, near the Idaho line; good-lookin' outcrop but no values; and while I'm out a-showin' them the place, Si an' Ralph can slip out quietly and I'll meet 'em after I dump the Patrick outfit. Then the fireworks begins, and where the end is goin' to be the Lord only knows.

"Yes, sir," he continued, "Ralph is to be the boss and the schoolma'am is to hold the claims in trust for us, and maybe Ralph'll marry the schoolma'am. By jiminy! if he has any sense and sand, he will, providin' she's willin'. I'll deed him, or them, an extra interest in the claims, for the kids. Let's see—Si Proctor's got a quarter, Ralph's got a quarter; I got a half. I'll give the schoolma'am a eighth, and a sixty-fourth for each kid up to three. But say—how'n hell am I goin' to tell the schoolma'am what I got in my head, afore I know they's really goin' to hitch up? Well, I just naturally got to hold the whole business under my hat. Maybe they'll call one of the kids 'James' after me. Jimmie for short! If he makes good, darned if I don't make him my heir; but nobody'll ever know that until I'm laid away somewhere. Always did want a fam'ly of my own. Only way I'll ever get one now is to adopt Ralph and Mary. I ain't an old fool, like some old fellers; I know fifty-odd is too old to change habits. Besides, if anybody grabbed me, at my age, it wouldn't be for myself, you can bet your sweet life. Money makes the mare go, and I bet it would get me as many wives as old Brigham Young, and not one of 'em would be worth a damn! The real prizes ain't got that way."

As he walked along toward his cabin, his thoughts continued along the same line. "That's the stuff," he soliloquized, "give the schoolma'am a interest for holdin' the claims, and then work like blazes to tie the two of 'em for life. Nobody's got nothin' on me as a matchmaker. Whatever I do, Si Proctor'll do too, so there you are! Lord knows *I* don't want much. Guess I wouldn't know what to do with myself if I couldn't git out behind my old burro and tromp 'round over them hills. Maybe some day I'll want to quit, but 'tain't time yet. Anyway, if the time ever should come when I get old an' rheumaticky and want to sit by the fire in a little house somewhere 'round San Francisco Bay and get up in the mornin' when I darn please, and have a Sam Hing to cook for me and bring me breakfast in bed—well, it would be mighty fine to have enough money to pay the bills. But what a hell of a life for a man to lead; the only worse thing at my age would be to have a woman 'round tellin' me what to do—or tryin' to, which amounts to 'bout the same thing. Well, maybe I shan't ever strike it—and then I'll just keep on prospectin' till they put me in the county poorhouse or plant me in a redwood box out there in the sagebrush a mile from town, where there's all kinds of company to suit any taste. None of 'em cares, now, whether the old camp's in bonanza or busted wide open; and they'll all be just as comfortable there as anywhere on earth. Those that's left will be gone from these here haunts some day—no more pay, mines played out, folks just natchally pullin' up stakes and movin' on; and only the wolves and the coyotes and the fallin' down buildin's and caved-in tunnels and shafts and the rottin' headboards out there in the cemetery. Just silence and the desert."

In the shade of his cabin Shorty seated himself on a rough wooden bench, looked around, lit his pipe and began reading the copies of *The Territorial Enterprise* and *The Weekly Bulletin* which he had bought. As the afternoon waned, he continued to sit there with papers scattered about him, contentedly smoking his pipe.

His reading finished, Shorty carefully folded the papers, laid them on the table in his cabin, swept the floor, tidied things up a bit and threw out a lot of rock that littered table and shelves. Then he locked the door and started for Sam Hing's restaurant.

As he stepped up onto the board sidewalk in front of the restaurant, Shorty found himself face to face with Ike Proctor, Si's brother. Ike was tall and slender, without an ounce of superfluous flesh, straight as an Indian, his clean-cut features indicated firmness in character. Gray eyes verging on a blue, set wide apart, showed him a fighting man. Ike Proctor in his early twenties had risen by sheer merit to the foremanship of one of the largest cattle ranches in Nevada. His dress, from the wide-brimmed felt hat to the high heels of his boots, was that of the cowman.

The Proctor boys hailed from Texas. Their father, a colonel in the Confederate Army, had been killed at Gettysburg, and the boys, then not old enough to join the army, had grown up under their mother's care on the family ranch in the Texas Panhandle. But after the war, when debts could not be met, the ranch passed into other hands and Mrs. Proctor died. The boys, then seventeen and nineteen—Ike was the older—were cattlemen every inch of them, habituated to the hardships of the frontier, dead shots, and loyal to their friends. They had drifted into Arizona and southern California, and had come over to Nevada with several carloads of thoroughbred stock for the Circle R ranch, where Ike was now foreman.

The greetings of the two men were cordial.

"Hello, Ike! Where's Si?"

Grubstake

"Hullo, Shorty. Oh, Si? Swampin' for Jim Langford. They went out to the railroad and ain't got back yet. Expect 'em 'most any time, now. We been runnin' Langford's horses on alfalfa for a spell. Some of 'em had collar-galls, t'others got poor feet. What you want to see Si for?"

"Oh, just a grubstake he's in on, and I wanted to tell him I was back in town."

"Out of grub and wantin' more? Or to tell him you got a bonanza all staked out for him?"

"Not exactly that, but I wanted to tell him where I've been and what I seen."

"Oh, I know, Shorty. Same old story. I savvy long time. Been bit myself. Well, never mind, old hoss. There's one thing I will say for you—if you *do* find it, I bet Si gets a square deal. Which is a damn sight more than some of 'em 'round here would give any one.

"Had your supper yet?" he went on. "No? Well, come along; let's feed together. Then I got to light out for the ranch. Just keeps me plumb busy, these days, holdin' that crew o' mine in till the Fourth. They'll all be in town tomorrow, and me after 'em. Beats hell how they want to get into town and likker up, 'specially 'long about the Fourth of July."

Still talking, Proctor pushed open the swinging screen door and found a stool in front of the counter. Shorty climbed up beside him, and the smiling Sam Hing came forward.

"What you likee?"

"What you got, Sam?"

"Oh, me got loast mutton, loast beef, stuffin' goose, cullie ham, licee——"

"Aw, we don't want none of your mutton nor beef nor

goose nor curry and rice. Give us a couple of T-bone steaks, some fried potatoes, and coffee," said Proctor.

"You no likee stuffin' goose, cullie ham?"

"Nope, we don't want none of them things you keep cooked by the week. Cut 'em all out and give us steak."

"Say, Ike, you ever get time to make a trip out into the country, prospectin'?" asked Shorty.

"Me? Not on your life. I got pretty close to ten thousand head of cattle over there on the Circle R, and what with lookin' after the gang that's punchin', and every so often gettin' a bunch of steers to the railroad for shipment, I just ain't got no time to fool around on any of this here prospectin' business. Besides, I wouldn't know pay ore from greasewood."

"But, Ike, that ain't what I mean, exactly. I mean, s'pose I ever did make a strike and some galoots started in to jump my claim, would there be any chance to get you and a few of your punchers to help me hold down the locations?"

"Oh, a sort of bodyguard, eh? Well, I'll tell you what I'll do, Shorty, whether my brother Si is in with you or not, if any of these smart ellicks 'round town get gay with you, just you let me know and I'll turn out a bunch of punchers that'll start 'em towards Mexico and they'll never stop goin' till they cross the Rio Grande. But say, Shorty, don't you think the first thing for you to do is to find this here bonanza before you call for a army?"

"Why yes, of course, Ike. I know I got to find her first, but you never can tell; maybe I will, some day."

"And maybe you won't, old hoss; but if you do, my agreement stands. Which I guess ain't no great responsibility on my shoulders."

Ike turned to his T-bone steak and the conversation ended.

The meal finished, Ike started toward the corral, while Shorty wandered homeward. It was not yet seven o'clock, and Shorty knew he could not expect Lee for a good two hours.

"She's just *got* to assay," he muttered. As he trimmed the kerosene lamp, he thought of his experiment with the piece of rock and how the globules of silver stood out on it as it heated up. It wouldn't be long now, he thought, before he would know whether his dreams were coming true.

It began to grow cold. "Never was a finer climate in the world," he thought; but at recollection of the winters with the thermometer twenty and thirty degrees below zero, he shivered and turned involuntarily to see if he had enough blankets on his bed. Well, he could always get a job pushing cars if—but there was no if. He had a mine—he was sure of that, and it wouldn't be long now before he knew.

The hoisting works up on the hill disappeared in the shadows as the sun dipped below Mount Pierce. As the shadows lengthened, they covered the town, touching first Simpson's Corral and last Shorty's cabin as they crept on across the valley. The purple-tinted sky faded to a deeper and deeper hue. Lights began to glimmer in the hoisting-works and mills. The indistinct outlines of the buildings vanished into the blackness of the night. And, over it all, the hush of the desert lay brooding and unbroken save for the distant and subdued hum of the stamps dropping, dropping, dropping upon the dies in the mortars, crushing the flint-like quartz into minute particles and releasing the metal to be caught on the silvered plates or carried to the pans, there to be ground with quicksilver into amalgam.

It was nine o'clock. Shorty trembled with excitement.

His brow was damp. Gradually, out of the blackness came the crunch of boots digging into the gravel of the dry creek. As he listened, there came bounding up to him a dog that almost upset him in his desire to greet his friend. Following Spot, Ralph emerged from the gloom.

"Well, Shorty. I didn't know whether you were home or not. Let me see your face. I've got some good news for you." And, no longer able to contain himself, Ralph grabbed Shorty by the shoulders, and, while shaking him, said:

"Where'd you get those samples from, you old geezer? Know what they go? Well, they average over $200—60 per cent silver, 40 per cent gold! I want to know all about it, quick."

Shorty's face paled, his eyes assumed a glassy stare, his knees shook, and he almost collapsed as he dropped on the bunk inside the cabin door. Resting his left arm on his knee, he dropped his head in his hand and waved Ralph away with his right hand.

"Gimme a few minutes to catch my breath, Ralph. Please don't speak or do anything. Just let me alone. To think that after all these years and years of trampin' over the hills of Nevada and tryin' and tryin' to strike it, gettin' more and more discouraged, growin' old and gray, and seein' the poorhouse a-starin' me in the face, I've struck it at last! It's too good to be true! My God, Ralph, you're sure there ain't no mistake? You didn't mix my samples with some mine samples, did you?"

"Never a mix, old timer. I only ran the one batch this afternoon—the four you gave me. There can't possibly be any mistake—unless you've 'salted' yourself somehow."

"No, Ralph, I ain't 'salted' nothing. I took them samples

myself, across the vein in four places about a hundred feet apart. Just think of it! A shoot of ore more'n 400 feet long and eight to twelve feet wide and good for $200 a ton! Good Lord, Ralph, it's the biggest find in Nevada in years, and even if it only goes down a couple of hundred feet, we got enough to make old age comfortable and more besides. Let's get a piece of paper and put it all down and talk it over. I can't believe it yet, Ralph. Gimme a hand, youngster. I feel shaky."

Shorty rose with Ralph's help and stumbled over to the table.

"Put that pup of yourn outside, Ralph, and shut the door and come here and set down."

Ralph called Spot and, walking out some ten feet from the door, said, "Watch 'em, pup!" With a knowing whine and a wag of his tail, the dog took his station.

Returning to the cabin, Ralph found Shorty with his elbows on the table and his head resting on his hands.

Springing to his feet abruptly, Shorty brought his fist down on the table with a bang. "I want a lot o' drinks. But no, by God! not another bust till this thing's fixed; an' if you see me full, Ralph Lee, before we get this business settled, you take that old army Colt of mine and fill me full of holes. Sit down on that stool. What's them assays? Number one first, then two, three and four."

"Number *one*—gold $102.67; silver 206 ounces."

"Sufferin' Moses!"

"Number *two*—gold $97.26; silver 164 ounces."

"Gosh A'mighty!"

"Number *three*—gold $67.18; silver 120 ounces."

"Never could've dreamed it!"

"Number *four*—gold $70.47; silver 122 ounces."

"And ore at both ends! I knew she was a humdinger, Ralph, but I never expected this."

Shorty handed the paper to Ralph, as he whispered: "Four hundred feet from number one to number four, and eight to twelve feet wide every foot of the way, and ore at both ends! And there's plenty of timber and wood for the boilers and a stream of water not over a mile away."

He was very quiet for a moment, then he said, "Now, son, we got a lot to do! First, we got to make out a deed to the schoolma'am, and then we got to draw up a contract between her and us. Get busy with this pen and paper." Shorty pushed over to the assayer some blank deeds to mining claims, the ink and the penholder.

"You write down what I tell you to." When finished, the document read as follows:

For and in consideration of ten dollars to me in hand paid, and other valuable consideration, I, James William Peterson, a citizen of Sulphide, Nevada, do hereby grant, sell and convey to Mary Clark, of Sulphide, Nevada, all those certain mining claims located by me and being in the Peterson Mining District, County of Elko, State of Nevada, and known as the "Stampede," "Rattlesnake," "High Hopes," "Fourth of July," "Bucking Burro," "June Bug," "Desert Queen," "Moonlight" and "Rising Sun," more fully described in the notice of location thereof recorded in the office of the County Recorder of said County of Elko on the twenty-eighth day of June, 1874, and which said record is hereby referred to and made a part hereof.

Witness my hand and seal this second day of July, 1874.

"I ain't no lawyer, Ralph, but I seen lots of deeds and location notices and such like, and I'll bet my boots that deed'll hold water."

Then he drew a long breath and said, "Gimme that pen."

"Well, that's all right, partner," said Ralph, "but would you just mind telling me what it's all about and what you're scared of?"

"Bet I will, Ralph. But first, I ain't scared of nothin'—but I'm gol-darn cautious! You see, it's this way: if we get that deed on record, and anything happens to me, you folks is safe. There'll be a contract for the schoolma'am to sign and everything'll be in ship-shape condition. By tomorrow noon, or maybe sooner, that Patrick outfit'll be putting up all kinds of jobs to get them claims! I think Randt's crooked and in cahoots with Patrick, but I gave Randt samples 'cause I wanted to find out for sure. They don't know where they're located, so they'll try to get me full and euchre me out of 'em; and I'm a-goin' to fool 'em, and take 'em off on a wild-goose chase while you and Si get on the ground and be in possession by the time the storm breaks. Ike Proctor's got to get into this, too; he wanted to know if I wanted a army to help hold the fort, and I'm goin' to tell him I do. Let me get this thing signed, and you can put your seal on as Notary. Thank the Lord you got that appointment! Then the schoolma'am can ship the deed off tomorrow by Wells Fargo, so it'll be recorded before any one suspects anything. Now, then, we'll draw up the agreement for her to sign, and things is fixed up all hunky-dory."

"Here's the copies of the location notices that's posted on each claim," he went on. "I put the originals in piles of rocks on each claim. I left a set for record with the County Recorder in Elko, and told him to keep them for me until I came back, when I'd call for 'em or ask somebody else to call for 'em. Anyway, they are of record; and it don't so much matter whether we ever get 'em or not."

Shorty handed Ralph nine notices, each being identical in form with the others, save for the description of the claim and its name. Ralph read them carefully and laid them on the table with the other papers. After some time and effort expended jointly by them the following document was duly transcribed and read by Lee:

Whereas, Miss Mary Clark is the owner of and in possession of those certain mining claims known as "Stampede," "Rattlesnake," "High Hopes," "Fourth of July," "Bucking Burro," "June Bug," "Desert Queen," "Moonlight," "Rising Sun," located in the Peterson Mining District, Elko County, Nevada, and of record in the Records of Mining Claims of said County, to which record reference is hereby made; and

Whereas Miss Mary Clark is holding said claims in trust for J. W. Peterson, Ralph Lee, and Silas Proctor;

Now Therefore, it is agreed that the said Miss Mary Clark will, when requested by said Peterson, Lee and Proctor, deed said mining claims to a corporation to be organized by the said Peterson, Lee and Proctor; and it is agreed that the interest of each shall be:

Peterson, one-half
Lee, one-quarter, and
Proctor, one-quarter.

"Sounds all right, Shorty," said Lee.

"No, damn if it does. We forgot the schoolma'am. We're goin' to add a clause like this:

"And it is also agreed that said Peterson shall pay to said Mary Clark one-fortieth of his share in these claims as compensation and that said Lee and Proctor each shall pay the same proportionate amount of their share.

You see, Ralph, the schoolma'am is our pardner."

"Well, you can't make me mad with such a proposal, Shorty. I'm for it, old hoss." And Ralph wrote it down just as Shorty had dictated it. "Only I got a confession to make. Miss Mary wanted to get in on a grubstake, so I sold her a small part of my interest."

Shorty smiled knowingly and remarked, "Seems we somehow hit on the same idea, only you got it first. Well, that's all right, only if the 'old man' finds out you let her in on the gamble, you'll pretty near get fired. He don't take no stock in grubstakes; says they're too long shots."

"But they win sometimes," suggested Ralph.

"Well, not enough to do any harm," replied Shorty, "although we seem to have struck it this time."

Shorty handed the documents to Lee, saying, "You take this transfer, put it in a strong envelope, and address it to the County Recorder at Elko. Get Miss Mary to take it to the express office and send it off on the stage tomorrow. Get her to sign the agreement, and tell her to keep one copy and you keep one, and give me one. You'll have to write the other two copies when you get home. Tell her to keep this hid where nobody can find it, for we got to keep her out of this just as long as we can. Maybe it would've been better to do it some other way, for I got a notion hell's a-goin' to pop, sooner or later, over this thing. And tell her to keep her mouth shut."

Shorty went on, "And before you go, Ralph, here's the rest of them samples; I want you to be sure not to forget to run 'em. The four I gave you are the two ends and the two half-way between on either side of the discovery monument, they represent the ledge where it outcrops. I think it's covered with wash as it goes down the hill, and with debris from the mountains as it goes up the hill; anyway,

I'm sure there's more of it than I've sampled. It don't make so much difference now, about them other samples I took to Hans Randt; we got enough results right now to know what's what, and if that Patrick bunch should steal 'em now it won't do 'em no good 'cause we *know* there's a payshoot there."

"Well, they won't get them, Shorty," said Ralph. "I'll sleep with them tonight and tomorrow morning they'll go into the furnace."

"That's the stuff, boy. And now it's time for you to vamoose."

Ralph stole away into the darkness with the sack over his shoulder, followed by Spot. Shorty yawned, lit his pipe, and remarked to himself, "That's the first milepost left in the rear."

Chapter VI

It was shortly after daylight when Ralph awoke after a restless night's sleep in which his dreams were a jumble of bonanzas, gun-fighters, gamblers, and stampedes to a new strike.

It took him a few minutes to gather his senses together and realize that somehow it was, after all, more than a mere dream. Tumbling out of bed, he dressed hurriedly and, pulling the bag of samples out from under his bunk, started for his assay office a short distance away.

At the assay office, he started a fire in the assay furnace and turned on the steam leading from the hoisting-works boiler. This steam drove a small engine that operated a crusher and a grinder which made it possible for him to turn out far more work than he could have done if he had had to "buck down" all his samples by hand.

Starting the machinery, he crushed the samples, weighed out the assay charges, filled the crucibles and put them in the furnace, now hot enough to melt them. While the first batch was in the furnace he made himself some coffee on the small stove used for drying purposes, cooked a couple of eggs, sliced himself some bread, and ate a hasty breakfast.

It was nine o'clock by the time he had completed the run. Before him were the buttons adhering to the çupels, small, glistening beads of light-colored gold, made almost white by the silver content. Carefully he looked at them, pried them loose with a pair of pincers, picked them up, turned them over—almost breathless with excitement.

"Every one is a pay sample—and big pay, too. It's easy to see that, without weighing them. There's not one of 'em that'll go less than $50—and from that up to $250. Shorty was certainly right; there will be hell popping when Patrick gets this information."

It was after ten o'clock when the weighing and the parting of the buttons were completed and the calculations made and tabulated. When finished, Ralph sat long in contemplation of the figures. He knew perfectly well what they meant—a vein of that size and good for over $150 a ton, for the whole distance sampled, was a bonanza of the first class. Twenty tons of ore a day of that quality meant $3,000; it could be worked for $35 a ton, even if they had to haul to the railroad and ship to the Salt Lake Smelter, and for less, if they had a mill; so it would be safe to figure $90 a ton *net*—or $1800 a day for the twenty tons. $54,000 a month, perhaps $600,000 a year! And twenty tons a day was nothing to take out and mill. The possibilities staggered and bewildered him. It was too good to be true. Yet there were the results before him; there could be no doubt about it. And by this time Bill Patrick probably knew it, and the whole town would know it before very long. Information of this kind was too startling to be kept quiet for any length of time.

"I must hunt up the schoolma'am," he thought, as he pocketed the assays and tabulations, sealed the deed in a large envelope, and started to find Mary Clark, who would probably be at the school house.

It was now nearly a year since Ralph, fresh from graduation from the Columbia School of Mines, had come to Sulphide as surveyor and assayer for the Sulphide Consolidated. He made friends rapidly, becoming especially attached to John Macklay, superintendent of the "Con."

Grubstake

Macklay had come to California in 1850 as mate on a sailing vessel. The crew deserted, like many others, and stampeded for the gold diggings. There was nothing for him to do but to go ashore, report to the ship's agents, and then start for the mines himself. He tried his hand at placer mining with indifferent success, and from this drifted into hydraulic mining. Soon he became foreman of a hydraulic mine near Nevada City. Later he went into quartz mining, in Grass Valley, and in 1862 he joined the rush to Washoe. In Virginia City he soon found work as a mine foreman, and for the next few years was in and around Virginia City, Gold Hill, Dayton and Silver City as mine and mill foreman and superintendent. He became superintendent of the Sulphide Consolidated when the mine was being developed. He supervised the building of the hoisting works and mill. He saw the shaft go from the one hundred foot level to the seven hundred, watched the drifts on the vein lengthen, the stopes gradually creep upward from level to level, and the ore cars in a never-ending stream, pushed by the top men, move over the track to the top of the mill. Here they passed through the jaw crushers to the mortars, whose batteries of five stamps each to the total number of thirty dropped day and night in a ceaseless roar, —1—5—2—4—3, crushing the ore into minute particles and releasing the gold and silver to be recovered later as amalgam. This amalgam (quicksilver, gold and silver) was brought to the assay office where the assayer retorted it, driving off by heat the quicksilver and leaving the gold and silver to be melted and poured into a brick which would be shipped to the United States Mint in Carson City.

Macklay was teaching Ralph Lee practical mining; Lee could have had no better teacher.

Grubstake

Mrs. Macklay frequently invited Ralph to meals. The home atmosphere and the home cooking were welcome relief from the monotony of his bachelor life and Sam Hing's restaurant. Since the arrival of Mary Clark some six months previously he had looked forward to these invitations with growing eagerness. Mary Clark had caught the get-rich-quick fever and, after hearing of Ralph's grubstake venture, begged so hard to be allowed to participate that Ralph reluctantly permitted her to invest twenty dollars in it. No one else knew of this until Ralph told it to Shorty.

Ralph could see the schoolhouse and its open door from his office, and as he slid and scrambled down over the waste dump, he could see some one moving inside. As he turned the corner of the building and entered the doorway he almost collided with Mary Clark, coming out with a large basket of wastepaper.

"Goodness me, Ralph Lee, you 'most upset me! And tell me what *you* are doing here this time of day?"

"Well, the first thing I'll do is relieve you of that basket and dump it for you; the second is to ask you to step inside and sit down quietly and listen to me make a speech—the finest speech you ever heard."

Taking the basket from her, he walked a few steps away, dumped the contents, touched a match to them, and returned to the schoolhouse. Placing the basket beside the desk he turned to Miss Mary. "You remember that some time ago you insisted on sharing in a grubstake with Si Proctor, Shorty Peterson and me?"

"Why, yes, of course I do. And you wanted to present me with an interest, but I refused and put up my own money just like the rest of you."

"Well—Shorty's back, and he's struck it rich."

"Oh, really?"

"Yes, really."

"Not really and truly?"

"Yes, *ma'am!* Really and truly, cross my heart and hope to die! Your twenty-dollar investment, cast upon the desert, bids fair to return to you after many days in the form of a good fat interest in the Peterson Consolidated, the coming bonanza."

"Hurrah!" she exclaimed, her eyes dancing and face flushing with excitement; she was a truly alluring picture, as she stood there in a dark blue dress and white apron deftly caught up at one corner.

"But seriously," he said, "please sit down and stop dancing about, and don't get so excited—although I must say red cheeks are most becoming to you."

Whereupon, her face suffused with blushes and her breath still coming rapidly, she sank down on a bench, saying meekly: "Yes, sir; but tell me everything, every bit about it all, and don't keep me in suspense."

"Well, then, first of all I'm going to be very frank and emphatic and tell you that the lives of some of us will, in all probability, depend upon your keeping absolutely silent about this whole thing. I'm not joking; it's all in dead earnest from now on, and success depends in a large degree upon you. You see, it's this way: Shorty gave me some samples to assay, and if they represent the true value of the vein, it's the biggest strike made in eastern Nevada in years. So big, in fact, that it's going to start a stampede and incidentally bring a crowd of vultures around who'll try to pick the meat off Shorty's bones and clean him out completely. Shorty gave Hans Randt, the assayer, some check samples, which I think was a mistake, but it's done and can't be helped now; and by this time Bill Patrick no doubt knows the results of Randt's assays and is beginning to scheme to get the claims. Patrick's a square gambler, all right, but this thing is so big I'm afraid he'll stop at nothing to get Shorty's claims. It's important you should play the game with us according to instructions. I've got a deed and an agreement for your signature. You see, Shorty has deeded everything to you to hold for all of us."

And so during the next half-hour Ralph Lee told her the story of their grubstake and the part she must play.

"I've got the deed here ready for you to take to the express office; and here's the agreement in triplicate for you to sign. You're to keep one copy, one's for me, and Shorty gets the third. You'll have to get down to the express office and get this envelope off on the one o'clock stage."

Somewhat dazed, Mary Clark took the papers. The envelope she concealed somewhere in her dress; and the agreement she signed with a pen taken from her desk, giving two copies back to Ralph and retaining the third one for herself.

"Now, not a word of this to a living soul, not even Mrs. Macklay," said Ralph. "The stakes are too high to take any chances. Besides, Mr. Macklay would skin me alive if he knew I had let you in on a grubstake; he thinks the chances are too slim."

"I must get back to work," he ended, "so good-bye till noon." With a wave of his hand he started back across the sagebrush toward the mines.

Returning to the office, Ralph Lee plunged into his daily routine. The courses and distance of a survey made the day before must be calculated; then the results had to be transferred to the mine map; stope maps had to be brought up to date; and last, the daily grist of assays must be prepared and run. A large drafting table with its maps occupied the most prominent place in the room; a desk with numerous drawers, a bookcase holding a number of technical books, several chairs, and the assay balances completed the equipment. The cases holding the balances were protected with oilcloth covers and stood upon timbers sunk in the ground through holes cut in the floor to keep them free from vibration.

Just before noon Ralph paused every few moments to glance through the window in the direction of the schoolhouse. But it was not until some ten minutes after the noon whistle blew that Mary appeared. Ralph picked up his hat and arrived in front of the superintendent's house just as she put her hand on the gate leading into the small enclosure surrounding the house. The fence protected the garden from the town billy-goats that wandered at will about the streets, picking up scraps here and there and living on the sagebrush when nothing better offered.

The simple garden, which Mary Clark had helped to cultivate, was not approved by Macklay. He looked with disfavor at the sprinklers constantly watering the flowers and lawn; he realized how fruitless were attempts to beautify ephemeral mining camps.

"It's all right, Mother," he would say with a twinkle in his eye, "but don't forget, if we happen to run low on water, we can't turn grass and flowers into bullion, and we can't crush ore without water, so I'm afraid the grass and flowers will get the short end of it."

At the gate leading into this oasis Ralph said to Mary Clark, "Remember, all you have to do is to take the deed to the Wells Fargo office after you have your dinner and give it to the agent. Instructions are inside. Just tell him to send it to Elko for recording. You must get there before one o'clock."

"By the way," she replied, after nodding her understanding, "Mrs. Macklay and I are going to the Bay for a visit pretty soon. Maybe we'll go to the seashore someplace. They say there are perfectly delightful places at Santa Cruz, Monterey and Santa Barbara. You can drive there or go by steamer from San Francisco."

Her tone was bantering, and there was just a suggestion of mischief in her eyes. But Ralph was too intent upon the problem in hand to heed lighter things or notice her look of disappointment as she realized that her banter had gone unnoticed.

"Well, good luck to you, partner," said Ralph. "I'll run along now to my dinner; and, please, don't forget to keep absolutely quiet about what's going on."

Chapter VII

Hans Randt was efficient. Disciple of German Kultur, philosophical cynic, he lived his daily life largely along the lines of his early training. The summer morning found him up and early at work. The fire in his furnace was well started; the muffle for the cupels was beginning to show a cherry red; the samples, including Shorty's, had been "bucked down" the previous afternoon with mortar, pestle and bucking-board until they would pass through a hundred-mesh screen. Each sample had been carefully mixed upon a piece of oilcloth, quartered, and small quantities taken from each quarter. These had been mixed, weighed and, with the necessary borax, flour and litharge, again mixed and placed in one of the crucibles ready for the fire.

Each sample having been treated in this way, the row of crucibles stood upon a shelf near the furnace. Taking them up one by one with a pair of tongs, he inserted six of them into the fire, banked fresh charcoal about them, and replaced the furnace lid.

In this manner all the samples were fired and, when satisfactorily melted, each crucible was lifted out and the molten contents poured into a conical iron mold, there to set and harden until ready to be turned out as a small conical mass of slag. Each piece of slag he placed on a small anvil and struck smartly with a hammer so as to crack the glass-like mass and release the small button of lead, gold, silver and other metals that composed the tip of the cone. Each of these buttons was placed in a numbered cupel, carried to the muffle furnace, and slid into the white-hot receptacle.

With the lead driven off in the muffle, Randt was ready to weigh up, preparatory to parting the gold and silver and reweighing the gold separately in order to calculate the values of each. He sat in front of the scales, contemplating with obvious interest the buttons representing the samples Shorty Peterson had brought in. Poking them loose, one by one, from the cupel bottoms, he muttered to himself as he worked:

"Mein Gott, vat has dis tam Peterson caught for himself dis time? By chiminy, if I didn't been an old-timer vat has seen before such tings dat amounts to nix, I gets mineself all excited aboud it alretty, before I knows yet vedder it iss somedings oder noddings. Dose sambles, I bet iss more as one hundred fifdy dollars to a ton, und if der fool brosbector has got plenty tonnage of dot kind, Oh! vat a time ve iss all goin' to have after ve euchres him oud of it. Dot Patrick gives me somedings in wridings aboudt mine inderest before I tells him somedings."

As he weighed the buttons, parted the silver and reweighed the gold, Randt continued to mutter to himself. Finally the last buttons were weighed, the calculations completed and the figures jotted down on paper ready for copying on the assay certificates. Eight of the samples were from various local prospects and were quickly disposed of. The four remaining Peterson samples Randt copied first upon a piece of blank paper, as follows:

(1)	Gold	$ 99.80	Silver	210 oz.	Total	370.70
(2)	Gold	101.07	Silver	160.03 oz.	Total	307.40
(3)	Gold	65.12	Silver	118 oz.	Total	217.34
(4)	Gold	74.67	Silver	128.10 oz.	Total	239.79

Then he wrote the following assay certificate:

Miners Assay Office
Sulphide, Nevada
July 3, 1874

Gold $20.67 *oz.*	*Silver* $1.29 *oz.*	*Lead* %	*Copper* %	*Total Gold and Silver*
Number (1)	Gold $2.26	Silver	$5.16	$ 7.42
Number (2)	1.17		4.27	5.44
Number (3)	3.56		5.23	8.79
Number (4)	5.12		7.18	12.30

(Signed) Miners Assay Office
Hans Randt
Proprietor.

"Und dat's vot Mr. Pederson gets for his money, und *dis* is vat Mr. Padrick gets ven he signs de agreement dat coundts me in on der deal." He patted significantly the piece of paper on which the true figures were written and which he put carefully in a pocketbook.

Just then Slim Wilson came in and said, "Well, Hans, what luck?"

"Nix, yust yet. I got to finish first a bunch of sambles for der 'Holy Terror,' vich iss a vildcat oudt by der slaughder-house und de only richness vat dey effer gets iss der rich smell from der offal oudt dere. But neffer mind, der suck-ers ain't all dead yet, und assessment money comes easy. Dose sambles for Padrick is goin' to be ready before noon. You tell him to be in der brivate room at der Rest und I comes in ven I shuts up to go eat, aboudt twelf oder twelf-fifteen."

"All right; but say, Hans, what do they look like? You

got 'em out of the furnace by this time, ain't you? You can guess something about what they're goin' to go."

"Nix on guesses, Wilson! I toldt you de sambles vould be retty aboudt noon, und dat's der finish of it. Get oudt! I got work to do, und besides, Shordy Pederson himself is liable to be in here priddy soon now. You ain't got no business here ven he comes around."

"See here, Randt, I'm in on this deal too, and I got a right to know what's doing."

"You have, ven somedings iss doing. Yust now noddings iss doing."

Wilson argued, pleaded, cajoled, but to no purpose. Randt was obdurate. In disgust, Wilson finally left the assay office and headed for the Miners Rest. There he found Hank Bartle, as usual, engaged in polishing and arranging glasses behind the bar.

"Where's Patrick, Hank?" he asked briskly.

"Upstairs in his room. Maybe he's asleep, maybe he's gettin' up, I don't know. I ain't seen him yet today. Too soon for him to be around."

"Well, I've got to see him," said Wilson, opening a side door that led into a hall from which a flight of stairs ascended to the floor above. He knocked at a door and a voice called, "Come in." In the room over the mantelpiece, beautifully mounted, hung a deer head, a buffalo head, and Indian baskets, bows, arrows, shields, and tomahawks. There were a cabinet, containing some fine specimens, a sideboard equipped with glasses and bottles, a lounge, chairs, and a large table covered with papers, magazines, and books.

Patrick, minus coat and vest, sat in a large easy chair by the window, reading the latest San Francisco paper. When

Wilson entered, he looked up and said, "What's on your mind this morning?"

"I just been to see Hans Randt asking him about them samples that Shorty Peterson brought in. He wouldn't tell me nothing about it, and said to have you in the private room downstairs a little after twelve o'clock and he'd come down here and tell you himself about it. Says they ain't done yet."

"I'll be down there at twelve o'clock," said Patrick. "I want to take on Randt myself, first. After I get things clear in my own mind and find out what he wants, and come to some sort of an understanding with him, I'll have you fellows in and tell you about it."

"Well, all right, but just what do we get out of it, if it's worth while?"

"What's your idea, Slim, asking that question? You know how we divided up on that 'Nevada Belle' deal, don't you? And you know I run the show, don't you? And that I fix the interest each one of you is to have, don't you?"

"Yes."

"Well, if you know all that, why ask questions?"

"Why, I thought——"

"Don't think, Slim. Save your brains, and take what's comin' to you."

Patrick resumed reading his paper, and Wilson, after a moment's hesitation, said, "Well, that's all right," and walked out of the room.

Arriving at the bar, he persuaded Hank Bartle to stand treat, drank his whiskey, and started for Sam Hing's restaurant for breakfast.

Meanwhile Shorty Peterson was headed for Hans Randt's office. The night before Shorty had rolled and tossed for hours before falling into fitful naps, in which he built hoisting works and mills, fought with Bill Patrick and his gang and awoke in a cold perspiration. He had had to strike a match on two occasions and look at the figures under his pillow to sleep on, for good luck.

As Shorty entered the office, Randt was seated at his desk copying some figures on assay blanks.

"Hello, Hans," he said.

"Hello, Shordy. How iss yourself today, anyvay?"

"Never better. Got that assay certificate ready for me?"

"Yah, here she iss." Randt handed the certificate to Shorty.

After contemplating the sheet for a moment in silence, Shorty raised his head, and, looking squarely at Randt, said: "Is this the best you can do, you durn Dutchman? Is that all I get for my last two months' work? Just enough gold and silver to fool a tenderfoot and not enough to pay or get excited about?"

"Id ain't my fault if you picks up barren quartz, iss id?"

"No, it ain't your fault, Hans, but I did think I was a sure winner that time."

"Vell, Shordy, you been in dis business long enough not to get discouraged yust because you gets one dot ain't vat you tinks she ought to be."

Without replying, Shorty laid six silver dollars on the counter, put the assay certificate in his pocket, turned on his heel and went out. Randt watched him as he walked away, and whispered to himself: "Dot feller certainly knows a brosbect ven he sees one. Py chiminy, I vonder if he's got suspicions?"

Randt returned to his figures. Out of sight of the assay office, Shorty Peterson thought: "That damned crooked

Dutchman! Trying to do me up like that. Now I know it's his regular game and the only reason he hasn't got away with it is because there ain't been no prospect found up to now that he thought worth while."

Shorty went to his cabin, picked up a paper, sat down in the shade and began to read.

"I can't afford to go downtown much today," he muttered, "because if I do, there's a chance I might get full; and I can't afford to get full at this stage of the game. I'm goin' to sit right here till the whistle blows for noon, and then I'm goin' over to Sam Hing's hash-house and get some grub and meet Ralph. Gosh, I wish Si Proctor was here. I certainly will feel better when he shows up with that old Colt of his."

At the sound of the noon whistle, Shorty rose and started down for Sam Hing's. He found the place filled with the usual crowd of shift-bosses, mill men, carpenters and a sprinkling of town residents.

"Mebbe you likee small chicken, Missee Peterson? Velly fine small chicken today; he am stew. Some flied potatoes, coffee?" asked the Chinaman.

Shorty nodded his head in assent, and joined in the general talk about the coming celebration.

"Say," remarked the postmaster, "when Tom Fitch gets going strong on that oration of his you just naturally get up on your toes and turn loose. Talk about your galvanic batteries! He ain't called the silver-tongued orator of Nevada for nothin'. He can make more chills run up and down your spine than any durn battery ever made. No, sir! I ain't goin' to miss that speech on no account. We raised $250 dollars to bring him over from Virginia City, besides his expenses. I calc'late it'll cost the town $350, and it's well worth the price."

Here Nick Trevethan chipped in with, "Say, postmaster, what'll you bet me on the drilling contest? We got a team up at the 'Con' that looks good to me. Like to make you a little bet, if you start your oration at one end of town and the drilling contest at the other, that your orator won't draw fifty people."

"Bet you nothin'," was the reply. "First place, there ain't goin' to be no such fool arrangement; second place, I ain't goin' to bet on no drillin' contest that you know all about."

Trevethan, however, had started something. The mine foreman and others took a hand in the discussion. Bets were made, and the money was put in the hands of the postmaster to hold. During the heat of the argument Ralph Lee came in, and in the conversation as well as in the betting, he and Shorty joined most heartily.

After finishing his meal, Shorty went out on the sidewalk in front of the restaurant and engaged in an argument with the boss carpenter from the "Con." Ralph Lee joined him just as the carpenter walked off. Shorty asked, "What did the balance of them samples go, Ralph?"

"Average of the bunch about $200," replied Ralph.

"She's a real bonanza," said Shorty. "But don't stay here too long, Ralph, and don't talk as though we were in earnest about anything; make out you're joshing me. Don't get excited, just listen to what I've got to say. That damn Dutchman is trying to stack the deck on me, just as I suspected. He gave me an assay return that showed just enough gold and silver to excite a tenderfoot, but no good. I seen Slim Wilson coming out of Randt's office, and I bet anything he was in there gittin' advance information, and that they got some kind of a deal on with Bill Patrick. Slim came out of the shop and headed straight for the Miners Rest."

"Doing a little detective work for yourself, eh?" said Ralph, grinning.

"You bet I am, an' I'm goin' to do some more. Now you back-track to the mine, an' keep your mouth shut."

Ralph laughingly replied that he understood everything and started toward the mine, calling to Shorty as he went, "All right, it's twenty dollars even money on the drilling team from the 'Con,' and ten dollars on Johnnie Forbes to win the footrace?"

"Sold," called Shorty after him, as he started down the street.

Chapter VIII

Shortly after twelve o'clock, Randt locked his door and walked to the Miners Rest. As he entered, he nodded to Hank Bartle, who remarked, "Patrick says you're to go in the back room and I'm to call him downstairs for you; he says he wants to see you as soon as you come in."

Randt went into the private room while Bartle scurried upstairs to inform the boss.

"You go down and tell him I'll be along shortly," remarked Patrick. "Let him sit there and cool his heels for a while. Don't give him a drink unless he asks for it; the less Dutch courage he has aboard, the better it'll be."

"All right, boss," replied Bartle, as he left the room. "I'll take care of him till you come down." Crossing the saloon, Bartle put his head in the door and said: "Bill'll be down in a few minutes. Says you're to make yourself at home. Here's a cigar to keep yourself company with." All he got in return was a grunt, as Randt accepted the proffered smoke, bit the end off it somewhat savagely, and applied a match.

It was some ten or fifteen minutes before Patrick, suave and collected, pushed open the door and, nodding to Randt, sat down remarking: "Well, Hans, what's the news?"

"Der news? Vell, I tells you dot py und py. Yust now ve iss going to haf a understanding aboudt vat share I get in dot prosbect vat ve iss going to took ofer vrom dot Shordy Pederson."

"So it *is* good, is it?"

"Who said it vas?"

"You said so, just now. If it was no good I don't think you'd be figurin' on taking it over or sweating about what you were to get out of it."

"Vell, maybe dot's so, und maybe it ain't. Vat I vant to know iss vere do I come in?"

"Where do you come in? And you want to know right now?"

"Dot's der idea. Ven I gifs de information aboudt dis prosbect of Pederson's, I vant somedings from you in wriding, dot I can keep. Dere is no shenanagin aboudt dis von."

The small, piggy eyes of the assayer snapped through the thick glasses; the cigar was chewed almost to a pulp.

As he worked himself up to a climax and banged his hand on the table, Patrick looked at him with amused tolerance; then, sitting back in his chair, half facing the table, he said mildly: "So, it's a real mine, and you want it all down in writing. Well, bring out your contract and let's look at it. Of course, you've written it all out, haven't you?" Still the same bantering tone on Patrick's part, quite unmoved, entirely self-possessed, his features as unemotional as those of a wooden Indian.

"Yess, I haf godt it down in wriding alretty."

Reaching into an outside pocket, Randt produced a document, which he offered to Patrick.

"No, you read it. I'll listen and see what kind of a lawyer you are."

"All rightd, I read it to you," said Randt.

"I, William Patrick, do hereby agree with Hans Randt, as follows:

"In consideration of information given me by Randt regarding a prospect belonging to Shorty Peterson and his associates,

I agree, if I buy said prospect or in any way come into possession of the same, I will give Hans Randt one-tenth interest in such claim or claims, and that I will organize a company and give Randt one-tenth of the stock."

"Well, Hans, is that all?"

"Yah, dot's all."

"Let me see that paper," said Patrick, leaning forward and taking the document from Randt's hand. After looking at it for a moment, he calmly tore it into bits and flung the pieces on the table. Then, squaring around, he pointed a finger at Randt, saying: "What do you think I am, Randt, a plain damn fool? I've never signed any papers yet in our deals, and I never will. You'll get an interest all right, but you'll get it in my way and when I get good and ready. And you'll take it or leave it, just that way."

Randt's face turned purple, his hands twitched nervously, his body tensed, as he leaned forward and said: "You tink you're smart as hell, don't you, Mr. Bill Padrick? Vell, I goes to Shordy and tells him der whole business, und den vere are you at, eh?"

"Oh, no, you won't! You'll play this game with me in my way, or in twenty-four hours this town'll be too hot to hold you. I'll tell my own story, about your fake assays and how you came to me and I turned you down. Then you'll not only get nothing, but the boys'll run you out of town on top of it. Your kind of cheating in a mining camp is about as popular as horse stealing. I've got you dead to rights, Mr. Assayer, and if you'll think it over for a few minutes, you'll realize it for yourself."

Tipping back in his chair, Patrick seemed quite oblivious to the surroundings, save that never for an instant did he cease to keep his eyes fixed on Randt.

Muttering and stuttering, Randt squirmed in his chair. Once he started to get up, but sank back and finally lapsed into ineffectual silence.

"Now, just one word more, Randt. I don't think myself smart as hell, but I know I'm a damn sight smarter than you, and I'm going to run this thing my own way and cut the division whatever way suits me. You'll get your share and put up your money like the rest of us. Now, hand over those assays."

Randt hesitated, looked furtively about, and after several moments of uncertainty, reached into his pocket and fished out a paper which he reluctantly handed to Patrick.

Unemotional as he was, and accustomed to controlling himself under all circumstances, Patrick could not entirely suppress the impression the figures made on him.

"Know anything about where it's at, or the size of the outcrop?"

"Noddings. Dot Shordy iss a smart ellick himself, und I dinks he smelled a rat somevhere."

"What did he tell you?"

"Absoludely noddings. Excebt it vas over by der Idaho line, vich iss a long line and means nix. Und he says der claims ain't recorded. Says dot costs too much money."

"Didn't he tell you anything else?"

"Nix, noddings. I tries him oudt, und gets left. You got to find dot oudt for yourself."

"Any idea who's in on this grubstake?"

"Yah, he iss got Si Proctor, who iss swamping for Jim Langford."

"Anybody else?"

"Not dot I know aboudt. Don't tink dere iss anybody else. Von of der poys told me he asked him to come in on der grubstake und said dere was only Proctor in, und if he couldn't get nobody else he'd pack der rest himself."

"Well, it might be better, and it might be worse," said Patrick. "I ain't stuck on that Proctor outfit, ever since Ike Proctor pulled a gun on Slim Wilson in a poker game."

"Vell, I don't do no gun fighting," said Randt with emphasis.

"You're right you don't. That's not your game, and you'd last about ten seconds in a real gun scrap."

"Vell, dot's your job, Patrick. I told you aboudt der assays, und now it's for you to find vere de claims iss und get possession. I'll do der assaying, but excuse me if I don't come so close dot my hair stands up on my head. Anyhow, ve got a agreement, und dot being seddled, vat's next?"

"Well, you go out and round up any of the boys you can find and bring them in here at four this afternoon. I guess you won't have to go far to find them," added Patrick significantly.

Randt got to his feet.

"By the way, Hans," Patrick called to him, as he put his hand on the doorknob, "if you talk to Anderson or Wilson or Bartle, you better cut these values in half. No use getting them too wildly excited."

"Dot's a good idea, Bill," said Randt approvingly. "Der least said, der better," and he turned and went out. After he left the room, Patrick reached for the assay certificate and read again and again the figures written thereon.

Chapter IX

Up on the hill at the residence of the superintendent, dinner was over and Mary Clark was helping Mrs. Macklay clear the table. In the adjoining room John Macklay was seated near a window scanning the latest San Francisco paper and smoking a cigar.

"Anything new about the parade on the Fourth, Mary?" he called through the open door.

"No, not that I know of. The children have a rehearsal this afternoon, and that will be the last one before the parade."

Mrs. Macklay came in and seated herself near her husband with her sewing basket in her lap. "You've no idea, John, what a struggle Mary has had to overcome her innate modesty and take the part of the Goddess of Liberty in the parade. She doesn't like to 'become the cynosure of all eyes,' enthroned on that float, surrounded by her prize scholars; she thinks sitting up there quite the most terrible task she has ever undertaken. George Washington in full Continental uniform will ride on horseback in advance."

"Yes, and the orator of the day will ride just ahead of us," added Mary, who came into the room at that moment, "and at the end the 'Horribles,'" she added, smiling. "Every small boy in town is making himself some sort of a costume and mask.

"Well, I must go down town to mail a letter before rehearsal," she said. Taking her hat from a peg in the hall, she walked out through the garden and started down the hill.

Sulphide, like all other mining towns of the West in those days, boasted a Wells Fargo Express office that handled not only parcels, but letters as well. No one who has not been part of that period and is not familiar with the atmosphere of mining camps can have any conception of what an institution Wells, Fargo & Company was. Its employees prided themselves upon their honesty, upon the promptness with which they discharged their duties, and upon the accuracy and certainty with which they carried out commissions entrusted to them. The Sulphide office, like many others, consisted of a counter running the whole width of the room, a gate at one side through which employees might enter, empty pouches and bullion boxes, the safe used for the protection of valuable property until it was delivered to the owners or shipped out on the stage; a desk, tables, a few chairs, and some lamps made up the remaining furniture. Under the counter were a brace of pistols and a sawed-off shotgun. The agent was a man who had come up through the ranks and had been assigned to Sulphide because of past satisfactory record; his name was Will Gault. As Mary entered the office, he was engaged in writing out some way-bills for the material that was to be shipped out on the afternoon stage.

"How do you do, Mr. Gault," she said.

"Why, how do you do, Miss Clark. What brings you here?"

"I would like to send this letter and get a receipt for it."

Looking at the envelope, Gault saw that it was addressed to the Recorder of Elko County, with instructions on the envelope to record the documents enclosed and return them to Sulphide.

"I don't know just what the charges will be, but you can

pay for it when the document is returned," Gault said. "I suppose it will take a week or ten days to get it back again, but I'll send you word when it comes."

Mary saw the envelope safely deposited in one of the locked pouches. Then she walked rapidly on to the schoolhouse. It was almost one o'clock, and the children would soon assemble for the last rehearsal before the parade on the morrow. It would be a busy afternoon, but she was in no mood to concentrate on parades, Fourth of July, school children, or much of anything other than Shorty Peterson's strike. To think of it! She, a tenderfoot, and on her first venture to "strike it rich"! She had read that there was a "tenderfoot luck," and only a few weeks ago Mr. Macklay was telling about the "Green Emigrant Claim," on the North Fork of the Feather, and how some old-timers, in derision, had suggested to some new arrivals, when asked by them where to prospect, that they go up on the side of the mountain a hundred feet or more above the level of the creek, and in guileless simplicity the greenhorns had done so, to the huge amusement of the old-timers who thought the joke was quite the best of the season. To their consternation, however, and the delight of the tenderfeet, it was but a few days before they struck "bench diggings" (simply another and earlier creek-bed that had become obliterated), enormously rich. Well, perhaps her luck would be equally dazzling! Ralph had spoken of $100 a ton, and if they got out one hundred tons a day, and if it cost $50 to work it, that would leave a profit of $50 to the ton, and that would be $5000 a day, or $150,000 a month, in which she would have a fortieth interest—or almost $4000 a month!

With the realization of it, she stopped short with a gasp. Her eyes were dancing, her color heightened, and her whole body tingled as she hurried across the barren flat to the schoolhouse, built apart from the town in order, as John Macklay said, "that the schoolhouse won't burn up with the darn town when she goes."

Meanwhile, Hans Randt had found most of the members of Patrick's inner circle, and instructed them to be on hand at the Miners Rest at four that afternoon. Having done this, he stopped at Sam Hing's to eat and then returned to his office to await the time set for the gathering in Patrick's private room. As the hands of his office clock neared four, Randt rose, locked the drawers of his desk (there was some stolen high-grade ore there, tucked away under some loose papers), dropped the latch on the outer door and started down the street.

He found Slim Wilson, Hank Bartle, and Gus Anderson engaged in desultory conversation; Hank, as usual, was behind the bar, the other two standing in front of it. Nick Trevethan could not be present because of his work underground at the mine.

As Randt joined the others, Bartle remarked: "Patrick's in the private room, Hans; says you're to come in as soon as you all get here."

"All right," answered Randt, "ve vill go in mit der lion's den." He led the way to the private room, where they found Patrick sitting idly drumming on the table and gazing abstractedly out of the window. Patrick was no miner and had no desire to operate a mine. As a gambler he thought only of stock speculation. He had a couple of hundred thousand dollars safely "salted down" in San Francisco, some of it on deposit with the Hibernia Savings and Loan Society which, like Wells, Fargo & Company, was an institution of peculiar standing with the Nevada miners.

In those days the Hibernia Bank paid nine per cent per annum interest on deposits. Loans at one per cent a month were common in those days; two was not unusual, and three per cent was obtained on occasion.

Bill Patrick was not going to jeopardize his cash resources by any speculative ventures. If he could get hold of a promising prospect, it would not be difficult to put it on the San Francisco Stock Board; all he would be out would be the first payment on the mine; the balance would come out of the sale of stock. Perhaps four or five thousand dollars would be the total of his out-of-pocket expense, and the income from the Miners Rest for a month or two would easily care for that. If he could clean up another $200,000 he would be ready to quit.

Patrick looked up as the men pushed into the room. Randt said, "Hello, Padrick," as he seated himself, and Patrick quietly replied, "Hello, Hans."

Wilson and Anderson slipped into chairs.

"Anybody else coming?" Patrick asked.

"No, I guess not," replied Wilson. "Hank's outside, Nick's on shift, and we're all you can count on now."

"All right, let's begin, then. First of all, you tell the whole story over again, Hans."

This the assayer did, in minute detail, winding up with the declaration that Shorty had located a "preddy good prosbect," good for $50 a ton, and that it was up to Patrick to get possession of it. Wilson and Anderson nodded acquiescence.

"Well, now that you fellows know all that there is to know, what's to be done about it, and who's going to do it?" asked Patrick, as he looked inquiringly from one to the other, but each in turn shook his head and shifted uneasily in his chair. Even Randt remained subdued, and merely remarked, "You boss der job, Bill, und ve foller your orders; only me—I don't be a gun-fighter, so coundt me oudt on any of dose bad-man performances."

"You won't get mixed up in no gun-fights, Hans. You and your forty-horsepower eyeglasses wouldn't be worth a damn in any such a game, so we'll leave you out at the beginning.

"Well, then," Patrick went on, "if I'm to boss this job, I am boss just one hundred per cent. I'll cut you all in for good shares; how much depends on how it works out. I can't say now. Each one of you does as he's told, and no questions asked."

"That suits me," said Wilson.

"And me," said Anderson.

"Me, too," echoed Randt, "only noddings like a gun-fight for me mit dose Circle R cowboys."

"Well, it's not likely that the cowpunchers from the Circle R will ever have a chance to get in on this. We're not going to do business that way. Diplomacy wins more battles than guns. Besides, it will be all over before the cowpunchers know what's what. Here's my plan: tomorrow is the Fourth of July; things are beginning to liven up already, but it's not much use to start today. Tomorrow Hans will make it his business to get hold of Shorty and get him started drinking. From what I know of him he'll be maudlin before long. You stay with him, Hans, and bring him in here to me after the parade, or any time during the afternoon, and I'll get an agreement out of him."

"Well, what about Proctor's interest in the grubstake?" asked Wilson.

"We'll have to take care of that some way; Proctor won't

have over a quarter, probably, and if we get possession of three-quarters, we'll just naturally fall heir to the other quarter, some way."

"But you know, Bill," answered Wilson, "these grubstakes is mighty particular things, an' monkeying with one of them—that is, tryin' to do somebody out of his interest—ain't so popular; in fact, it's just about as popular as horse stealin' or cattle rustlin'."

"I know that, and I haven't the slightest intention of denying that Si Proctor is one of the owners. We've just got to accept that as a fact and plan accordingly. There's one thing we must know, however, as soon as possible, and that is—how many interests there are in this particular grubstake, and who owns them."

"Couldn't buy the whole thing from him and let him settle with his pardners, could you?" asked Wilson hopefully.

"You could not," replied Patrick. "Shorty's got no more power to sell out his partners than you have. Whatever their interest is, it's theirs to do with as they please. All they got to do is prove they are interested and for how much."

"Do you suppose there's any agreement in existence?" asked Anderson.

"No doubt of it. I've been in on one grubstake with Peterson," said Wilson, "and he's got a regular form he draws up that says what's what and how much interest you got. I know, 'cause I had one."

"My plan," continued Patrick, "is to make a stock company, list it on the San Francisco Stock Exchange and whoop her up for awhile and then unload. Many a good prospect has been spoiled by too much digging. However,

I don't calculate we're going to knock the bottom out of this one by any such foolishness. Get a shaft started and then unload on the strength of the showing. Lots of 'mud hens' will figure that the values will go to the centre of the earth, and will buy accordingly. Let 'em have it, is my motto! We'll get Nick Trevethan to lay off for a week and go out with Shorty and sample the claims; then, when he gets back and we get the assays, we'll pay Shorty his money. In the meantime, we'll have to make some kind of a deal with Si Proctor. You better bring him in here later in the afternoon and I'll give him the once-over and see if I can't make a trade with him as well as with Peterson. Between the two of them we ought to get pretty near the whole story—where it is, whose it is, and all about it. Now, just one thing more—you've all got to remember that if any one opens his mouth the whole business is up the spout! Just let a suspicion of this get to Peterson, and you won't see him for dust."

"Yah, dot's so," interjected Randt. "Dot tam prosbector iss a wise fella. I been thinking he smells him a rat alretty yet. He vas too tam secretive ven I tried to gross-examine him. Dot Shordy Pederson, even if he *iss* full, ain't going to forget everything he knows. I bedt you, Padrick, you iss in for a hell of a time before you gets him to sign somedings."

"Well, there's one thing sure, we ain't going to get anywhere by just sitting here and talking about it," replied Patrick.

As they walked through the saloon, they stopped and had a drink "on the house" at the invitation of Hank Bartle, to whom Anderson related the conversation with Patrick.

"Well," said Bartle reflectively, "you'll get a square deal, all right, from Patrick. His word's better than most men's bond—but I don't know about that Shorty Peterson. He's a stubborn cuss, anyway, and maybe if he gets full he'll be twice as bad."

"Well, here's hoping," said Anderson, and all hands silently lifted their glasses and drank to the success of the prospective deal.

Chapter X

SHORTY PETERSON was torn between a desire to begin celebrating the Fourth of July on July third and a determination to await the arrival of Si Proctor and post him on the occurrences of the past few weeks, culminating in the receipt from Hans Randt of the false assay certificate.

He drifted rather aimlessly down the street, stopping here and there to talk with some one and to buy some fruit from California, which he carried in his hand in a paper bag, eating the contents as he walked and shying the cherry stones and apricot pits at vagrant dogs that wandered freely up and down the main street of the town. He passed the stores and found himself at the end of the board sidewalk, with Simpson's Corral a short distance ahead. Having nothing better to do, he walked on toward the corral, where he found Simpson leaning over the gate inspecting some horses.

Standing six feet three or four inches in height, Simpson must in his younger days have been a formidable antagonist. Now, somewhat stoop-shouldered, his still black hair somewhat straggling, with gray, drooping mustache, angular features and piercing gray eyes, he was a typical American frontiersman. He had been a sharpshooter in the Confederate Army and still retained his ability to shoot straight and quickly. They wanted to run him for sheriff, after he had headed a posse that captured the three highwaymen who had held up the stage about a year before.

But he declined, simply because he was an easy-going Southerner who preferred to take life more quietly than would be possible for the sheriff of Elko County. He was good natured, warmhearted and, by instinct, a respecter of law and order.

As Shorty came up, Simpson turned and greeted him. "Hello, Shorty, where'd you come from?"

"Oh, I just come down here to see what you fellows was doin' and find out if anybody had heard anything about Langford's outfit."

"Yeah," said Simpson, "cowboy came in here 'bout a hour ago and left his cayuse and said he'd passed Langford on the road; he calc'lated they'd get here 'bout dinner time, today. What you got to do with Langford, anyway? He ain't haulin' any freight fer your mine."

"No, not yet; but maybe he will some day."

"Well, when he does, Shorty, I'll apply for the job of drivin' your four-in-hand. Wear one of them uniforms and top-boots, like a picture I seen in the paper the other day."

"Aw, go to hell; I may have a mine yet, someday."

"Yeah, maybe you will. Say, come on, let's go in the office and sit down; it's too darn hot out here."

The corral stood on the edge of the high-road, with the sun beating down upon it. Shorty and Simpson went into the cool office. A desk covered with old newspapers and magazines, pieces of harness scattered about the floor, a Henry repeating rifle hanging on the wall, a lamp suspended from the ceiling, three or four wooden chairs and a bench much cut up by whittling constituted the office equipment.

Seating himself in one of the homemade wooden chairs with high sloping back and broad arm-rests, Simpson bit off a large chunk of chewing tobacco and offered the plug to Shorty, who helped himself liberally.

"I calc'late we're goin' to have a real celebration on the Fourth," remarked Simpson. "Tom Fitch is comin' over to make the oration, and there's goin' to be a reg'lar rip-roarin' time with fireworks at night and firewater all day."

"Say," remarked Shorty, "which one of them broncs out there is liable to win that mile race?"

"Well, I don't rightly know, you see, 'cause they ain't all there yet, and a lot of them that's goin' to run won't come to the corral at all; but as fer me, if I was a-goin' to bet, I'd pick that bay mare that belongs to a feller that's been in here for a month sort of lookin' up prospects, he says. I don't know what he's doin', but I notice he goes ridin' with tol'ble reg'larity, and if he ain't trainin' that mare for a hoss race, I just don't know hosses when I sees 'em."

After a time, as Shorty was thinking of going back to town, he noticed a swirl of dust rising beyond the summit of the first hill. Idly watching it, he saw it become more and more distinct until there came into view a freight team consisting of sixteen animals, a wagon, and a trailer.

"Hello! Maybe that's Jim Langford's outfit now," exclaimed Shorty.

Simpson unwound himself from his chair and squinted out of the door, remarking: "I calc'late that's just about right, Shorty; it won't take long now for him to get in. I don't know of any other outfit that's expected right now. Reckon it must be Langford."

Enveloped in a cloud of dust, the freight team toiled onward toward Sulphide. To the collar of each leader was attached a piece of bowed iron carrying three bells, firmly riveted on. Soon the jingle of these bells could be heard, and now Shorty could distinguish Jim Langford himself, guiding the nigh wheel-horse, with a jerk-line firmly grasped in one hand and a huge blacksnake whip in the other. Perched on top of the load sat Si Proctor. The huge leading wagon, with high sides and canvas cover, carried the smaller articles of freight. Upon the trailer was a large sinking-pump. When the outfit was abreast of the corral, the two occupants of the office emerged to greet the teamsters as they passed by on their way up to the hoisting-works on the hill. With an exchange of salutations and a friendly wave of the hand, Langford urged his team forward, while Si Proctor, catching sight of Shorty, clambered down from the wagon and jumped to the ground.

Walking with gliding steps, his whole body synchronized into perfect action, Si Proctor was the embodiment of the frontiersman, whose movements might be characterized by the words "chain lightning." He was taller and slightly broader across the shoulders than his brother, but his whole build was adapted to rapid motion. He was two years younger than Ike, not quite twenty-two, but every inch the frontiersman: calm, quiet and self-possessed. He had grown up in the saddle; the rifle and the six-shooter had been his constant companions. It was a toss-up as to which one of the boys was the better rider or the better shot. Certain it was, however, that as riders, ropers and marksmen they had few equals and no superiors.

Shorty rapidly advanced to meet Si, and walking side by side, they kept pace with the team as it went on up the street.

"Jiminy, Si, I'm glad to see you back; been waiting for you the best part of two days now."

"What you waitin' for me for?"

"Oh, just to tell you about the prospect I've located. It looks pretty good."

"Seein's believin', Shorty. I ain't goin' to get excited about this business yet. Swampin' or punchin' cows is 'bout the surest job I know of."

"Well, of course, that's your job, Si, but, jiminy, you're a-goin' to have a darn sight better job than that."

"What do you mean, better job?" queried Proctor.

"Well, I've located a prospect over near the Ruby Range, and the samples've been assayed by two people, Hans Randt, who gives me a value of seven or eight dollars a ton, and Ralph Lee, who gives me a result of over two hundred dollars a ton! The vein is about eight to twelve feet wide, and the pay-shoot is over 400 feet long, so far. And there you are!"

"Gosh, if you've got a mine like that, Shorty, you sure got a real mine. But how does it happen that there's such a difference in them assays?"

"Reason is Hans Randt's a crook, standing in with Bill Patrick and that Miners Rest gang. Patrick wants to grab the mine and dump us out in the cold."

"The hell he does! We'll show 'em a few tricks ourselves."

"That's what I want to talk with you about. We've got to play a mighty fine game, Si. Every fellow's got to do just as I tell him. You're one of them people, and I don't calculate you're goin' to get left any more than I am or Ralph Lee is. We're all in together, and we're goin' to sink or swim with this prospect."

"Well, that suits me," said Si.

As they talked, they approached the town, and as they

came to the first houses Shorty said, "Si, I'm goin' to leave you here. You come over to my cabin tonight and we'll talk things over. Come any time you like. But you got to do one thing, though; you got to keep your mouth shut so doggone tight that a fireproof safe would look like a sieve in comparison. If anybody sees you and talks with you about it, you tell 'em you don't know nothin' much about it an' you guess maybe the grubstake's blown up, as they generally do, and that vou're kind of sour on the whole business."

"All right, Shorty," said Si, "I'll carry out your instructions," and he hopped onto the wagon and resumed his seat.

Rivulets of fine alkali particles trickled down the sides of the canvas cover and lost themselves in the clouds of dust rising from the wheels and from the hoofs of the horses. The sweat of the horses was caked on their backs in gray patches. Langford and Proctor were covered from head to foot with dust. Their eyes looked out from under eyebrows and eyelashes gray with the dust of the desert; their hair was powdered with it.

As the outfit rolled along the street up through the town, men in their shirtsleeves, standing on the sidewalks, nodded to Langford and Proctor, and, in some instances, exchanged greetings with them. Both men were well known in the community; the one as a middle-aged man, steady and reliable, the owner of the outfit he drove; the other as an enthusiastic youngster, essentially honest, frank and straightforward, raised upon the cattle ranges of Texas where he had learned to take care of himself.

They stopped at the foot of the hill near the mine. Here Proctor uncoupled the back action; this they left behind while the outfit went on up the steep ascent. Arriving at the mine, the animals were unhitched from the wagon, driven back down the hill, and the back action, in turn, pulled up the steep slope.

"Come on, Si," said Langford, "rip the canvas cover off and let's set them packages out on the ground."

They began to unload the miscellaneous assortment of freight in the front wagon. Ralph Lee came and sat on a couple of boxes of candles and began to check off the packages as they were piled on the ground.

So they labored on, checking out candles, caps, fuse, powder, picks, shovels, hammer handles, drill steel, and miscellaneous other articles used in mining operations. Unloading the pump from the trailer took considerable time, as it weighed well on to 8000 pounds. Prying it up from the bed of the wagon, they inserted short lengths of two-inch pipe as rollers and, using a pinch-bar, gradually worked the pump over the tail end of the wagon, down an improvised skidway of timber, and onto some pieces of 12 x 12 posts which they had piled up in the form of a crib. Here the pump was allowed to remain, later to be dragged into the hoisting works and to the collar of the shaft, where it would be swung beneath the cage and lowered safely to the 700-foot station.

The unloading completed and a receipt given to Langford by Lee, Langford entered the office and handed it to the superintendent, who gave him in return a check for the amount of the freight.

"When will you be ready to start back for another load?" asked the superintendent.

"Well, Mr. Macklay, you see it's thisaway—tomorrow bein' the Fourth o' July, I calc'late it'll take us 'bout two days after that to get straightened around; so, let's say that I get away before noon on the sixth."

"That's all right," replied Macklay, "but don't make it much longer than that, for there's a load of stuff there that we've got to have, and have pretty quick."

"All right," answered Langford. "We'll get away by that time."

He folded the check and put it in a dilapidated wallet. Then he went out, leaving Macklay with Ralph Lee checking over the list of freight which had just been unloaded.

"Ralph, tomorrow all hands are going to celebrate," said Macklay. "There will be nobody underground, and there will be no work going on on top; all that will be done is to keep the mill shift at work on the ore in the storage bins. We've got them all well filled, so there won't be any shortage, if it takes longer than I expect to get the crew back to work again after the celebration. The pump men will be on shift to look after things and see that fire is kept in the boilers and to stand by in case of any necessity. You can take a day off along with the rest of them and see the show."

"Thank you, Mr. Macklay. There are some things I want to see—or rather, see and hear. I want to hear the oration —they say Tom Fitch is a real orator; and I want to see the drilling match. There is a tremendous amount of interest among the men, and from all I can gather, it's going to be a nip-and-tuck contest. The boys have been getting ready for it for weeks—sharpening and tempering drills, practising changing, trying different speeds and, in short, using every device to make themseves as nearly invincible as possible."

"Yes, I know that," answered Macklay. "The boys have

asked me to act as referee, and I have agreed to do so. I wish we could have more drilling contests and similar athletics and less of other contests that go on downtown, especially those that are staged in the Miners Rest. It takes this crew just about a week to get back to normal again after the Fourth of July, and while I am a first-class American, even if I am Scotch, I must say that the Fourth of July can raise more hell with a crew of men than any other one celebration I ever ran up against. Foot-races, drilling contests, the oration, the 'Horribles' and the parade—I don't mind those things at all; but it's the amount of whiskey consumed that raises particular Hail Columbia with this whole outfit."

Chapter XI

MEANWHILE, Proctor had headed the two wagons down the hill. With the aid of the two wheel-horses and with the use of the heavy brake, he negotiated the steep descent from the mine dump to the gently sloping hillside that marked the edge of the town. From there he continued down the main street to Simpson's Corral. Stopping the wagon in the rear of the corral, he unhitched the horses, led them to the feeding shed, deposited the harness in a small room partitioned off from Simpson's office and then slid himself onto the much-whittled bench, prepared to absorb the latest gossip.

The main topic of conversation was the horse races. The camp gossip, possible new discoveries, and the like were all quickly dismissed; the orator of the day was not even mentioned; the drilling contest received some attention, as did the foot races. The horse races, however, were minutely discussed; bets were made and stake-holders selected.

The meeting broke up just as the sun touched the distant peaks to the west and the long shadows began to creep across the valley and up the gentle foothill slopes toward the hoisting works.

"Well, Sim," remarked Si, "reckon I'll go clean up, have a real shave at the barber's and get ready to celebrate. Got to get my hair cut, too. Ain't nothin' like the Fourth to make a feller slick up, 'ceptin' you got a best girl—and I ain't." He moved up the street to a rooming house and deposited his bag, rescued from Simpson's storeroom where many such kits were left while their owners were away.

Si washed, put on the clothes taken from his bag, and started out. The Miners Rest was his first stopping place, and there he deposited a quarter on the counter, with a nod to Hank Bartle and a "Hello, Hank, gimme a drink."

Hank had spotted Jim Langford's outfit as it toiled up the street earlier in the day, and promptly reported to Bill Patrick. "Get Proctor in here," was Patrick's terse rejoinder. "Get him full and we'll buy his interest, or play poker for it."

"He don't drink much," ventured Bartle.

"Well—poker, then."

"Don't forget what Ike Proctor did to me once," interrupted Slim Wilson ruefully.

"Well, this ain't Ike," retorted Patrick.

"No, 'tain't; but Si's yust so goot a gun-shooter vat iss Ike," remarked Hans Randt, who had dropped in while the consultation was in full swing.

"We ain't goin' to have any gun-shootin'," fired back Patrick. "This a game of diplomacy."

Proctor helped himself liberally from the bottle set in front of him and drank the liquor with evident gusto. "What's the news, Hank?" he asked.

"Oh, nothin' much; same old thing. Ain't heard of any new discoveries, have you?"

"Naw, I ain't heard of nothing. Seen a good many prospectors between here and the railroad, but nobody seems to have been lucky."

"Ever go prospecting yourself, Si?"

"Me? No! I put up a grubstake once in a while just to get rid of my spare cash, but never got anything back yet—don't expect to any more, neither."

"Well, you never can tell, Si. Generally they turn one up when you least expect it."

"Well, it's about time for me, then, 'cause I sure don't expect it," answered Si, as he headed for the door. "Got to get shaved and get a haircut now. So long, Hank."

Calling his helper, who was in the cellar filling bottles with whiskey from barrels, Hank said: "Hi, Jimmie, come up here a few minutes to keep bar for me."

Walking rapidly across the room, Bartle opened the door leading to Patrick's living quarters and taking the stairs two at a time, rapped hurriedly on the door of Patrick's room.

"Come in. Well, what's up now?" asked Patrick.

"Just had a talk with Si Proctor. He don't suspect a thing."

"How could he?" asked Patrick. "Peterson himself don't know anything, and if *he* don't, how could Proctor suspect anything?"

"Well, I didn't know but what Peterson had an idea the find was some good."

"After getting the assays Randt gave him? No, Hank; there's not a chance."

"Well, I thought you'd like to know, anyway, Bill."

"Of course, I'm glad to know. Get all the information you can; every little bit helps."

"Well, I hope so," ventured Bartle, as he departed, shaking his head. Returning to the barroom, he found a number of people beginning to celebrate the Fourth. Jimmie, in anticipation of the coming thirst that would overtake residents and visitors alike tonight and on the morrow, took his basket and descended to the cellar for more whiskey. It would be the busiest two days of the year for the Miners

Rest. Patrick himself would help behind the bar and Hank Bartle and the others would be on hand almost constantly for the next thirty-six hours.

The advance guard were even now lining up at the bar, intent upon demonstrating their patriotism by consuming large quantities of the liquid for which the Miners Rest was famous.

Proctor entered the barber shop that occupied a room on the main street, adjoining the Golden Eagle Hotel. Business was brisk, every one was cleaning up for the Fourth, and Si was compelled to wait.

Of the waiting group there were only three Si knew—a miner from the "Con," the postmaster, and a cowboy named Frank Lowry from the Circle R.

"Hello, Frank, how's the bunch at the ranch?"

"Well, most of 'em's headed for town. Ike'll be here right soon. Comin' in to be on hand to see we don't clean out the town or land in the calaboose. He's got a job on his hands to keep that bunch from goin' on a reg'lar bust!"

"Reckon he don't calc'late on keeping 'em from goin' on a bust," replied Si. "Only sort of wants to see they don't get into no shootin' scrapes. Keepin' a gang of cowpunchers sober on the Fourth o' July is a good deal like tryin' to keep this town from puttin' up grubstakes. Just naturally can't be done, nohow. Grubstakes and Fourth of July busts is part of the programme in every mining camp in the West, and you bet your life the boys have a hell of a fine time on both occasions. Generally end up the same way, too—swearin' off and a headache. Reminds me of a feller I tried to sober up once; took him upstairs and left him in his room—and him promising never to touch another drop—so I left him and went down the front stairs and stopped in the office to speak to a feller and then went into the barrom, and I swear there he was, standin' at the bar! He skipped down the back stairs and got there before I did. He fell out of a window over in Reno afterwards and broke his neck."

"I knew a feller like him," said Lowry. "Used to get the jimjams. We roped him out in the desert once or twice, and hogtied him while he was seein' snakes. Say, but they do see the damnedest snakes you ever heard of, if you can believe what they tell you. Pink and blue ones, big around as your body and 'bout twenty feet long, at least."

The cry of "Next" broke up the conversation, and Proctor climbed into the chair. As he left the barber shop, the five-thirty whistle was blowing at the "Con," notification to all the town that supper would soon be ready.

The whistle was a signal for Proctor to go to Sam Hing's, where he was sure to meet Peterson and Lee.

Soon Peterson came in. "Hello, Si," he said, as he climbed upon the stool next to Si.

"Hello, Shorty, how're they coming?"

"Oh, 'bout as usual; nothin' to holler about. Hello, there comes Ralph Lee," he continued. "Come on over here, Lee, an' sit down," Peterson called to him. Lee nodded and took the place at the end of the counter. The room was filling rapidly now, and the talk was of the coming celebration. Peterson, Proctor, and Lee joined in the talk, and having finished, left the place together. As they stood on the sidewalk, Peterson said hurriedly, "You fellers be at my cabin tonight just after dark. I got to talk to you."

Ralph made no reply, but waved his hand as he walked off. Proctor muttered "Keno" and started down the street to care for his horses.

Shorty drifted into the Miners Rest, sat in a poker game for an hour or so, had one or two drinks, declined an invitation "to have one on the house," and ran into Patrick standing in front of the bar.

"Well, Shorty, did you clean 'em out?" he asked.

"Not so you'd know it," Shorty replied. "Winning much of a stake at poker's a lot like strikin' bonanzas—you do all the work and gen'rally come out the little end of the horn—'ceptin' maybe Slim Wilson and a few more professionals."

"Well, anyway," said Patrick, "have a drink on me—Fourth of July tomorrow, you know, and all good Americans must celebrate."

"Well, seein' it's you, Bill, don't mind if I do."

Patrick pushed the bottle over to Shorty, who helped himself and passed it back. Patrick poured out a small quantity and raised his glass, saying as he did so, "Here's to your bonanza, Shorty."

"Bet your life I'll drink to that," replied Shorty as he drained his glass.

Patrick had no intention of going further with Shorty at that time; he simply wanted to get him started drinking, to feel him out a little. So when Shorty started for the door, he made no effort to stop him. The Miners Rest was filling rapidly, the poker tables were well occupied, the faro and keno layouts had commenced operations, the bar was doing a rushing business, and Patrick had plenty to think about without taking the responsibility for Shorty Peterson on his shoulders. No one else could, very well. They were all too busy.

It was almost dark by this time. The streets were dimly lighted by a few kerosene lamps here and there. There was no inducement to linger; it was either go into one of the stores or saloons or go home. Shorty walked up the street past the stores and saloons without stopping.

"I vunder," soliloquized Randt, "vot dot Shordy iss goin' home dis time of day for? By righds, he should be takin' in der town, und here he iss goin' home before der night iss begun yet."

"He's got some one coming out to see him," Patrick surmised as Randt reported to him. "Say, Hans, can't you find out who it is?"

"Vell, I might sneak up by his cabin und vatch."

Chapter XII

It was now quite dark, and Shorty had scarcely reached his cabin before footsteps on the gravel announced the coming of Si Proctor. They had hardly exchanged greetings before Ralph Lee appeared, with his dog, who, as before, went on watch some little distance from the cabin.

"I'm mighty glad to see you fellers," Shorty remarked as they seated themselves around the table. "Boys, we've got a mine, if all signs don't fail. We've got a shoot of ore over 400 feet long and over eight feet wide. That'll make pretty close to 250 tons for every foot in depth. If she averages $150 a ton, that'll be $37,500 gross for every foot she goes down, or $3,750,000 for every hundred feet in depth. Take off $50 a ton for expenses of every kind, and we'd net $2,500,000 for every hundred feet."

"Say, Ralph," interjected Si, "is Shorty givin' us the real steer? Don't sound possible to me. What would be my share of that first hundred feet?"

"You bet he's giving you the real thing, Si; and your part would be around $800,000 to the hundred feet."

"Holy sufferin' wildcats! Do you mean to tell me if she holds out for a hundred feet, an' it's like them assays you give Shorty, that I get $800,000 out of it, all for myself?"

"That's about the size of it, Si."

"Why, I could buy a ranch and stock it with 5000 head and be a sure-nuff cattle king, and have Ike and the Lowry boys, Bill Gale and Ted Wilson and the whole crew a-workin' for me."

"Yes," added Shorty, "and if she goes down 200 feet, you can have two ranches."

"Holy smoke, I never thought of that. Say, Ralph, how deep is the 'Con'?"

"Ore in the bottom in the 600, and opening up the 700 now."

"Gosh! S'pose this one of ourn goes down that deep! Why, say, fellers, we'll just naturally have so much money we'll be lousy with it—stinkin' lousy. I pass, Shorty; you deal 'em," said Si weakly, as he settled back in his chair with a sigh.

"I know how you feel, Si; felt that way myself, only more so, when Ralph gave me them assays. I've had time to think it over and sort of get my bearings, as it were; settle down to business and get to thinkin' how we're going to hold on to what we got. We've got to get on the ground just as quick as we can, get survey stakes set and things properly marked, so's no one can beat us out with another survey and claim possession. We got to see that the vein goes out over one end line and comes in over the other end line. We want all the extra-lateral rights we can get.

"Now, this is what we got to do . . ."

Just then came a growl, a bark and a snarl from Spot. Shorty hastily left the cabin. A dim figure was retreating in the direction of the town. Spot stood rigid, with hair bristling. It was too dark for Shorty to see who it was, so he returned to the cabin after patting and praising the dog.

"Some one's been over here, spying round, but Spot chased him off," he announced as he re-entered the cabin.

"Bet it was some of Patrick's outfit," said Ralph.

"Shouldn't wonder," returned Shorty. "Patrick knows what them assays went, too. What he don't know is where they come from or that Ralph Lee ran duplicate assays. Well, as I was sayin', we got to get a few men over on them claims; get some holes dug and a showing made as quick as we can and get ourselves settled in possession before they light on to where it is. Ralph, you got to get a lay-off and do that surveying. Si'll build a camp and do the teamin', and I'll boss the miners. Anybody got any money to buy tools, powder, fuse, caps, and camp outfit?"

Si and Ralph looked blank at this suggestion; they had not realized that even the richest of bonanzas requires money to start things going.

"I got $200 when I get paid off," volunteered Si.

"I've got over $1,000 invested in San Francisco," said Ralph, "but only about $300 here. I could borrow $1000, I guess."

"I guess you won't," said Shorty. "You go out and borrow a thousand dollars and somebody'll want to know what you want it for, and the first thing you know it'll be all over town; and that's just what we don't want. The less said about what's goin' on, for the next few weeks, the better it'll be for all of us. I got a couple or $300, myself; your $300, Ralph, and Si's $200 makes $800—but that ain't enough. We got to have enough to pay six men for a month, that's say $750; hiring a team to haul'll cost $300 more. We got to have 'bout $300 worth of powder, picks, shovels, drill steel and general hardware. Camp outfit, includin' grub and sundries'll take another $1000. That's more'n $2000 to get her a-goin'."

"Might sell some stock," suggested Si.

"Nope, can't be done," said Shorty. "I know all about that game. You got to incorporate and deed the property, have stock certificates, keep books and all that kind of stuff; and we ain't ready for anything of that kind yet. This is just for us three and the schoolmarm. Got to think up some other plan."

"Who's got $2500?" asked Si hopefully. "Maybe we could take in a pardner."

"We ain't goin' to have no pardners," answered Shorty. "Tell you what we might do—get Patrick to advance $2500 on account for a first payment when he tries to buy the prospect. He's trying to freeze us out. What's the matter with our getting him to put up the money to start us off with?"

"That's the stuff," exclaimed Si, slapping his leg. "Say, wouldn't it be slick to get him to put up the money for us to start mining with?"

The humor of the situation appealed to Si immensely, and apparently to Ralph; but Shorty looked dubious.

"I don't know, fellers," he said, "whether, on second thought, I exactly like the plan or not. You see, it's gettin' too near to a grubstake proposition, and a grubstake's a grubstake, no matter how big a crook your pardner is; and I can't hardly bring myself to take that money in cold blood and then throw Patrick down."

"He'd throw *you* down, Shorty," said Si.

"Well, he would and he wouldn't. Bill Patrick runs straight games; his word's as good as his bond, if he gives it to you. You could give him $100,000, if you had it, and he'd hand it back to you when you called for it. He wouldn't let no card-sharp deal phoney cards from a cold deck, nor he wouldn't stand for any crooked work about his saloon. Bill's word is good. He's got his code, so have I; and mine is, when I go in on a grubstake I play on the level all the way."

"Well, but ain't he a-tryin' to swindle you out of your strike, Shorty?" asked Si.

"Of course he is, but that's part of his code; he thinks it's all right to do something different where you ain't put him on his honor and he ain't give you his word, you see. That's the way he looks at it. I ain't quarrelin' with his standards, but I don't want to play a skin-game just because he does. I'll play the game to the limit, to euchre him out of what he's tryin' to do, but this seems sort of like a grubstake proposition; leastways, it's too close to it to suit me."

"Oh, hell, Shorty," Si remonstrated, "you got to fight the devil with his own weapons."

"Yes, I know that, but there's a point where you got to draw the line, and grubstake's the line with me."

Ralph nodded approvingly. "Guess you're right, Shorty. We can't turn blacklegs just because the other fellow's that kind of a bird. Might borrow it from him, though."

"What kind of a chance do you think we've got of goin' down to his saloon and saying: 'Please, Mr. Patrick, loan us $2500 to bust up your deal with'? Think you'd get it? Not in a million years!" replied Shorty.

"No, you wouldn't," answered Ralph. "But I wasn't thinking of doing it that way; I was thinking we could treat the payment he makes you as a loan, and when we got out a shipment or two we could return it to him with interest at two per cent a month."

Si evidently saw something comical in the suggestion, for he rocked with laughter. "Say," he finally managed to gasp, "I want to be 'round when you hand that money back to him and tell him what it's for. When you do, if he don't have apoplexy I bet he nearly busts a blood vessel. Better have me come along, Shorty, to get the drop on him if he wants to commit murder. I bet he'd rather have 'most anything happen to him than get his money back. That story'd go all over the state, an' Bill Patrick'd be a busted sportin' man. Why, he'd have to leave the country. You simply got to negotiate that loan, Shorty," he said.

"Surely, you won't object to that, will you?" chimed in Ralph, who had been sitting quietly listening to the argument.

"No, I don't know that I object to that kind of a deal," said Shorty, "only you fellers got to understand that it's only a loan and we pay it back just as soon as we get the money."

"Agreed," said Ralph.

Si added, "I wouldn't miss that play for any amount; and say, the kiddin' he'll get."

"Bet he will," said Shorty," an' I guess you're about right, Si, that he'll have to leave Sulphide, anyway, and maybe the state. I'm goin' to write it down, though, and you fellers can witness it, and I'll seal it up and Ralph can keep it up at the 'Con,' to show if the occasion ever arises. I'm goin' to give you somethin' else to keep, too, Ralph, an' that's the assay certificate. If this thing ever gets into a lawsuit, that piece of paper may be mighty handy. Bet they'll be after it tomorrow."

"Well, now we got the money, what's next?" asked Si.

"But we ain't got it yet," retorted Shorty, "only got a plan. Maybe it'll blow up. Better not count your chickens, Si, till they're hatched."

"Oh, well, I'll take a chance, Shorty."

"Well, I won't, Si, if I don't have to; and if we work this thing out right, we don't have to take any chances. There'll be enough, without manufacturing extra ones.

Anyway, let's go on with the plan. I get Patrick to put up $2500 cash as a first payment. You got to keep sober, Si; Ralph will, anyway; and somehow I got to slip you that money. Soon's you get it, you start for the railroad. Ralph will go over and join you, after you get your camp established. You ride out from Elko, Si, locate the place, and go on to Eureka for supplies. You can't miss it. It's about fifty miles from Elko and about the same from Eureka, I guess. Ride out to Hale's ranch and then go on southeast till you see three small hills near the main range; on the other side of them three hills you'll see a stream comin' out of the main range. That's to be the camp site. The mine is on the hill nearest the water. There's all kinds of room for bunk houses, hoisting-works, mill—and a town, too, if the camp ever gets that big. There's enough timber in the main range for all the building we'll ever want to do, and for mine timbers and fuel, too. When you get the mill located, Ralph, we can drive a tunnel into the vein and run the cars out on a level with the top of the ore bins; dump 'em into the grizzly and send the coarse stuff direct into the jaw-crusher and the fines to the stamps.

"You can get men and buy everything you want in Eureka. Nick-o'-the-Woods has got plenty of teams. The hauling in and out of Eureka, including charcoal for the smelters and pig lead, is takin' a pile of teams and one more or less won't be missed. I hear they got about 10,000 people there now. Eureka'll be better than Elko. More men, mining town, too; you can get anything you want, and Ralph can join you there. Now, let's figger time. When do you go back, Si?"

"Well, Langford wants to leave here on the afternoon of the fifth or morning of the sixth. I'll be ready. We'll be at the railroad on the eighth or ninth. I can get started for the mine next day, and in Eureka by the eleventh; rustle an outfit by the twelfth and have supplies bought."

"That's fine," said Shorty. "You arrange to meet him there on that day, Ralph. You can ship your surveying outfit by Wells Fargo, soon's you can, an' pick it up there and go on with him. Then get your survey made and stakes set. I'll turn up when I can at the mine or Eureka."

"I'll speak to Mr. Macklay," said Ralph. "I'm sure he'll let me off. I'll have to explain it to him, though."

"That's all right," said Shorty, "only tell him to keep mum. By the time Patrick finds out where we are, we'll have a couple of shipments out and some money in the bank. Then we'll be ready for fireworks."

It was now after ten o'clock, and Ralph rose to go, saying: "If you have no more instructions, Shorty, I'll mosey along and see if I can find Mr. Macklay."

"No, I don't think of anything more," said Shorty. "Here's that assay certificate I want Mr. Macklay to keep for me," handing the document to Ralph, "and now each one of us knows his part."

"Correct," affirmed Ralph, "and now good-night and good luck to both of you," he said, shaking hands. He stepped out into the darkness and started toward the mine office. Si followed shortly, but struck off in the direction of the Miners Rest.

Left alone in his cabin, Shorty sat for some time thinking intently over the events of the past few days. Rapidly his mind wandered over his career as a prospector; the hopes, fears, joys and sorrows that comprised the emotions attendant upon years of tramping over the deserts of Nevada, and now, after all the illusion had pretty well worn off, after the hope of striking it rich had grown fainter and fainter, he had struck it richer than he had ever dared to dream.

"Well, any way you look at it, it's goin' to be a mighty interestin' time," he said, as he blew out the lamp and climbed into his bunk.

Hans Randt had beaten a hasty retreat back to the Miners Rest, where he told Patrick what had occurred.

"Couldn't you see the dog, Hans, and tell who it belonged to?"

"No. Der tamn dog begun to growl when I vas a hundred feet from der tendt, und I could see noddings at all. It was aboudt as black as ink oudt dere."

"Too bad, Hans. If we knew who owned that dog, we might find out who's in on the deal with Peterson. You go back and keep your eyes open and when the party breaks up, maybe you can get a look at the outfit."

Randt's vigil was, however, in vain, as Lee on leaving the cabin, struck off up the hill to the mine, leaving only Si Proctor to walk in the direction of the town. Randt saw him pass on down the main street and enter the Miners Rest. He waited until the light in the tent was extinguished, then walked to the saloon where he reported his failure to Patrick.

Chapter XIII

Al Perrine, the night foreman at the "Con," had undertaken to fire a national salute of twenty-one guns at sunrise on the morning of the Fourth. His aide, one of the powdermen at the mine, was to prepare twenty-one sticks of giant powder. The operation was simple: a round stick about the size of a pencil was used to make a hole in one end of the cartridge, a piece of fuse was inserted into the cap, the edges of the cap were "crimped" to hold the fuse in place, the cap was inserted in the hole in the stick of powder, and the powder was pressed tightly around the fuse. The pieces of fuse were to be exactly the same in length, so that the time between explosions would be the same as the time between the lighting of the fuses.

In the east was the first faint glow of dawn. Perrine came up from underground and stood near the mouth of the shaft, watching the loading of some timbers on the cage. A locomotive headlight, set behind the hoisting engine, illuminated the shaft opening and showed the engineer standing motionless at the engine, waiting for two taps on the gong, the signal to lower. The indicator dial, with its pointer and station marks set on the circular rim, cast long shadows across the floor toward the air-compressor room. From the shaft the hot air, ascending and striking the cooler surface currents, condensed into a mist that rose slowly and disappeared, finally to be carried out through the lattice openings over the head frame that carried the pulleys on which the rope travelled from the winding drum to the cage.

About the works there was utter quiet save for the dropping of the stamps in the mill. In the boiler-room the fireman sat, with heavy leather mittens on his hands, ready to feed more wood into the furnace if the steam gauge showed any signs of reduced pressure.

Perrine, judging it to be about time to begin, called to Johnson, "Bring on your cannon, Harry."

Johnson went out and walked rapidly to a small powder-magazine cut in the side of the hill several hundred yards from the building. The magazine was an underground room, perhaps six feet square, sealed—sides, top and bottom—with tongue-and-groove flooring and protected with two heavy wooden doors, with an air-space between them. This precaution was necessary to keep the powder from freezing. In this cellar, small quantities of explosives were kept for a day's use, brought from the main magazine, half a mile away.

Opening the doors, Johnson picked up a box containing the sticks of giant powder already prepared for firing, and walked back past the hoisting-works and out to the waste dump of the mine. As he passed the end of the building, he called in through the open door, "All aboard, Al."

Reaching the end of the mine dump, he deposited his box near the end of the car track and laid out the twenty-one sticks of powder on a timber truck.

Now the mountain tops to the westward reflected the sun's rays. Looking at the powder, Perrine remarked:

"What for did you cut the sticks in half, Harry? Thought I told you yesterday to have twenty-one sticks."

"You did, Al, but you see the 'old man' come along while I was gettin' 'em ready, and asked me what I was up to, and I told him 'gettin' ready for the Fourth.' 'No use burnin' up so much powder,' says he, 'cut 'em in two, Harry, and use half a stick for a gun, instead of a whole one. It'll make plenty of noise to wake the town, and we'll save a lot of powder.' So I done what the 'old man' told me to."

"Well, I might of known what'd happen, without asking you," Perrine replied. "Might of known if that old Scotchman saw twenty-one sticks of powder bein' fixed to burn up, he'd immediately begin to wonder how he could save some of it. In this case, the answer's easy, and here it is," he continued, as he picked up a half-stick and examined it carefully.

"Well, I got 'leven sticks, 'stead of ten, anyway," said Harry. He wanted me to use ten sticks and cut one in three pieces, but I sneaked the extra stick."

"Yes, and when she goes off he'll know by the noise it's a whole stick, an' you'll get hauled up about it. It's those kind o' things, though, that have made him a superintendent and keeps him at the top. He can make a dollar go further than any other man in eastern Nevada, and he knows what's a full day's work, too. You bet the boys can't pull any wool over his eyes!"

Perrine pulled his candle-stick out of the side of a timber used as a "bumper" at the end of the car-track, and remarked to Johnson: "I'll count ten between shots, and you hand me the next one soon as I throw the one just lighted. All set? Let 'er go!"

He applied the candle to the end of the fuse, saw that it was well lighted, and began to count as he threw it from him.

Meanwhile, Johnson picked up another half-stick and handed it to him on the count of ten. He applied the candle to the fuse and again threw the charge from him. So, at intervals approximating ten seconds, he lit the fuses and threw the twenty half-sticks, reserving for the twenty-first shot the whole stick. As he threw it, he remarked to Johnson, "Bet the drinks the old man'll comment on that last shot."

As the last shot exploded, the engineers at the various mines tied down their whistle cords. The resulting din of whistles in different keys was kept up for several minutes, finally dying away. The town band, standing in the street in front of the postoffice, struck up the "Star-Spangled Banner." Then they paraded up and down the main street playing "Marching Through Georgia," "Rally 'Round the Flag," "Yankee Doodle," and "Hail, Columbia." A goodly crowd of small boys paraded behind the band, as well as a heterogeneous assortment of grown-ups.

The parade ended in front of the Miners Rest, and Hank Bartle, who had been up most of the night, invited the band in to have a drink. To a man, they took whiskey.

Coming back from breakfast, Ralph met Mr. Macklay on his way to the mine office, where he was going for an hour's work before making the rounds of the plant.

"Well, Ralph," he remarked, as they met in front of the gate leading to his cottage, "getting ready to celebrate?"

"Not quite yet, sir. I thought I'd work in the office for an hour or two before going downtown. Besides, I have something I'd like to speak to you about."

"Better come into the office now, then. I want to start out soon and go through the mill and the hoisting-works to see that things are moving properly before the men go off for the day."

In the office Mr. Macklay sat down at a large flat-top desk and looked inquiringly at Ralph.

"What's on your mind, son?"

Then Ralph told him the story of the grubstake, of the plot and counter-plot and of Mary Clark's interest.

When he finished, Macklay paused a moment and then said, "Well, if it should turn out, son, that you boys have happened to drop onto any such prospect as your samples indicate, all I can say is you have a bonanza, and I congratulate you! As for Mary, probably if I had known what was up I'd have given her a good talking to, and you, too, young man, for letting her throw her money away on a grubstake. You seem, however, to have got her in pretty deep; the milk's spilt; and, not content with that, Peterson goes and deeds her the whole thing! I can't say I follow his reasoning, and I don't like the situation, especially if the claims are worth anything. Between you, you've kicked up a nice mess. Why didn't Peterson leave town, instead of staying here and deeding his claims?"

"I don't know, sir, except perhaps he wanted to be in town over the Fourth and didn't think it safe to keep the claims in his own name. You see, he has an ambition to out-general Patrick. He's terribly hostile at the way they've gone after him, calls the whole outfit a set of crooks, and proposes to fool Patrick by selling him these worthless claims he has over near the Idaho line."

"And how are you going to finance your operations?" asked Macklay.

Ralph launched into a description of the part each was to play. When he had finished, Macklay leaned back in his chair with an amused smile on his face.

"My son," he said, "your partner Peterson is honest, of course, but I can't say I admire his judgment. He seems to me to have picked out about the most fool way of going about this thing that I can imagine. I don't admire his deeding the property to Mary, as he has; it's putting her in an unnecessarily dangerous position—and it puts Peterson in a very dangerous position in that he intends to get at least partly full during the day, and if he loses his head and describes the locations, Patrick will have a crew over there to jump the ground and move all the stakes, and he'll be taking out ore before you people know it. Why on earth didn't you come to me, in the first place, and I'd have fitted out a crew for you and sent them over there before any one knew a thing about it. And why give samples to Randt for assay?"

"Well, you see, sir, Shorty never really knew that Randt would turn in false assays until I gave him my check assays. He had a suspicion, but it was only after he got that certificate that he knew Randt was crooked, and then it was too late. Then when he really found out what was the situation, after getting my returns, he became obsessed with a desire to beat Patrick at his own game. You can't imagine his emotions when I read the results to him! His dreams of years had all come true, apparently, long after he had almost abandoned hope. He's like a young mother with her first child. You can't reason with him. He's going to work it out in his own way. His whole life is wrapped up in two things: first, holding those claims, and second, beating Patrick at his own game. You can't argue religion and love,

Mr. Macklay, and you'd be arguing both if you attempted to get Shorty headed in another direction. Prospecting has been his love, these claims are his bride, and his religion is to beat Bill Patrick.

"He has an idea that they may try to 'get him' during the melée, and he thinks he has it fixed so that if they do they won't benefit by it. I might add that he wants the three of us to share the property equally, if anything should happen to him."

"Humph!" said Macklay. "Not content with trying to get Patrick to slaughter him, he makes an additional inducement for you and Proctor and Mary to start a conspiracy to remove him."

"Oh, Mr. Macklay . . ."

"No, of course, I don't think anything of the kind! And now, my boy, I want to give you some good advice. Good mines are not found every day, and they are getting scarcer all the time. There hasn't been a good strike for a long time, notwithstanding the army of prospectors who have been going out from Virginia City, Eureka, Pioche, Austin, Tuscarora, Sulphide, and lesser camps. You can't afford to get excited over this thing; it may peter out and it may not —only time and work will tell the story. You'll have all kinds of proposals to sell out, or form a company, or take in partners. Don't do anything in a hurry, and if you feel like coming over and talking to me about things, I'll always be glad to give you my honest opinion on any proposition, or advise you in planning your development work. If the vein is as rich as your assays indicate, you won't need any outside capital to develop the mine. Go at it slowly; increase your shipments by degrees; build up a good surplus; use a horse-whim and hand-drills. After a while you can put in a steam-hoist, an air compressor for power drills, and finally you can erect a stamp mill in which to reduce your ore. It'll take you a year or two to do all of this, and in the meantime you'll probably have a law suit or two, attempts will be made to jump your claims or pre-empt your water or harass you in divers and sundry ways, with the object of getting possession of your property."

Chapter XIV

IN the meantime, Mrs. Macklay had been making Mary ready for her part in the parade as the Goddess of Liberty. Now, fully armed and equipped, Mary sat in the front parlor awaiting the time when she would ride down the hill in Mr. Macklay's rockaway, duly covered with a robe and Mr. Macklay's great overcoat. The excitement of the occasion had brought the roses to her cheeks and animation to her eyes, and Mrs. Macklay looked at her with an approving nod.

"You'll do splendidly, my dear, if you look as well in the parade as you do this minute. All the gay young blades in town will be making sheep's eyes at you, and if you haven't won all their hearts by this time, you certainly will today."

"Nonsense, Mother" (Mary had long since begun to call Mrs. Macklay "mother"). "There are lots of girls in town who would make a better Goddess of Liberty. You let your affection bias your judgment, I'm afraid—but I love you just the same," she added impulsively, as she threw her arms around Mrs. Macklay and kissed her again and again.

"My, that'll do, Mary. You 'most took my breath away. And now we must get Father to come and pass judgment. You stay here and I'll run over to the office and get him. No, you can't go in that costume. I'll go myself." At the office, she found her husband in close consultation with Ralph Lee.

"Come over to the house, John. I want you to see Mary. She looks radiant in her costume."

"All right, Mother, I'm coming. Suppose, Ralph, you come, too, and have a preliminary view? Sort of family dress rehearsal."

They all went over to the house. Mary, somewhat perturbed, wore a white costume with red, white, and blue stars all over it. Her long hair flowed in masses that rippled over her forehead to be caught at the back with a red, white, and blue ribbon, and fall luxuriantly to her waist. White shoes and stockings completed the costume, save for the shield and spear which lay upon the sofa in the corner.

"You look like a real queen, Mary," remarked Mr. Macklay approvingly, as he walked around her, critically looking at her from head to foot.

"Gosh, but you look like a million dollars," Ralph breathed, as he gazed at the girl in her simple, home-made costume.

Compliments brought blushes to her cheeks and caused her eyes to sparkle. "Oh, I'm so glad you all like my costume. Mother is responsible for its success, though; without her aid and advice I should never have dared to take the part, nor could I have made the costume without her assistance."

"Nonsense, Mary, you'd probably have done quite as well without me," interjected Mrs. Macklay, obviously pleased.

"Well, Mother, Mary is going to take the town by storm, sure enough. If on top of that the town finds out she's an heiress, she'll have so many beaux there'll be no living in the house."

"How do you mean, heiress, John?"

"Oh, of course, you don't know about that yet; but Ralph

has just been telling me about a prospect Shorty Peterson has located in which Mary has an interest."

"Mary in on a grubstake?"

"Yes, just that. Only, this time it looks like a winner, if it comes up to Ralph's assays."

"Did she ask you about it first, John?"

"She did not—luckily for herself. If she had, I'd have told her to keep out of it. She and this assayer of mine have been plotting behind our backs."

"Well, John, don't you think you'd better tell me all about it?"

"Why, of course, Mother, but let's sit down, for I want to tell Mary a few things, too."

Macklay told his wife in a few words the story of Shorty Peterson's discovery and admonished her to make no mention of the matter.

"My wife, Ralph," he said, "knows everything I know. She is a jewel of discretion, and besides, her advice is worth more than that of any man I ever knew. If you do as well some day, son, you'll be in luck."

Mrs. Macklay stopped his mouth with her hand and kissed him tenderly on the top of his fast-graying head.

"Mary, I've given Ralph a lot of good advice about this prospect. Mother will do the same for you, and will tell you just about the same things I've told him, so I won't stop now to deliver a lecture; only I do want to say, before I go, that 'silence is golden.' You may have stumbled onto a real mine. You can't afford to take any chances at this stage of the game; and, if it is a real mine, the surest way I know of to lose it will be to talk about it.

"I'll see you all later downtown," he added. "I must run over to the plant again for a little while. When Mary's ready to go, Mother, you call Pratt and he'll bring up the rockaway and drive you both down. Tell him to put the top down while he's waiting for you so we can have a good view."

Ralph, with a final look of admiration at the fair young Goddess of Liberty and a parting "You do look lovely," turned and walked with Mr. Macklay to the office.

Left alone, the two women sat quietly for a few minutes, Mrs. Macklay breaking the silence by saying, "If it should prove to be a real mine, Mary, don't let your good luck turn your head. More women have been made fools of by riches than by anything else. I'd rather see you poor, just as you are, than rich and spoiled by your riches."

"It's all so sudden and so wonderful that I hardly know what to think about it. I can't believe yet that it's true!"

"It isn't true yet, my child, and perhaps never may be; so don't build castles in Spain. Wait and hope, and maybe it will all come true some day. I've been through the mill too often not to know that there's many a slip 'twixt the cup and the lip. I married John in Grass Valley, when we were both much younger than we are now. We had our day dreams, too, in those days. John thought he had a quartz mine once, over on the South Fork of the Feather River. We sank all we had in it, and it failed. He tried again in a hydraulic mine, but that didn't pay either. Then we came over to Gold Hill, on the Comstock, and there"—her voice trembled and her eyes filled with tears—"I lost my little girl. That was the greatest loss of all—everything else didn't matter, but just that. I felt I couldn't go on. I wanted to get away from the mines and the desert and hide somewhere, forever and ever. But we went on; I had to go on for John's sake. He was so patient, so kind, so gentle, that it made me ashamed to think how selfish I was, in my grief; and so I fought it down, and we went on together there, and then over here."

She was crying softly as she finished. Mary's arms were around her.

Chapter XV

THE Miners Rest had had a most satisfactory night. No one had been killed—which was more than the most sanguine could have hoped for. Luck had run with the house; the percentage had been large; trade at the bar had been good; and, all in all, Bill Patrick had nothing to kick about except that he had not yet got hold of Shorty Peterson. That was the important business. It must be done within the next twenty-four hours, come what might.

Patrick had gone to bed just after the national salute had been fired, and now, at nine o'clock, he was finishing breakfast in his rooms over the saloon and mapping out his day's work. Most of his crew had turned in about the same time; a few had gone earlier, but most of them, knowing of the racket of dynamite, firecrackers, whistles, and horns that would break loose about sun-up, wisely concluded it would be useless to attempt to sleep prior to that outbreak.

Patrick had had about four hours sleep—enough to carry him through another twenty-four hours. He was ready to begin the most strenuous day of the year. Stretching himself and yawning languidly, he went downstairs. The saloon was comparatively deserted; a few "hold-overs" slouched about in chairs, asleep. Looking them over quickly, he said to Bartle, who was still tending bar, "Why don't you get those drunks out of here, Hank?"

"I'm a-goin' to, Bill, soon's the bouncer and some of the crew get back from breakfast; I can't leave the bar to tackle 'em alone, and the boys'll be back 'most any minute now."

Grubstake

Two or three men were standing in front of the bar, drinking either an eye-opener or a night-cap. The windows at the back of the room and the swinging front doors were open, but the odor of stale beer and tobacco smoke hung over the place.

"Seen anything of Randt or Anderson or Blake, this morning, Hank?"

"No, Bill. Gus went home to get some sleep 'long 'bout half-past four, Blake quit an hour or so earlier, an' Randt ain't been around since you were talkin' to him last night."

Patrick looked at his watch; it marked a quarter past nine; in an hour things would begin to move. He stepped out onto the sidewalk in front of the saloon and looked up and down the street. Even now there was a drift of children in the direction of the corral. The grown-ups would be along later. As he looked, Big Sim, the Marshal of the Day, rode past accompanied by two aides. He was wearing a gaudy red, white, and blue sash across his shoulder caught at the waist in a large bow-knot with loose, gold-tasseled ends. His hat, a broad-brimmed slouch, was encircled with a red, white, and blue ribbon. His high top riding boots shone. The saddle and the bridle of his beautiful horse were heavy with silver mountings. Sim waved to Patrick and called to him that he had better come and ride in one of the carriages with other prominent citizens.

"No thanks, Sim," he replied. "I got too much of a job on hand here."

As he turned to re-enter the saloon, three of his bouncing crew came down the street from their breakfast.

"Here, you fellows," he said, "clear out this crowd and dig up a constable or a deputy sheriff or two and get 'em to clean up the street."

One of the men set out to find a constable. The others began shaking the sleepers, dragging them to their feet, either to stagger out onto the sidewalk unaided, after Bartle refused another drink, or to be dragged out by the two men and dropped at the edge of the sidewalk. They would be picked up shortly by the town constable, making the rounds with a small freight wagon borrowed for the occasion, and carried off to the calaboose to sleep off the effects of their spree.

About the time the Miners Rest had been cleaned up, Hans Randt came in. Patrick greeted him with, "Well, what's the news, Hans?"

"Noddings, dis morning, Bill. Shordy iss up py der restaurant gedding himself some breakfast. I talked to him, und he vill be down dis vay priddy soon.

"Well, see to it, Hans, that he gets plenty of encouragement in his drinking. Loosen up, yourself, and stand treat. You can blow in that six dollars you got from him for assays. Maybe it'll ease your conscience to get rid of it that way."

"My congscience iss not troubling me at all, Padrick."

"No, I guess you're right, Hans. Well, it's all the same to me, only see he drinks plenty."

Randt turned to talk to some newcomers, and Patrick thought, "That damn Dutchman would sell out his own mother! I'd as leave steal horses as play the trick he did. Not for me! Beats hell how some people look at things."

It was close to ten o'clock. People were beginning to dispose themselves along the sidewalks that, raised some eighteen inches above the street level, afforded satisfactory seats from which to view the parade. American flags were strung on ropes hung across the street, drooping from flagpoles on roofs and projecting from second-story windows. Red, white, and blue bunting, draped from porches, hid some of the ugliness of mining-town architecture.

Down by Simpson's Corral the parade was forming. The town band, augmented by several players from outside towns, stood in position at the head; next came members of the G. A. R. in their uniforms and carrying muskets; then came the orator of the day, in a resplendently decorated rockaway, escorted by the leading local lawyer. A small boy dressed to represent George Washington rode on a pony in advance of the flag-bedecked float on which sat the Goddess of Liberty, surrounded by numerous attendants, consisting of boys and girls, including whites, Indians, negroes, Chinese, and Mexicans.

Behind the float, acting as a rear guard of honor, came the local fire company, resplendent in leather fire-helmets, red shirts and white patent leather belts with large buckles. They were led by the Chief, carrying a silver trumpet. Thanks to the water pressure from the reservoir on the hill, the company did not need a fire engine, but contented themselves with a most elaborate four-wheel hose-cart, gaudy with red paint and gold stripes, mounted on which a large reel carried several hundred feet of fire hose. Two of these carts and a smaller two-wheeled cart were dragged by ropes. Behind the fire brigade came prominent citizens, and bringing up the rear of the parade were the famous troop of "Horribles," numerous small boys and young men masked and wearing the most fantastic and grotesque costumes; they wore cast-off women's clothing, old flour and grain sacks, and anything else that would serve as a disguise, the more uncouth the outfit, the more desirable.

The Marshal and his aides were galloping up and down

the line, busily "showing off." With a final inspection and a dash from the rear to the front, the Marshal installed himself at the head of the parade and gave the signal to start.

It was not far to the outskirts of town, and as the band didn't know many tunes, it proceeded in silence until nearing the first buildings. Ahead of them stretched the one main street, gay with the national colors, the sidewalks crowded with sightseers. The balconies above the street were full and people were perched on many housetops. Near the first buildings four aides, galloping in advance, crowded close in to the sidewalks and pushed back, here and there, a too enthusiastic spectator. The marchers were now abreast of the first straggling houses, mostly deserted for more central locations further up town. The fire company had wet down the street, and the parade moved forward free from dust.

Lifting his hand, the Marshal motioned to the band leader, who in turn signalled to his men, and with a crash of brass and drums the band burst forth into the martial strains of "Marching Through Georgia." People on the sidewalks, in windows, on porches and on roofs began to wave their hats, to cheer and to applaud. The prominent citizens, the Goddess of Liberty, her attendants, and the fire company, each won applause. The Goddess of Liberty float won the highest praise, perhaps because the parents and relations of the children surrounding the Goddess were all assembled and applauding vigorously and vociferously, and because of the popularity of Mary Clark and her undeniably striking figure.

Mrs. Macklay had started a few moments before the parade began to move, and her team soon covered the ground between Simpson's Corral and the town. She turned into an alley and brought the rockaway to a halt just clear of the main street. Her husband stepped into the vehicle and seated himself by her side.

"Well, Mother," he said, "everything going off all right, so far?"

"Oh, yes, John, splendidly. Mary looked really radiant, and the children for once in their lives all have clean hands, faces, and clothes. I don't suppose they'll stay clean for an hour, but now they all look really very sweet—red, white, black, and yellow, all of them on their good behavior and as docile as lambs."

Ralph Lee had come up and stood in the street by the rear wheel.

"You must applaud the Goddess of Liberty, Ralph," said Mrs. Macklay.

"Yes'm," he answered. "I came down the street from the mine, just now, with some of the men; several of them have children on the float, and they have enlisted those who haven't to help make a noise. Sam Hing has a couple of kids parading, and he's lined up every Chinaman in town to applaud. Jose, the porter at the hotel, has canvassed the few Mexicans in town, and between them the Goddess of Liberty won't be overlooked."

As they passed the corner, the band changed to "Columbia, the Gem of the Ocean" and marched on up the street. Ralph applauded wildly as the float passed, and so did Mrs. Macklay and her husband. They were rewarded by an almost imperceptible nod and a smile from the figure seated rigidly on the bedecked chair borrowed from Mrs. Macklay's front parlor. The parade passed on up the street, out toward the mines, counter-marched back through the town, and swung off at the lower end of the street, after passing the reviewing stand of the judges, who were to award the prizes. There was one prize for the most original "Horrible," one for the best-looking costume on the float, and several other first, second and third prizes.

Sandy Bowers, two years ago, had knifed one of the judges for not giving the award to his kid; Sandy was full, the judge recovered, and the matter was dropped by common consent. The result, however, was that the award was changed from the handsomest child to the best costume, at Sim's suggestion. "People naturally won't kick so hard if it's a costume that gits the award," he explained.

The committee, without dissent, awarded a prize to the "Chinese twins"—"Sam Hing's kids," explained Sim. "We certainly can't afford to pass up that combination if we expect to get anything to eat in Sam's hash house. He gave us some money for a prize, too, so we just naturally got to recognize his kids. Had a bright idea, though, the committee did—got 'em to come as twins, and we made the prize cover both of 'em. Result, everybody happy. Sam got his five dollars back—or the kids did, which is the same thing. They can split it, two-fifty each; no jealousy, nothin' to kick about; everybody pleased. That's what you might call a fine Eye-talian hand—only none of the committee is dagos."

The parade passed in review, prizes were handed out, and all assembled around the reviewing stand to listen to the Fourth of July oration.

Those were the days of emotional oratory. It was expected that Bunker Hill and Lexington would open the oration; that Valley Forge and Yorktown would be duly dwelt upon; that the War of 1812, so far as the sea fighting was concerned, would be chronicled; that the Alamo and

Chapultepec would be mentioned; and that the days of '61 to '65 would be reviewed; that the glories of the days of '49 and of Nevada would be painted in glowing colors; and it ended finally with a peroration that "just made you want to raise up on yer hind laigs and turn loose," as one of the cowpunchers remarked as the crowd began to drift away. There was close attention, much applause, some cheering, and a generous outburst of wildly expressed appreciation at the end of the address. Tom Fitch was not called "the silver-tongued orator" without reason. He was master of the art of swaying human emotions. He had even been known to hold an audience spell-bound in a downpour of rain, and as his speech and the day were ideally suited to the occasion, the oration was a complete success.

Chapter XVI

It was now past noon. There would be nothing more doing until one-thirty. A good many of the crowd drifted over to Sim's Corral, to look over the horses and pick up what gossip they could; others started off to hunt up some grub against the rush that would soon commence; and still others made tracks for the Miners Rest, where Patrick, for this occasion only, provided a free lunch of crackers, pickles, ham sandwiches, cheese, and herring.

"Keeps 'em near the bar," Hank Bartle explained, "and maybe the salt herring'll give 'em a stronger thirst. Sky's the limit today. They can buy likker as long's they can stand up."

"You don't think much of the Fourth of July, do you, Hans?" remarked Patrick to the assayer, who was standing at the bar of the Rest talking to Bartle.

"Not much," grunted Randt. "I stays here und gets me ahold of dot Shordy Pederson for you, Bill."

"Well, it's about time you began on him, Hans. Grab him when he comes back from the parade. Don't let him get out to the sports this afternoon, if you can help it. Things'll be kind of quiet here until after the sports are over. That's the time to get in our work. I have two or three forms drawn up ready to use, if I can find out which one he'll sign. You get him in here and start him drinking; then we must work it out as we go along. If I can get him into the private room alone, he's done for, if I don't miss my guess."

"I'll stand oudside und vatch fer him," said Randt. He went out and stood watching the people beginning to straggle back from the reviewing stand—children still wearing their "Horribles" costumes; Indians; Chinese; foreigners, mostly Cornish, Welsh, and Irish; cowboys; G. A. R. veterans; wives, washerwomen, and women of doubtful morals. It was the typical Western mining town crowd of the years of the "gold rush" and of its backwash that followed with the feverish scramble for silver, lead, and copper.

It was not long before Shorty appeared, walking up the middle of the street with others who wished to avoid the crowd that thronged the sidewalks.

Randt hailed him as he was passing, "Hello, Shordy!"

"Hello, Hans."

"Been oudt by der speech-making? Come on und haf a drink."

"Yeah," Shorty answered, as he turned and stepped up on the sidewalk. "It was a bully speech, too. Just naturally made you glad you belonged in the old U. S. A. Great country, Hans."

"Yah, I guess so; bud Chermany iss a priddy goot coundry, too, Shordy."

"Y-e-s, I guess so. Never was there yet. Maybe some day when I strike it rich I'll take a trip over there and look around them old castles and museums and things. Ever see old Bismarck, Hans?"

"No, I neffer did. Bud how aboudt a drink, Shordy, to celebrate der Fourth mit?"

"Well, I don't mind if I do, Hans; but it's goin' to take

more'n one drink fer me to celebrate on and drown my sorrows. I certainly expected you was goin' to give me some good assays on them samples I brought in, an' all I got was a skunk."

"Vell, nod qvite a skunk, Shordy. Maybe if you dig on her deep enough you strike her rich yet."

"Not on your life. I seen too many fellers always insistin' all you need to have was depth, and then I seen some of 'em dig to prove it. Somehow, the pay ore seems to start on the surface and go down a ways and then quit. You give me the first five hundred feet in depth on a vein and you can have the rest of it clean down to wherever hell is."

"Vell, some feller mighd buy you oudt, und take a chance."

"Lead me to him and see what happens!"

They had crowded their way into the Miners Rest and edged up to the bar behind which Hank Bartle and his assistants were busy passing the whiskey bottles from hand to hand. Standing at one end of the bar, Bill Patrick, with cigar in mouth, was apparently keeping watch over the crowd. But he was devoting his attention almost exclusively to Shorty and Randt. If those claims turned out at all like what the assays indicated, the Miners Rest and its contents in comparison were worth about one white chip. Hank Bartle spotted Shorty and Randt instantly, and deftly flipped two glasses in front of them.

"How's tricks, Shorty?"

"Oh, so-so, Hank."

"Well, help yourself," he remarked as he turned to other customers. There was no time for more than a mere salutation.

Filling his glass, Shorty pushed the bottle to Hans. Hans

raised his glass. "Here's looking ad you, Shordy, und goot luck to all of us."

Shorty replied: "Here's to the Fourth of July, to the U. S. A., and to my bonanza—when I find it."

Setting their glasses down on the bar, each of them wiped his mouth with the back of his hand and drew a long breath.

"Bill certainly does have good likker, Hans."

"Yah, dot iss zo. Haf anoder one, Shordy?"

"Don't mind if I do, but it's on me this time." He clasped his hand around the glass, looked quickly away, saw that no one was paying any particular attention to him, and tipped up the bottle, allowing only a small quantity to flow into the glass. Randt poured out a generous helping.

"Once again, Hans."

"Here's to you, Shordy."

Shorty flung a fifty-cent piece on the counter and Hank swept it into the till.

"Let's play a little faro, Hans."

"No. I vatch, Shordy. I dondt haf no luck at all at dot game. You go ahead, und I gets me a sandwich.

Shorty walked over to the faro table, while Hans went to the lunch counter and helped himself to a sandwich and a pickle. These he contentedly munched as he edged over to where Patrick stood by the corner of the bar.

"I got him started, Bill. Maybe he vill keep righd on going, oder maybe he vill skip oudt to see der races und drilling matches; bud I get some more whiskey into him before he goes."

"Keep after him, Hans," said Patrick, without moving or changing a muscle of his face.

"You bet I vill." Randt drifted over to the faro table,

where Shorty had a fair-sized pile of chips in front of him.

"How's she coming, Shordy?"

"Breakin' good, so far. Watch this one."

"Well, that's enough for me for once, so here's where I cash in," he remarked as he gathered in his chips and quit about $50 to the good.

"Now come and have a drink on me, Hans."

Again he helped himself to a small drink and again Randt helped himself liberally.

"Let's go get some grub," Shorty remarked, after pocketing the change from a five dollar gold piece he had laid on the counter.

"Dot suits me," remarked Randt. So, arm in arm, they wandered over to the free-lunch counter and helped themselves to pickles and sandwiches.

The room was now full to suffocation of miners, cowboys, Mexicans, and teamsters. At the bar, the speaker of the day, Big Sim the marshal, and several members of the reception committee were drinking with Patrick. Ike and Si Proctor discussed with several other punchers the merits of the horses entered for the races. Near them a group of miners argued about the teams entered for the drilling contest. The town was taking advantage of the breathing-spell to "likker up," feed, and discuss the events of the afternoon. The contests would be over by four and then all hands would continue to "likker up," either to drown their sorrows or to celebrate their good luck.

"Come ofer und haf anoder drink, Shordy," suggested Randt.

"Naw, Hans, not now. I got a good load already, and I want to see them races and drilling matches first; and then I'm comin' back here and make the eagle scream. See you later, Hans." Shorty walked over to the Proctors and entered into the arguments about the drilling contest and the horse races.

Randt drifted aimlessly around for a few minutes and finally stopped near Patrick.

"He's goin' to take in der drillin' und der races, und says he's comin' back here to make der eagle scream afterwards. He's had three oder four drinks alretty and has got der taste in his mouth. I bet ve vix him before night."

Patrick gave a barely perceptible nod, and remarked: "Keep right after him, and call for help if you need it."

After the parade Mrs. Macklay had picked up Mary Clark, still dressed in her Goddess of Liberty costume. Mr. Macklay had taken the reins and with Ralph Lee at his side had driven out to listen to the oration. Afterwards they all had gone back to the house and, while Mary was changing her clothes and helping Mrs. Macklay prepare a hasty cold lunch, Mr. Macklay and Ralph had walked through the hoisting-works and down through the mill to see that everything was in good shape. There was no one underground; an engineer and a fireman were the only men on top, except the mill crew that was to change at one-thirty, so that one shift could have the morning free, the other the afternoon.

Coming back to the house after their inspection, they found lunch waiting for them.

"Mary made a lovely Goddess of Liberty, didn't she, John?", Mrs. Macklay remarked as she poured the tea.

"Yes, of course she did; and the children all looked fine and behaved themselves like little angels."

"Couldn't last very long, though," chimed in Ralph. "A couple of them got to fighting for a place to hear the oration and I had to separate them. The language they indulged in was anything but angelic, and as for cleanliness—you should have seen them after rolling over in the dirt and mud once or twice. I heard lots of nice things said about the Goddess of Liberty, though," Ralph continued, with a glance of admiration that brought the color to Mary's cheeks.

"Well; if to all the admiration you have already stirred up, Mary," Mr. Macklay interjected, "you add the fact that you are a prospective heiress, you'll be swamped with suitors."

"As if she hadn't plenty now," retorted Mrs. Macklay disdainfully. "Seems to me all the young men in town and some of the old ones, too, who ought to know better, are spending a lot of time tramping in and out of my front gate, asking to see 'Miss Mary' or 'Miss Clark.' "

"Well, what else can you expect, my dear?" her husband inquired. "It's a free country, and youth must have its romance. You'd be the first one to object if Mary didn't receive attention, and you know it."

"Well, I suppose I would, but that's no reason I should be nice to some old fools in this town who ought to be thinking of heaven rather than matrimony."

" 'No fool like an old fool,' my dear," Mr. Macklay answered.

Looking at the clock, Macklay noted that it was a quarter past one. "Drilling contest in fifteen minutes," he remarked, getting up from the table. "Come on, Ralph; Mother, you and Mary come as soon as you're ready. I can't wait for you."

"You run along with them, Mary. I'll clear up," said Mrs. Macklay.

"No, indeed I won't. I'm going to help you and we can go down together. Besides, it won't take ten minutes to pick up here. We'll join you shortly," said Mary, as she began to clear the table while Mrs. Macklay got out the dishpan.

Chapter XVII

MR. MACKLAY and Ralph walked rapidly down the hill to the main street. As they passed the Miners Rest Ralph paused, saying, "I think I'll run into the Rest for a minute, Mr. Macklay, and see if I can find Shorty."

Inside he found the bar crowded, the gambling tables surrounded. Bill Patrick was still standing by the bar; in the corner on the left as he entered, Ralph found Shorty standing near the cabinet of mineral specimens in a heated argument with one of Ike Proctor's cowboys over the mile horse race.

Ike and his band of cowmen had arrived early in the forenoon, had taken part in the parade, and were now preparing to celebrate with the town. Si had been at the corral when Ike arrived, and as they walked up town, he told him of Shorty's strike.

"You're my pardner in the whole business, Ike, of course, and whatever I get, half's yours."

"Shucks, Si, I got a good job and don't need money. Anyway, if I do and you get some, I know you'll loan it to me, so I ain't much excited about being your pardner."

"Well," replied Si, "we ain't goin' to quarrel about it, only I want you to know all about it, and you got to help in this business. And, of course, you got to keep your mouth shut. Never was much for talking, Ike, you know, and I reckon this ain't one of the times when a fellow ought to have much to say."

So, as they went on up the street, they discussed the plans for the future.

"I'll kind of stand around and look on," said Si. "All you fellers got to do is to call for me, and I'll come a-runnin.' "

As Ralph joined the crowd in the saloon, he asked, "Going out to see the drilling?"

"You bet I am," replied Shorty.

"Oh, I don't know," said Ike Proctor, speaking for the collected group of cowpunchers; "we ain't so hell set on this drilling match, but we're certainly waiting for them hoss races. Guess I'll head my bunch out there if I can. The less time they spend in this joint, the better off they'll be tomorrow, but I'll have a hell of a time getting some of them away from that bar and them card tables."

"I'll take them what'll go," volunteered Si, "and you can stay here, Ike, and keep an eye on the rest of 'em. When the hoss races begin, the whole crowd will move out themselves without any coaxing, and when that's over you might as well go on home so far as holdin' 'em in is concerned."

"Yes, I reckon so," replied Ike doubtfully, "but I got to stick around here, anyway, as much as I can. Don't calc'late there'll be any shootin' if I can stop it. Them punchers is goin' to get plenty full by night, an' if they can't be held until they gets dead to the world, why, we can pack 'em off to the calaboose and leave 'em there for twenty-four hours and then round 'em up and head 'em for home."

"Fine time you'll have, rounding 'em up," interjected Ralph. "They'll be scattered from Sim's Corral all the way up to the other end of town. You'll get some of 'em all right, here and at the other saloons and joints around town, if you want to go digging them up; but I'll bet you're short a few tomorrow night."

"Yes, I reckon so," replied Ike; "but we'll get away for the ranch with enough of 'em to keep things movin'. Fourth of July is one hell of a time for a ranch foreman."

"Well, come on, you fellows that's going to see the drilling," said Ralph, turning toward the door.

Shorty, Si Proctor, one or two punchers, and several miners joined him, and they all straggled off in the direction of the corral. Shorty was extremely talkative, somewhat pugnacious and disputatious, and attempted to start an argument with Ralph as they left the saloon. For several minutes he stood in front of the entrance, arguing in a loud voice the merits of one of the drilling teams and offering to back it with cash. Meantime, the rest of the crowd had drifted off down the street, leaving Ralph and Si as his only listeners, except those standing in the saloon near the door and those coming and going. No one paid any attention to Shorty except Ralph and Si as he stood and argued while they vainly tried to persuade him to move on.

Patrick, standing by the bar, saw the group as they stood there, and beckoned to Randt, who was standing close by. "Shorty's got a good start, Randt, but it'll wear off a lot in the next two hours or so. You keep him in sight and get him in here before he goes to supper. Don't lose sight of him, and separate him from those others if you can."

"I'll keep Shordy in sight, Padrick."

Shorty finally yielded to the pleading of his friends, but insisted on walking in the middle of the street. He locked arms with Ralph and Si and started toward the corral. They had walked well out of earshot before Shorty said, "It's workin' all right, fellers, I ain't full; just feel a little gay an' frisky. It'll all wear off before I get back to the Rest. Don't stay too close to me. Randt'll be after me, pretty pronto, and you got to let him take me in tow. You can devote yourself to the schoolmarm, Ralph; and you can mix with your own bunch, Si. So long as you keep away from me, you can do as you please. I'm goin' to stay out here till the sports is over. Then I'm going back there and let Mr. Patrick put up a couple of thousand dollars on account."

"Here comes Mrs. Macklay and the schoolmarm," interjected Si, who had been looking up the street.

"Well, that's your signal to vamoose, Ralph," said Shorty.

Ralph joined Mrs. Macklay and Mary Clark. Shorty moved off with Si.

The crowd had already gathered in the open space between the town and Simpson's Corral. Here three blocks of stone had been set up. A platform some three feet wide surrounded each. A rope had been stretched to four stakes set some ten feet away from the platform. Within this space were the judge, the timekeepers, and the teams that were to open the contest. The first match was the double-handed three-man contest: two strikers and an assistant to hold the drill, clear the hole and change. The drills of various lengths were laid out in order on the platform; cleaning spoon, water, and hammers—ten-pound sledges—all carefully arranged. A row of chairs for contestants had been placed on two sides of the roped-off area. On the other sides chairs had been arranged for such distinguished guests as the orator of the day, the marshal of the parade, Big Sim, and the superintendents of several mines, with their wives. Among the last sat Mrs. Macklay, Mary, and Ralph Lee.

The time of the contest was to be fifteen minutes; the

prizes, $500 first money; $200 second money. By common consent the teams had been limited to three: one each from the "Con," the "Desert Queen," and the "Nevada Belle." The men composing these teams were all known for their ability; they had been training for weeks; their drills had been sharpened with the greatest care by the mine blacksmiths under the personal supervision of the contestants. Each mine crew backed its own team, not only with words, but with money. The saloons of the town, Bill Patrick's in particular, were holding thousands of dollars in stakes. Excited partisans in the crowd were proclaiming the merits of their favorites and bets were still being made.

It was now within five minutes of one-thirty, and Mr. Macklay was about to mount the platform to announce the rules of the contest. As he started toward the steps leading to the platform, Big Sim, as marshal of the day, stopped him.

"Let me say a few words first, Judge. I want to tell this crowd where they get off." He mounted the steps with deliberation, walked to the middle of the platform, and surveyed the crowd standing about on all sides. He stood erect, six feet four, lank of frame, grizzled of countenance, with a quizzical smile lighting his face as he lifted his hand for silence.

"Fellow citizens," he began, "this here Fourth of July celebration is under my direction as marshal. We have had a bully parade and a bully oration. The day, so far, has been a grand success." Then, pausing, he hooked one thumb into the armhole of his vest, worn only on rare occasions, and added, "And she is goin' to be a success for the rest of the day. I ain't sayin' a thing about tonight. We have ladies here present,"—with a sweep of his hat and a bow in the direction of the reserved seats—"and Sulphide is goin' to uphold the tradition of courtesy to and for the fair sex." Then in stronger tones he continued: "But any galoot that gets gay, gets run in. I got half a dozen aides circulatin' 'round in the crowd, and if any of you starts any fuss, you lands in the calaboose. Your turn, Judge," he concluded, as the hand-clapping died away and he descended the steps.

Mr. Macklay mounted the stairs, stepped to the middle of the centre granite boulder, raised his hand and began: "There will be three events today: the two-handed three-men event; the one-man striker and helper; and the single-handed no-helper event. The first event is the three-man contest, time fifteen minutes. There are three teams entered, one each from the Sulphide Consolidated, the Desert Queen, and the Nevada Belle. The drilling will begin at the crack of the pistol and will stop at a similar signal. Holes are to be cleared by contestants; measurements will be made by me. No substitute will be permitted. Strikers and helpers may not change places. Usual rules will govern in all cases. In the event of a tie, five extra minutes time will be allowed for deepening the holes of the tied teams. Sim has already told you we must have order. Come on, boys," he said, turning to the contestants, seated inside the rope waiting for the signal.

Rising, the men threw off the coats they had wrapped around themselves and mounted the steps. Long hours underground had whitened them. The constant swinging of hammer on drill had developed their muscles until they rippled and swelled like bands of steel beneath the almost marble whiteness of the skin. Bare-headed, bare-chested, they wore only knee-pants, stockings, and shoes.

Selecting the first three, Macklay led them to the centre and announced:

"Joe Tredenick and Nick Pentworthy, strikers, John Gee, helper; representing the Sulphide Consolidated."

A pandemonium of applause broke out from the other Cornishmen present. then silence as the next team stepped forward.

"Michael O'Toole and Timothy O'Connor, strikers, Patrick Mulcahey, helper; representing the Desert Queen."

Again a storm of applause from the partisans of the Irish team, and again silence as the third team stepped forward.

Joseph Spongoli and George Ambrazzo, strikers, Pete Mombelli, helper; representing the Nevada Belle."

There was generous but perceptibly less applause this time.

"You will draw for positions," continued Macklay. "I have three pieces of paper in my hat, with a number on each piece. The numbers are 10, 50, and 75. The high man has first choice; the middle man, second choice. You will not open your slips until the last man has drawn."

He passed the hat in turn to each helper, who drew a slip of paper and nervously fingered it, waiting for the signal to read the number. Each team crowded around its helper.

"All right," spoke up Macklay, and three sets of hands feverishly opened the slips.

One position was as good as another, but the drawing of the high number was regarded as a lucky omen.

Italy won the choice, followed by Cornwall, with Ireland last. The Italian helper danced about waving his arms, while the strikers grinned and signalled to friends. The other two teams, apparently unaffected, waited for the winners to select their position. This was quickly done. The second team took its stand, and the third team took the unoccupied block. Drills, hammers, and water were moved into position. The strikers nervously fingered their hammers. The helpers, down on their knees with drills in hand and eyes on the judges, waited for the pistol shot.

"All ready," announced Macklay, as he raised the pistol above his head. Muscles tightened, drills came into position, the pistol cracked, hammers fell simultaneously.

With marvelous precision and speed the hammers rose and fell. The training for weeks past and practice in changing drills without the loss of a stroke had brought perfection. The drills bit into the granite at astonishing speed. The helper turned the drill with both hands, or with one hand, as he fed a little water, picked up a longer drill with one hand and substituted it for the shorter and blunted drill in the hole, between hammer strokes, and cleared the hole of accumulated muck. The contest was the perfection of team work. Each man had his allotted movements that must absolutely synchronize with other movements timed to the fraction of a second. The striker stood with right foot advanced, the sledge-hammer grasped firmly with the right hand perhaps a foot or eighteen inches from the hammerhead, the left hand near the end of the hammer handle. His whole body swayed from the waist, up and down, in rhythmic time, one hammer rising while the other fell, the helper turning the drill between the strokes.

The audience, composed in large part of experts, followed the cutting of the drill into the rock with tense interest. Words of encouragement, cheers, derisive comments, all mingled. Bets were offered, taken, refused, as the contest progressed toward conclusion. The last five minutes climaxed in a wild delirium of excitement. Hammers rose and fell faster and faster, chests heaved; the hah-hah-hah of the strikers, uttered with each blow, took on a more sinister tone of labored effort, until the pistol cracked at the expiration of the fifteen minutes. Instantly the strikers lowered hammers to the ground, stood erect, and gulped in great mouthfuls of fresh air, while the helpers began carefully to clear out the holes. Using first the spoon and then a swab, the helper freed the hole of every particle of grit or muck that might have accumulated as the result of the final few minutes of cutting. Clean water was poured in, removed with the swab, and the swab was examined to see that there remained no loose particles to lessen by even a minute fraction of an inch the depth of the hole.

"All clean?" asked Macklay, as he looked at the three helpers, who had ceased their labors and were squatting close to the holes.

"Yes, sir," they replied, almost in unison.

"Very well. Stand back there, clear of the stone."

The crews stepped back, leaving open the space immediately surrounding each hole. Taking a foot-rule from his pocket, Mr. Macklay deliberately opened it and beckoned to Ralph, saying, "You take down these figures, Ralph, as I call them off."

He then knelt down by the hole nearest to him and carefully bottomed it with the rule, and then read the figures on the scale to the top of the hole:

"Team No. 1, from the Nevada Belle, 38½ inches."

Tense silence followed the announcement.

"Team No. 2, from the Desert Queen, 37 inches."

A cheer followed this announcement.

"Team No. 3, from the Sulphide Consolidated, 37¾ inches."

Grubstake

The Nevada Belle team had won. Handshaking among the contestants, free expression of opinions among the spectators, paying of bets, and much good-natured and some ill-humored banter greeted the announcement by Mr. Macklay:

"First prize of $500 goes to Spongoli and Ambrazzo of the Nevada Belle. Second prize of $200 goes to Tredenick and Pentworthy of the Sulphide Consolidated."

"'E need good blacksmith to sharpen tools, boys," called one downcast Cornishman.

"Ah, 'tis some good Irish muscle ye need, bys, bad cess to ye," answered a brawny Irishman. And so the talk went on, while the contestants for the next event prepared for their match.

This was to be the hundred-yard foot race. It had been arranged that there should be first a drilling match, then the hundred-yard dash, then the second drilling match, then the two-twenty dash, then the last of the drilling matches, the mile run, the tug-of-war, and finally the half-mile and mile horse races to wind up the afternoon.

Shorty won some money on the three-man drilling match and also on the hundred-yard dash. As he was wandering back to the drilling match, where the single-handed contest was about to be staged, he met Hans Randt, also wandering in an aimless fashion toward the roped-off arena.

"Vat you tink aboudt dis match, Shordy?"

"I'm betting on a Cornishman from the 'Con,' Hans."

"Dis von-handed drillin', vere a fella iss his own striker und helper mit no odder help at all, keeps him aboudt so busy as a jack-rabbit chased py a coyote. He iss got to do everydings at oncet."

They edged into the milling crowd and awaited the pistol shot that signalled the beginning of the contest. Again the heavy breathing of the contestants, the encouraging cries from the crowd and the final pistol shot. In this case Tom Dugan, an Irish miner from one of the outlying wildcats, won the contest, and since he was a friendly soul and well known to many of the onlookers, the award was greeted with cheers.

And so the events, one by one, were completed; the tug-of-war and the horse races bringing to a close the sports of a glorious day.

Chapter XVIII

Hans Randt had hung tenaciously to Shorty. The assayer carried a flask of whiskey in his pocket, which he frequently tendered to Peterson. Apparently nothing loath, Shorty accepted and appeared to drink liberally with seeming gusto. He even neglected twice to return the bottle to Randt, dropping it into his own pocket, from which he surreptitiously twice removed it and spilled some of its contents on the ground while Randt was busy watching the contests. The liquor seemed to have a potent effect on Shorty, for by the time the last drilling match had been decided Shorty had become extremely loquacious and affectionate. He babbled on to Randt in a most confidential way about his plans.

"Goin' to find that mine, some day sure, Hans. Thought I had her last time, till you knocked the bottom out of it with them assays."

"Vell, maybe she's a mine yedt, Shordy, if you dig on her avhile."

"Maybe she is, but I'll sell out cheap on the chance she ain't."

This was exactly the information Randt had been looking for. Shorty would sell. It was now up to Patrick to do the rest.

"Guess I've had enough of this for one day, Hans. Let's go back to town. I got over a hundred dollars I won and I want to try my luck at faro."

"All righd, Shordy; gome along. I'm gedding kind of tired of it mine own self."

Linking his arm in that of Randt, Shorty started off uptown, headed for the Miners Rest. Others had had their fill of the sports. A thin dribble of folk was beginning to flow toward town, drawn by gambling, whiskey, and the hurdy-gurdy girls.

Ignoring several maudlin invitations to have a drink, the pair wended their way up the street toward the Miners Rest. Curiously, the walk had apparently made Shorty, if anything, more garrulous and confiding.

"Once a year, Hans, maybe oftener, I have a hell of a time. Always on the Fourth of July. This is Fourth July. Make a coyote's howl sound like nothin' a-tall when I turn loose. You goin' to join me in celebration?"

"Vell, I feel priddy goot alretty, mineself, und maybe I'll haf a hell of a time alzo yet."

They turned into the Miners Rest, which was well filled but not overcrowded.

"You ged your san'wich, Shordy, und I gets us a drink," and Randt turned to the bar where Patrick was standing, and said to Hank Bartle, "Drinks fer two of us, Hank." Then, with a furtive glance at Shorty, he remarked sotto voce to Patrick: "Shordy's got a goot load, alretty. I took me a bottle oudt by der sports, und he helped himself to most of it."

"Except what you didn't drink yourself, eh?"

"Vell, nod so much as I ain't kept sober."

"Oh, all right; keep him going. I'll look on for a while. Here he comes," cautioned Patrick.

"Hello, Bill," Shorty exclaimed as he walked up to the bar with an engaging, if somewhat vacuous, smile on his face.

"Hello, Shorty; had a good time?"

"Sa-a-y—won $100, an' I'm goin' to bust your old faro bank."

"Well, good luck to you."

"Here's your drink," interrupted Randt.

"Have one on me, Shorty," remarked Patrick, motioning to Bartle, who instantly placed three glasses and a bottle in front of them. Patrick, as usual, concealed his with his hand and poured a very small quantity into the glass.

"Here's how."

Shorty had now had two large drinks. The first one had been poured by Randt; the second he had poured for himself while both Randt and Patrick were watching him closely. His loquaciousness quickly increased, his smile became more winning and his manner more affectionate and confidential.

"Goin' over and play little faro," he remarked.

"Better have another drink for good luck," said Patrick.

"Not annuzer one, right now. Can't see cards, pretty soon. Mus' bust your bank."

He wobbled rather than walked toward the faro table, while Patrick, Randt, and Bartle all watched him eagerly.

"He's got a good start, all right," opined Bartle.

"Yes," replied Patrick, "but we've got to find some way to keep him going and not let him out of here. Let him alone for a few minutes and then you see if you can't steer him into the back room, where I'll join you. You've had enough, Randt," Patrick warned, as he laid his hand on Randt's and firmly removed it from the bottle out of which he was preparing to pour himself another drink. "It's your job to get Shorty full—not yourself."

"Oh, all right. I goes ofer und vatches him play," muttered Randt, as he reluctantly gave up his drink.

For the next half-hour Shorty continued to buck the tiger. His luck ran fairly well; he had doubled his money in the half-hour's play. The heat of the room and the fumes of the whiskey, however, seemed to be more than he could combat. With increasing frequency his head dropped forward, only to be snapped back with a shake.

"Come on, und I plays you a game of poker, Shordy," Randt finally suggested, as he took him by the shoulders and shook him to his feet.

"All right. I can beat you with one hand tied behind my back." So saying, he started for a poker table that stood near the door leading to Patrick's private room.

"Ve'll go in der back room und shut der door," said Randt, as he guided Shorty to the door standing conveniently ajar. With his foot he pushed it open, and gently propelled Shorty into the room.

A single window admitted light and air. A table and a few chairs constituted the furnishings. Shorty dropped into a chair with a grunt of satisfaction.

"Got $100 this morning. Got $200 this afternoon. Now got $400. Lot of money, but goin' to have more. Goin' to bust the bank soon's I bust you playin' cards. Come on, you old stiff."

Shorty picked up a pack of cards, shuffled them with uncertain hands, and promptly began to lose.

"I'm goin' to get a cigar," said Randt, as he got up and left the room.

"Dot tam prosbector is priddy near goin' to sleep," he reported to Patrick.

"You go back now. I'll be in in a minute and take your hand and play. Then you vamoose."

"Got too durn much whiskey in me now; but not full

by a hell of a sight," said Shorty as he sat alone in the room.

With cigars and matches, Randt re-entered the room. Shorty was lolling back in his chair gazing at the ceiling with feet outstretched beneath the table, almost asleep.

"Have a smoke," said Randt as he passed Shorty a cigar and resumed his seat.

Shortly after they had lit their cigars and commenced a new game the door opened and Patrick entered.

"Hell, I'm tired," he remarked, dropping into a chair beside the table and lighting a cigar. "Just like to sit here and rest a few minutes."

"Take a hand in the game?" suggested Shorty, with a vacant smile.

"You fellas play awhile," said Randt, rising from his chair. "I'll come back priddy soon." He left the room.

To Hank Bartle he confided, as he stopped at the bar, "Padrick's got him now, und it's his pardy."

Patrick began to shuffle the cards with the sure touch of the professional gambler. Quietly he dealt them, and for some time the two played on almost in silence. The stakes were not large and the luck seemed to vary.

"Pshaw," Patrick at last remarked, throwing down his cards. "Nobody is ever going to get rich at this game, Shorty. My saloon is more like a mint, but after all there's nothing like a good mine to roll out the coin. Don't come very often, though, and you usually go broke waiting for the real one to come along. My saloon don't make it as fast, maybe, but it's a whole lot surer, I guess.

"Some day you'll find a real mine, I hope," Patrick continued, "one that will put you on velvet for the rest of your life."

"Well, I hope so," Shorty replied, as he swayed uncertainly in his chair. "Thought I had one sure enough last trip, but assays knocked it into a cocked hat."

"Haven't you ever sold any claims, Shorty, after all the time you've been tramping around making locations?"

"Nope, never sold dam' one. No tenderfoot ever seemed to come my way."

"Maybe you'll meet up with a tenderfoot some day. Fact is, I got a letter from the Bay the other day, telling me about a fellow who's coming over here trying to see if he can't get a group together and stock it for the Pine Street market. Tell you what I'll do. You give me an option on your last bunch of locations you was just talking about and I'll try to sell 'em to this sucker when he lands in town. What do you say?"

"Options not so much good. Only sell for cash. If I don't get cash to begin with and fellers dig hole, it's good-night to cash 'cept you got a real mine; then you don't sell at all till you done some development."

"Well, but what'll you take for your group?"

"Sell 'em for cash?"

"No; give me time to turn 'em over to this fellow that's coming up from below."

"You gimme $2500 cash now and $7500 when you sell 'em."

"Not today, Shorty."

"Nossir, I'm not goin' to sell them claims 'cept I get some cash. No cash, no sell!"

Shorty now assumed a somewhat belligerent mood; apparently his pride had been hurt.

"Me stayin' out in summer—wander all over hills—hotsh sun, all for nothin'? Tramp all around State an' get bilked by s'loonkeeper? Nossir! I keep them claims till some feller pays me some cash for privilege of prospectin'. I'm goin' play faro," he said indignantly, as he started to rise.

"Hold on a minute, Shorty. Tell you what I'll do. I'll play you one hand to see if I get a free option or I don't."

"Bill Patrick, you're a good friend of mine. Like you very mush, but if you was my brother, you'd have to make me cash payment."

"Well, tell you what I'll do, Shorty. I'll give you $1000 cash and $5000 more when I sell 'em again."

"No, sir."

"Well, hell, what's your lowest figure?"

"Take $2000 cash, $8000 when you sell; $10,000 for whole bunch. That's final."

"Too much, Shorty."

"Call her off, then."

"Damn it, you're not anxious to sell, are you?"

"Good lookin' claims. Maybe dig on 'em a while; strike it rich. Guess I'll go play faro."

"Oh, well, have it your way, then; $2000 cash and $8000 when I resell them. Good for six months."

"You said it, Bill."

"Well, you sit here and I'll get a form of agreement."

It was rapidly growing dark now. The lights in the saloon were lighted. The place was crowded, the air thick with tobacco smoke and the reek of liquor. Randt stood near the end of the bar, and as he passed him Patrick vouchsafed, "I got him!"

Randt whispered it to Bartle, and then went off to the other end of the room to inform Anderson.

Ike and Si Proctor stood by the specimen case; Ike was keeping a fatherly eye on his punchers to prevent trouble if possible. Big Sim had strolled in and stood talking to them.

"I reckon it would be a good plan, Ike, to just go down the line from one end of town to the other and confiscate every damn gun and keep 'em till the boys sober up. We got eight or ten hombres locked up in the cooler now. Most of 'em was packing some kind of a gun, from a Colt .44 down to a two-barrel pocket derringer."

"All right, Sim; but a few of us has got to hang around ready for trouble, in that case. I don't calculate to have my punchers disarmed and then have some town pimp take advantage of the situation and bore holes in 'em. You got some specimens in this town I'd like to help you get rid of, anyway. Some's only fit for a necktie party, dangling at the end of a good rawhide riata. Wouldn't waste powder on some of 'em."

"You ring a bull's-eye, Ike. Well, maybe I'll come back after a bit and swear in a few of you fellers and clean up."

Just then Patrick quickly crossed the room and opened the door leading to the stairs which gave access to his sleeping quarters; he was evidently going after something.

"Slip around the side of the house and see if you can spot Shorty," Ike whispered to Si, who immediately nodded and left. He walked quickly down the alley that ran at the side of the building and glanced in at the open casement. Shorty was standing facing the window, stretching himself and yawning. Catching sight of Si, he paused abruptly and said:

"Keep moving. I'm all right. Come back when you see this newspaper laying on the ground. It won't be till after Patrick's gone, maybe not then. I'm goin' to try to get him to leave me alone here a while after I sign this option. Maybe that damn Dutchman'll be back here. If so, I'll come out front. *Vamoose!*"

Si retreated to the sidewalk and the saloon. Randt was in his old place by the bar. Patrick closed the door to his rooms and started across the saloon to the private room. Declining several invitations to drink, he pushed his way through the crowd and entered the room, where Shorty was sprawled out in a chair, arms on the table and head on his arms, apparently asleep.

"Hell," Patrick muttered, under his breath, "hope he isn't dead to the world."

He wiped the table off with a newspaper, flung it into a corner, put the document he was carrying on the table, fished the ink-bottle out of his pocket, inspected the pen, and sat down. For several moments he contemplated the sleeper, and then turning his attention to the paper in front of him, read it carefully. The document was ready for Shorty to sign. Leaning over, he took hold of Shorty's arm and shook him vigorously.

"Hey, Shorty, come to, and look at this paper."

A grunt was his only answer. Again he vigorously shook the prospector, but with little better result. With an oath he got up and using both hands shook the snoring Shorty into a sitting position. Only then did the sleeper open one eye, which he solemnly winked, while a quizzical smile slowly spread over his countenance.

"Guess I must been 'sleep."

"I don't guess at all. You were damn well asleep. Here, wake up and look over this paper."

Shorty settled back comfortably in his chair, folded his hands over his stomach, stuck out his legs under the table, looked vacantly at Patrick, and remarked in a most persuasive tone, "You read it, Bill, I'm seein' double. Everything goin' round 'n' up 'n' down like ship at sea. Thash good feller, you read it."

"All right; here she goes, word for word, just as you agreed before I went out."

"Thash mush be long time ago you went out and wrote all thash paper. I mush been sleep long time." Another wink and an inane smile.

Without deigning a reply, Patrick began:

"'James Peterson agrees with William Patrick, in consideration of $2000 cash paid to said Peterson and $8000 to be paid within six months on resale of his claims by said Patrick, to give and does hereby give Patrick the exclusive right to buy the group of mining claims known as. . . .'

"What do you call 'em, Shorty, and where are they?"

"April Fool group, Bill. Six claims: April Fool, May Day, You Bet, Sulphide Girl, Mary Ann, an' Sister Sallie. Not in any minin' district; just over north near Idaho line, 'bout fifty miles. You go out past Circle R ranch and keep on almost northeast. I go show 'em to you."

Patrick duly wrote in the description and continued: "'And recorded in the records of said county. . . .'"

"Not recorded at all yet, Bill," broke in Shorty. "No use recording till you know what's the value. Costs money to record mining claims."

"All right, Shorty. We'll take that part out." He continued, "'and now owned by said Peterson. It is further agreed that Peterson will make out a deed to said claims and put in escrow with Wells Fargo & Company, to be delivered on payment of the $8000. In the event said payment is not made within six months from date, the $2000 shall be kept by Peterson as forfeit money and Wells Fargo shall return the deed to said Peterson. During the term of the agreement, Patrick may prospect the said claims in any manner he may desire. In the event he shall ship any ore, the proceeds after deducting freight and treatment charges shall be paid to said Peterson in full and by him shall be applied on the purchase price.'"

"How's that, Shorty?"

"Sounds all right—I guess I can sign her, but I got a pardner in this deal. You go out and find him and bring him in here. Let him read agreement. If it's all right, I'll sign. His name's Si Proctor. You know Si? Fine boy. Got brother Ike."

"Yes, I know Si; but why not sign now and tell him about it afterwards?"

"No, sir. Grubstake's grubstake. Si's entitled to know whash goin' on."

Shorty drew himself up with comical dignity and tried to rise, but gave it up as a bad job and subsided into his chair.

"You go get Si," he said, shaking his finger at Patrick. "You get him, Bill, or I got to get him."

"Oh, all right. I'll get him, Shorty."

Patrick rose and left the room, and walked across the saloon over to the specimen case where Ike and Si were still standing.

"Say, Si, I wish you'd come into my private room a minute. Shorty Peterson has talked me into taking an option on some mining claims of his, and says you're in on a grubstake and he won't sign without seeing you first."

Si looked at Ike, and said, "I don't think much of Shorty's claims, Bill, but if you want 'em, I'm willing. How much you payin' for 'em?"

"Just taking an option for $10,000; $2000 cash, balance when I resell."

"Come on in, Ike," said Si, as he turned to follow Patrick. "You might as well be in there as out here for awhile."

The three men pushed their way through the crowd and entered the room, where Shorty sat contentedly leaning back in the chair. He gave them a comical grin and a nod of the head as they entered and waved his hand, saying, "Hello, fellers."

"I brought your friends in to have Si look over the agreement, as you wanted him to," said Patrick. "Come on, brace up, and let's get the agreement signed."

Shorty, with considerable effort, pulled himself together while Patrick handed the document to Si Proctor.

Ike looked over his shoulder as he read it. Having finished reading it, he passed it back to Patrick and remarked to Shorty, "If this suits you, old hoss, it's all right with me. It's your funeral; I'm agreeable to most anything."

"Whazzit say, Si?"

"Why he's goin' to give you $2000 now an' $8000 sometime in the next six months, if he sells the claims."

"Thash a sousan' for you an' sousan' for me. Lot of money, in cash. Nuzzer four sousan' for each of us, when he sells claims. Suits me, Si. How about you?"

"Suits me, all right, Shorty."

"Gimme pen, Bill."

Patrick dipped the pen in the ink and handed it to Shorty.

"Where's money?"

"Got it all for you here in greenbacks," replied Patrick.

"Greenbacks?" repeated Shorty, with a rising inflection in his voice. "No, sir. Gimme gold twenties."

And it was not until Patrick again left the room to get the gold that Shorty would be appeased. As Patrick closed the door and went to the safe behind the bar, Shorty looked up at the brothers and remarked quite soberly and intelligently, "I got some load on all right, fellers, but I ain't plumb full. I'm about ready to bust a-laughin', though, to think how Patrick's swallowin' it all. I'm goin' to divide that money right here under his nose. Don't mention Ralph's name," he cautioned, and then relapsed into apparent stupor again.

"You're sure a actor, Shorty," remarked Ike in a tone of respect as he looked at the huddled figure in the chair.

When Patrick re-entered the room he found them all in the same positions as when he left them, except that Shorty had slumped down in the chair again.

Patrick stacked up the glittering twenty-dollar gold pieces in piles of five each, twenty shining piles.

Shorty looked up abstractedly, fingered some of the gold, and taking up the pen, laboriously signed his name. He tossed the paper over to Patrick, and motioned to the brothers, saying, "Here, you fellers, is where we divide—here's your sousan', Si, "and he pushed some of the gold over to his partner. "You keep mine for me, Ike," he said, pushing the remaining pile toward the foreman of the Circle R.

"Them bills is easier to carry," remarked Ike. "Say, Patrick," he said, "you gimme bills, an' if Shorty wants gold later, you'll trade him back, eh?"

Patrick agreed, and as Si seemed to want his in bills also, he took the entire amount back to the safe and exchanged the gold for greenbacks.

When Patrick returned he found Ike examining the agreement and Si helping Shorty light a cigar.

"Better give the boys a copy of this agreement, hadn't you, Patrick," Ike asked.

"Yes, of course. I'll write out another and sign it, and Shorty can have it any time."

"That's fine, Patrick," Ike replied. "Your word is as good as gold with me."

He knew that if Patrick gave his word he would live up to his promise if it broke him. He took the document, looked at the signature, asked Ike to sign as a witness—which he did—stuck the paper into his pocket, and remarked, "I've got to keep moving around, boys, if you'll excuse me. You stay here as long as you like."

After Patrick left the room, Shorty sank into a chair and laughed till the tears rolled down his cheeks.

"He swallered it all, fellers," he gasped between paroxysms, "just ate it up alive. We got our money, and I ain't so full that I can't enjoy a joke. I'm just full enough to be happy, light-hearted and gay."

"You got to go out, Ike, to them claims of mine north of the Circle R, and get them location notices changed. I'll give you a set of notices before you go, and I won't leave here until you have had time to get there and change them."

"All right, Shorty," replied Ike. "I'll take care of that for you, but you got to give me a good head start so I can get this crowd of wild Indians of mine back to the ranch, first."

Shorty nodded his head as he got up, and taking Si by the arm, he walked out into the saloon.

"Si's goin' take me to Hing's hash-house and get some coffee," he said to Patrick. "Come right back," he added, as he clung to Proctor and started toward the door. "Hello," he said with a leer, as they passed Randt near the end of the bar. "Hope you're feelin' as good as me, Hans."

"Guess dot must be feelin' priddy goot, Shordy," Randt replied.

They walked out of the saloon and up the street, Shorty clinging affectionately to Si's arm.

Chapter XIX

At the hoisting works Macklay and Ralph found everything quiet. A watchman had the fire-hose out and was busily engaged in wetting down around the works, giving particular attention to the roofs of both the hoisting works and the mill, as well as to the scattered buildings in the immediate vicinity. The weather was so dry that a fire once well under way in the wooden buildings could not be extinguished. Both mine and mill fire-hose had been unreeled early on the Fourth and frequently used during the day. It would not be taken up again until the afternoon of the fifth. Inside the hoisting works all was silence. The engineer on watch was the only man in sight. He had volunteered to keep up the fire in the boiler, thus releasing the fireman. The mill was running on reserve ore in the bins. All that was needed was to keep up enough steam to run the pumps and hoist the cage, should the pump-man underground want to come to the surface.

At the mill the ceaseless drop of the stamps, and the millmen moving from place to place feeding a little quicksilver here, adjusting the screw of a pan there, quickening or slowing the ore feed, examining the tailings, all gave evidence of continued and smooth operation. Of the entire mine and mill crew there were not over six men on shift. But a few prolonged blasts on the whistle of either mine or mill would bring the men up from the town on the double-quick. In the meantime, the watchman would keep things well wet down.

After walking through the plant, Macklay stopped at the

office, as a matter of habit, and hastily ran over the daily reports lying on his desk.

"Not much news here," he remarked, "and there'll be less in the reports tomorrow. Cars of ore hoisted—um-m; cars of waste—um-m; feet drifts advanced—um-m; assays —um-m."

Picking up the *Daily Alta California* he looked over the stock list, noted the transactions and prices in his own stock, and after another rapid glance at the headings of the news columns, lit his pipe, and leaned back in his chair.

"I've been thinking all day about that grubstake of yours, Ralph," he said. "It sounds as though you had stumbled on to something good. It's not going to take so much money, either, to find out. You won't, of course, permit Mary Clark to put in any more money; you fellows have got to pack that load, and if you lose you must see that she doesn't. That's the penalty I'm going to exact from you for taking a woman in with you."

"I intended that Miss Mary should not put up any more money, but she says she has several hundred dollars saved up and she wants to contribute her share," replied Ralph.

"She's got the money, safe enough. At least I've got it for her and have it on deposit in the Hibernia Savings Bank in San Francisco, where it's drawing interest at the rate of nine per cent per annum*; and," he added dryly, "so far as I know, it's going to stay just where it is."

"You must remember, Ralph, that you're going to have all sorts of attempts made to get your mine away from you. Bill Patrick is only the starter of what's going to happen. Mines such as yours don't grow on every bush. In fact, you can name those in Nevada almost on your two hands. You

* The Hibernia Bank paid interest at the rate of 10 per cent in 1870–71, and 9 per cent in 1872–73 and '74.

can, in fact, if you name camps instead of single mines. Virginia City, of course, with Gold Hill, is in a class by itself; then there's Eureka, but that's silver-lead; then Austin, Pioche, Hamilton, Tuscarora, and Sulphide. That's about all the big ones, and some of them are not so very large. Then you have Cerro Gordo and Tybo and Belmont, and that's about all.

"If your prospect turns into a real mine you'll have 'em piling in on you from all those places and a lot more; all intent on making a stake for themselves—some honestly, a lot of 'em by any means at hand. Lawsuits, jumping your claims, labor troubles, every device you can think of, will be used to try to dispossess you. Your safety lies in being on the ground, getting your monuments up, protecting your lines on all questions of extralateral rights. Get up your hoist, begin to ship ore, settle down in possession, and then hang on!

"Patrick has one bad man in his employ, Jim Graves, his chief bouncer. That fellow is a killer; came here from Montana. I'm trying to get his full pedigree now against the time you may have use for it. Sim knows something about him, but not a great deal; says he was chased out of Montana after a killing scrape over in Alder Gulch."

"I've been thinking, Mr. Macklay, that I'd like to have you identified with us. Can't we make some arrangement with you, so you will be an interested party?"

"No, son; you boys just hang on to what you have and don't take in any more partners. I haven't anybody to leave what I've got to—just me and the wife; and there's enough in sight to keep us as long as we live. This job will last for a while yet. I've made money in stocks, both here and in Virginia City, and we could retire now any time we wanted to. Our tastes are simple, and there's not much we need to keep us contented and happy."

He rose as he spoke and started for the door. "Guess it's about time to eat," he remarked, as they began to walk toward the house.

Below them the town lay in the shimmering heat waves of the July afternoon. To the west, the sun was dropping toward the mountain tops, casting long shadows about the mill, the hoisting-works, and the buildings of the town. Save for an occasional burst of a bunch of fire-crackers the place might have been a mirage or the painting of a master upon a gigantic canvas.

"It's a wonderful country, Ralph; you'll have it in your blood always, and you'll be glad you've lived in it and lived in these times."

He expanded his lungs as he spoke, gulped in great draughts of the pure desert air, and swept with a glance of sympathetic understanding the scene before him. They had reached the gate. He lifted the latch and they walked up the gravelled path to the house.

"Come on, Mother, with your victuals," he called, as he pulled out a chair and seated himself at the table. "Ralph, you sit over there, opposite Mary."

"Wonder what's going on downtown," remarked Mrs. Macklay as she poured out the tea.

"Well, the saloons are doing a land office business, for one thing," replied her husband. "Pretty good place to stay away from right now, as a matter of fact," he continued. "The town's full of strangers from a hundred miles around, and what between the cowpunchers, the miners, and the prospectors, to say nothing of the Mexicans, there's likely to be several killings before morning."

"I wonder what Shorty is up to," said Ralph. "I think I ought to go down there and stand by, ready to take a hand if needed."

"Si and his brother will be all the bodyguard Shorty needs," Macklay replied. "If you appeared on the scene and Patrick saw you hobnobbing with Shorty, he'd begin to smell a rat right away. You're about the only assayer in town, with Johnson of the 'Queen' laid up in the hospital. If Patrick ever took it into his head that you had been doing any assaying on those samples, he'd cause all kinds of trouble in no time. You stay right here, and we'll watch the fireworks from the porch."

A month or two before, a subscription paper had been handed around for the purpose of raising funds with which to purchase fireworks. The donations had been liberal. Everybody contributed something, even Sam Hing. A large assortment of skyrockets, Roman candles, bombs, and other devices had been imported and were to be set off just below town. A space had been roped off, and the ubiquitous Sim was master of ceremonies, as usual. It didn't make much difference what was going on—wedding, funeral, election, fight—Sim always seemed to be more or less directing things, and always in the interests of order, honesty, and fair play.

As they sat on the porch the twilight faded into dark; lights began to twinkle. Soon the first bomb exploded, and for the next half-hour the display was continuous. Finally the noise died down and the last rocket was discharged.

"That winds up the Fourth of July celebration in the year of Our Lord 1874," remarked Ralph.

"Well, yes, I guess it does, so far as the official programme goes," Macklay said. "But there'll be plenty of unofficial celebrating the rest of the night and well into tomorrow. The crew won't all be back at work for several days," he added, ruefully, "and some of those who do come back won't be worth a dollar a day. If we get off without some kind of an accident, we'll be in luck. Well, that's the end of the Fourth, folks," he said, rising. "Let's go inside and have a game of cribbage."

"It's almost too pleasant out here to leave," remarked Mrs. Macklay.

The heat of the day had given way to the inexpressively pleasing coolness of a desert night in summer. Overhead the Milky Way and other stars shone with a brilliance unknown to dwellers in eastern States. The stars, twinkling with luminous radiance, seemed very near. The distant mountains even seemed to be surrounded with an indefinable something that attracted and held the attention of the onlooker. About everything was the fascination and spell of the desert, which, once experienced, can never be entirely forgotten.

They rose, almost regretfully, and went into the house, where under the light from a suspended kerosene lamp they spent an hour or more in playing cribbage.

"Remember," remarked Mr. Macklay, as Ralph was leaving, "you keep away from Shorty. Ike or Si will be up here in the morning to report. The trail behind the hoisting works cuts off a good mile of the road to the Circle R, and the riders mostly go this way. Ike can stop here as he passes, or Si may come up to see about freight from the railroad. They'll get word to you, some way, without your hunting up Shorty."

"You're right, sir, and I'll follow your suggestions, although I can't promise to sleep much tonight. There don't seem to be any sleep in me. I'd much rather go downtown and spend the night with my eyes open than go to bed."

"But that would be giving notice to Patrick that something unusual was going on. You're not a sufficiently regular habitué of his saloon to have your presence pass unnoticed. Everything has worked out just right, up till now. Let it alone. You run along to bed, forget all about grubstakes and assays, and have a good night's sleep."

"Easier said than done, sir; but I'll try to do it."

In bed he tossed restlessly about until he sank into disturbed slumber, to dream of prospect holes, assays, and of Mary Clark perhaps more than of anything else.

Chapter XX

SHORTY and Si went on up the street to Sam Hing's restaurant where, thanks to the lateness of the hour, they found seats. Drinking coffee and eating ham and eggs did not consume much time, and they were soon headed for the Miners Rest. This time Shorty would really enjoy himself, in celebrating not only the Fourth of July but also his triumph over Bill Patrick and, most of all, Hans Randt, for whom he had conceived a particular aversion.

"You and Ike be sure to get me home when I get full," he said to Si before they entered the Miners Rest. "I'm feelin' so darn good that if some one don't hold me down, I'm likely to walk up and spit in Patrick's eye and tell him to go to hell."

Men were standing three and four deep in front of the bar. The gambling tables were running full blast. There were men in all conditions from utterly drunk to utterly sober. Bouncers now and then carried some one who had "passed out" to the sidewalk and deposited him there, to be picked up later by "Sim's patrol," as the boys had facetiously dubbed the team which passed along the street at intervals and gathered up the casualties.

It wasn't all play, either. Down at Mexican Pete's, at the lower end of town, mescal had been consumed in large quantities. One Mexican was dead with a knife through his heart, another was suffering from a bullet wound inflicted by one of Sim's deputies, and an incipient race-war was in the making. Sim had gone down the street on the run, picking up his aides here and there as he went. They had charged the saloon, guns in hand, and were now engaged in disarming the crowd. Herding them all into one end of the room and keeping all exits guarded with armed men, Sim marched the mob, one at a time, past a table set in the middle of the room and quickly searched each man. A miscellaneous assortment of weapons had been collected and tagged.

"We'll just keep this collection as a souvenir of the occasion," Sim remarked. "You all can get back your hardware by callin' on me day after tomorrow."

He swept the collection into a gunny-sack and handed it to one of his aides, remarking, "Here, take this sack and lock it up in the calaboose till we get ready to refund."

At the Miners Rest Shorty was performing entirely according to programme. He bucked the tiger and drank frequently. Randt had long since succumbed, and was now peacefully sleeping in a chair crowded back against the wall. A few of the more eager gamblers, especially those playing poker, were not drunk. They couldn't be drunk and play the game. They preferred the thrills of gambling to those of alcohol.

The town was now putting the finishing touches to the day's festivities. In the street, firecrackers, large and small, were being exploded. Roman candles and pin-wheels were being set off by the small boys and grown-ups. And, on the outskirts of town, sky-rockets and bombs—to say nothing of anvils that were being fired with disturbing frequency—all added to the din.

"What's the next move, boss?" asked Hank Bartle of Patrick, as they stood together momentarily at the bar during a lull in the drinking caused by a fight over a poker game.

"Nothing for the present. Just let things cool off. I've got my option, and that's the main thing. Nobody is in any condition to do anything now. Look 'em over! There's Randt, asleep. Nick Trevethan, who will go out to sample the claims, is over there playing roulette and headed for a bust that will take him till day after tomorrow to recover from. Slim Wilson's going to get full by morning, to relieve the strain of the last two days."

Bartle nodded and turned to care for the rush of customers that swamped the bar now that the fighting poker players were disposed of.

It was well after midnight. The crowd was beginning to thin out a little. Some wandered off to other saloons or went home.

Shorty had long since ceased playing cards or bucking the tiger or playing roulette. He had importuned Ike and Si to drink with him, and had gone through the various stages of intoxication until he was on the verge of collapse. He had begun to turn morose and ugly.

"I'm goin' to tell that Bill Patrick what I think of him," he vociferated to Si. "He can't steal my claims, not by a damn sight. Jus' goin' to tell him to go to hell an' fin' out where them claims are for himself."

Things were beginning to get tense. Shorty might spoil it all, even at this late hour. Ike nodded to Si, and the two brothers closed in, one on either side.

"Come on outside and cool yourself off a few minutes," Ike suggested.

"Just get a little fresh air, and you'll feel better," added Si. "You can lick Patrick when you come back. Pour a little cold water on your head—it'll make you see straighter."

So, talking, coaxing, and pushing, they got the obstreperous Shorty out onto the sidewalk and headed him up the street. Protesting and hanging back, he insisted on returning to the Miners Rest and wiping up the floor with the proprietor. He had become obsessed with but one idea: that Patrick had tried to do him out of his claims. He proposed, therefore, to administer an unmerciful beating to him.

"Aw, come on home, Shorty," protested Si. "You won his money buckin' the tiger, you done him in on the sale of them claims; you got everything comin' your way. What in hell more do you want?"

"Wanna lick Bill Patrick," protested Shorty.

"That'll do you a hell of a lot of good! You go in there and start something and his bouncers'll land you in the street, and maybe you'd be just damn fool enough to shoot off your mouth and give the whole business away. Want to spoil everything, at this late date, eh? You keep a-goin' up the street with me. I'll take you home and put you in your little bed, where you can't do no harm."

The argument waxed warm, but in the end Shorty went up the street, steered by Si.

"Shorty gone home?" inquired Patrick, indifferently, as Ike returned to the saloon.

"Yep; he got to the fightin' stage, an' we run him out."

"Who was he going to lick?"

"Oh, you. Said you bought his claims too cheap; wanted to make you put up another couple of thousand. Si led him home."

Arriving at the cabin, Si tried in vain to mollify the usually placid Shorty, who insisted on telling his troubles, until finally Si yelled, "Oh, shut up, you make me tired with your drunken talk."

By degrees Shorty calmed down and sprawled out on the table, arms extended and head on arms, dead to the world.

After a few minutes Si threw back the blankets and dumped Shorty into the bed, pulled his boots off and covered him over. He found some extra blankets with which he made himself a bed on the floor near the door.

"Guess you won't move before some time tomorrow, old hoss, but I'm takin' no chances on losin' that cow ranch; so I'll camp between you and the door, an' you'll have a hell of a time gettin' a-past me without my knowin' it."

Then he blew out the kerosene lamp, rolled up in the blankets on the floor, and was soon sound asleep.

Chapter XXI

Meanwhile, at the Miners Rest, Ike, intent on keeping his punchers within bounds, mingled with the cowboys and other patrons of the resort.

"I don't mind," he said to Sim, "if the darn cusses will only keep away from the bar; they can gamble as much as they like, if only they'll leave the whiskey alone."

"But you know darn well they won't, Ike, so what's the use of hopin' for the impossible?"

"Oh, I know they won't; only I got to shoo 'em off from the bar whenever I can. Wait a minute," he said, as he stepped toward the counter, where one of his men was getting into a somewhat heated controversy with a miner.

Stepping in between them, Ike drawled, "Hey, you fellers, what's all this discussion about? You don't know nothin' about mines," he said to the cowboy, "and your friend here don't know nothin' about punchin' cattle, so why try to argue about it?"

" 'E says 'e can lick any miner in Sulphide," said the Cornishman excitedly. "I been a-tellin' 'e thot 'e is a dom liar! Coom us along out in street an' I'll show 'e a few tricks."

Putting his hand on the cowboy's arm, Ike said soothingly, "No, Bill, you know perfectly well that you ain't a-goin' to get into no row while I'm around, so just mosey over to that keno game and see if you can't win a few dollars. You always were pretty good on keno, Bill." He gently pushed the resisting cowboy in the direction of the card tables. "And he don't mean nothin'"—turning to the miner —"Fourth of July is always a time for the boys to get a little full, you know. It beats hell how a little whiskey'll make a cowpuncher think he can clean up the universe! You don't want to pay no attention to him; he don't know nothin' 'bout fightin', 'cept with a gun. He's a daisy with a rope, if he had one, and can throw and tie a critter 'bout as quick as any feller I ever seen. But you'd have him licked to a finish in a fist fight."

Thus he praised the prowess of the miner and at the same time cautioned him about the prowess of the cowboy. The miner permitted himself to be pushed in the direction of the door leading to the street, muttering to himself, meanwhile, that he could lick any cowboy in town. With one of them seated quietly at the keno table and the other wandering aimlessly up the street toward another saloon, Ike was free to continue his watch.

Patrick nodded to him as he turned away. "Much obliged to you for keeping them cowboys of yours in order. The drinks are on the house whenever you'll have them."

"Thanks, but I reckon I better not drink while this band of wild Indians of mine are runnin' around this town loose. Somebody's liable to get into trouble before the night's over. Guess I can best take care of the situation by confinin' my celebratin' to tobacco. I'll take a cigar on the house, if you don't mind."

"Certainly," answered Patrick, as he called to a barkeeper, "hand me over that box of our best cigars."

He passed the box to Proctor, who took one and contentedly began to exhale the smoke.

"Ain't all of my crew here," he remarked. "Some of 'em's scattered promiscuous-like around town, but I got the most likely ones corralled right here. Oh, hell! what's broke loose now," he said, as the obstreperous cowboy who had recently begun to play keno rose from the table and jumped onto the chair in which he had been sitting. From the holster on his side the cowboy drew a large Colt revolver. Waving this above his head and keeping it pointed toward the ceiling, he shouted, "Been a-playin' keno off and on ever since I come to town and I ain't had keno yet. I get tired of listenin' to other fellers yellin' 'Keno' just about the time I'm ready to take a trick. Jus' want to give notice that the next son of a gun yells 'Keno' ahead of me gets plugged. Gentlemen will keep their seats and go on with the game."

After considerable difficulty Proctor persuaded the irate cowboy to sit down in the chair. Nothing, however, could induce him to quit the game.

"You brought me over here a while ago, Ike, and broke up a little argument I was a-havin' with a fresh Cornishman that I was a-goin' to beat up; and now you're tryin' to spoil my keno game. I'm just a-goin' to stay right here, and the next feller that yells 'Keno' gets plugged. And nobody is goin' to quit the game, either," he added with significance, as one or two players started to leave the table.

"Tell you what I'll do, Bill," suggested Proctor, "you play one game and if you win, you quit; and if you don't win, you can play until you do."

"All right," replied Bill, with drunken solemnity, "but if any feller yells 'Keno,' he gets plugged."

The game began again, with Proctor standing at Bill's right elbow, prepared for action should any one complete his cards before the cowpuncher finished his. No one, however, seemed to have any luck; and shortly, to his great delight, Bill won.

"Whoopee," he cried, as he gathered in his winnings and executed a jig-step. "Let's likker up," he said to those nearest him. Whereupon those around the table rose, to a man, and joined him at the bar.

"Can't you cool him off a little?" suggested Patrick.

"Yeh, I'm goin' to try. Say, Bill," he said, "go on up to the hash-house and get yourself some supper. Here, Jim," he called to one of his trusted aides, "you go with him."

"You bet I will," said Jim, taking his cue from Ike. "I'm hungry as a wolf. Come along, Bill."

Taking the somewhat befuddled cowboy by the arm, he led him toward the door, while Ike deftly removed the six-shooter from its holster. "I'll keep this for you for a while, Bill," he said.

Protests and arguments were of no avail, and the puncher went off up the street.

"If he comes back and tries to start anything, reckon we'll have to get him locked up in the calaboose over night," remarked Ike, as he watched the two figures disappear.

"He won't make any trouble without his gun," replied Patrick.

"No, probably not. Here, wish you'd lock this thing up till tomorrow," he said, as he handed the weapon to Patrick.

"All right," said Patrick. "I'll cache it behind the bar, and he can get it before he starts back to the ranch."

Chapter XXII

LATER, Ike Proctor was so vigilant that there was no undue disorder. The only near clash came when Jim Graves attempted to throw out one of Proctor's men.

"Just kinder let go of that feller, Graves, and I'll take care of him," Ike said, taking hold of Graves' right arm with his own left, as Graves was about to run the befuddled cowboy towards the door. "I got his gun, Graves; took it from him early in the evenin'; maybe saved your bacon for you, too, in doin' it. Howsoever that may be, the point now is that if any of my men is to be run out, I'll do it myself."

The room went suddenly quiet, as the two men stood facing each other. Cards were dropped; the roulete wheel ceased to spin; the drone of the faro dealer was hushed. Hank Bartle stood as if carved of stone, grasping the neck of a bottle he was just about to place in front of a customer, and ready to dive to safety behind his protection of boiler plate the moment anybody reached for a gun. Patrick was the only live man in the room. Every one else was transfixed, watching the two men in the centre of the room and ready to drop to the floor the instant a gun was drawn.

Patrick had been standing looking at a poker game. Instantly, as the room froze in rigid attention, he wheeled around, and, sensing the situation, stepped forward saying, "That's all right, Graves, Proctor will take care of his own men."

Graves hesitated, but finally dropped his hand, saying as he did so, "Oh, all right, boss, if you say so."

He had no particular desire to quarrel with Proctor, whose reputation was not unknown to him. He may have realized, also, that he was helpless as he stood. Proctor knew it. With his left hand resting on Graves' right arm he could block any move to draw a gun, while at the same time his own right arm was free. He could pull and use his own gun long before Graves would have any chance to draw.

And Patrick knew there would have been no time wasted if Graves had made a sudden motion. Proctor's gun would have been out of its holster before Graves' hand had moved half-way to beneath his vest, where he carried his own gun. Any attempt to stop a killing after the first move had been made would have been worse than useless because of the speed with which the drawing and firing would have been done. Patrick saw instantly that his killer was at the mercy of Proctor, and he did not wait on formalities but began to walk and talk at the same time.

With Graves' acquiescence the tension relaxed instantly. Bartle let go his hold on the bottle and pushed the glass towards the customer; the roulette wheel began to spin again; the faro dealer resumed his cards, and the players went on from where they had left off. A general sigh of relief swept over the room as the actors parted. It had been a near squeak, but hadn't quite come off.

"Say," remarked Bartle to Patrick some time later as they stood talking during a momentary lull, "did you see the way Proctor got himself set for that bad man of yourn, Bill? Graves wouldn't have had a Chinaman's chance, if he'd tried to start anything. Proctor would have killed him before he could've got his gun out from under his vest. Guess he knew it, too! You can bet some of the other fellers saw the situation. Well, I'll say one thing, Bill, that makes Graves Proctor's enemy for life. If they ever should come together you won't have to sic 'em on, so far as Graves is concerned."

"Might be worse things than that, Hank."

"Sure, there might be."

Patrick turned on his heel and walked away. The episode did not please him. Proctor had shown that under certain circumstances he was Graves' master; and, what was worse, Graves knew it. The odds would be in favor of Proctor if they ever met again.

Patrick's next move was to stop a town roustabout who was attempting to buy liquor by the bottle.

"You get out of here," he ordered. "Thought I'd told you before not to come 'round here trying to buy whiskey for Indians. We don't indulge in that trade in this saloon, and you ought to know it by this time."

"Aw, I ain't a-trying to buy no likker for Indians," remonstrated the partially intoxicated individual. "Just want it fer myself and a few friends."

"Well, you can't have any for yourself or your friends. Your trade ain't wanted. Do you go, or do we throw you out?"

"Aw, I'll go."

"You bet you will, and be quick about it."

Midnight saw little slackening in the pace. It was two o'clock in the morning before the crowd began to thin perceptibly. Not before daylight did the gambling cease and the attendants begin to clean up.

The money had been gathered up and placed in the large safe that stood between the end of the bar and the front wall of the building. Besotted customers were shaken to their feet and pushed out of doors to reel away or sink in helpless stupor on the sidewalk. Those utterly helpless were dragged out to be carted off to the calaboose. Patrick and most of his assistants went off to bed. A couple of attendants who had not been on duty all night took possession of the place. Daylight was breaking.

Before leaving the room Patrick turned to Bartle and said, "Where's Randt?"

"Oh, I had McCabe and one of the bouncers pack him off to bed about four o'clock. I'll have him routed out about eleven."

"Well, do that. Have 'em get him down here by noon, so I can talk to him. We can't lose any time. This expedition starts tomorrow morning without fail. Send word to Nick Trevethan I want him here, too, at the same time. We'll have him and a helper out of town by eight o'clock tomorrow. I don't intend that Randt shall go with the party. Nick and one more man, and Shorty to show 'em the way. I would send Graves, but he's no good as a miner. Trevethan's got to get somebody he knows to go along and swing a pick and help sample. Randt or Graves would only be in the way on a job of that kind."

Bartle stopped to speak to McCabe, who was on watch, and tell him what he wanted done. Patrick disappeared through the door leading to his living-quarters on the floor above. Things had quieted down and were rapidly assuming their normal course. Tomorrow most of the celebrants would be back at work, some of them in too poor condition to do much real work. A few of them would be entirely out of commission for some days. Two would find final resting-places out in the sagebrush where they would sleep, unmolested and alone, with the desert around them.

Chapter XXIII

"Come on, Randt, get out of that."

McCabe, carrying out Bartle's orders, was standing by Randt's bed in the cabin where he lived, vigorously shaking the sleeping assayer.

Heavy-eyed, Randt looked up at his tormentor. "Vat der hell iss you tryin' to do mit me, eh?"

"Bill Patrick wants you over at the Rest at twelve o'clock. It's eleven now, an' I'm goin' to stay here till you get out on your feet."

"Aw, go to der deffle."

Randt rolled over with his face to the wall and clasped the blanket tightly around himself.

"I will not, and you can't stay here any longer. You get out of that, pronto, or I'll run a hose in through the window and drown you out."

"Go suck yourself some eggs," was the sleepy rejoinder.

McCabe grabbed the drowsy Dutchman and dexterously hauled him, blanket and all, to the floor. His efforts were greeted with a flow of profanity, in German and English. Randt was dragged to his feet, rubbing his inflamed eyes, and blubbering, "Gott damn! Gott!" He was fully dressed save for his boots.

"Vat's all der row aboudt, anyvay?"

"I told you before, Patrick wants you over at the Rest at twelve o'clock."

"Oh, all righdt," he replied, beginning to collect his senses. "Yust get me a pitcher of cold water. I am so thirsdy as like nefer vas."

Slowly he began to put on his boots.

McCabe returned with a pitcher of water, from which Randt drank greedily, and then seated himself on the edge of the bed with his hands on his knees.

"Come on, now, stick your face in cold water, and brush your hair, and then we'll go over to the barber's and let him shampoo your head for you."

"You go along, und I comes lader," Randt replied, as he looked longingly at the bed.

"Not on your life. I'm goin' to stay right here with you till you get out on the street and into the barber's chair. You'd be asleep in five minutes if I left you here alone."

"Oh, all right. I'll come."

He yawned and stretched himself, poured some water into a washbowl, and plunged his head into it with much splashing and grunting. Even then he endeavored to persuade McCabe to leave him, but all to no avail. Finally, he adjusted his crumpled clothes and started out.

"Let's get some coffee," he suggested.

"Do you good," commented McCabe. Coffee, toast, and an egg at Sam Hing's brought him out of his stupor.

McCabe left him at the barber's, getting a shave and a head rub, with a warning to be at the Miners Rest at noon sharp.

At the time when McCabe was hauling Randt out of bed, Bill Patrick's efficient and silent Chinese servant entered his bedroom and gently pulled at the sheet, remarking, "Him 'leben clock, Misser Patlick. Allee samee time you get up."

Persistently but gently he continued to shake the sleeper, repeating his remarks until Patrick answered, "All right, Ling. I'll be up in a few minutes. You have me some breakfast in half an hour."

He stretched himself, yawned prodigiously, and finally kicked off the bedclothes and rolled out of bed. Patrick had drunk comparatively little. Tea often masqueraded as whiskey when the opportunity offered, but even at that he felt the effects of the night's work. Slowly he went about his dressing with much yawning and stretching.

"Hell of a life," he muttered, "but it ain't going to be necessary much longer, if this option is any good." He felt in his pocket to assure himself that the document was there. "Just going to carry it around with me till I get a deed. Won't even put it in the safe. Got twenty or thirty thousand cash in there now, and this is worth more than that, a good many times over, if I ain't fooled. It stays right with me, and I'd like to see anybody get it away from me."

His toilet completed to his satisfaction, he walked out into his living room, where he found the table set for breakfast, and Bartle waiting for him.

"Come on with the coffee," he called through the open door, as he dropped wearily into his chair and began to eat some fruit already on the table.

"Trevethan's downstairs, Bill, an' McCabe says he's just left Randt over at the barber's gettin' his head rubbed; he told him to be here at noon."

"All right, Hank, I'll be down in a few minutes. Take Trevethan into the private room, and put Randt in there if he shows up."

He finished his breakfast, lighted a cigar and went downstairs. There were a few customers in the saloon, some sitting dejectedly about, two or three standing at the bar taking a morning bracer. He crossed the room quickly, with a nod and a "Hello, boys! Feeling a little rocky this morning?" One or two grunts and an affirmative or two answered him. With a laugh he went into the private room, where he found Trevethan and Bartle waiting for him.

He had scarcely seated himself when Randt came in and with, "Goot morgen, efferybody," took a seat by the round table and turned expectantly to Patrick.

"Vell, here I am, Bill. Vat's oop?"

"I've got Trevethan here to arrange about that trip and I wanted you to sit in and listen."

Slim Wilson, who had also been dragged out by McCabe, here joined the circle.

"According to Shorty Peterson," Patrick began, "the claims he has located are over somewhere near the Idaho line. Nick, you are to go with him, and take a good man along to help you sample. I want you to get your stuff together today and be ready to start early tomorrow morning. Randt, you go over and dig Shorty out and get him in shape to make the trip. You can hire some horses from Simpson and load Shorty's burro with grub, blankets, and your sampling outfit. He says it's about fifty or sixty miles from here, and you ought to make it in two days. You and one man, in one full day, can take enough samples to tell us all we want to know. You should get back here in five or six days. Randt can take care of the samples at once; he'll be waiting for you. And then we'll be ready to get down to business.

"I am prepared to make the final payment as soon as

Randt reports," he continued, "and I will want you to start right back with an outfit, Nick, and take possession and go to work. There'll be plenty of stampeding, soon's the news gets noised around. We can't keep it quiet for long, and as soon as it's known you'll see a rush that will just about cut the population of this town down one third.

"You look out that everything's located that is necessary, Nick. Take up a mill-site, too, and don't be backward about plenty of ground; we don't want any undesirable neighbors to cause us trouble with apex litigation."

"I'll look out for all that, Bill," said Trevethan. "I'll have to go up to the mine and get a lay-off for a week. Hardly think the old man'll have any serious objections to my bein' away. Anyway, if he does I can draw my time and quit. Gettin' kind of tired of that job, anyhow."

"Rolling stone, Nick," said Patrick. "Better stay where you are as long as you can. We'll all have to move some day, but Sulphide is good for another year anyway."

"Yes, more than that, Bill; but the town's beginning to lose population already. The wildcats is startin' to peter out on the assessment game; the boys and the public are gettin' tired payin' assessments. Something's got to happen pretty soon, or you'll see a lot of vacant houses standin' 'round here."

"Well, if this new camp of ours amounts to anything, Nick, you can tear down some of those houses and move 'em over there. There's houses here that have been moved two or three times already. No reason why they can't stand another move or two.

"Here's some money to buy grub and anything else you'll need, Nick," he said.

Trevethan took the hundred dollars Patrick handed him and rose to go.

The meeting broke up. Patrick went out with Randt. "You go and get hold of Peterson," he said. "Tell him to get ready to start in the morning and bring him in here; I want to talk to him."

Chapter XXIV

It was long after sun-up before Si Proctor stirred in his shake-down on the floor. It took him some time to get his wits together and realize where he was. He sat up and looked at Shorty, sound asleep.

"You'll have a fine head on you, old hoss, when you wake up," Si drawled. "You had a real load on last night, sure nuff. More'n you could carry. You never would've got home by yourself. Well, sleep on, pardner; as fer me, I'm goin' to rustle myse'f somethin' to eat."

It was after nine o'clock, and the sun was beating down on the canvas roof, making the cabin uncomfortably hot. "Got to fix this, or Shorty'll roast," Si said, as he kicked off the blanket and scrambled to his feet. He threw the door wide open, went around the sides and untied the strings that held the canvas down, and having loosened them, lifted the canvas a foot or so, permitting a freer circulation of air.

"That's better," he remarked, as he seated himself near the fireplace. "Seems to me I'd like some coffee. Wonder what there is to eat in the house. Find out by lookin', maybe."

On the shelves he found coffee, sugar, bacon, potatoes, crackers, and a loaf of bread.

"Say, this is made to order! All I need now is a match, an' we'll have something to eat in no time."

Before long he had a fire going and water boiling. In short order he had a pot of coffee on the table, some bacon cooked to a turn, and potatoes roasted in the coals of the fire.

"Guess Shorty won't want much to eat this morning; a cup of good strong coffee and a cracker'll be about his style. Nothin' the matter with *my* appetite, though." (Munch-munch-munch.) "Beats hell how some fellers'll go off and get full when they get a chance." Si shook his head. "I'll just set this coffee-pot by the fire and keep her good and hot, and if he don't come to, pretty soon, I'll have to shake him up. Too bad to disturb him, though, for he certainly won't feel like no spring mornin' when he gits on his feet."

He washed up the dishes and threw out the dish water; then he sat down on the bench by the cabin door, carefully loaded his pipe and leaned back as he blew the first mouthful of smoke into the air.

Ike Proctor had not gone to bed. By nine o'clock he had located eleven of his crew, and had begun to take stock of the situation. "Four down in the calaboose, five asleep in Julia Ann O'Neal's lodging-house. That's nine, two gone back to the ranch—that's eleven. Well, that's not so bad. I'm only short four, an' I'll bet I know where they are, but I ain't a-goin' after 'em. Guess I can get this crowd headed for home by two or three o'clock. Get 'em home to bed and give 'em a full night's sleep, and they'll never know they was out on any Fourth of July spree. That damn cook is goin' to give me the most trouble, as usual, and maybe we'll have to rope him and tie him on his hoss and just natchally lead him home, whether he likes it or not. Bully good cook, too; we can't afford to lose him. Anyway, he's down in the calaboose so darn drunk that it'll be a wonder if he can sit a hoss before a week."

It was nearing ten o'clock when he emerged from the restaurant. "Too early to stir anybody up, for a while yet," he said to himself as he walked down the street. He looked into each saloon as he passed, thinking that he might find some trace of the missing punchers. By eleven o'clock he had made the rounds, without success.

"Reckon I'll run over and see how Si and Shorty's makin' it. It's time fer Si to be up, anyway. Wonder why he hasn't been over."

He walked rapidly up the street and was soon out in the open. Across the dry arroyo he could see Shorty's cabin and, sitting on the bench in front of it, his brother, contentedly smoking his pipe.

"Well, somebody's around, anyway. Good old Si! They don't make 'em any finer than he is. Hope for his sake this mine pans out."

He rapidly covered the intervening space and was soon sitting on the bench beside his brother.

"How's Shorty this morning?"

"Oh, he's still dead to the world. Don't you hear him sawin' wood?"

"Sure do! Any feller that can make a noise like that ain't dead for keeps, anyway."

"Him? You bet he ain't dead for keeps. We'll go in an' stir him up in a few minutes. Say, what did you do with his spondulix?"

"Oh, I got it here, in my inside pocket; and that's one thing I want to talk to you about, Si. I ain't a-goin' to lug that cash around any longer than I have to. You better take it. You're his pardner, I ain't."

"Shucks, Ike, you make me laugh! Of course, you're his pardner. Whatever's mine is yours. Dip in and help yourself to a million."

"Well, Si, we won't quarrel about that now. We've been through some pretty tough deals together, and I reckon if I needed help you'd come to the rescue all right."

"What time you goin' to pull out for the ranch?"

"Sometime this afternoon, soon's I can get my bunch of wild Indians in shape so's they can sit a hoss; and they've got to be in dern bad shape if they can't do that. Cook's the only one I just got to drag home; maybe we'll tie him on his cayuse, if we have to; but he's just got to be on hand tomorrow mornin'. Reckon some of 'em would stay here drunk for a month if they had the cash—but they ain't. I went through 'em all, and what cash they had left I give to Patrick to keep for 'em. I'll get it before we start for home this afternoon, and hand it over to them in about a week. They'll be a surprised bunch when they find out they've got any money left. Say, if they knew they had any coin I'd have a hell of a time gettin' 'em out of town."

"Let's go in and stir up Shorty."

"First, let's settle about this money I got in my pocket. I ain't a-goin' to carry it 'round no longer. I told you that already."

"Well, I tell you what you do. You stop as you go by the mine office and give it to Mr. Macklay and ask him to keep it for you. Tell him it's Shorty's, and that Shorty'll tell him what to do with it."

"That's all right. I can stop there as the procession rides by on our way to the ranch. I'm goin' to bring up the rear, anyway, so's nobody can turn back, and I can run in the office for a minute or two just as well as not."

"Sure. Well, let's go wake up Shorty."

They entered the cabin and surveyed the sleeper.

"He's havin' such a good time it seems a pity to disturb him, but let's get him up anyway," said Ike.

After some effort and much remonstrance, they got the prospector on his feet. Some hot coffee and a few crackers brought him around to something approaching a rational frame of mind. They brought him a basin of cold water, gave him some more coffee, and got him outside on the bench, which they had moved into the shade.

"Gosh, fellers, I feel rocky," Shorty said. "My head's as big as a balloon. I'm thirsty enough to drink a river, and my stummick feels like I was at sea."

"You had a real celebration last night, Shorty, and now you're feelin' the after effects," commiserated Ike.

"How'd I get home?"

"Me and Si drug you most of the way."

"I must've been pretty far gone."

"You was, for a fact. Just couldn't stand up."

"Did I say or do anything I hadn't orter?"

"Didn't give you no chance. 'Bout the time you was gettin' ready to fight Patrick we run you out and headed you for home. You wanted to fight us, too, but we didn't agree to that notion none, so you turned sullen and lay down on us, and by the time we got you over here you was dead to the world. We pulled your boots off an' dumped you into bed—and there you are."

"Much obliged, boys. Say, my plan must of worked fine, didn't it?"

"Sure did. We got the money for you, me and Si. I calc'late to leave my part of it with Mr. Macklay as I ride by this afternoon."

"That's fine. You'd better do the same, Si, and when you want it you can send for it. Take some with you, and send for the balance as you need it."

"Suits me, Shorty. I'll get to see Mr. Macklay before we pull out for the railroad. Don't see any reason why we can't pull out by sun-up tomorrow morning."

They rehearsed again the plan of campaign and tried to provide for every contingency. Ike was to come over to the claims as soon as he could arrange to be relieved. Si was to leave Langford at the railroad and make a beeline for Eureka, after finding the locations on the way. He was to outfit in Eureka and pick up Ralph. Shorty was to give the sampling party the slip at the Circle R ranch and cut across country to the railroad.

"Well, I got to be goin' back to town," remarked Ike.

"I'll go along with you and find Langford," added Si. "Then I'll get up to the works and leave this money. Shorty better stay here for a while and see what happens. They'll be after you soon enough. Let 'em come to you! Don't show any anxiety, by goin' and huntin' them up."

"Well, I don't feel much like huntin' anybody or anything, boys. Guess I'll lie down and snooze for a while. If they come over lookin' for me, they can drag me out if I fall asleep. Guess you better take this agreement, too, Si, an' give it to Mr. Macklay to put in the safe along with the other things; he's got the assay certificate, and you give him the money and this agreement, and when the deeds come back you tell the schooolmarm to give them to him, too. Then he'll have the whole shooting match safe."

"I will, Shorty. Well, so long. May not see you again till I meet you at the mine. Take good care of yourself, and don't let that Patrick outfit get you in no hole."

The brothers waved a parting farewell as they turned away and disappeared around the corner of the cabin. Left alone, Shorty sat for some time apparently engrossed in deep thought. Then he got up and went into the cabin to lie on his bunk and doze.

Hans Randt approached Shorty's cabin with considerable curiosity. He saw the door open; evidently some one had already been there.

"Von of dem Broctor poys, prob'ly. Dey lugged him home last night, Padrick said; und I guess von of dem has been on der chob alretty today."

He peeked in cautiously. Shorty was lying on the bed, apparently asleep. Walking in, Randt stepped over to the bunk and shook the sleeper, saying, "Hi, Shordy, it's time you vas gettin' up. Don't you feel like eating somedings?"

Shorty rolled over and gazed at Randt with lack-luster eyes. "Naw, I ain't hungry. Si and Ike was here a while ago and fixed me some coffee. Ain't never goin' to want to eat again, the way I feel now. Just want to be let alone and sleep it off."

"Vell, you has priddy near done dat, alretty, Shordy. It's after two o'glock now, und you ain't goin' to stay here all day, iss you?"

"Might as well. Ain't good for nothin' else."

"Aw, come und take a walk round town und you vill feel bedder."

"Oh, hell, no, Hans. I don't want to take no exercise, today; maybe not tomorrow neither."

"Vell, you got to go oudt und show dem claims vat you sold to Padrick."

"By jiminy, I forgot all about them claims. That's a fact, I have got a trade on. What did I get for 'em, Hans?"

"You told me last night you vas to get $10,000."

"Gee, that's a lot of money. My share'll keep me for quite a long time. Well, well; so Patrick's goin' to buy me out? What did he do that for, Hans?"

"Tamd if I know, Shordy. You better come on ofer to town und ask him yourself. We'll stop at Sam Hing's und you eats a liddle somedings und drink some coffee und you feels bedder. Den ve go down und see Padrick."

As there seemed to be no reason why he should not go with Randt, Shorty locked the door and started for town. They stopped at Sam Hing's, where Shorty and Randt both had coffee, poached eggs and toast. From Hing's they wandered to the Miners Rest.

Si Proctor was coming out as they reached the door. "Hello, Shorty," Si called to him.

"Hello, Si. Where are you goin'?"

"Oh, I just been talkin' with Jim Langford and he wants to pull out first thing in the mornin'. I'm goin' up to see Mr. Macklay and find out what freight he needs the most. Just been talkin' with Bill Patrick, inside; he says he's goin' to start a bunch out tomorrow to sample them claims of yourn."

"Yourn, too, Si."

"Oh, well, I got a interest, but you boss the job, Shorty. Bill says he figgers on makin' a right smart turn."

"Well, if we get our price, I reckon Patrick's entitled to all he can get out of it."

"I reckon so too, Shorty. So long."

Proctor started up the street, and Shorty and Randt entered the Miners Rest. There were not many people in the saloon, and the gambling games were all idle. Hank Bartle stood listlessly behind the bar and nodded to the two men as they came in.

Randt looked vaguely around. Shorty appeared quite uninterested.

"Vere's Padrick, Hank?"

"He's in the back room. Want to see him?"

"Yah."

"Well, go knock on the door."

Randt walked over to the door and rapped on it vigorously.

"Come in," called a voice.

Opening the door, Randt discovered Patrick sitting in an armchair tilted back against the wall reading a paper, his feet on the table in front of him.

"Hello, Padrick. Me und Shordy yust dropped in. Shordy wants to talk to you aboudt his claims."

"Oh, well—come on in, the two of you."

Randt beckoned to Shorty, and the two men entered the room.

"Sit down," he said.

"Shordy is vondering vat you're goin' to do aboudt dem claims of his."

"Why, going to have them examined, of course. I had Nick Trevethan in here a while ago and made arrangements for him to go out and look 'em over. You about ready to go with him, Shorty?"

"Me? Oh, yes. I'm ready to start 'most any time. When was you figurin' on us makin' the trip?"

"Trevethan says he'll be ready to go by tomorrow morning. How'll that suit you?"

"Suits me as good as any time. Is he rustling up a outfit?"

"Yes, he's getting things together. You can load your burro with the outfit, can't you?"

"Yeah, sure."

"What about a horse for yourself?"

"I reckon I can git Sim to hunt me up a hoss somewheres. Anyway, I'll go out and hunt him up and ask him. I'll come back and let you know what he says."

Shorty slouched out of the room and went out to the street. He stood for a moment, undecided, and then turned toward Simpson's Corral; there he found the cowboys from the Circle R ranch getting ready to pull out. Catching sight of him coming down the road, Ike advanced to meet him. They stood at some distance from the corral, while Shorty gave Ike the latest information regarding their plan; he also reminded Ike it would be necessary for him to get out to the claims as soon as he could and change the location notices. These he had prepared and handed to Ike, saying, "Don't want them old notices there for Nick to find. He would smell a mouse then, sure."

"All right," Ike remarked, after listening to Shorty's explanation, "I'll get there ahead of you and fix it. I've got two or three extra hosses and I can leave one for you as well as not; Sim's got the saddle and bridle, and I'll tell him to give 'em to you when you want 'em."

During this conversation they had been walking slowly toward Sim's office. There Ike said to Sim, "Shorty's goin' out on a expedition, and I'm goin' to loan him a hoss. You let him have that saddle and bridle of mine that you got here, and he'll bring it back to you all right when he gets through with it; and let him have that pinto hoss of mine."

Sim stopped chewing tobacco long enough to spit in the general direction of the open window, and remarked, "All right, Shorty. You can have that hoss any time you come for it.

"Shorty got you hooked on some prospect, Ike?"

"Naw; him and my brother Si is in together. Shorty's goin' out to the claims, an' I agreed to lend him a hoss."

"Well, so long, fellers," Ike called, as he turned and walked toward the corral where his horse stood saddled and bridled and where the other cowboys had finished saddling and tightening cinches. They all mounted and started up the main street.

Chapter XXV

THE Circle R punchers rode up the street with Ike at their head. They had come into town on the gallop, spurs jingling, whooping and yelling, as they rode down the street. Now they were going back in a much more subdued frame of mind, at a slow trot, in silence, feeling decidedly rocky. They were all young, however, and a day or two of regular living at the ranch would put them back once more into thoroughly first-class shape.

As they neared the centre of town, Ike pulled out to one side, slowed up his horse and allowed the rest to pass him, with his most trusted man at the head. He went to the rear of the procession, so that there would be no stragglers left behind. His brother, standing on the sidewalk in front of the hardware store, waved to him as he passed.

"So long, and good luck, Ike," he called.

"Good luck, Si. See you later."

The cowpunchers left town by the road leading to the Sulphide "Con." The leader took the trail between the hoisting works and the superintendent's residence, leading up the side of the mountain, and soon disappeared around a projecting mass of rocks that marked the shear-zone in which the Sulphide Consolidated vein occurred.

Ike had instructed Bill Boyd, the leader, to keep moving while he stopped to speak with Mr. Macklay. He had gradually dropped further and further behind as they came up the hill, and now, as he saw the rear of the cavalcade disappear behind the projecting rocks, he pulled up his horse in front of the mine office, allowed the reins to drop to the ground, and entered the building. Taking the money from his pocket, he said, "This is the money, Mr. Macklay, that the boys wanted you to keep for them."

Methodically, Macklay counted the pile of greenbacks, and remarked, "$2000. I'll give you a receipt for it, Ike."

"I don't want no receipt from you, Mr. Macklay. You just take the money and keep it, and when the boys want it you know how and when to give it to 'em."

"Well, I'll take good care of it," said he, smiling. "I'm genuinely glad that you have concluded to be in the vicinity of these claims of Shorty's in case something happens. Shorty can take care of himself all right, in ordinary circumstances, but when it comes down to dealing with a crew of gun-fighters, I'd much rather have you on hand."

"Well, I reckon I can take care of myself, all right, under them conditions, Mr. Macklay, and I reckon that if Shorty needs any help I can take care of that job, too."

He shook hands with the older man, left the building, picked up the reins that were dragging on the ground, threw them over the horse's head, jumped into the saddle, and was off at a gallop up the trail.

Nick Trevethan had bought his supplies at the grocery store and McGurn was putting up the order. It was the usual collection of grub that a prospector would take with him, and the quantity was enough to last for about a week.

"Goin' in for a grubstake, Nick?" he asked.

"Oh, maybe so. I'll pay you for the supplies and you can send 'em down to Sim's Corral before dark."

Then Trevethan ordered from Gillig's hardware store a few sticks of giant powder, some fuse and caps, so that he could put in a few shots if he found it necessary in sampling the out-cropping of the ledge.

"We're going out to the powder-house this afternoon," remarked Gillig's clerk, "to get out some powder for delivery to two or three prospectors, and we'll deliver the powder for you down at Simpson's Corral sometime late this afternoon. You know we don't keep any powder here in the store."

"Yes, I know that," said Trevethan. "It will be all right if you get it there any time before dark."

Like all mining camps, Sulphide refused to permit local merchants to carry much (if any) powder in their stores. On the outskirts of every mining town there was to be seen the inevitable powder-house. In the larger camps there might be several such structures built usually into the side of a bank if the configuration of the land permitted it. If not, the structures were built of brick or of wood with the walls thoroughly insulated to keep out the extreme cold of winter, because of the danger of freezing where temperatures fell to twenty or thirty degrees below zero. These structures stood as trademarks on the outskirts of every mining camp in Nevada. Frozen dynamite presents a problem the attempted solution of which has resulted in the loss of numerous lives. The correct method of thawing, by the use of hot water, was well known. The necessary paraphernalia was always at hand. But, notwithstanding this, venturesome folk had frequently tried short cuts and had not lived to tell about them.

Next, Trevethan went up to the office of the Sulphide Consolidated and got from Mr. Macklay permission to take some drills, hammers, picks, and shovels that belonged to the mine.

Trevethan had picked up a miner he knew, who was temporarily out of a job, to go with him as assistant. Shorty would provide his own horse and the burro to pack supplies.

It was well on toward dusk before Trevethan had completed his preparations and the supplies had been delivered to Sim's Corral. "Must be a-goin' prospectin'," remarked Simpson, suggestively, to Trevethan.

"Oh, no; just goin' out to look at Shorty Peterson's claims."

"Think he's got anything?" asked Sim.

"No, I don't think so. We're just tryin' to get up a group to sell to some tenderfoot who's expected in here before long."

"Oh, I see," replied Sim. "You're not expecting to make your money out of the mine but out o' this tenderfoot."

"Well, that's about the size of it."

"I was goin' to bet you the drinks," said Sim, "that you wouldn't find a mine. Leastways, most fellers that go out don't. If every feller that went out on a trip like yours came back with a real mine, there'd be so dern many of 'em in Nevada that gold and silver wouldn't be worth nothin' at all."

After seeing that his outfit was ready to load, Trevethan walked up the street to the Miners Rest, where he informed Patrick that the expedition was ready to start in the morning.

Turning to Randt, who was in the saloon when Trevethan arrived, Patrick said, "Hans, chase around and find Shorty and bring him here so we can have a final talk."

Randt set out and Trevethan went to get some supper, promising to return as soon as he had finished.

Hank Bartle was behind the bar, polishing and arranging glasses as usual. Patrick stood in front of the bar, abstractedly drumming with his fingers.

"Boss," said Bartle, "I kind of got a little bit nervous 'bout somethin' I seen 'round here last night. Did you notice that Si Proctor didn't have but two or three drinks all night, and he stood mighty close to that cowboy brother of his?"

"I noticed that, all right. And you don't know it, because you were too busy at the time, but I had Jed Blake working on Si Proctor trying to get him full, as I got Peterson. Somehow or other, it didn't work. He explained to Jed that he was acting as lieutenant for his brother and that, between them, they calculated to keep that bunch of wild Indians of Ike's in order so they wouldn't shoot up the town or get themselves into any kind of a bad fix."

"Well, maybe that's the reason," said Hank.

"I think it is, because I talked with him about the claims and he told me that whatever Shorty did was all right with him."

Trevethan came back shortly. Hans Randt found Shorty and brought him in. Patrick talked to Shorty about Si's interest and suggested that he ought to sign the paper giving the option.

"Well, I guess there ain't no objection to that," said Shorty. "As a matter of fact, the claims all stand in my name and Si has said that whatever I do will be agreeable to him."

"Well, we'll ask him anyway."

"He's got to speak for himself," said Shorty, "so you better talk to him."

At this point Si arrived. Patrick put the matter up to him at once.

"Well," said Si, "I ain't got nothin' but Shorty's word, and that's good enough fer me. He can do as he pleases and when it's all over he'll give me what's mine, and there ain't a scratch of pen or paper between us. Guess you'll have to be satisfied with that, Patrick, and take my word just as I've taken Shorty's; and we'll let it go at that."

Patrick was not pleased with the situation, and said so rather plainly. "I've bought this group of claims under an option and paid $2000 down, and I can see no reason why you refuse to sign the agreement."

"Hell, Patrick," replied Si, "them claims is Shorty's. All I got is a grubstake interest in 'em. There's just a verbal agreement between me and Shorty; that's good enough fer me. Whatever Shorty says, goes; and no writin' will make it any stronger 's far as I'm concerned."

Patrick appealed to Shorty, who had been an interested listener to the conversation, but he simply shook his head and said: "That's correct 'bout Si havin' only a verbal agreement with me. Maybe it ain't exactly accordin' to law, but you bet yer life it'll stick as far as either of us is concerned; an' if Si takes a notion that he's goin' to deal with you in the same way, you can bet it will be better than any agreement that might be drawed up, 'cause courts sometimes busts agreements and what Si says he'll do, he'll *do*. No damn courts or nobody else will ever get him to change."

The details of the expedition having been thoroughly gone over, it was agreed that Shorty would start with the burro early in the morning and would be overtaken by Trevethan during the day. They would camp for the night at Duck Creek or the Circle R, and push on the next morning.

"There's an old log cabin near the forks of Willow Creek," Shorty said, "where we can stay the next night and make our camp; the claims are about a mile and a half or two miles from there."

When the arrangements were completed, Patrick turned to Bartle and said, "Set 'em up for the crowd, Hank."

Each of them took one of the glasses that Bartle set upon the counter and helped himself from the bottle that was passed from hand to hand.

"Well, here's how," said Patrick.

"An' here's to the success o' my prospectin' trip," said Shorty. Whereupon all hands drained their glasses.

Later Shorty asked Si, "Why didn't you sign the paper for him, Si?"

"Well, mostly pure cussedness, I reckon; but he made me mad when he seemed to think he could hold me better with a signed agreement than he could with just my word." And they went off together.

Trevethan waited a few moments for some final instructions from Patrick. Hans Randt stood about, talking in a subdued voice, but in a highly excited condition, with Bartle.

"Py chiminy, Hank, it looks like ve vas fixed for der rest of our lives!"

"Well, I hope so," remarked the skeptical Hank, "but I've seen a lot of them prospects blow up and I don't believe nothin' no more till it happens."

Shorty and Si sat long in conference in the cabin that night. They went over the entire programme in subdued whispers as they sat on opposite sides of the wooden table. Finally, Si rose to go, and shook hands cordially saying, "Good luck, Shorty. Next time I see you it'll be on our own mining claims, and I hope that we'll be gettin' ready to work our bonanza."

"Gee, that sounds good, Si. I hope it will all come out as we expect. Good-bye and good luck."

He watched Si disappear into the darkness, and went to bed.

Chapter XXVI

On the morning of the sixth Jim Langford started for the railroad with his sixteen-animal team, with Si Proctor swamping. Nick Trevethan completed his arrangement preparatory to starting out to sample Shorty's claims. And Shorty got up early and went to Sam Hing's for breakfast. There he found Ralph Lee. Since no one else was in the restaurant, he began immediately to discuss his plans with Ralph.

"I'm goin' to get goin' pretty pronto now, Ralph; Trevethan'll catch up with me over at the Circle R, and we'll go on from there together. Everything's ready down at the corral. Only have to load my burro and pull out. Ain't got a single thing to say, Ralph, only what I said already."

"Wonder how long it will take them to locate you after Trevethan gets back," said Ralph.

"Have no idea, but not very long after our first shipment gets to the smelter. You can't keep that kind of news dark very long."

So they chatted on until Shorty had finished his breakfast. They left the restaurant together, Shorty going down the street to the corral, Ralph going to the mine.

"Well, you're pulling out this mornin', too, are you, Shorty?" asked Sim.

"Yes, I'm goin' out on a little expedition with Nick Trevethan to sample some claims of mine. You got to keep tryin' if you expect to find a mine."

"You bet you have, Shorty. It ain't every feller that gits a reward, but if reward comes to them what deserves it, you are certainly goin' to draw a 'grand prize' some day."

"Well, somebody's got to draw one, once in a while, Sim. Just as well be me as somebody else."

Shorty got his equipment out of the building and loaded his burro. He took a turn of the halter-rope around one of the stakes of the corral and went after his horse. It was in an adjoining corral. Sim brought a riata, roped the animal, and led it to the building where the saddle and bridle were kept. It took but a few moments to saddle up. Shorty mounted. Sim untied the rope by which the burro was hitched and tossed it to Shorty, who took a couple of turns of the rope around the pommel of the saddle and started off up the street.

The sun was well up above the horizon by this time. People were beginning to stir in the town and, as he passed, Shorty greeted several whom he knew. Sam Hing stopped him a moment in front of his restaurant.

"You go out ketchy plospect, Shorty?"

"Why, yes, I'm goin' out on a little trip."

"You likee mo' help in glub-stake?"

"Well, I can't do it this time, Hing. I got a couple of pardners. But maybe next time it'll be all right."

"All lite, Shorty, sometime you go ketchy plospect, me takee glubstake all same Melican man."

"Well, Hing, I think you'd make a darn sight better pardner than a lot of white men I know."

"All lite, Shorty. Me likee you. You velly good plospector. Hope you ketchee plentee gold."

"When I do, will you come and cook for me, Hing?"

"Oh, mebbe so. Mebbe sometime all people move some other camp. No mo' lest'lant here fo' me. Mebbe so I cook fo' you."

Shorty took the same road that Ike Proctor had taken the day before, between the superintendent's residence and the hoisting works. Near the office Shorty dismounted and went in. Mr. Macklay and Ralph Lee were standing over the drafting table examining a mine map.

"Well, Shorty, you're on your way, are you?" remarked Mr. Macklay.

"Yes, sir; pulling out for the famous bonanza," he answered, with a twinkle in his eye and a broad grin on his face. "Trevethan and his helper are coming along late in the day and I'm goin' on ahead with the burro and the outfit."

"Ike told me yesterday," said Mr. Macklay, "about your arrangement of having him go there and change the location notices and stick around in case you need him. You won't have any trouble with Trevethan; that will come later."

The three men talked a few moments, then walked out to the burro together and stood for a moment exchanging a few parting words. While they were standing there, Mary Clark came out of the gate leading to the superintendent's house, and, seeing them, walked rapidly over to the office.

"Now that we're partners, I think, if you don't mind, I'd like to call you 'Shorty,' too," she said as they shook hands.

"You bet I'd like it," he said, obviously pleased. "You can call me Shorty, of course, just like the others do. And now, long's you're my pardner and call me Shorty, mebbe I might call you 'Mary,' too. You see, I'm old enough to be your pa, and it really don't mean nothin' if I call you Mary, 'cept that I like you a lot and you're a pardner in our mine and pardners oughtn't to stand off at arms length."

"Why, of course," she replied. "I should be delighted if

you would do that. And, Shorty, Mrs. Macklay and I have been talking and we've made a plan that, when you get over to the mine and get some kind of a camp established, we'll get Mr. Macklay to take us over there for a few days so that we can see everything for ourselves. Would that be all right, Shorty?"

"Well, that'll be just fine," said Shorty, with great enthusiasm. "Couldn't imagine I'd like anything better than just to take you up on the hill and show you that vein and let you take some samples for yourself and have Ralph assay them; then you'd know from your own personal examination what that old burro done for us."

"That's a bargain, then," said Mary. "When you are ready for visitors, just let us know and we'll come over."

They shook hands on it, laughing. "Well, I must be movin'," Shorty added, reluctantly. "I've got quite a day's journey ahead of me, an' if I'm to get into camp 'fore dark I ain't got no time to spare. You'll see Trevethan and his helper comin' along here, afterwhile, headed in the direction of the Circle R ranch."

Shorty started off up the hill, waving his hand in reply to the farewell salute of his friends, who stood watching him until he passed behind the pile of rocks and disappeared.

"Well, that's that milestone passed, anyhow," said Mr. Macklay, "and now it's about time that we went to breakfast."

They started toward the superintendent's house, leaving Ralph alone, watching them as they went. He turned as they disappeared, and re-entered the office building, and began the daily routine of his work.

It was not long before Mr. Macklay came back, on his

way to the mine and the mill and for his usual daily trip underground. "Ralph," he called, as he passed the open door, "I told Mary to keep a lookout for Trevethan and when he comes up the hill to see who is with him and let you know."

Macklay walked on towards the hoisting works, and Ralph resumed his work until interrupted by Mary several hours later. "I can see Nick Trevethan coming up the road towards the works," she said.

They stood talking, watching Trevethan and his helper as they rode up the trail from the town.

"Did you ever think," ventured Mary, "just what you would do if it should turn out to be a real mine?"

"Of course, I've thought about it. I'd like to stay there and see it developed, equipped with a plant and producing bullion, and I'd like to be superintendent. After that, some day, I'd like to take a trip to California, go around and see the State, perhaps go back east to New York and Washington; and perhaps, some time, some day, after the mine is going in good shape, I'd like to take a trip to Europe. But I don't allow myself to think much about those things now."

"Well, neither do I," said Mary; and there was perhaps just a tinge of disappointment in her voice.

Nick Trevethan by this time had climbed the hill and was passing up the trail between the hoisting works and the office.

"How strange," remarked Ralph. "There are people who have gone over that trail in the last few hours who are going to have quite an influence on our lives. There's Ike and Si and Shorty, and now Trevethan. The rival forces have begun to manœuvre for position, all right, and," he added with a sigh, "I've got to stand idly by and watch them, for the time being. I wish I could get more actively into this thing, somehow."

"Oh, you must have a little patience," she replied. "Your turn will come soon enough; and you've quite an important part to play at the proper moment. Well, I've got to be getting back to the house. I ran away and left a lot of things undone, and if I don't get back pretty soon Mrs. Macklay will begin to do them herself."

"Good-bye, Ralph," she said.

"Good-bye, Mary," he called, as she disappeared around the corner of the building. And each of them wondered why the other had not said more.

Chapter XXVII

After leaving Sulphide and getting well started on the trail, Shorty dismounted and took the lead-rope from the pommel of his saddle and tied it to the pack on the burro's back and turned the animal loose. He managed to keep the animal moving at a fair rate. There was nothing of interest in the journey. The country was made up of the low, rolling hills characteristic of northeastern Nevada. Animal or vegetable life was lacking, save for the sagebrush that dotted the hills as far as the eye could reach.

The Circle R ranch was located in a small valley enclosed on three sides by gently sloping hills. Through the valley flowed a small stream of water that eventually found its way into the Owyhee River. The stream had been dammed and the water turned onto the flat ground where alfalfa had been planted. A grove of cottonwood trees surrounded the ranch buildings, affording welcome shade during the summer months. There was a ranch house for the owner, bunk-houses for the cowboys, a cook-house, and the various buildings that go to make up the headquarters of a great cattle ranch.

Smoke was ascending from the chimney of the cookhouse, and Shorty could see, as he approached along the road, a group of men sitting about under the shade of the trees, evidently awaiting the signal for the midday meal. After reaching the floor of the valley, he rode between fields of alfalfa. Finally, crossing a small bridge that spanned the creek, he came to the end of the road and into a large yard around which the various buildings clustered. Several of the men sitting on benches in front of the cook-house knew Shorty and gave him hearty welcome.

"Where's Ike?" he asked.

"Out riding the range," was the reply. "Goin' to stop for grub, Shorty?"

"Guess I will. Goin' over to some claims of mine beyond Duck Creek. Got a party coming out from town to sample 'em."

"Well, make yourself to home, Shorty," said one of the cowboys, who acted as an assistant foreman. "Drive your burro and your hoss over to the corral and turn 'em loose; then come on and have some chuck."

After disposing of the animals, Shorty came back just as the cook began to hammer vigorously on the large steel triangle that hung by the door. The men trooped into the mess house. They seated themselves at the long table, on long wooden benches that ran the full length of the table on either side.

"How you fellers feelin' after your Fourth of July celebration?" asked Shorty.

"Like hell, mostly, I reckon," volunteered one of them. "Nobody just ain't been no good for nothin', so far. By tomorrow, though, they'll be all ready to go to work again, in good shape."

After the meal, Shorty gossiped a while, then loaded his burro, saddled his horse, and pulled out. Late in the afternoon, as he was climbing the slope of a hill, he looked back across the flat country that he had been traversing and saw two horsemen descending the opposite slope.

"That's Trevethan all right," he said, as he watched them for a moment. Soon Trevethan and his helper caught up with him.

After six o'clock they reached the banks of Duck Creek and made camp for the night.

"You rustle up some dry wood, Nick, and I'll get things unpacked, and we'll make a fire pronto and have us some grub," said Shorty.

The horses had been unsaddled, the pack removed from the burro, and the animals staked out close to the creek, where they could drink their fill and nibble the grass that grew along the water's edge. Shorty had pitched camp a little up-stream from where the animals were staked, and in a few minutes a fire was blazing and everything ready to cook the evening meal.

"We got to let that fire burn out a little first, Nick," he said, "until we can get us some good live coals. You rustle up a few big flat rocks that we can put around them coals and set the coffee pot and the fryin' pan on, when them flames die down."

Within a short time the fire, now a bed of live coals, was surrounded by a few large flat stones upon which the coffee pot was singing and a pot was boiling, as Shorty was frying bacon. Boiled potatoes, coffee, bacon, and hardtack composed the evening meal.

"Tomorrow, when we git over to the cabin, I'll fix up a mess of beans in this here pot. We can cook our potatoes in the ashes and be real comfortable. There's some bunks in that old cabin, and if they ain't full of bugs we can make a pretty slick camp. Lots of times, in them old camps, there are so darn many bugs you got to move out into the sagebrush if you want to sleep in peace," said Shorty reflectively, as he shook the bacon from the frying pan onto the tin plates upon which he had already put some of the boiled potatoes.

"Some fellers don't seem to mind bugs," said Trevethan.

"Yeah, I know that," replied Shorty. "Never could understand why, though. I been in some places where I bet any feller would've minded 'em. I remember one time I was down in California and I come back over the Kingsbury Grade and stopped at one of them stations that had bugs like nothin' I ever seen before or since. People had fed them bugs so much that they had become real educated animals. I got some old tin cans and put some water in 'em and set the legs of the bed in the cans and put the mattress on the floor and threw my blankets down on the slats and laid down and went to sleep. Well, sir, them darn bugs figgered it all out, and they just naturally clumb up the side of the wall and walked along the ceilin' till they got right over my head, and then they let go and hit me square on the face. Maybe you don't believe that story, Nick."

"Sounds kind of queer, Shorty."

"Yeah, I know it does; but that's what happened just the same."

It did not take them long to finish their supper. As the twilight deepened they sat about the fire smoking their pipes.

"Guess I'll turn in early, Nick," remarked Shorty. "Had kind of strenuous time last couple of days; feel I'd like to have a little sleep. Won't mind either if we take it kind of easy in the mornin', will you, Nick? We can make the old cabin all right and anyway there won't be no time to go up to the claims tomorrow."

"Well, if we can't get there in time to do anything tomorrow, it won't make much difference what time of night we make the cabin," replied Nick.

"We'll be there in time for supper, anyway," said Shorty, as he rolled himself up in his blanket, put his head on his saddle and quickly dropped off to sleep.

The next day was a repetition of the preceding one. The country through which they travelled was of the same gently rolling character as that of the previous day. They saw no signs of life other than an occasional band of cattle grazing on the hillsides. Their midday meal was quickly prepared and dispatched, and in the late afternoon they arrived at the old log cabin on Willow Creek.

This had originally been the home of a cattleman whose holdings had been purchased by the Circle R. It was now used, upon occasion, by that outfit for headquarters during the branding season, as it was more convenient to round up and brand many of the cattle here than drive them to the home ranch. Most of the time, however, it stood silent and deserted. There were an earthen floor, a large stone fireplace at the far end of the cabin, a few bunks around the sides, built out of odds and ends of lumber, a rickety table and two or three homemade stools.

This was to be their home during their stay. Shorty had brought with him, among other things, a few old gunnysacks into which he had stuffed a quantity of dry alfalfa.

"Kind of luxurious for a prospector, Nick," he remarked, "but I sort of thought you fellers wasn't used to sleeping on the soft side of a plank, so I brought along a few of them old sacks that you can throw into them bunks and spread out and get a few soft spots under your hips, anyway; and you might use one of them sacks for a pillow."

After a fire was built on the hearth, the pot partially

filled with water, and some beans poured into it to soak, the prospecting outfit placed in one corner of the cabin, the animals staked out where they could get both feed and water, the men settled down preparatory to spending the night and getting an early start in the morning for the claims. Either the cabin was free of bugs, or the men were too tired to pay any attention to them, for they were all shortly asleep and rested undisturbed until morning.

When Trevethan awoke he found Shorty already up and engaged in preparing breakfast. As he sat up in his bunk, blinking his eyes, Shorty remarked to him, "I was just gettin' ready to call you and tell you it was about time we was on the move. Breakfast'll be ready in another five minutes, and I'll take a coffee-pot and a few things along so we'll have something to eat at noon."

The sun was showing above the distant mountains as they set forth. Shorty led the way, driving his burro, followed by Trevethan and he in turn by his helper. The chill of the early Nevada morning was in the air as they splashed across the narrow creek. Deep shadows lingered around the few scattered trees that marked the water course, and over all was the brooding silence of the desert. They kept on until they came to the foot of the hill on the opposite side of the little valley.

"I got a monument 'long here somewhere," said Shorty, "where we turn off up into the hills. It's an old tin can, stuck on a stick in the top of a pile of rocks."

"Guess that's it, over there," said Trevethan, pointing to the flash of a sunbeam reflected from some polished surface.

"Yeah, so 'tis," said Shorty, as they pushed on toward the object. It proved to be the sought-for monument, and turning abruptly up the hill Shorty led the way over the rough ground in the direction of a prominent pile of rocks clearly outlined near the crest of the hill.

"That's the place, up there by them rocks," said Shorty, pointing to the boulders above them.

"Well, if the vein dips this way," said Trevethan, "you can get a good tunnel site down near the bottom of this hill, and it ain't goin' to be much of a trick to bring that water from the creek to where we'd put up the mill. Taken altogether, it looks like a favorable location, to me."

"Yes, it is," said Shorty, " 'bout as good a location as anybody could want for a mine, but I wouldn't give much for all the favorable things about the location of a quartz ledge if it didn't carry a lot of mineral."

They climbed in silence for another ten minutes, when Shorty said, "Guess we'll stop here, Nick, and leave the animals."

They dismounted. The burro was unpacked, the horses unsaddled, and staked out, and everything made ready for the day's prospecting.

"It'll be an all-day dry camp for them, all right. They'll have to wait till they get back to the creek this evening before getting either water or feed," said Shorty. Shouldering the picks and shovels, and carrying the hammers, moils, and sample sacks, the three men started up the steep slope. Coming to a mass of rocks, Shorty threw down his load, seated himself, and remarked as he waved his hand toward the outcrop, "Well, that's her, Nick."

Trevethan and his helper began to survey the surroundings with a critical eye.

"Guess I'll walk along the outcrop a little way, Shorty, and see what it looks like."

"Fine, Nick. You'll find her outcropping for several hundred feet, and she's five or six feet wide; some places a little more, I guess, and other places not quite so much."

Trevethan and his helper, taking prospecting picks in hand, walked along the outcrop of the vein, now and then stopping to chip off pieces of rock and examine them. Shorty watched them as they moved along, but did not volunteer to go with them. He lit his pipe, found a comfortable seat, and sat in quiet contemplation of the activities of the two miners. Trevethan took about half an hour to walk along the outcrop of the vein, and then returned to the spot where Shorty was seated.

"I didn't go along with you, Nick, 'cause I thought you prob'ly might like to be alone. I don't calc'late to butt into this examination of yours, in any way. Don't want no question 'bout my tryin' to have you pick the best; and when you get your samples I want you to keep 'em, so that when you get back to town nobody can say that me or none of my pardners had a chance to do any "salting." I'll kind of walk along with you and keep back when you're takin' your samples, or I'll stay here all the time, just as you say."

"Come along, Shorty. Maybe I'll have some questions I'll want to ask. Only, of course, when I'm cutting down my samples, you can sit ten or fifteen feet away, then there won't be no question 'bout whether anybody dropped any high-grade into 'em."

"That's agreeable to me, Nick," said Shorty; and so it was arranged, and the sampling of the claims began.

"I figger I can trace this outcrop, good and plain, for about 300 feet," said Trevethan, "so I'm goin' to take a sample every twenty-five feet along the vein. That'll give me twelve samples. Then maybe I'll take some sections in the vein to see whether she's all pay or whether there's a rich streak runnin' through it and a lot of barren stuff. But anyway I don't think I'll need over fifteen samples."

Trevethan paced off approximately twenty-five feet and himself began to take sample number one. The usual method of chipping an equal quantity as nearly as possible from each section across the vein was followed. The broken rock was gathered, broken into smaller pieces, mixed, and quartered. With part rejected, the process was repeated until there remained a final sample of a few pounds. This was placed in the sack and labelled, and the sack was securely tied. Trevethan placed the sample in a leather bag, very much like a mail pouch, passed the strap through the metal rings, and securely locked the bag.

"You can carry this bag, Shorty," said Nick, handing it to him. "I'll take charge of it when we come back to the cabin tonight. Guess nobody can get at them samples, even if they want to," he said with a grin.

"You're right, Nick. Nothin' like taking all the precautions. I don't mind at all."

"Wonder who that feller is, over there, on the horse," remarked Trevethan, as he paused and looked up.

Shorty looked in the direction Nick was pointing and saw a horseman coming across the valley at a gallop.

"Must be one of the cowboys from the Circle R ranch," said Shorty. "Let's hail him."

Standing up, he waved his hat and began to shout. Evidently his signals were heard, for the rider paused and looked about and, finally locating the party, turned and started up the hill toward them.

"B'lieve that's Ike Proctor," said Shorty as the man came nearer.

"So it is," said Trevethan. "Wonder what he's doin' in this part o' the country."

"Oh, out ridin' the range and seein' what's goin' on, I reckon," replied Shorty.

Soon the rider came within hailing distance and called out, "Hello, Shorty."

"Hello, Ike, come on up and sit a while."

Proctor approached, dismounted, dropped his bridle rein to the ground and sat down close by where Trevethan had his sampling canvas spread out on the ground.

"I never seen one of them ledges prospected," said Ike. "Say, I ain't got very much to do today, and I'd like to stick around and see how you do it, so's if I come across one of 'em some time myself, I'll know what to do with it."

"You can stay if you want to," said Trevethan, "I ain't got no objections."

"Well, I ain't," said Shorty. "You'll find out all about it in a little while, Ike, and we can give you some grub at noon."

Trevethan and his helper toiled on, sampling the outcrop of the vein, to the intense interest of Proctor.

"Gosh, you fellers take a whole lot of trouble, chippin' them pieces of rock up and poundin' 'em down," he remarked. "What's the idea, Nick?"

"Well, you see," said Trevethan, "we're tryin' to get an average of this whole thing, right across the vein, to see what the assay value of it will be. Wouldn't do no good just to pick out one piece somewhere and have it assayed, because you wouldn't know what the rest was goin' to do. Lots of fellers come in with a piece of rock in their pocket about as big as a hen's egg, just stuck plumb full of gold, and show that to you and think you got to take it as a sample of what the whole darn ledge is goin' to go. That's the biggest fool idea on earth. What you got to do is to get equal quantities right across the vein and take lots of samples and then have 'em assayed to find out what the average of all of it is goin' to be. That gives you a notion of what you can expect when you begin to take out a big tonnage."

"Well, I swan,' said Proctor. "I never had no idea that was the way you done it. I just thought you went out and picked up a lot of pieces of rock and give 'em to the assayer and got the results."

"Lots of people got it figgered out that way," said Shorty, "but it's wrong. Nick's goin' at it in the right way, and when he gets through he's goin' to have a good idea of what this whole thing's worth."

At noon the sampling was suspended while Shorty prepared coffee and the party consumed the grub that he had brought with him in a sack. Lighting their pipes afterward, they sat around on the ground talking over the business of mining and cattle raising, finally coming to an agreement that the best thing to have was a good mine, but that it was about the hardest thing there was to find.

As the sampling progressed during the afternoon, Trevethan became more and more uncommunicative. By the time he had finished and they were ready to return to the cabin, he had lapsed into complete silence.

"Throw that bag of samples of yourn across my saddle, Nick," said Ike, "an' I'll pack it down there to the burro and save you the trouble."

Trevethan made no comment, but hoisted the sample sack onto the empty saddle, and Ike, holding the bridle in his hand, started down the steep slope toward the staked-out animals. As they rode back toward the cabin, Trevethan and his helper went on somewhat in advance but not out of sight of the burro carrying the bag of samples.

"I bet you a dollar, Ike, that Nick is wondering about them samples and what they'll go," said Shorty.

"What makes you think so?"

"Well, the further he sampled, the quieter he got. I seen him a-shakin' his head several times an' lookin' at some of that rock, an' I'll just bet my boots that he's got a notion that that stuff ain't goin' to assay and that maybe they've been whipsawed and Bill Patrick has spent some good money for nothin'. You can get some idea, sometimes, just by lookin' at rock whether it is likely to assay big or not; and between you and me, this stuff is about as hungry lookin' as you can find in Nevada. I took some of it once and had it assayed, an' got about $2. It's just hard, glassy, dead stuff that you kind of feel won't pay; and Nick's got that feelin' now, you bet your boots."

It did not take them long to reach the cabin, where Shorty promptly went to work preparing supper. After supper they sat and smoked, discussing the day's work and the programme for the next day.

The next day they pushed on to the camp on Duck Creek, where they spent the night. In the morning Trevethan was up at daybreak, making his preparations for a quick trip to Sulphide. He divided his samples into two lots, and wrapping them up securely in flat oblong packages he tied one lot behind his own saddle and the other lot behind the saddle of his assistant.

"No use of our waitin' on that burro of yours," he said to Shorty. "We'll just go ahead with these samples, and you take your time and get into town as soon as you can."

"All right, Nick. I'll follow along. I'll stop with Ike Proctor tonight, and come in tomorrow."

Swinging into the saddle, Trevethan said, "Well, goodbye, Shorty; we'll see you in town some time tomorrow."

"Yes, I guess so," said Shorty, as he waved his hand.

"Nick didn't have much to say about it, that's a fact," he soliloquized. "Don't know as he could, exactly, seein' that I ain't supposed to know nothin' about what them samples really did assay."

He ambled along behind his burro, chuckling to himself now and again and watching the two riders as they disappeared in the distance.

"Well, mule," he said to the burro, "we got to be movin', ourselves."

When Shorty arrived at the ranch he found Ike Proctor waiting for him.

"Trevethan went through here about three hours ago," Ike announced. "Didn't stop nor nothin'; just give his horse a drink at the creek and kept on goin'. If he keeps up that pace he'll get to town by three o'clock. I calc'late he can't keep it up, though, but he'll be there by four, all right."

"Well, that's what I was a-figurin' on," said Shorty. "I kind of thought he'd get there 'bout four. If he does, they'll have them samples assayed by six. Guess there ain't no use in my tryin' to go back to that town now. I'm goin' to leave this burro of mine here with you, Ike, and I'm goin' to light out for the railroad. Wish you'd get one of your boys to drive him to town next time some one goes in, and unload him and turn back them things that's been borrowed."

"All right, I'll take care of that."

"And, by the way, Ike, your trip out there with them location notices was time wasted. Nick never looked at one of 'em."

"Well, he might," replied Ike. "What's your plan now, Shorty?"

Grubstake

"I'm going over to Halleck on the railroad and go out to them claims. It'll take me two days to get to the railroad and a day more to get south of the railroad to the mine. I figger me and Si'll be on the ground about the same time."

Shorty pulled out early in the afternoon, headed for the railroad. There were several ranches on the road where he knew he could stop, and there were one or two camping spots where there was water. As he carried with him a small amount of grub, securely packed behind the saddle, he gave little thought to the journey ahead of him.

In the afternoon of the second day he saw in the valley ahead a cluster of buildings and a cloud of smoke that moved rapidly in an easterly direction. It was the station of Halleck, the smoke of a locomotive pulling an eastbound train.

Chapter XXVIII

Nick Trevethan pushed on rapidly to Sulphide, arriving there between four and five o'clock in the afternoon. He halted in front of Randt's assay office and carried in the packages of samples. He pushed through the swinging gate leading behind the counter and went on through the glass door and entered the room at the rear, where Randt, with his back to him, was feeding some charcoal to his furnace.

Randt turned and exclaimed, "Vell, you get back alretty yet, did you, Nick?"

Dumping the two packages of samples upon the floor, Trevethan said, "I got two bags of samples for you, and you can get busy and find out what's in 'em—which ain't much."

"Vot for you tink I iss not goin' to get some assays oudt of dem sambles? Vhy ain't I?"

"Well, because the quartz don't look lively. It's a dead hungry kind of looking stuff that you might expect to get two or three dollars out of, but if you're going to get any bonanza, my guess is it ain't going to come out of them claims."

Randt was now in a frenzy, his face flushed, his hands trembling. "Ve vill find oudt mighdy quick aboudt dis," he exclaimed. "Open up der sacks und giff me some of dose sambles dot I get dem pulverized up mighdy quick."

Trembling with excitement, the German began preparations to treat the samples. "You go down right avay by dot Miners Rest, Nick, und see Bill Padrick and tell him vot you haf been telling me."

Trevethan left him at his work and went out on the street and on to the Miners Rest.

"Hello, Nick," said Hank Bartle as Trevethan entered. "Got back already? What'd you find?"

"Oh, I found the place all right, took some samples and brought them in, and Randt's got them now, working on them."

"What's it look like to you, Nick?"

"Oh, I don't know. Where's Patrick? I want to talk with him about it."

"He went down to the barber shop."

"Well, I'll walk in there and tell him I'm back and when he gets through he can come up here and talk to me." Trevethan started to go, but Bartle called, "Have a drink, Nick, before you go out, and be just a little sociable. You might give me a little encouragement. I'm in on this thing just like you are."

"Yes, I know you are, Hank, but I ain't got nothing to say until Randt gets his assays out."

"Well, have a drink anyway." Over the drinks Bartle again asked him, "Have you got any idea, Nick, about what that thing is going to do?"

"Well, Hank, I don't want to hurt no one's feelings, but if I was going to give a guess I'd say that somebody had salted a lot of samples and put up a nice job to do Bill Patrick out of a couple of thousand dollars."

"Hell! You don't mean to say you think the thing ain't no good?"

"Well, I'm not saying exactly, yet, but it don't look any too rosy to me. I got to find Patrick now and tell him about it."

He walked out, leaving Bartle dazed. Trevethan found

Patrick in the barber chair. He showed no sign of surprise, but simply looked at Trevethan and remarked, "Hello, Nick; back, are you?"

"Yes, I got back a little while ago. Went in to see vou and Bartle said you was down here."

"All right, I'll be back to the saloon in a few minutes. You go in the back room there and sit down and wait for me." He began looking at the pictures in *Harper's Weekly,* a copy of which he was holding in his hands. His toilet completed, he rose leisurely, paid the barber, lighted a cigar and strolled up the street to the Miners Rest. As he passed the bar he said to Bartle, "Give me three or four cigars, Hank. Is Nick Trevethan in the back room?"

"Yes, he's there waiting for you, Bill."

"Have a cigar, Nick," he said, as he entered the room, holding out the fistful that he had taken from Bartle.

"Thanks, Bill, don't mind if I do."

Seating himself, Patrick said: "Well, what did you find, Nick?"

"We found the place all right, just as Shorty described it to me. A good location, with a very plain outcrop; and I took enough samples to tell you all you want to know. But if that outcrop is pay ore, I'll eat it."

He dived into his pocket and pulled out three or four lumps of rock. "Look at these," he said, "and tell me if you think that's highgrade."

"Well, I'm not much of a judge of these things, Nick. It's a little bit out of my line, but I got a cabinet full of specimens out front there, and I must say I wouldn't put this kind of stuff in my cabinet as a specimen of highgrade."

Dropping the rock on the table, he said, "We'll forget

this thing till Randt comes down here. He'll probably be here within an hour or two. What kind of a trip did you have? Tell me about it."

Trevethan launched into a description of his trip, going over the details step by step.

"I ain't had anything to eat since breakfast, Bill. I guess I'll go out and get something and come back in a little while. I'll get back here before Randt gets his assays done."

"All right, come back when you get through; just sit around till Hans shows up with his results. We'll know something definite then, anyway."

Meanwhile Randt had been working feverishly, pulverizing and preparing his samples. His furnace would hold six crucibles at a charge and he accordingly prepared six samples first, and put them into the fire to melt. Heaping the charcoal around them, he replaced the covers, opened the draft, and went about the preparation of the other six. He had examined the quartz minutely; a few of the pieces were sufficiently large to permit this. He had taken a magnifying glass out of his drawer and, going to the window for a better light, examined the rock under the glass. The more he looked, the more excited and ugly he became.

"By chiminy, I bet my life dot Nick Trevethan was right about dese sambles. I vonder vere dot damn Shordy got dot bunch of sambles from dot he brought in here to me."

Muttering and gesticulating to himself, he went on with his work. With each step in the process Randt became more and more excited. The fusing and pouring of the molten sample finished, he removed the little buttons from the slag cones and put them upon the cupels, which he deftly slid into the muffle.

Once or twice he opened the muffle door to look at the samples, and finally considering them ready, he took up the tongs and gingerly removed them one by one. Instead of the large buttons of gold and silver similar to those on Shorty Peterson's original sample, he saw adhering to the bottoms of the cupels only minute specks much less in size than the head of a pin. He was now thoroughly enraged. Muttering oaths under his breath, he viciously poked the buttons with a small pair of pincers, saying as he did so, "Dem damn sambles—day won't go more as tree oder four dollars a ton."

They had cooled by this time, and setting them again upon the board, on which the numbers had been painted in squares, he muttered to himself, "Der iss yust no use parting dese buttons to see how much gold und silver der iss. If I parts dem dere yust wouldn't be noddings left."

He placed button number one carefully upon his scale.

"Yust might so vell not veigh dem at all," he muttered. He continued the operation until the six were weighed and he had the weights on paper before him. Making some rapid calculations, he again called down imprecations upon Shorty Peterson's head as he looked at the results.

"If dose buttons is all gold, she don't go over $10.00 a ton, und if I take dem at their probably ratio of gold midt silver, I get me aboudt two oder tree dollars. Dot's a hell of a bonanza, ain't it?"

Neglecting the furnace, leaving the balance of the samples untreated, he walked rapidly out of his office, not even pausing to put on his hat, and went down the street to the Miners Rest. Bartle nodded his head in the direction of the private room and said, "Bill's in there, Hans. What you get?"

"Go to hell," was his answer, as he walked past and entered the private room.

Nick Trevethan, who had returned from his meal, was sitting with Patrick. Glaring at them both, Randt slapped the piece of paper he was holding in his hand down on the table in front of Patrick, then lifting his hand, he slammed it down on the paper, saying, "Und dot's vot ve get for all our troubles."

Patrick picked up the paper and ran his eye over the figures. As he handed the paper to Trevethan, Patrick remarked, shrugging his shoulders, "You're a hell of a fine mine sampler, Nick, if that's the best you can do."

"Well, I can't put value into the rock if it ain't there," said Trevethan, as he looked at the sheet of paper. "I ain't surprised, though, at what them assays show. I told you that already, and I told Randt, too."

"Vell, vot iss ve going to do aboudt it, anyvay?" asked the German. "Dot Shordy Pederson he brings me some sambles dot has got a hell of a lot of gold und silver in dem, und I make dose assays und you got dem. Vot I like to know iss vare dot quartz come from anyvay."

"Might have got it up at the mines on the hill," said Trevethan.

"No, it didn't come from there," said Patrick. "It happens that we saw him when he came into town and we watched him until he left his samples with Randt. Wherever those samples came from they didn't come from the hill. What we've got to know now, or what we've got to try and find out, is where they did come from. By the way, where is Shorty?"

"He's coming along behind me with that burro of his. I left him and come on ahead. He won't get in here until some time tomorrow."

"There isn't anything we can do till we get hold of him," said Patrick. "You better calm down, Randt, or you'll have a fit of apoplexy the first thing you know," he said, turning to the assayer. "Just go on and finish up the rest of these samples and call it a day's work."

"You iss a hell of a fine smart elleck, Bill, dot sits und takes it like it was a big joke."

"What's the use of getting excited about it, Hans? It won't do no good. We've just been whipsawed, that's about all; and if anybody can figure out just what it all means, I wish they'd let me know. I'm going to do some thinking about it myself, but just at the minute I don't get it. I don't think Shorty Peterson would start out deliberately to swindle me, just for the sake of getting a couple of thousand dollars. He's a mighty square prospector, that fellow. All we can do is wait till he comes back to town."

"Vell, maybe he don't come back at all."

"Well," said Patrick slowly, "if he don't come back, we'll certainly know we've been bilked. But what I would like to know is whether Shorty had any idea of what was in those samples he left with you."

After Randt and Trevethan had gone Patrick and Bartle had a council of their own.

"What do you think about it, Hans?" Patrick asked.

"Bill, I don't know— I just can't make it out. Do you think that Shorty knowed anything about what the real value of them samples was?"

"Well, if he did, somebody else in town must have done the assaying for him."

"The only assayers in town outside of Hans Randt is Ralph Lee at the Sulphide Con and Dick Johnson at the Nevada Belle."

"Do you suppose that either of them fellers did any assaying for Shorty?"

"No, I don't think they did. If they had there wouldn't have been any reason for his taking his samples to Randt."

"Maybe he took them to Hans first, and not getting satisfactory results he took them to one of those other fellers."

"Well, whatever the truth is, we're not going to find it out by guessing about it. We've just got to wait and see what happens from day to day. If he don't turn up here by tomorrow afternoon, we can be sure either that he has some claims staked out, somewhere, that's got highgrade in 'em or that he has pulled up stakes and left the country. Shorty couldn't stay around here, after doing anything of that kind. That's obtaining money under false pretenses, and he's either got to produce the real thing or I'll put him in the penitentiary for getting my money under false pretenses."

"Bill, you're getting excited and just don't know what you're talking about. Shorty wasn't working on no false pretenses. He was working on that assay certificate that Hans Randt give him."

"I guess that's so, Hank. I got a little ahead of the game. The next thing to do is to find that assay certificate. We've got to get hold of that thing and destroy it, because as long as Shorty's got it in his possession, he's got an alibi."

"He's either got it with him or it's over in that cabin of his."

"Yes, there's a job for Jim Graves. We'll send him over there tonight to go through that place and just see what he can find."

That night, acting under orders from Patrick, Graves

visited Shorty's cabin, loosened the ropes and climbed in through the opening between the boards and the canvas. Two hours spent in careful search produced nothing. The missing assay certificate could not be found. Books were removed from the shelf and carefully examined, the trunk was opened and its contents thoroughly inspected, the bedding was removed from the mattress, the mattress taken out of the bed, the drawers of the table emptied, the flooring taken up where it showed any signs of having been disturbed, but all to no purpose. Graves reported to Patrick in his room over the Miners Rest about two o'clock in the morning.

"Guess Shorty's got that certificate in his pocket."

"By the way, Graves, I want you to be ready to leave town on short notice and hunt Shorty and maybe the Proctor boys."

"That suits me. I'm just lookin' for a chance to get that Ike Proctor square in front of me once. He kind of got me unawares downstairs the other night, but I ain't forgot it."

"No, I didn't think you would forget it, Graves; but don't forget that those boys are chain lightning with a gun. Remember what he did to you once."

"He'll never get another chance like that," replied Graves, as he turned and left the room.

"No, I don't suppose he will," mused Patrick as he sat alone.

Chapter XXIX

THE day following Nick Trevethan's return Bill Patrick and his followers focused their eyes more than once on the road leading up from the main street to the trail that, climbing the mountain side, disappeared behind the jutting outcrop of the Sulphide Con. They figured it would be one or two o'clock before Shorty could arrive. The sun gradually reached beyond the zenith, and yet no sign of him. Hans Randt had been early on the street, nervously pacing backwards and forwards between his assay office and the Miners Rest. As the noon whistle blew at the mine his excitement approached fever heat. He had been early at the Miners Rest to talk to Patrick, but Patrick had not yet put in an appearance and Hank Bartle flatly refused his request to go upstairs and interview him in his living room.

"Take my advice, Hans," he said, "and let Patrick alone. He don't fancy being disturbed upstairs. When he gets ready he'll come down and you can talk to him down here. If you went up there now you'd probably get thrown out. Won't do you no good and might do some harm. Bill's a mighty cool customer, he don't get rattled at nothing, and he's generally able to take care of himself; you best let him alone."

The hands of the clock crept around, marking the hour of one, yet no signs of the missing prospector.

Randt could no longer contain himself. He had no thought of eating, as he nervously paced his office, now and again looking up the street in the direction of the mine. Again he went to the Miners Rest and, in a belligerent tone, said to Bartle, "I dink it's aboudt time dot I saw dot Bill Padrick."

"Well, hold your horses for another five or ten minutes, and you'll see him all right. He's down at the barber shop getting shaved. He's been gone fifteen or twenty minutes now, and it ain't going to take him much longer. He left word if you come in to set down and keep your shirt on."

With a shrug of his shoulders and a shake of his head, Bartle turned to his glasses.

Bill Patrick came in, cool and collected. "Well, Hans," he said, "what ails you today?"

"Vot ails me? Dot damn Shordy Pederson iss vot ails me. Vere iss dot damn prosbector gone to anyvay?"

"I don't know," said Patrick, with a scarcely perceptible smile. "I'd tell you if I did, Hans. We've just got to wait, that's all."

"Vait, vait! Vait und lose der piggest ponanza dot iss in eastern Nevada?"

"Well, you don't know whether it is a bonanza or not, Hans. Maybe he just picked up some highgrade and put over a neat trick on us."

"Go search the records and see if they tell anything about where the claims are located," suggested Bartle.

"No good, Hank," said Patrick. "I asked Shorty and he said that he had not recorded them yet, and wouldn't until he knew they were good for something."

Twenty-four hours after Nick Trevethan had returned, Shorty was still missing. The entire crew at the Miners Rest was obviously under intense strain; even Patrick himself became morose and silent beyond his usual custom.

Early in the afternoon Randt took a pair of field-glasses and climbed up to the top of Mount Pierce, from which he could see almost to the Circle R Ranch. The wagon road unrolled before him as it wound its uncertain course through the desert. Carefully he followed its crooks and turns. On the road there was not a living thing.

He returned late in the afternoon and said to Patrick, "Dot damn prosbector gives us der slip. You must send somebody oudt to der Circle R und find oudt vere dot Pederson iss gone to."

"Oh, well, give him time, Hans," replied Patrick, looking up from the paper he was reading and calmly blowing a cloud of smoke into the air.

"Vot for you vant to giff him more time? It's too long time alretty."

A flood of vituperation on the part of the assayer resulted in Patrick's putting his hand on his shoulder and saying quietly but firmly, "You open your mouth just once more and you're out in the cold. I've given Graves his instructions, and he will leave here early tomorrow morning and will get back tomorrow night. In the meantime, I don't want to see you around here until he gets back."

Muttering threats, the German slunk out of the room.

The sun descended, the shadows lengthened, twilight faded into night. Darkness came. The stars in the unclouded sky began to twinkle with all the radiance so characteristic of the heavens as seen from the desert country.

Randt was fast becoming a nervous wreck. Late in the evening he began to drink and soon became unbearable. Bartle finally said to him in desperation, "Aw, take a bottle and go home and go to bed and drink yourself to death. Anyway, whatever you do, get out of here and don't come back till tomorrow. You don't get nothing more to drink from me." Randt disappeared.

Late in the evening, Graves came for a conference with Patrick.

"You ride out there," he instructed him, "and see what you can find out, and come back and advise me; or, if you can find out where Shorty's gone, follow him, and see what he's up to. I think he switched prospects on us and skipped with my $2000."

"All right, boss," said Graves, "I'll do the best I can, and what will I do with him if I find him? Shall I bring him in dead or alive?"

"No, you don't bring him in dead or alive. Find him if you can, and try and get all the information you can, but the principal thing is to find out where those claims are. Shorty dead doesn't do us any good unless we got the claims; and, besides, he's got a lot of friends around here who would make it so damn hot for anybody who killed Shorty, accidentally or otherwise, that you might find yourself hanging at the end of a rope. That's not the game. The thing to do now is to find Peterson and find those claims, if they exist."

"All right, I'll find him, if he is to be found, and bring him back with me if he will come peacefully; if not, I'll come back and tell you."

Chapter XXX

EARLY next morning Graves rode alone in the direction of the Circle R ranch. He made quick time and before noon saw the ranch house in the valley ahead of him. It did not take him long to reach it and tie his horse to a convenient hitching-post. After loosening the cinch, he walked over to the corral where a group of cowboys were engaged in breaking some saddle animals.

"Anybody seen Ike Proctor around?" he asked.

"Yes, he rode down the creek this morning, towards the lower end of the valley. He'll be back by dinner time anyway," volunteered one of the cowpunchers.

Graves took his horse, removed the saddle, and turned him into a corral, after arranging for some hay which he threw over the fence with a pitchfork. Later, when the animal had cooled off somewhat, he would water him and have him in good shape to return to Sulphide in the afternoon. He stood talking to the cowpunchers working with the horses they were breaking and tried to bring out some information without appearing to ask for it. The information he was looking for came unexpectedly when one of the punchers remarked casually, "I'm going into Sulphide tomorrow. You could go back with me, if you're staying over, only I got to drive in a burro."

"Goin' to pack some supplies? I thought you brought all your supplies out in a wagon."

"We do, but this ain't our burro. This is the burro that

Shorty Peterson left with Ike and asked him to send to town the next time anybody was going in."

Graves had sense enough not to show any undue excitement. "What happened to Shorty?" he asked casually.

"Nothing; he was out this way the other day with some fellows from Sulphide sampling some mining claims. He come back this far and asked Ike to send his burro into town and he skipped out on his horse the same afternoon."

"He ain't coming back here?" asked Graves.

"Guess not—he told Ike to send his burro into town. Said he'd meet up with it there some day. Maybe he told Ike where he was going, but I don't know nothing about it."

As the sun climbed to the zenith, and just as the cook was busily hammering the steel triangle in front of the mess house, Ike Proctor rode in and turned to meet Graves, who had walked over from the corral where the cowpunchers were still busily engaged in horse-breaking.

"Hello, Graves," remarked Ike as he came up. "Didn't expect to see you around here."

"Well, the fact is I'm lookin' for Shorty Peterson. He came out here a few days ago to sample some claims for Patrick and was going back to town. Patrick has been waiting for him for two days and asked me to come out and see what has become of him."

The two men eyed each other with unemotional faces.

"Yes, Shorty came in here all right, and stayed with us the day Nick Trevethan rode on through to Sulphide. Nick left him when they broke camp in the morning. He came through here quite a spell ahead of Shorty. He took the samples with him when he left the camp and had 'em on behind his saddle and his helper's saddle. They was making pretty good time, considering the load they were packing. I don't know where Shorty went to. He said he wanted to go and look at some ground that he knew about and that it would mean doubling back if he went into town, and so he asked me to send his burro in for him next time any one was going in. Shorty got on his horse that afternoon and rode out. I didn't ask him where he was going. I reckoned it was none of my business if he didn't want to tell me, but it wasn't in the direction of Sulphide, 'cause he said he would have to double back if he went into town with his burro."

This was the sum total of the information that Graves gathered. Proctor's statements were verified by the earlier statements of the cowpuncher at the corral, and Graves had no reason to doubt them so far as Shorty's arrival and departure were concerned. If Proctor knew more than he had told, Graves knew it would be useless to question him about it. Ike must know the true story, of course, but getting it out of him was quite another thing.

Graves had learned nothing more when he left the ranch after dinner on his way back to Sulphide.

It was Randt who finally brought the news of the return of the scout. He had been standing on the sidewalk in front of the saloon at intervals, now and then coming inside to indulge in some remark or get a drink or light another cigar.

"Here he comes," he cried, bursting through the doors and into the back room where Patrick sat imperturbably playing solitaire.

"Well, sit down and don't kick up a row about it," said Patrick, without looking up. "Go tell Hank to send Graves upstairs to me."

Randt went on his errand and Patrick went upstairs to his rooms.

Graves rode down the trail and finally tied his horse to one of the supports of the wooden awning over the sidewalk.

"Where's Patrick?" he asked.

"He's upstairs in his room," answered Bartle. "You better go up there and see him."

Graves turned to the door leading to Patrick's living quarters above the saloon and went upstairs.

"Well, I got back," he said, as he entered the room in response to Patrick's "Come in."

"What did you find out?" asked Patrick quietly.

In a few words Graves related the result of his trip to the Circle R and hazarded the opinion that Shorty had whipsawed the outfit.

"Guess you're right, Graves. We've been bilked. Shorty's given us the slip and gone off somewhere. He has skipped out with my $2000 and he has taken us to the wrong group of claims.

"I'd like to make a small bet that he's gone to the place that those samples came from that Randt assayed."

They then went downstairs and found the gang in the private room. A few words explained the situation. Various plans were offered but none of them seemed to meet with Patrick's approval.

Patrick said, "I figure that Si Proctor will be back with Langford's team in a couple of days, then maybe we'll find out what's doing. Anyway, we'll get hold of Proctor and try and find out something. I guess he'll know all right, but getting him to tell is another thing. Who come in on the stage today?—driving, I mean."

"Gus Lake," said Slim Wilson. "I seen him on the street a little while ago. I'll go out and hunt him up and see if he saw anything of Langford on the road, and if so, whereabouts."

Wilson slipped out of the room. The others sat in more or less desultory conversation, apparently at a loss to know what course to follow. Wilson returned shortly, obviously agitated.

"What do you think," he said, as he burst into the room and slammed the door behind him. "I seen Gus and he says he met Jim Langford in Elko loading his outfit and Si Proctor ain't swamping for him no more. He's got a new swamper."

Randt sprang to his feet, hammered his fist on the table, exclaiming, "Dot's anoder one of dem fellers dot's gone off, und der two of dem iss by dis time together somevere. Ve got to find out vere dot somevere iss."

Not noticing the interruption, Patrick turned to Graves and said, "You go out on the stage in the morning and when you meet Langford question him and see what you can find out. There's no use looking up the records. Shorty said he hadn't recorded his claims yet."

"All right, boss," said Graves. "If I'm goin' to leave in the mornin' I have to go now and get ready."

"There's nothing else this outfit can do now," said Patrick, "so we'll call it a day."

Early the following morning Graves went out of town on the stage. In the late afternoon they met the sixteen-animal freight team. He had arranged with the driver to stop when they met Langford. He got out and walked back to where Langford had stopped at his hail. Graves wasted no time on preliminaries.

"See you got a new swamper, Langford."

"Yeh. Proctor took a lay-off in Elko for a trip or two. Said he had somc business of his own that he wanted to attend to. I don't know what."

"Is he stoppin' in Elko?"

"No, I don't reckon he is. I don't know exactly where he did go. You looking for him?"

"Yes; he's interested in some claims Bill Patrick wanted me to see him about."

Graves had secured the information he wanted.

Chapter XXXI

SHORTY had arranged for Ike to send a cowboy into Sulphide with a note to Ralph Lee. The day after Shorty's departure, Ike called one of his most trusted riders and said, "Here, Slim, take this letter and ride down the creek towards the lower ranch, and when you get down by the trail leading into town, you turn off and go on to the Sulphide Con and dig up Ralph Lee and hand this to him. Don't tell anyone where you're going, and after you get to town don't tell anybody there why you came in. You can come back afterwards the same way. It's particular you must keep your mouth shut."

"I savvy," remarked the rider, as he took the letter. Carefully tucking it inside his shirt pocket, he rode off down the creek toward the lower ranch.

In the afternoon the cowboy dropped from his horse at the Sulphide Con and handed the letter to Ralph, saying, "Reckon I've got a letter here for you from Ike Proctor over at the Circle R. Ike told me as I was passing by here to hand it to you. Don't need no thanks," he added hastily, as Ralph started to express his appreciation. "Just goin' by and dropped in to leave it for you." He turned and left the office, mounted his horse, and rode down the street.

Ralph read the following:

Shorty left here yesterday for the railroad. He left his outfit here and told me to send it to town. He thinks he better get out of the way as quick as he can as he sure thinks when Bill

Patrick gets them assays he's going to be right mad about it. I reckon I can leave here in the next week. I spoke to the boss already about it and we are looking up a new foreman now. Well, so long, and I hope to see you over at Shorty's claim pretty pronto.

IKE.

This was what Ralph had been waiting for. He had already shipped the surveying outfit by Wells Fargo Express to Eureka, and, keeping in mind his understanding with Si and Shorty that he was to meet Si in Eureka, he figured it was time for him to go. He began, therefore, at once to get together an outfit. He would do the surveying, get his notes in shape, get the corner stakes of the claims tied in to some prominent monument by transit bearings, and complete his work as to the validity of Shorty's locations. During the afternoon he talked with Mr. Macklay about the trip, and found that the plans he had already outlined in his own mind met with the approval of the older man.

"If you're going off on the stage in the morning, Ralph, you'd better come over and have supper with us tonight."

"Thank you, Mr. Macklay, I'll be very glad to."

The conversation at supper was of nothing save Shorty's claims and the events that had come so thick and fast since Shorty had returned from his prospecting trip. Trevethan had reported to the superintendent the afternoon he returned, ready to go back to work. He had volunteered the information to Mr. Macklay that he did not have a very high regard for the claims he had sampled and expressed the opinion that it was another wild goose chase.

"I have noticed Hans Randt," remarked Mary, "walking up and down the street like a man possessed. He seems entirely beside himself in his excitement."

"Bill Patrick don't take it with any outward signs of excitement, though," Mr. Macklay remarked dryly. "I've seen him once or twice in the last couple of days, and he seems to be as calm and cheerful as ever."

"He has wonderful nerve and control of himself," said Ralph.

"He wouldn't be the successful saloon owner and gambler that he is if he didn't have that control," answered Mr. Macklay.

Having thoroughly discussed Patrick, they turned to ways and means of warding off threatened dangers from their opponents.

"I really don't think you need to worry a great deal," said Mr. Macklay. "That assay certificate that I've got locked up in the safe, and the story that you could tell if it ever gets into court, would be sufficient for a jury to give you a verdict. There are only two things they can do. One is to take forcible possession of the property, claiming 'by location'; the other is to secure someone's interest by hook or crook. They may try one or both methods, but if you will make the survey, Ralph, and tie your corners in to some mountain peak or prominent landmark, so that any other surveyor can reproduce the bearings, I think you need have no fear on the score of prior locations. If it comes down to a question of a gunfight, it seems to me we are all hitting at shadows, because title to the group of claims rests in Mary. While it is true that it is a mixed-up affair, the way Shorty has handled it, still I believe it will work out somehow. I think I'll go over to the office," said Mr. Macklay, "and do some work. You can stay here and talk with the folks, Ralph. It will be some time before you get back and have another chance."

"I think I'll go around with you, John," said Mrs. Macklay. "I want to get out into the cool of the evening for a little while."

The two older people left Ralph and Mary sitting on opposite sides of the dining table, now cleared of the supper things.

"I'm going to pull out in the morning," said Ralph, "and I don't know what chance there will be to get any word back, but if there is I'll drop you a line."

"I wish you would, Ralph; I shall be dreadfully worried about all of you, and if you can manage to send us word you will add very much to our peace of mind."

So they talked on for the better part of half an hour, about Shorty's prospect and their hopes and fears. They almost, but not quite, reached romantic declarations, as the minutes slipped away and the hands of the clock marked off another half hour. At the end of that time Mr. and Mrs. Macklay returned. Mary was sitting in a low rocking chair on the porch, and Ralph sat on the flooring, his feet on the ground and his back against one of the posts that supported the awning overhead. No one spoke for some time, until Mrs. Macklay remarked, "Heaven's sakes, I never saw two such dumb critters as you two young folks."

It was just after sunrise next morning when Ralph emerged from his cabin with his pack slung over his back. He was on his way to the restaurant for an early breakfast, after which he would catch the stage that was due to leave at five-thirty. Mary was standing on the porch of the superintendent's residence as he passed to say good-bye.

"I have a sewing outfit for you, Ralph, on which I have embroidered your initials," she said, "and I wanted to give it to you this morning before you left and to tell you . . ." she hesitated a moment, a blush suffusing her face, "and tell you I wish you all the good luck in the world and a safe return."

"I'm terribly obliged," he said, as he took the package and held it nervously in one hand while he fumbled with his hat in the other.

"I'll be thinking a lot about you, too, Mary, while I am over there; and when I get back we'll have the best talk yet —and I'll tell you all that has happened, and a lot about everything." He hesitated a moment, gave her hand an extra and unduly long shake and stammered "good-bye" as he started off.

The stage pulled out promptly. At that early hour none of the Patrick outfit were on the street. Ralph Lee left town unknown to Bill Patrick.

Chapter XXXII

All day over the sun-baked alkali desert the stage carrying Ralph Lee to the railway toiled laboriously forward. Save for the occasional clouds of alkali-laden dust that the vagrant currents of air drifted over the stage, the trip was not uncomfortable. Halfway they stopped for dinner. This and the occasional freight outfits they passed going loaded to the mines, or coming out empty, were all that broke the monotony of the trip. Late in the afternoon they passed Jim Langford's outfit. Ralph noted that a new swamper occupied the position formerly held by Si Proctor.

At the railway Ralph took his canvas-covered roll of blankets and boarded the train for the west. He paid the conductor the train fare demanded, but he purposely avoided buying a ticket. There were several who had bought tickets to San Francisco, so that any attempt to trace his movements would be difficult. He could lie over in Palisade all night, taking the stage from there in the morning for the ninety-mile trip to Eureka.

Palisade in those days was a busy centre. The mines of Eureka were producing a large tonnage of lead-silver ore that required an endless amount of supplies for the mines and the town, which claimed a population well on to 10,000 people. It was this business that made Palisade one of the busiest railroad stations between San Francisco and Ogden. Travellers on horseback, in light buggies, six-horse stages, sixteen-animal freight teams, with their back actions coupled to the heavier front wagons, lined the road. Hay ranches, cattle ranches, stations of one kind and another, charcoal burners burning charcoal for the smelters at Eureka, all helped to add life to the ninety-mile stretch of hill and valley that intervened between the banks of the Humboldt River, where it flowed through the Palisades that gave the station its name, and the famous lead-silver mining camp, which at that time fixed the price of lead throughout the world. In those days it was an all-day stage ride from Palisade to Eureka in the choking dust of the Nevada desert.

After dark Ralph arrived in Eureka. He had arranged to meet Si at the livery stable owned by Frank and Dick Carrington. Ralph found the place and said to the man whom he judged to be the boss, "Can anybody around here tell me where I can find Si Proctor? He came in here a day or two ago with a horse, and I had an arrangement to meet him here."

Dick Carrington, one of the proprietors, passed an appraising glance over Ralph and remarked, "You're the fellow he's looking for, are you? He was in here a short time ago, and said he would come back. You might sit around and wait for him, or I'll tell him when he comes in that you have been here and maybe he'll wait till you come back."

"I'll just leave this roll here with you, if you don't mind; got my blankets and a few other things in it; and I'll walk down the street and see if I can find him."

"Put your blanket over there in the office," said Carrington, with a wave of his hand in the direction of the space that had been partitioned off and used indifferently as an office, a storehouse, a baggage room and general utility quarters for the travelling public.

The sidewalks were crowded, many people walking in the streets. Crowds congregated in saloons, drinking, gambling, or looking on. At the postoffice a line of impatient men stood waiting the distribution of the mail which had come in on the evening stage. Ralph walked on down the street, looking in the saloons and scanning the passing crowd, but without catching sight of Si. Stopping at the lower end of the street, where the two smelters were located, he stood fascinated by the glow of the molten metal as it was being tapped from the furnaces, by the rumble of the trucks, and by the crash of the red hot slag as it was dumped over the end of the track onto the slag dump. The arrival of the ore teams from the mines, teams loaded with charcoal, flux and other supplies, the rapid movement of the men about the plant, all served to present a spectacle to be seen nowhere save in a few mining camps in the West. After several minutes Ralph turned and retraced his steps. When he had again travelled the length of the street and come within sight of the stable, he encountered Si, walking slowly down the centre of the street, gazing at the passing throng. Si slapped Ralph on the shoulder, and said, "Gee, I'm mighty glad to see you. Got things pretty well ready for starting out. I hired a four-horse team, loaded her with camp equipment and grub, and got everything ready to pull out as soon as you got here. We can get away in the morning slick as a whistle."

They walked back to the stable, Ralph relating to Si the events of the last few days.

"Reckon Shorty will be at the mine by the time we get there," said Si. "I found the place all right, and she looks like a humdinger. I don't know much about mining, but from Shorty's description I could see the thing is just like he said it was. I am terribly anxious for you to get out there and look it over yourself and give me your opinion about it. There ain't no accommodations to be had at the hotel, so I rustled around and found a house where there was a room to rent. It has a double bed in it, and we can camp there tonight, get something to eat in some restaurant, and pull out early in the morning."

They went around town together, while Si notified the crew of their early morning departure. He explained he had found an old friend in the teamster who used to freight into Sulphide.

"I knowed him over there, before he came over here. There's more business over here because of the freight that's got to be hauled to keep them smelters going and the hauling of the ore from the mines and the lead-silver bullion to the railroad, and there's no trouble for him to keep busy all the time. Reckon I'd have had a hard time finding anybody, if I hadn't knowed him; but he agreed to take a lay-off and do some freighting for us. I got a horse for you all right. Miners can ride on top of the freight wagon. I got a couple of tents; we can use one for a cook-house and sleep in the other. I'll do the cooking for a while anyway, and Shorty can cook when I'm not there, if I have to go out for anything. Thought we'd start in kind of slow and get a cook when we have a little money ahead."

"Speaking about money," said Ralph, "I have $500 with me if you need any."

"Don't need none; that $1000 I got before I started bought all the supplies that we need and more and I got some money left. I told the miners that we would pay them once a month, and we'd bring the money out from town to them, or I'd leave it in town anywhere they said. Told me I could deposit it for them in the Eureka County Bank."

It was long after midnight before they completed their arrangements and went to the room that Si had hired, and turned in for the night.

Daylight the following morning found the four-horse team loaded with the camp outfit, powder, caps, fuse, drills, picks, shovels and charcoal, on its way down the main street. The miners were perched on top of the load and Si and Ralph rode their horses. They had picked up the survey outfit at the express office.

All day long they travelled slowly over the desert, following the road that led in the direction of Elko. At night they camped at a well that had been sunk for stock. The next day, after leaving the main travelled road, they turned off to the east and about noon came to the campsite on the edge of the stream where Shorty had camped while making his location.

As they approached the spot, they saw a man moving about and a horse, hobbled, nibbling the grass on the edge of the stream.

"Bet that's Shorty," exclaimed Si. "Knew the old geezer would be on time."

Shorty received them with signs of wildest delight.

"Gosh," he exclaimed as they galloped up. "I'm mighty all-fired glad to see you fellers. Been looking for you for quite a spell. Been over on the claims doing some work and tryin' to hold 'em down till you folks got here. What did you bring on the wagon?"

Si enumerated the articles that made up the load, and, as he called them off, Shorty nodded his head in approval.

"Well, come on, let's get the team unloaded," he said, as

the outfit drove up and came to a halt. After shaking hands with the four miners and the teamsters, Shorty took command and bossed the unloading and assembling of the contents of the wagon. Tents were soon erected, materials sorted out, and by dusk things were so arranged that it was possible to cook supper and serve it on a home-made table.

They talked until late into the night, and turned in with the agreement that in the morning Shorty would take Ralph over the claims, leaving Si with the miners to complete the camp, find a place for the explosives, and make things ready for a long stay. They would come back for dinner in the middle of the day, and in the afternoon all hands would go out and begin work on the claims.

Next morning after an early breakfast Shorty and Ralph started out leaving Si to lay floors with the lumber they had brought and build bunks, tables and chairs.

When Shorty and Ralph returned at noon, Si asked excitedly, "Well, what do you think of her, Ralph?"

"As far as I can see, Si, Shorty has given a very accurate description of things as they are. I found the location notices undisturbed, just as he described them, the monuments all in place. In fact, I am sure there has not been a soul on the ground since he was there. We can go out this afternoon and begin work."

"Of course, I've got to go along with you and see you start this business," said Si, as he busied himself putting the midday meal on the table. There was a piece of oilcloth spread over the table, with knives, forks, plates and tin cups in place, and there was bacon, potatoes, hard tack and coffee. "Grub's ready," remarked Si, and all hands fell to.

They had left their mining supplies in the wagon and,

after finishing their meal, the horses were harnessed and the load was driven over to the foot of the hill as near as possible to the outcrop of the vein. Here they unloaded and packed their supplies up the side of the hill to a place that Ralph had selected as the location of the shaft. The powder, caps, and fuse were piled some distance away, and a rough covering of boards erected to protect them from the sun's rays. The forge and anvil were set up; a barrel cut in half was filled with water, into which to dip the drills and picks for tempering while they were being sharpened, and all preparations made to begin work.

Placing the miners along the ledge, Ralph instructed them to begin to strip it and pile up anything that looked like ore so that it could later be sacked and packed down the hill on horses, there to be loaded on a freight team and hauled to the railroad for shipment to the smelter.

"We'll have to do some surveying," Ralph said, as he took his transit out of the case and began to set it on the tripod.

"I don't know nothing about surveying," said Si.

"Well, you don't have to. You just take this rod and hold it where I tell you to, and I will motion to you with my hand whether to move it to the right or to the left. All you do is to hold it as nearly perpendicular as possible, and I'll do the rest. We'll set up here at the discovery monument and run out a course 750 feet each way, and then turn off at right angles and set the corner stakes." He had been working while he talked; having his instrument satisfactorily adjusted over the discovery monument, he instructed Si to walk out until he thought he was in line between the two stakes and then to stop.

"I'll line you up from there," he said, "and you move

either right or left as I wave my hand, and when I wave both hands above my head and bring them down to my sides you stay there and plant the stake at the point where you are holding the rod. Then come back here to me and we'll measure out the distance. It's got to be exactly 750 feet from where the instrument sets to the centre stake of the end line."

Si lined in and set his stake as directed. Coming back, he took the steel chain Ralph handed him and walked ahead as Ralph followed, holding the other end of the chain. Arriving at the stake set by Si, Ralph found that Shorty had overrun the distance. Measuring back to the indicated point, he had Si again hold up his rod while he lined him in with his instrument.

"Just drive that stake into the ground, and drive a nail into the top of it," he said, "and we'll run out the two corners and get 'em set."

This done, the instrument was again set over the discovery monument and the line run out in the other direction and the other two corners located. Ralph found a lone tree on the side of the mountain two or three miles away, and this he used as a monument to which to tie in his corners. It was now beginning to get dusk. Work for the day was discontinued, and the crew went back to camp, where Si had preceded them to prepare supper.

Chapter XXXIII

The second day's work was a repetition of the first, with Ralph carefully setting his stakes by the aid of the instrument and the miners working upon the vein and piling up the ore as they worked, stripping the ledge of the loose float that had broken off as the vein disintegrated. By degrees they cleaned up the surface, leaving only the solid quartz ledge in place. This they would have to drill and blast.

Shorty's delight was almost childish. He refused positively to leave the miners and assist Ralph in his surveying except for short intervals. He busied himself going from one miner to the other, helping them to pick up and pile the ore, examining pieces and breaking them with his hammer, his face beaming with smiles.

At camp he talked to Ralph and Si by the hour about what they were going to do. He had located in his mind the hoist, the mill, the various mine buildings, the camp, the bunkhouses and the superintendent's quarters.

"We've got to get all them claims surveyed," he said, "get them corner stakes tied in to the lone tree of yourn, get the maps out, and get them notes locked up in Mr. Macklay's safe. We just ain't goin' to take no chances on nobody droppin' in on them claims and movin' our monuments."

"Every day makes it less liable to happen," said Ralph.

"It will take us a day or two to start a shaft," Shorty said. "Somebody's got to go back to town and buy a whim, a bucket and some rope and bring out some more timber.

We can get her down quite a ways with a hand windlass, but it ain't going to be long before we'll need a horse whim, so's we can hoist fast."

"We've got ten tons of ore piled up by this time," said Ralph. "I was measuring it today and calculating it, and if the assays run like that you brought over to Sulphide, Shorty, we've got over $2000 stacked up there already. Good for U. S. gold coin as soon as we can get it to the smelter."

"Yes, and most of the ore that we got piled up was float that we just picked off the croppings," said Shorty.

"I've located the shaft," continued Ralph, "at the discovery monument. We'll start the shaft down in the vein—a single compartment about six by six feet, inside the timbers. That will probably give us size enough to take in the whole width of the vein, and the ore that we get out as we sink will much more than pay all expenses. The shaft should give us about six tons of ore to the vertical foot. Six tons of ore at $200 a ton is $1200. It won't cost us, any way you figure it, over $50 a foot to sink, including everything, so there is quite a handsome profit even sinking a shaft on this kind of a ledge."

That afternoon Shorty built a hand windlass such as was common on every prospect in the West. A space was cleared, drilling began, and shots were fired. Before long there was a well-defined excavation in the ledge. As the material taken out was practically all ore, it was carefully piled to one side as the work went on.

The next day, from the hole that was to be the working shaft, they extracted and sacked a quantity of what was obviously high-grade ore, and by the end of the week it became necessary to erect the windlass which Shorty had built. One man below loading and two hoisting would comprise their crew for the time being. When not engaged in hoisting, two miners would be in the shaft drilling and one would be sacking ore or sharpening tools.

A week passed. The monuments were all duly placed, distances were carefully measured, bearings were taken with the transit to the lone tree, and the whole was tied in so completely by surveyors' notes that there could be no question as to the location of the property.

"I've got to be getting back to Sulphide," said Ralph. "My work is done here. We can begin to ship any time now and, of course, as soon as we do, the news of the discovery will be in every paper in the State."

"We can't keep it quiet much longer, that's a fact," said Shorty. "As soon as that carload of ore gets over to Salt Lake, and they get the assays out, things'll begin to crack."

"I'll get away just as quick as I can find somebody to take my place and come right back," said Ralph. "I'll take all these survey notes, work 'em out and make the map, and deposit the original notes with Mr. Macklay in the safe."

"Better make a package of that assay certificate, them agreements and your notes, and send the whole business by Wells Fargo down to the Bay and have them kept there in some bank," suggested Shorty.

"I guess that's a good idea," replied Ralph. "I'll speak to Mr. Macklay about it."

"We'll load that wagon we came out in with ore and send it back to Eureka and ship what there is of it to the smelter, get it run through the sampling works, and find out what it is worth. And, incidentally, they can send us the money for it," said Shorty.

"It'll help," said Si reflectively.

The next day the wagon left for Eureka. Shorty went with the teamster. The survey instruments were carefully packed so that they could be shipped back to Sulphide from Eureka. Ralph saddled the horse Shorty had ridden over from the Circle R, and with his survey notes carefully tucked away in his pocket and his pack strapped on behind his saddle he struck off to the northwest in the direction of Elko.

"You can make town by night, all right," said Si, "if you keep moving right along. If you don't you can stay at the ranch where I stayed over night. They will be glad to see you. Tell them you are a friend of mine—that's all that's necessary—and I'll stay here and hold the camp down till Shorty gets back. Between my Henry rifle and the two six-shooters, I reckon nobody is going to run away with the mine while you fellows is gone."

The sun was just rising above the mountains when both Shorty and Ralph waved good-bye to Si. Si turned and walked up the hill toward the claims.

"I ain't much of a miner yet," he soliloquized, "but, by jiminy, I'm going to learn."

Chapter XXXIV

WHEN Graves arrived at Elko, he discovered that Si Proctor had bought a horse and left town and that Ralph Lee had been seen getting off the stage. Beyond that, the trails vanished. He wired Patrick the following morning as soon as the telegraph office opened. Before noon he had a reply instructing him to return to Sulphide. The following day, just as the whistles at the mines were blowing the noon signal, he arrived in Sulphide.

"Where's Patrick?" he asked, as he walked into the Miners Rest.

"Upstairs in his room," replied Hank Bartle. "You'd better go see him. He's waitin' for you. Don't seem to have had much success, Patrick says."

Without replying, Graves disappeared through the door leading to Patrick's living-room.

"Well, I got back," he said as he entered the room to Patrick's "Come in."

"Yes, so I see; but you don't seem to have got very far."

"I got as far as I could, or as far as anybody else could."

"Well, you proved one thing, anyway—we've been flimflammed."

"My notion is," said Graves, "that Shorty took Trevethan to the wrong bunch of claims, and that the whole outfit, Shorty, Lee, and Proctor, have skipped out to wherever the real claims are."

"That's probably the truth, Graves; and, if we ever do get the truth, we'll find that Lee did some assaying as well as Randt."

"Then they must have knowed all the time what you knowed?" asked Graves.

"Yep, I guess they did."

The only answer Graves could think of was, "Ain't that hell!"

"That's all for the present," said Patrick.

Graves returned to the bar and confided to Bartle that Patrick was one cool, nervy boy, to which the bartender agreed.

It was well into the afternoon before Patrick appeared in the saloon and proceeded to the private room, where Graves, Wilson, Bartle, Randt, and Trevethan were waiting.

"Well," he said as he closed the door, "you all seem to be on hand, anyway."

"You bet ve iss," answered Randt, "und ve vant to know somedings."

"So do I," said Patrick, "so let's begin. In the first place, you know by this time as much as I do, which ain't much. Now let's see just what we do know. We know Shorty's got a pretty fair prospect somewhere. We know he's disappeared, after taking Trevethan on a wild-goose chase, and that his partners, Lee and Proctor, have also vamoosed. If Lee was in on it he must have done some assaying, so they know everything we know—and more, for they know the location of the claims, and we don't. I don't know how we are to find them or the claims, except by letting time work it out. It'll be public before very long. We must get Randt's assay certificate back if we expect to have a leg to stand on. Meanwhile, keep your eyes and ears open, and if you hear anything let me know. The drinks are on the house," he added, as he rose and led the way to the bar.

Days passed. Cautious inquiries failed to reveal anything. Shorty Peterson, Ralph Lee, and Si Proctor had disappeared utterly.

Among the people who planned for the future was Mike Sullivan, proprietor and editor of *The Sulphide News.* He had been through several rushes and outlived several boom towns. Gossip was bound to drift into his office, and recently he had collected some rather discouraging information concerning the local mines. He was beginning to have doubts as to the future, and to think it might be well to look about and see what the prospects were elsewhere. He determined, therefore, to visit Elko, Eureka, Reno, and maybe Grass Valley and some of the other California mining towns. He owned his equipment (such as it was) and moving it from place to place involved no serious problem. Too poor to buy a building, he had rented space; so the problem of moving, should he find a new location, was a simple one. Elko, he found on inspection, offered nothing encouraging, so he went on to Eureka. The editor of *The Eureka Sentinel,* an old acquaintance, had invited him to lunch.

As they walked down the street to get a drink, preparatory to eating, the team on which Shorty was coming into town for more supplies came up the street, and Shorty dropped off near the saloon for which the newspaper men were headed.

"Hello," remarked Sullivan, "there's Shorty Peterson. Wonder where he's coming from."

"Let's find out," answered Skillman, the news instinct asserting itself. Quickening their pace, they overtook the prospector.

"Hello, Shorty. What you doing in Eureka?"

"Hello, Mike. Oh, just prospecting around some. Doing a little work on some claims I got located out east of here."

"Been out with a team?"

"Yeah. Fixin' up to spend a month."

"Charlie Smith in with you?" asked Skillman, referring to the driver.

"Oh, no. Just hired him to freight out a load," replied Shorty, who, declining to have a drink, went on his way.

The next day the freight outfit, having unloaded the sacked ore and loaded the supplies bought by Shorty, started for the mine. True to his promise, Shorty went back with the outfit sober. At almost the same hour, the stage for Palisade pulled out carrying Sullivan. He had crossed Elko and Eureka off the map as offering him no inducements. Reno and California were still possibilities, but in the meanwhile, he must write some items for *The News*. Of course, he would mention that Shorty Peterson was doing some work on a promising looking group of claims between—"Hum, let's see—northeast of here, did he say? That would be in the Elko direction . . . yes, on a group between Elko and Eureka in the Ruby Range." That would cover it and the Ruby Range sounded good, anyway.

So, a few days later, *The News* contained an item to the effect that the editor while recently in Eureka had met Shorty Peterson, who was in town loading a freight outfit with supplies for his new prospect in the Ruby Range between Eureka and Elko. "Shorty informs us he figures to spend a couple of months prospecting the group. We understand he has a promising showing." The item was neither long nor in a conspicuous place, but it created a sensation among some of its readers. Mrs. Macklay saw it and showed it to her husband and Mary Clark.

"Well," said the superintendent, "it had to come out some time."

Ralph saw the item and went over to Macklay's house from the office with the paper in his hand, to find the others discussing it.

"Won't be long now before things begin to happen," he said. "They've been trying to pump me ever since I returned, and Hans Randt has been absolutely comical in his eagerness to find out something and, at the same time, to appear unconcerned. I wonder," he went on, "just what they will do."

"The first thing they'll do," replied Macklay, "is to find out where the claims are located, and then they'll make an effort to get possession."

"You forget, John," interrupted Mrs. Macklay, "that the claims have all been deeded to Mary."

"No, I haven't overlooked that, either," said her husband, "and so far as I'm concerned, I wish to goodness they hadn't."

"Well, but I'm a partner, too, you know," added Mary.

"If they find the place," said Ralph, "and get such samples as I brought back, and have them assayed, they'll know that Shorty's first samples were not picked specimens by any means."

"I rather think," interrupted Mr. Macklay, "that you'd better pack up, Mother, and go down to the Bay for a few weeks with Mary. There's no telling how tense this situation may become before it's over, and it's no mess for a woman to be in."

"I'd rather stay here, Mr. Macklay," said Mary. "I should feel safer close to you and Mother and Ralph and Ike and Si than I would in San Francisco with no bodyguard."

"Well, you'll have plenty of bodyguards here, Mary," said the superintendent. "If necessary, we'll get Big Sim to organize a vigilante committee. There won't be many on the other side, and those who are might just as well be run out of town now as at any other time. It would do the town good, and might save some of them from decorating the end of a rope sooner or later."

Hans Randt found the item as he sat in his office trying to divert his mind from the ever-recurring question of the location of the claims. Upsetting his chair in his haste, leaving the door open behind him, he rushed down the street to the Miners Rest.

"Haf you seen it?" he vociferated, waving the paper wildly in the air. "Idt's ofer in der Ruby Range by Elko."

"Gimme the paper," said Patrick quietly, "and shut up."

"Here idt iss," said the distracted German, pointing with his finger to the item. There was no one in the saloon at the moment save Bartle.

Patrick spread the paper out on the top of the bar, remarking, "Hank, it will interest you, too; at last we seem to have the answer. We know now Shorty hasn't skipped with the money, we know he has struck it, we know where the strike is located, and I think the sooner we declare ourselves in on it the better it is goin' to be for us. Go out and round up the crowd, Hans," he said, "and we'll hold a council of war."

It was not long before the private room off the saloon was filled with an excited crowd. Hank Bartle had turned the bar over to an assistant; Jim Graves had been found in the barber shop; Slim Wilson and Nick Trevethan had been rounded up in Sam Hing's hash-house by Randt, who, tense with excitement, was chewing the end off an unlighted cigar while he fidgeted in a chair pushed back against the wall.

"Well," remarked Patrick, as the last of the group arrived, "you all know what this meeting's for?"

Grunts and nods of assent answered his question.

He proceeded. "It's up to us to get possession of them claims. I want you, Graves, to ride over there and see what you can find out. No rough stuff, yet, but get some samples and bring them back. After we find out if the property is worth fighting for, it will be time enough to work out a plan. I'll write to the recorder of Elko County and get an abstract of the location notices and see who the owners are. Get back as soon as you can, Graves, and get goin' at once. Go on the morning stage, hire horses in Elko, take two men with you, and lose no time getting back. I'll talk to Lee and see what I can get out of him. The rest of you keep quiet. Listen plenty, but don't talk. We've got to know our facts first."

The next morning Graves, accompanied by two men, hard-boiled like himself, was on the Elko stage. That night they slept in Elko, and the following morning, mounted on hired horses, they struck out for the Ruby Range that loomed in the distance.

In the mail that went out on the same stage was a letter from Patrick to the recorder of Elko County asking for a telegraphic abstract of title covering the claims located by Shorty Peterson. Two days later the information came back that the claims stood in the name of Mary Clark, deeded to her by Peterson. For once Patrick lost his gambler's poise.

"Damnation," he muttered to himself, "have we got to fight a woman? I never bargained for that, and I don't like the idea. It's not so bad fighting a bunch of men, but when you get a woman, especially one like Mary Clark, mixed up in it, it's certainly hell."

To Hans Randt, however, the situation took on an entirely different aspect.

"Vell," he remarked to Patrick, "I yust as soon fight a voman, maybe sooner if she gits scared und lets go."

"Well," said Patrick, "this one ain't that kind. I got her sized up to be as courageous as they make 'em. And besides," he added with a touch of menace in his voice, "don't you go fussin' round that woman, Randt. If you do, I'll fix you myself. I got some decency left in me, yet, and I draw the line at fightin' a woman. Don't let me catch you lifting a finger against her."

"Vell, she iss one of der enemy, ain't it?"

"Maybe she is, but I tell you she is a woman and a good one, and I don't make my livin' annoying that kind. What we get, we get from the men."

An effort at further protest from Randt was silenced by Patrick with a curt "Shut up!"

Randt went off muttering to himself and vowing under his breath that, Patrick or no Patrick, he would get something out of Mary Clark, if the worst came to the worst, even if it involved abduction and, perhaps, murder.

"All my life," he muttered, "I been vaiting to gedt me an inderest in a good brosbect, and now, py jiminy, no Bill Padrick, or any oder feller, is going to stop me ven I iss so close mit der ding vat I haf been vorkin' for so many years."

Chapter XXXV

MEANWHILE, Graves was busy scouting to find the location of the claims that were the source of so much anxiety. In his first attempt he struck the Ruby Range too far west and scouted in the direction of Eureka, instead of to the east. He searched draws and canyons in vain until in sight of Eureka he turned back. Several days had been lost in vain search.

"Let's try the wagon road to the east," suggested one of his companions, and so, without better guidance, they cut into the road and followed back on their tracks.

"Shorty must have come out on this road," remarked one of the trio, "and I reckon if we follow it far enough we'll find where he turned off and then all we got to do is to follow the tracks."

It was well on to dark when they reached a small stream, beside which they camped for the night. Starting early in the morning they soon discovered tracks leading off the main road and heading into the sagebrush in the direction of the mountains.

"I guess we got her at last," said Graves, as they turned their horses and followed the newly broken trail. After several hours the horsemen sighted the white canvas tents and the workings of the long-sought claims.

"Well, I swan," said Graves, "they ain't in the range at all. They're just out in the valley on a little lone butte standing up on the plain all by itself."

"And that's why nobody ain't found the place afore,"

remarked one of the others. "Nobody'd ever think of prospectin' out there. Wonder how Shorty ever came to do it."

"We might as well ride up to the camp," said Graves. "It's near noon, and we can eat first and get down to business afterwards."

Both Shorty, at the claims, and Si, at the cook-house, had seen the dust of the approaching horses long before the riders drew rein and dismounted. Si was standing near the cook-house observing them as they drove up.

"Howdy, Graves," he remarked as Graves dismounted and began to loosen his saddle cinch. "Which way you headin' now?"

"Oh, just scoutin' round lookin' for Shorty Peterson. Patrick's anxious to see him about some money he loaned him on some claims."

"Well, Shorty's over yonder, but I don't reckon Patrick has any interest in this group."

"No? Then what group is it?"

"Don't know for sure, or I'd tell you; but Shorty told me he'd been over north of Sulphide somewhere with Nick Trevethan before he came here. Maybe them's the claims Patrick is interested in."

"You know a damn sight better, Proctor. I'm goin' over there and talk to Shorty about it."

"Well, I'll go along, too," replied Si, and he stepped back into the tent and strapped on his six-shooters. He then strode on after Graves, who was now well in advance. The two men Graves had brought with him were close at his heels.

Shorty had been sacking ore all morning and packing it down the hill to where the freight outfit was waiting for a load. The burro he had been using stood on the dump close to the windlass. Two miners were in the shaft getting ready to fire the noon round of shots. As the men approached, Shorty seated himself on a pile of sacked ore. He had recognized Graves. The two other men he did not know.

"Three of them and five of us," soliloquized Shorty, "but the miners ain't got guns, so it's up to Si and me, two against three." He hitched nervously at his belt as he talked to himself, and made sure his Colt was loose in its holster. It did not take long for the party to cross the intervening space, and soon they were climbing the slope to where Shorty sat on the sacked ore.

"Hello, Graves," he called.

"Hello, Peterson," was the answer, as Graves paused for a moment to get his breath after the climb. He gained the level of the dump and rested himself on an empty powder-box, while his companions disposed themselves on rocks. Si quickly followed and seated himself on some sacked ore near Shorty. For several minutes the heavy breathing of Graves and his companions was the only sound that broke the silence, each party, meanwhile, eyeing the other and speculating on the possibilities.

"Well, Graves, what brings you over to this country?" asked Shorty finally.

"Patrick sent me to find you," was the short reply.

"And havin' found me, I suppose you have a message?"

"You bet I have. He wants to know what about his $2000, and when are you going to transfer the claims to him?"

"Why, he got his claims long ago. I took Nick Trevethan out to see 'em and he sampled 'em and took the samples back to Sulphide. I left him at the Circle R ranch and cut across country to do some work on these claims for the owner."

"Which I suppose is you and Proctor and Lee and maybe some more?"

"Not at all. The owner of these claims is Mary Clark, the school teacher. We're just hired help."

"You mean to tell me you didn't locate these claims?"

"You bet I did, but I deeded them to her."

"What's the use playin' that kind of a game?" replied the irate Graves. "These here claims is the claims you sold Patrick, and he wants them; and he sent me here to tell you I was to sample 'em and bring him the samples and tell you to show up in Sulphide pretty pronto and get the rest of your money."

"Well, I ain't goin' to Sulphide just now. I ain't got any money comin' to me at present, and if Patrick don't like the claims I sold him, I'll refund the money he paid on account. And lastly, you ain't goin' to sample these here claims 'cause you ain't got no right to."

"Like hell I ain't. I'll sample when and what I please."

"Try it," was Shorty's answer.

"You fill that bag with small rocks from that ore dump," Graves ordered one of his assistants as he rose and tossed him the bag.

"Better not try it," warned Shorty, who also stood up. But Graves, bent on completing the job and getting Peterson and Proctor out of the way, ordered his men to proceed. He had resolved to precipitate a fight, feeling sure that he and his men were more than a match for Shorty and Si.

As the man picked up the sack and started for the rock pile, Shorty reached for his gun. That move was the signal for general action. First a single shot, then two more, so close together that they sounded almost like a single shot. Then quickly there came another. Shorty and Graves fired almost simultaneously. Si, firing first, had dropped Higgins as he was drawing his gun. His second shot struck Graves as he was falling. The third man stood with hands high above his head, waving the white canvas sack as a sign of surrender.

The miners, swarming out of the shaft, found Si covering the third man, and Graves, Shorty and Higgins stretched on the ground.

"Take this fellow's gun," said Si to the miners, "and tie him up with that piece of rope." It was quickly done and the party now turned their attention to the men on the ground. Graves was dead, shot through the head by Si and through the abdomen by Shorty. Higgins was also dead. Shorty was alive. They laid him down on some ore sacks and Si cut away his flannel shirt and dressed the wound.

"It's above and to the left of the heart. You'll be all right, old hoss," he said, "but lie still and take it easy. I'll do all the talkin' that's needed round here. We'll fix up the wagon with a cot and start for Eureka with you. Charley will ride ahead and get the doctor to come and meet the outfit. The rest of you fellers stay here and go on with the work. I'll drive the team and take Graves' pardner along with us. As for them two," he said, pointing to the two dead men, "they'll do to start the new cemetery. . . . Two of you go out there in the flat, about a mile away, and dig a couple of graves and get these fellows planted before they become objectionable."

They rigged a stretcher and carried Shorty down to the

wagon. Charley started on horseback to fetch the doctor. Grub was rustled, canteens were filled, and Shorty was carefully placed in the wagon on a cot with a temporary awning.

The miners were given instructions to go on with the work and to hold the claims at all hazards.

"Ain't goin' to be no one here, though, before I get back," remarked Si. "Patrick ain't prepared to move till he hears from Graves, and he ain't goin' to hear from him for quite a spell. I'll get back quick as I can after I see Shorty in the hospital in Eureka. Of course, it'll be all in the papers day after we get there. But I can get back ahead of any outfit, and there'll be so many people hereabouts in a few days that there won't be no more attempts made to do any claim jumpin'."

"I'll drive careful as I can, Shorty," said Si, as he picked up the reins and started the team.

Far in advance, a lone horseman was speeding to bring the doctor.

The wagon camped for the night at a water hole and there, in the early hours of the morning, the doctor, driven by Charley, found them. After examining and carefully dressing the wound by the light of the lanterns held by Si, the doctor patted Shorty on the shoulder, and said, "Pretty close call, Peterson, but there is no reason why you won't pull through all right. No vital organs affected, and after we get you safely into Eureka and keep you in the hospital for a while you'll be good as new."

Shorty nodded his head and said, "Thanks, Doc. I ain't goin' to cash in yet. Got too much to live for just now."

"Well, you can tell me all about it in a day or two; meanwhile, take this drink and go to sleep."

The sleeping draught soon had its effect, and Shorty lay breathing quietly.

Sitting by the campfire some little distance removed from the wagon, Si asked, "Say, Doc, what's the real facts?"

"Just what I told him," was the reply. "It's a nasty hole, just above and to the left of the heart. I can feel the bullet under the skin of his back. We can get it out quick enough, once we get him to Eureka, and, unless infection sets in, he'll recover quickly."

"Well, you're the boss, Doc, and what you say goes, and I'll guarantee the rest of our crowd'll agree with me; so go ahead and do a good job. And say, don't forget he ain't no charity patient. He's got money, and so have the rest of us."

"Got a good claim out there?" queried the doctor.

"You bet we have, and that's why that outfit tried to jump it. I can't figure out, though, just what they was after. Wouldn't have done no good to kill us all off; there's more of us over in Sulphide and our deaths would only have resulted in several killin's or hangings, and wouldn't have changed the ownership of the claims any."

"I knew Graves in Eureka," replied the doctor. "In fact, I took care of him after one of his shooting scrapes. He was strictly a bad man with a gun, but had no sense or judgment. Couldn't see beyond the end of his gun as to what the consequence would be. Just naturally a killer who seemed to think that if he killed somebody, things would be all right. You can't figure anything out of his actions, other than that he thought the simplest way was to remove you people and take possession and let Patrick work out the rest."

"And, by the way," said Si, reflectively, "Patrick is going to be one mad hombre when he gets the news. He ain't no fool, and above everything he didn't want nobody killed. That's the one thing most likely to cause him trouble and bust up his game, and he knows it."

Soon after sunrise they were on their way again. That evening Shorty was lifted from the wagon and carried into the hospital, and Si found time to think of other things.

"I'd better telegraph Ralph first thing in the morning, soon as the telegraph office opens." The next morning he went to the telegraph office and sent the following message to Ralph:

> Graves tried to jump our claims yesterday. He and Higgins dead and Shorty in hospital here with shot in shoulder. I am going back this afternoon. Tell Ike to hurry up.
>
> SI.

Rumors of the shooting were already widespread, and Skillman, editor of *The Sentinel,* caught up with Si as he came out of the telegraph office and began to bombard him with questions. The result was a two-column story in the next day's edition. The location of the claims, the fact that they were shipping ore, and the very interesting fact that the claims stood in the name of Mary Clark, were all chronicled. The article wound up with a prophecy that a new and important district had been discovered.

The sheriff was also on hand, and tapped Si on the shoulder and suggested that he had better spend the night at the jail and make arrangements to go before the judge in the morning for a preliminary hearing.

"It just can't be done now, Sheriff," Si replied. "I got to get out of town pronto if not sooner and get back to them claims. Tomorrow's paper is going to have a piece about the shootin', and there'll be a stampede out there that'll take most half the town, and I got to be on hand to see that no funny business is attempted by them stampeders. We got all the ground layin' around loose, but what's in it I don't know. One thing is, I don't want nobody to try and attach themselves to what's ours."

"Well, I'll tell you what I'll do, Proctor. You get ready to leave town, and I'll meet you down below the Richmond smelter and go along to keep an eye on you and generally look after things out there. Guess the sheriff'll be needed there more than he will here for a while anyway. After a few days, when the rush has kinda quieted down, you can ride into town with me and surrender. Meantime, you got to promise me you won't try and skip the country."

"You know I won't, Sheriff," was the reply. "I got too much of a stake out there, and, besides, I ain't got nothing to be scared of. It was Graves or me, and I got him first."

"Yes, and I reckon you did a good job, knowing the gent as I do. Eureka's goin' to be mostly on your side when the trial comes off. Only don't say I said so, 'cause I got to uphold the law and condemn gun play in public, no matter what I think in private."

The sheriff would be on the ground early and there was nothing to prevent his making a location. Si would be under guard, and at the same time free to protect his property, and justice would be in no way outraged by the short delay in bringing Si into court. An hour later, Si, mounted on a horse he had rented at the corral, was ready to start. He had but a short wait before the sheriff, accompanied by two of his deputies, drove up in a buckboard.

"Just brought them along to help keep things quiet while the stampede's on. And now let's get goin'. The news is beginnin' to leak around town already, and in another hour or so the boys will be startin' to hit the trail. After the paper comes out in the mornin' the road'll be black with 'em. And I reckon the sooner we get through, the better chance there'll be to locate something." And the sheriff, now turned stampeder, put whip to his team and led the way down the Elko road. They camped for several hours to give their horses a rest, but were off again after a hasty meal of coffee and sandwiches.

Hard riding and driving brought them in sight of the camp by late afternoon. They could see one of the miners sacking ore, another at the windlass attending to the wants of the man in the shaft, but beyond that there were no signs of life. They hobbled their horses and turned them loose to graze along the banks of the stream.

Then the sheriff said, "Just show me your corners, Si, and I'll make a location or two myself; and I reckon we better get goin' quick, for by morning I calculate we'll have company."

Stopping at the shaft long enough to tell the miners about Shorty, Si pointed out the limits of their claims and left the sheriff and his deputies to their own devices, while he went back to the miners.

"You got the water located, Si?" asked the sheriff.

"Yep, Ralph located that before he left. We got water rights, mill sites, tailing dumps and mineral locations all sewed up. We got all the room we want for everything, including bunk-houses and office buildings. So let 'em come on and stampede."

"You got a mine all right, Si," remarked the sheriff that evening as they sat in the cook tent eating a late supper, "but there's got to be more'n one mine to make a big camp, and what the rest of us have got to do is find some more good prospects hereabouts. No tellin' what's out there under that wash that's covered up the extension of your vein. Guess the vein's there all right, but has she got pay in her?"

"Only way to find out is to dig," answered Si.

"Yep. And I guess we'd better begin diggin' early in the morning. We're goin' to sleep on our claims tonight so's to watch for jumpers."

Late that night the vanguard of the stampeders came galloping in, and after rousing the camp and asking a few hurried questions, they rushed off to locate some ground. By ones and twos they trickled in, and by morning the teams began to arrive. By noon the stampede was in full swing, and the sheriff began to exert his influence. His own outfit had arrived, his tent was up with a placard "Sheriff" prominently displayed over the entrance. Tents were going up in every direction and Si, with his six-shooter strapped on, was dissuading enthusiastic citizens from attempting to relocate over the original locations.

"What kind of an outfit is this, anyway?" queried one belligerent stampeder. "You got the claims, the millsites and the water, and what in hell is left for me?"

"Well, I see plenty of ground hereabouts," answered Si soothingly, "and all you got to do is to go out and stick some stakes in it."

"Yeah," answered the angry stampeder, "a hell of a lot of good it'll do me locatin' scenery."

"Well, it's all been here for a long, long time, son, and you could've located them claims any time since you was twenty-one if you had found 'em."

"Sure, your grandmother could, too."

"Certainly she could. Only you see, she didn't. Shorty Peterson came along and did, and I figure we all is goin' to hold 'em. You saw what's happened already, and it could happen again if any smart Alec gets promiscuous with location notices."

While Si and his miners were getting out ore and sacking it for shipment, the tide of frenzied men rose higher and higher. Eureka, Elko, Palisade, and Carlin were all represented, and it would be only a few days before Salt Lake, Virginia City, Austin, Sulphide, Tuscarora, and other mining towns would be pouring their quotas into the new camp.

"Better get some of your pardners over here," remarked the sheriff to Si on the second day. "I can't let you run loose much longer, and, besides, I got to get back to town. I figure on leavin' the boys to look out for the morals of the camp and maybe to keep an eye on some of them claim-jumpers I see dodgin' round."

"Ain't goin' to touch your claims, Sheriff," answered Si, "and if they do we'll give them a real interestin' time. But I'll be ready to go in a couple of days, an' I promise not to skip the country in the meantime," he grinned.

"No, I reckon you won't, Si. Leastways, not with a million dollars or two layin' loose to be had just for pickin' it out of the ground.

Chapter XXXVI

THE telegram to Ralph was received by Will Gault. He carried it himself up the hill to the mine office, where he found Mr. Macklay and Ralph going over some mine maps.

"I have a message, Ralph," he said, "and didn't stop to put it in an envelope even, but brought it to you at once."

He handed the paper to him as he spoke. After glancing at it hurriedly, Ralph read it aloud to Macklay. For a moment no one said a word.

Then Macklay remarked, "Well, Ralph, Graves' mad action has made everything public property. The story will be in the papers all over the West. There will be a thousand men in the new camp within a week. You must get Ike over there at once and have him take two or three men with him, even if the Circle R has to go without a foreman for a few days. You will have to ride out there and bring Ike back in the morning."

"I'll start at once," replied Ralph, as he reached for his coat and hat.

"By the way," said Macklay to Gault, "I wish you would say nothing about this telegram; it will be public property soon enough, and it is important to Ralph and his partners that this news be kept quiet as long as possible."

"It can't be kept long, Mr. Macklay. I have no doubt that when I get back to the office the telegraph instrument will be busy calling me to take a telegram for *The Sulphide Times* telling the story. They go to press at four o'clock, and by five it will be all over town."

"Much sooner, probably," said Macklay. "Sullivan or some of his office force will repeat the story before the paper is off the press and it will pass from mouth to mouth with the speed of a prairie fire. Well, it can't be helped, but hold it back as long as you can, Gault. Take the message, but don't give it to Sullivan until afternoon."

"I'll keep away from the office for an hour or two. No one but me knows how to telegraph. I'll do my best, sir."

"Well, come on, Ralph," called Macklay, "let's go over to the house and tell the news to the women folks. They'll be wanting to pack up right away and go and nurse Shorty."

The two men walked over to the house. Will Gault went back to town. They entered the superintendent's residence, where they broke the news to Mrs. Macklay and Mary.

"We must go at once," said Mrs. Macklay, "and take care of Shorty."

"I rather thought you'd say that," remarked Macklay, "but, in the meantime, put up two or three sandwiches for Ralph as quickly as possible. He has to ride out to the Circle R and get Ike and two or three of his men, and start for the mine to help Si in case of any further trouble."

The sandwiches were quickly prepared and Ralph was soon well over the hill on his way to the ranch.

"Well, I must go back to work," said Macklay. "There is nothing more to be done now. Events will simply have to develop themselves."

Arrangements for the departure were begun at once, and it was not long until the last bundle was tied up. The company hospital supplies were drawn on liberally. The store of canned goods Mrs. Macklay always kept on hand in large quantity was overhauled, and those things likely to help an invalid were packed in generous amounts, much to the amusement of Macklay on his return.

"You'd think, Mother," he said, "that there was nothing to eat in all Eureka, the way you are packing things."

"Well, I suppose there is, John, but it will do no harm to go well supplied for any emergency; and what we don't use we can send out to the mine."

Ralph, meanwhile, was riding hard in the direction of the Circle R. The horse he rode was Mr. Macklay's and one of the best in that part of the country and was always kept in perfect condition by the conscientious Pratt. It was early afternoon when he topped the hill and saw the ranch house in the river bottom below. Twenty minutes later he was greeted by a chorus from half a dozen dogs. Riding up and dismounting at the corral where Ike was working with some horses, he told the story.

"Of course, I'll go back with you, and take a couple of punchers with me. The new foreman's here, and I was figgerin' on gettin' away in less'n a week anyway. No reason at all why I can't leave now. You put your horse in the corral and give him some hay and a rest and we'll start back after a spell."

While Ralph was turning his horse into a vacant corral, the cowmen were talking things over among themselves, with the result that all hands proposed to go with Ike.

"I got to pick a couple of you," said the latter, "and you can draw lots to see who's goin'."

This was quickly done with pieces of paper, two of which had the word "go" scrawled on them. The papers were dumped into a hat and the drawing was under way when Ralph returned from feeding his horse. The two successful candidates emitted yelps of delight, while the others showed unmistakable signs of depression.

"Aw, say, Bull," remarked one of the unfortunates, "lemme go in your place. Give you $10 to boot."

"Huh! What do you think I am? Wouldn't miss this chance to help Si for the best hoss in the outfit."

It was late in the afternoon when, amid a volley of good wishes and parting advice, thev saddled up and started on the return journey.

"I just knowed that brother of mine had the real stuff in him," remarked Ike during one of the breathing spells. "Never was quarrelsome, or anything like that, but was always practising with his gun, and you can bet he's chain-lightnin', too."

"He's a good pardner," replied Ralph, "and the rest of us have always thought we were in luck to have him with us."

They pushed rapidly on towards Sulphide. At ten o'clock Macklay met them as they dismounted at the mine.

"Had a telegram from the doctor this afternoon," he said, "and Shorty is doing fine."

"Bully for him," ejaculated Ike, and Ralph echoed his sentiments.

Turning to the cowmen, who were listening to the conversation, Macklay said, "You boys take the horses over yonder to the company stable and Pratt will feed and care for them, and then you can come back here and we'll see what the plan is to be." As the punchers left, Macklay, Ralph, and Ike went into the office, where Macklay said, "I suppose you boys will want to pull out in the morning."

"Yes, that was the plan, if Mrs. Macklay and Mary will be ready," said Ralph.

"They'll be ready. Mrs. Macklay has been packing all morning, and Mary is over at the schoolhouse with the trustees talking over some school matters. Let your horses rest till two o'clock or so; you can pull out then and make the thirty-six-mile-house for the night. I have sent word out there that I want a change of horses. Ralph can ride in the rig, and Ike and his two men can ride their own horses."

"We'll be ready to pull out on time," said Ike, "and meantime, if there's nothing for my punchers to do, I'll let 'em go downtown and fool around a while. Hey, you fellers," he called to the two men sitting on a pile of timbers outside and idly kicking their heels, "if you want to go downtown a while, go along. Only be at Sam Hing's when the whistle blows, and we'll move along right after we feed. Don't bother with too much red likker, neither; this ain't no Fourth of July party nor a shivaree. It's strictly business."

"All right, Ike," one of them answered, "we'll be on hand when the whistle blows. You can bet we won't take more'n one or two drinks."

Ike sat talking with Mr. Macklay and Ralph for a few minutes, going over the news of the killing and the probable results, and speculating as to what Patrick and his gang were likely to do under the circumstances.

"I've got to go down to the mill," said Ralph.

Ralph and Ike went first to the stable, where Ike cast an appraising eye over the horses and talked with Pratt for a moment.

Ralph remarked, "I'm going to drive the team this afternoon, Pratt." Then he added, "And we'll leave soon after twelve-thirty."

The stableman nodded. "They'll be all ready for you, and fit to the minute."

Ike and Ralph turned and started toward the trail leading downtown.

The story of Shorty Peterson's discovery went out over the wire to every important paper in the West. The discovery of a new camp of undoubted merit was in itself news of first importance. When to that was added the dramatic story of the attempted claim jumping, a rare combination was offered that easily made the front page of every paper. Skillman of *The Sentinel* was besieged by editors in Salt Lake, Virginia City and elsewhere for additional news. A mining stampede of first magnitude was in the making.

The story of *The Sentinel* reached Sulphide by noon and was promptly set up for the edition of *The News* that afternoon. Long before the paper was off the press, the news had trickled out on the street. Within an hour stampeders were on the road to Elko, hoping to be on the ground before the big crowd arrived.

The printer, one of Patrick's scouts, acting as editor in the absence of Mike Sullivan, had read the story on its arrival and had lost no time in hunting up Patrick. Breathlessly he recounted the facts as brought in over the telegraph.

"Hank," commented Patrick, still as cool and unemotional as ever, after the newspaper man had departed, "Graves had to go and make a fool of himself and ruin everything, including himself and us."

"You don't think we're down and out, boss?" anxiously inquired the bartender.

"That's just the situation, Hank. I wouldn't give you a plugged quarter for all we'll ever get out of it now.

Chances were bad enough, but with all the publicity and a stampede on, and the sheriff on the ground—well, we may as well forget it, so far as owning the claims is concerned."

"Maybe if the camp's big enough we can open another Rest over there," said Hank.

"Well, it's got to be pretty big to attract me. Much bigger than a one-mine camp. Shorty and his crowd'll know the whole story—in fact, do now, I guess—and we'd have a fine chance in a camp with only one mine, and that owned by a crowd dead against us. No, Hank, it's keno for the other fellow this time."

The conversation was abruptly terminated by the arrival of Hans Randt, who literally burst through the door in a frenzy, waving a copy of the evening paper just off the press.

"Here idt iss," he vociferated. "Yust everydings vat iss wrong."

Patrick curtly interrupted the excited German, and taking the paper from him, began to read the account to himself.

"Read him aloud, Padrick," interrupted Randt.

"Now, see here, Hans," said Patrick, lifting his eyes from the paper, "you go to the bar with Hank and get yourself a drink and a smoke and sit down, and when I get through reading I'll talk to you, and not before. Now get out. I'm in no humor to argue with you, or anybody else." And he went back to his reading, while Randt, after one or two grunts, went to the bar and got his drink and cigar. Into the ears of the usually patient Bartle he poured his tale of woe, only to be told to shut up and let the boss run the job.

"If there's anything left to save out of the wreck, Patrick'll save it; there's just no use for you to say anything about it at all."

Having finished reading the story, Patrick called Randt into the private room and remarked, "Well, Hans, I'm through with the whole damn business; and my advice to you is to get out of town and hunt a new camp for yourself. Sulphide's goin' to be too hot for you when this story all comes out. Nobody will trust your assaying any more, and you'll just naturally starve to death."

"Und you don't make any more effort or noddings to gedt dem glaims?"

"Not another effort. Somehow, our connection with the business don't seem to have come out as yet. I don't know why, unless it's because they don't want the story of Shorty's sale to me ventilated yet. Anyway, until it does break, I shan't go down to the Bay, and maybe not then. I never was much of a hand to run, and I guess I'm too old to start running now. Don't bother me any more, Randt, and if anything turns up I'll let you know."

"Vell, I don'dt like vat you probose, Padrick. Vhy don'dt you go hold up dot school teacher some night und make her sign somedings. She iss der legal owner."

"I've told you before, Randt, I do not fight women, and the sooner you discover that the better off you'll be."

"Vell, I ain't afraid of vomen, und I goes und tackles her mine own self."

For once Patrick lost his self-control. Grabbing Randt by the throat, he backed him up against the wall, saying, "You dirty rat! Let me find you trying anything rough with that school teacher, or any other woman, in this affair, and I'll see you fixed so you'll never try it a second time. Now you get out of this saloon and stay out until I send for you; and that won't be till I have something of importance to tell you. You're not wanted here, so get out!"

He flung Randt from him. Randt stumbled and fell to the floor. He picked himself up heavily, peered at Patrick through his thick glasses, and muttered, "I fix you somehow for dis, Mr. Padrick. Vot you dink I am? A vorm for you to step on? You can go to hell, you und all your high ideas. As for me, I do vot I please."

He walked slowly out of the saloon, still muttering to himself.

"You ought not to have done that, boss," said Bartle. "That Dutchman's a mean devil, and there's no tellin' what he might do to you."

"Never mind me, Hank. It's the school teacher I'm interested in, for the moment. I'll just put Slim Wilson on to watch Randt for a while."

Wilson happened to come into the saloon shortly after Randt departed, and soon got his instructions from Patrick. He took up Randt's trail and located him in a nearby saloon engaged in the act of 'loading up.' He watched him till he saw him buy a whole bottle of whiskey and stagger up the street to his cabin. Wilson returned to Patrick with his report.

"Well, he's safe for the night, anyway," said Patrick, "and tomorrow he'll not feel like doing anything except getting sober."

Chapter XXXVII

THAT morning the school trustees had met with the school teacher and discussed arrangements for the coming school year. The schoolhouse where Mary taught was a one-room affair, built early in the life of the camp. Another more pretentious two-story school had been erected at the other end of town, but the old building, being convenient to the houses nearest the mines, was still maintained. Here Mary taught some thirty children, including those of Sam Hing, Manuel Lopez, Mike Slavick, Nick Trevethan and others.

The session had adjourned and the trustees had departed, leaving Mary alone. Her work finished, she was ready to return home and start for Eureka. Her mind dwelt continually on Shorty and his condition. Even the reassuring telegram of the early morning did not quite relieve her anxiety. Through the threads of her thoughts ran a constantly recurring idea—"Thank God it's not Ralph." She blushed, laughed a little, and went on with her work.

Well, why not? She had known for some time that her heart was given to Ralph Lee, and she suspected and hoped that his own case was equally hopeless. If only he would muster up courage enough to say so, she thought, with more blushes and an exclamation of dismay at her boldness.

"Only, of course," she thought, "he won't know how I feel until he makes up his own mind and has the courage to speak out."

Not more than a quarter of a mile away from the school stood the cabin of Hans Randt. He sprawled in the sun on a bench outside his door, recovering from the debauch brought on by the news of the killing of Graves.

His befuddled brain had taken cognizance of the departure of the school trustees, and he had speculated as to why they were at the schoolhouse. Mary Clark appeared at the door and started a little fire of old papers.

"Py jiminy," he muttered, "I make dot young lady sign me dot deed to dem claims vot I haff fixed up alretty, und den everybody can go to hell."

Getting up from his bench, he took from a box on a shelf in his cabin a deed he had previously spent some time in writing out, transferring the claims to himself. Stuffing the paper into his trousers pocket, he took some rope that had been tied around a trunk, and started in the direction of the schoolhouse. It took him but a few minutes to cover the distance, and finding the door open, he walked in and slammed it shut behind him.

"Vell, young voman," he said, as he crossed the room to where Mary was sitting at her desk, "der jig iss up, und now you iss going to sign me a deed for dem glaims." He leaned over the desk and leered into her face, as he pulled the deed from his trousers pocket, slammed it on the desk, and pointed to the place where he wanted her to sign. He stood threateningly beside the desk, unshaven, unkempt, his shirt open at the throat, his finger pointing to the place for her signature. Mary screamed and started up from her chair in terror.

"Sit down," he commanded, and his hand thumped the table, "or I put a halter round your neck und strangle you."

He leaned over the table and seized her by the wrist, pushing her back into the chair, where she crouched, trembling.

"For years und years," he said, "I haf been trying to get me an inderest in a mine, und now, my priddy lady, you iss not going to stop me. I haf dreamed about it. I haf vorked for it, und py Gott, I commit me murder if I haf to. So take up your pen and sign, und den I tie you up in der chair till I get oudt of town."

The years of waiting, of unsuccessful effort, the prize seemingly at last within his grasp, only to be snatched away, had been too much. Randt was a raving maniac.

Mary had but a dim realization of all this as she sat cowering in her chair, trying to pull herself together. If she could only get out of doors, she was sure she could outrun Randt.

"Where am I to sign?" she asked tremblingly.

"You iss to sign dere," vociferated Randt, stabbing his forefinger at one end of the document.

"And when I sign, what am I to do next?"

"You iss to sit still vile I tie you up mit dis rope," he snarled, shaking the rope in her face.

"But I will starve to death," she said, looking furtively around for some chance to escape.

"Und vat if you do? I don't care me for dot," he answered roughly.

"But I have no pen. It's over there in that desk, and the ink, too," she said weakly. "Oh, I feel I shall faint. Please get it quickly if you want my signature."

"Sit still, den," growled Randt, as he turned his back.

Instantly and silently she was on her feet, all signs of weakness and fear gone, as she dashed for the door. Randt heard her footsteps and turned with a growl of rage in pursuit. Mary always said afterwards that she covered the distance in two jumps, but whether two or more, she was out of the door and slammed and locked it. It was only a momentary respite, however, for the crazed man seized a chair, smashed a window sash, climbed through the opening and started in pursuit, bellowing like a bull, "Stop! Damn you! Stop!"

She dashed madly toward the house. Ralph Lee and Ike Proctor, coming down the path near the mine, heard the yell. In an instant they were racing down the hill.

Randt, seeing them coming, suddenly stopped and backtracked toward his cabin, leaving Mary to sink into Ralph's outstretched arms, her head on his shoulder and her face upturned.

It was Ralph's boast in after-years that he had never proposed to his wife. "You see," he would say, "she just said 'Kiss me, dear,' and I did, and that settled it."

Ike sped on after Randt. "I'll get him alive," he flung back to Ralph as he ran forward in swift pursuit.

"Go with Ike," said Mary.

Ralph ran on. Randt was well in the lead, Ike a few hundred feet behind, and Ralph not so far away. Behind Ralph streamed a dozen miners who had witnessed the chase. Mary followed them slowly and Macklay was a short distance behind her. She was at least 200 feet behind Ralph when Ike reached the cabin into which Randt had disappeared. Impetuous as ever, Ike threw open the door and rushed in.

There was the report of a gun and almost instantaneously another. A wisp of grayish smoke drifted out of the door and lost itself in the atmosphere. Ralph rushed into the powder smoke. Ike was moaning. Randt lay still, a bullet between his eyes.

Gently Ralph turned Ike over onto his back and, sitting beside him, lifted his head and rested it on his knee. Macklay, Mary and the others had come up.

"Get me some water," Ralph said to Macklay, while Mary, in tears, took the head of the dying boy in her lap and Ralph held the water to his lips.

"Reckon he got me," Ike said, and a wan smile passed over his face. "Never thought he'd be crazy enough to shoot. Give my love to Si, and tell him I would have liked to have helped him work his claims, but I reckon I can't. He's got to hoe the row alone, and I wish him and you all good luck and millions of money. Kinder wish I could have been there when you get that old mill a-goin' and have seen some of the gold and silver come out. I'm gettin' kind of cold, Miss Mary. Won't you hold my hand just a minute?"

Quietly she clasped his hand, as he gave hers a little caress and snuggled down like a tired child creeping close to its mother as the shadows of evening steal across the nursery floor. Outside an ever-increasing crowd was gathering. One had gone for the doctor. Slim Wilson had slipped away to tell Patrick. Macklay was posting guards to keep back the crowd, while inside the cabin Ralph knelt beside the dying boy whose head was in Mary's lap. She was using her free hand to keep away the flies that began to gather round the dark blotches of blood that dripped to the floor and formed an ever-widening circle. She made no effort to conceal her tears. Ralph sobbed.

"No cause to take on so," folks," Ike said with a feeble effort. "Nobody but me and Si left, and Si can take care of hisself."

They placed him on a mattress dragged from the bed, cut the clothes away from the wound, and staunched the flow of blood while waiting for the doctor.

"I'm goin' pretty quick, now," murmured the wounded boy. "Just sorter wish, Miss Mary, you'd kiss me once afore I go."

Mary leaned over and gently kissed the dying boy as he gasped out his last breath.

"Come, my dear," said Mrs. Macklay to the sobbing girl, "you must go home with me now. You can do no more here. We have to think of the living more than the dead."

Slowly she led the girl through the silent crowd, that parted respectfully before them, and slowly they went up the hill to the superintendent's house.

Chapter XXXVIII

Sulphide had had numerous killings. The graves out in the clearing in the sagebrush testified to that. But this was different. One of the town's well-known citizens had apparently attempted to assault or kidnap the school teacher, and when thwarted had committed murder. Then, too, Ike Proctor was not only a well-known figure as a cowman, but was a quiet, orderly, peaceable citizen and immensely popular.

Big Sim, deputy sheriff and town peace guardian, had been standing on the sidewalk in front of the post office when the pistols cracked.

"Well, now, who the hell is that a-cuttin' loose, I wonder, and just where was it?"

"Two shots, Sim," his companion remarked. "Must be over toward the schoolhouse; I see 'em runnin' in that direction."

"Well, I guess I'll have to look into it," said Sim. "But I ain't got no gun and maybe I'll need one." Stepping into the store next door, he remarked casually to the storekeeper, "Lend me a gun, Jim."

He carried no gun himself, except as occasion required. It was a habit of his to step into some store, or saloon, where he knew a gun was to be had, and appropriate it for the time being. He kept guns of his own at the corral, in the express office and at the hotel, but he was not near any of those places at the moment, so he got the nearest gun available and started for the scene of excitement.

Even Sim was startled on arrival at Randt's cabin. A crowd was already there, congregated around the door, and was being kept from entering by the men Macklay had posted. Inside, Mary Clark, seated on the floor, was holding Ike's head in her lap, Ralph was giving him water, Macklay was standing in the doorway. A few quick questions addressed to Macklay, and Sim was in possession of the facts so far as the bystanders knew them.

"And you say that Randt tried to kidnap the school teacher, and that he run in here when it failed, and that he shot Ike as he come in the door, and that Ike got him afore he fell?"

"That's about the size of it, Sim," replied Macklay.

"Guess that Dutchman must have gone plumb crazy to try anything of that kind," hazarded the foreman of the Con.

"He must have," remarked Sim. "A snowball in hell would have twice as much chance as he would when this town got onto what he was trying to do. And I guess the result of this business shows it," he added with emphasis. "Only I'd give a whole lot not to have had Ike took off like that. And him one of the best shots in the country, getting his from a skunk like this Dutchman. Things ain't always according to the rules," he added, with a tinge of bitterness in his voice.

"Well, one of you fellers run for the coroner, and let's get it over with. And," he added, as he caught the look in the eyes of the two cowboys who were to have gone with Ike, "I'm a-goin' to take charge of this business and run it myself. There ain't no accessories before n'r after the fact. If there is, I'll look out for 'em myself."

"That's all right, Sim," remarked one of the punchers, "we was just a-thinkin' that mebbe one of us ought to ride over to where Ike's brother is and let him know what's happened. And," he added, with a menacing stare, "if there's anything to be done about it, we reckon Si can take care of his own affairs."

"Well, I reckon so, too," replied Sim.

Among the early arrivals at the cabin was Slim Wilson. With staring eyes he viewed the scene, the full meaning of which was clear enough to him and caused him to depart in haste to the Miners Rest. Bursting through the door, breathless, he gasped out to Hank Bartle, "Randt's killed Ike, and he's dead himself. He tried some funny business with the school teacher, and Ike chased him into the cabin and he shot Ike, and Ike got him before he died. Where's Patrick?"

"Upstairs," answered Bartle, as he started for the door, with Wilson close behind him. Through the door and up the stairs they raced, and burst into the room where Patrick sat reading. Here Wilson stammered out the news that caused even Patrick to lose his nerve and show signs of agitation.

"My God," he ejaculated, "what has that fool Dutchman done? We're in a hell of a mess now, and no mistake."

"You certainly are, Patrick," said Bartle nervously.

"Yes, and what's worse," said Wilson, "Si Proctor will be here in a day or two. When he comes we better all be out of the State if we can get that far away before he shows up."

"Goin' to run away?" sneered Patrick.

"You bet I am, and so are some others, soon as they know

what's happened," answered the now thoroughly frightened Wilson. "I don't want to get into no gun fights with that outfit, and you bet your life that's what it'll be when they get back here and Si has talked with the schoolmarm and with Macklay. I'm going on the next stage, or sooner, if I can get a team. Ain't you coming along, Patrick?"

For a moment tense silence was the only answer, and then slowly Patrick looked at Wilson and replied, "No, Slim, I'm not going. I never ran away from anything yet, and I guess I'll have to stay this time and play out the hand."

"You ain't got a chance, Bill," said Bartle. "You better go."

"No thanks, Hank. I've played the game and, thanks to that fool Dutchman, I've lost; but I ain't no quitter, and I'll stay right here and face the music."

"Si'll kill you sure," said Wilson.

"Well, maybe he will, and maybe he won't. There's more than one gun in this town, and I'm pretty handy with one myself. Anyway, I'll take the chances and stick it out. I've gambled all my life, and been in some pretty tight places and seen lots of gun play and killings, and anybody always has some chance."

"Not in this game, with that feller, Patrick. He's quicker on the draw than you ever thought of being, even with your iron nerve. And it takes something more than nerve to win this hand, and that something is the quickest draw and straightest shooting."

"You've seen me shoot, Slim," was the reply.

"Yeah, I have; and you can shoot all right, but you can't draw like that feller can; and I tell you, Bill, you ain't got a ghost of a chance," was the reply.

"Well, suppose I haven't, and he does come here to do some killing. Do you expect me to run away? I could never show my face in the camp again. I have a stake here and I got a right to defend myself, if necessary; and, besides, I have my own self-respect, and Bill Patrick has to live with himself as long as he lives, and he couldn't look himself in the face if he turned tail and ran to cover. Any of you fellows that want to can go as soon as you like, but here I am and here I stay."

"I got to admire your nerve, Bill," said Bartle. "You got a hell of a sight the worst of the layout, and you know it. You can't count on much help or sympathy from any one. In fact, if Si don't get you, I guess the town'll string you up if they ever get the truth of the affair. Suppose you do kill Si. You don't think it'll end there, do you? That'll only make matters worse; and if they don't get you with sawed-off shotguns, they'll get you on the end of a rope, and the game'll be up good and plenty. Go on and get out while you have time, and let me stay here and keep the saloon going. They won't touch me. I ain't a prominent character in this here tragedy. They won't suspicion me as having any part in the business. Slim wants to go, and he'd better if he feels that way about it; but I'll stay and I guess I'll get by with it."

"You bet I want to go," interjected Wilson, "and I'm going now; and you fellers make me sick, making such fools of yourselves. Maybe you'll get away with it, Hank, but Patrick ain't got a chance. Better come along with me, Bill, and we'll get a team and I'll meet you down the road, and we can catch the train at Elko and go on to San Francisco and try it somewhere else—Arizona, or Mexico, or somewhere."

"You better go, Bill," repeated Bartle.

"No, boys, I've made up my mind. I took a gambler's chance on the thing, and I don't lay down my cards in the middle of the game."

"Middle, hell," said Wilson, as he edged toward the door. "This ain't no middle; this is the end, and bluffing ain't a-goin' to get you nothing, Bill Patrick. You got to hold the winning hand in this game if you want to win, and you ain't got it. Better come," he added, as he opened the door.

Patrick only shook his head, and the door closed behind Wilson, who clattered down the stairs, out of the saloon, and on down the street to the stage office, where he got himself a seat on the out-going stage and shook the dust of Sulphide from his feet forever.

Patrick sat for a few tense moments, gazing into space. Bartle stood silently watching him, making no attempt to break the silence, but waiting patiently, as he had always waited, for Patrick to give him his cue.

"Hank," he said finally, "I simply can't run away. It's against every principle I ever had. I've played the game according to my own code, and when I've given my word I've stood by it to the end. I've never flinched or run away from the consequences of my own acts. I don't suppose I'd pass for a parson or a Sunday school teacher, but in one way or another I've done maybe as much good as some of 'em have; and there's more than one down-and-outer, man and woman, who could testify to that. I've lived according to my own rules, and I can look any damn man in the eye and tell him to go to hell. I've never been a hypocrite, nor sung psalms on Sunday and short-changed the public the rest of the week, and I've never tucked my tail between my legs and run to cover from any man—and I ain't goin' to do it now. I'm goin' to stay right here, and if we have to shoot it out—well, I guess the town can't hang me for shooting in self-defense. You go, if you want to, Hank; I can get somebody in here they can't accuse of having any hand in this mess, and then after it's all over you can come back."

"No, boss, I ain't going to run away. I've follered you a long time now, and what I got I owe to you, and I stick the thing through right here. Lots of people don't have much gratitude—just take what they can get, and make use of a man while they can and then quit him cold when the pinch comes, or they get through with him or think they can't get anything more out of him. Well, I ain't that kind; and if I haven't had much bringing-up nor much education, and not much of nothin', anyhow, I ain't goin' to quit you, like you say I can if I want to. No, sir, that ain't my style."

"Good old Hank—I kind of thought you'd stick; and I guess it's me, not you, they'll be gunning for. If I get the chance, I'll clear you of any blame in the thing; and, anyhow, there's nothing much they could do to you except to tell you to leave town. All right, old sport, you stick if you want to. I shan't forget it."

Hank went back to the saloon, where he began polishing glasses and arranging them in long, shining rows under the mirror behind the bar.

Chapter XXXIX

In the dining room of the superintendent's cottage John Macklay and his wife sat talking over the tragedy. In the parlor on the black horsehair sofa Mary Clark sat with her head on Ralph's shoulder, hysterically sobbing. Ralph's arms were around her, and he tried to calm and comfort her.

On the porch the foreman and his wife were meeting the townspeople as they arrived, and assuring them that there was nothing that could be done. In twos and threes, and in groups, they stood around the gate, trying to puzzle out a reason for what had happened. The general opinion was that Randt had gone crazy from too much whisky, and, in a fit of delirium—jim-jams, they called it—had made the attack.

"It's almost too bad Randt died," remarked a townsman. "He would have looked fine dangling from the end of a rope, and you bet your life we'd have seen to it that there was plenty of rope handy."

"Better let them alone," Macklay had said once or twice as his wife had started to rise. "They want to be by themselves for a while. The best thing for Mary's nerves is to let her have her cry out. It'll cure the hysterics quicker than anything you can do, Mother." Mrs. Macklay had assented, sinking back into her chair, although with evident reluctance.

Coming up the hill Mary had told them of Randt's effort

to get her to sign a deed, and to them, of course, the tragedy needed no explanation. "Randt realized the game was up," said Macklay, "but whisky, consumed to drown his disappointment, was too much for him. No man in his right mind would have attempted a thing of that kind. There wasn't the slightest chance for him to win. The town would have made short work of him when they found out what was going on. And even if they didn't, the courts would have put a stop to his plans in short order. The whole story is bound to come out—Patrick's plot, the shooting of Shorty, and all that led up to today's killing. And when it does, Sulphide will be an almighty unhealthy place for several people."

"It's Si that concerns me most now," remarked Mrs. Macklay. "He never in the world will forgive Patrick and I'm afraid he'll follow him till he catches up with him, and then there'll be more trouble."

"Not much chance for Patrick, if he does," said Macklay grimly. "And he will, of course, and nothing on earth can stop him."

"Well, they mustn't meet," answered his wife.

"You go downtown, John Macklay, and tell Patrick he'd better get out of town at once. There's been enough killings over this mine already, without having any more."

"Probably there'll have to be another one, my dear," responded her husband. "Si's not the man to let a thing of this kind go by without seeking to even the score. It's born in him, and all his life he's been trained in the law of the frontier, with its crude but simple code of rapid justice —an eye for an eye and a tooth for a tooth. It can't be helped or stopped; and I've enough faith in Si and the outcome not to be at all enthusiastic about stopping it."

"Well, you ought to be in some better business than abetting murder, John Macklay," answered his wife disdainfully.

"It's not murder, my dear; it's the working out of the law of the frontier—the primitive law of primitive man. You can't judge this situation by the standards of New York or Massachusetts. I don't think that's derogatory to Sulphide, either. When the town folks know the facts, they'll take it as a matter of course that Si will fight; and if he should fail to—which he won't—he would be ostracized. The only chance is that Patrick will leave town, and to tell you the truth, I don't think there's much chance of that. Bill Patrick is a good deal of a man; he is neither a coward nor a weakling. He has a code of his own that might not meet your approval nor mine, but my guess is that his code will keep him in town to face the music and fight it out if necessary.

"Of course," he continued, "the last thing he would have wanted was for Randt to do just what he did. Patrick's no fool. He knows what the consequences are likely to be. He knows that there was no combination of circumstances that could possibly have occurred that would make Randt's action other than the wildest kind of folly. To that extent he's as innocent of Ike's death as you or I, but there's not one chance in a million that Si will look at it that way. Si's young, with all the emotions, enthusiasm and courage of youth, and when he learns of this there'll be but one thought in his mind. It's the primitive savage cropping out, and it's useless to try to stop it."

"Well, at least I can get Mary a cup of soup," answered Mrs. Macklay, in anything but a placated voice; "it's past noon, and it's time to give that child a little nourishment."

She prepared a simple lunch, which she put on the table. Then she went into the parlor. Mary had ceased crying and was sitting in utter dejection, exhausted and crushed.

"Come, my dear," said Mrs. Macklay. "I want you to have a little soup and then lie down for an hour or two and rest quietly. You needn't come to the table, but come to your room with me and I'll bring you something to eat."

As she spoke she gently took the girl in her arms and led her toward her own room. "You go out there and sit down with John, Ralph. You need food almost as much as Mary. I'm going to take her away from you for a while. There'll be plenty of time for you two to be together later."

"Mrs. Macklay is right, Mary," said Ralph to the reluctant girl. "You need rest and food."

"But I need you, too, my dear," she said simply, "more than anything else in the world."

"All in good time, Mary," said Mrs. Macklay, as she pushed the girl gently in the direction of the bedroom. "You lie down for a while. I'll sit beside you, and while I know I'm a poor substitute for Ralph, yet there might be worse, and besides, I want Ralph to talk with John." She led Mary away and motioned Ralph into the outer room.

As they helped themselves to the simple meal, John Macklay and Ralph Lee talked over the events of the day and attempted to forecast the future.

"Si'll never rest, sir, until he meets Patrick face to face."

"I'm afraid not," was the reply. "I've been talking it over with Mother ever since we came in. She wanted me to stop it, or do something to get Patrick out of town; but I told her it was utterly useless."

"You're right, of course, sir. Si won't let Ike go unavenged. And, as a matter of fact, the cowboys out at the ranch won't, either; they'll let Si lead, of course, and look to him for advice. It may end in a pitched battle, or Si may fight it out alone with Patrick."

"The latter probably," said the older man, "unless Patrick assembles a crowd and starts a general row. But I think that is unlikely. You and I'd better go downtown and see Sim and find out what has happened since the shooting. Patrick has been badly served. There was almost as much folly in what Graves attempted as in what Randt did. Neither effort had the least hope of success, and both made the final result a foregone conclusion."

After finishing the meal they went into the bedroom where Mrs. Macklay was sitting beside the girl. Mary's soup bowl was empty.

"I'm all right," she said with a wan smile, "just getting my nerves quieted down; but I should feel better still, Mother," she said, "if Ralph could hold my hand for a minute."

Mrs. Macklay smiled and moved aside, and Ralph took the vacant chair, kissing Mary as he sat down. Taking her hands, he said, "Mr. Macklay and I are going downtown, dear, to find out what has happened since we brought you home. Don't worry about us. We'll be back shortly, and in the meantime take a good rest."

As Macklay and Ralph went out, they passed the foreman's wife, sitting in a chair on the porch. "Jim's gone back to the mine," she said, "and I'm going to stay here for a while, and then one of the other women will come over and keep visitors away. Jim's going to have one of the men come over too, and he's coming back himself soon as he comes up from underground."

Macklay nodded approval, and he and Ralph went out

through the gate and down the hill towards the town.

The most pressing problem at the moment was how to get word of the tragedy to Si. Macklay's first impulse was to send one of the cowboys with the message, but second thought told him that this was a waste of time. The telegraph line to Elko would save hours, provided the right man could be found in Elko to carry the message out to Si's camp. It should not be difficult for any one at all familiar with the country to follow instructions and find the location. The road from Elko to Eureka passed close to the Hale ranch, and any one who followed that road for ten miles and then headed direct for the highest peak in the Ruby Range would cut the wagon tracks made by Shorty's outfit. From there on it was a mere matter of following those tracks to the camp.

There was no question as to the best plan to follow, but who was there in Elko to make the ride? Williams, the company agent in Elko, would know; he could be called to the telegraph office and Macklay could talk with him over the wire. Going to the telegraph office he stated the case to Will Gault, who opened his key while Macklay was still talking, and began calling Elko. Williams answered almost immediately. The news of the tragedy had been already flashed to Elko, so no preliminary explanation was necessary. In a few words Gault asked Williams what he could do in the matter of finding a suitable man.

"He says old man Hale's son, Will, is in town, and he's sure he can get him to make the trip," said Gault.

"Tell him to go out and get him at once," replied Macklay.

Again the instrument chattered and Gault translated. "Wants you to write out instructions, and also write the message to Si. While you're doing that he'll go and try to find Hale."

Quickly Macklay wrote out instructions for finding the camp, and also a message to Si telling him of the tragedy and advising him that the funeral would be postponed until he could reach Sulphide. To this he added his sympathy and that of his wife and of Mary and Ralph, and told him that Ralph would meet him on the road coming in to Sulphide. He had scarcely finished when the sounder began to chatter again.

"Says he's got Hale at the instrument, that he is ready to go and wants instructions."

Macklay handed Gault the sheets on which he had written the instructions and the message to Si, and these Gault transmitted at once.

"Wants to know if that's all, and says Hale will leave within half an hour," said Gault.

"There's nothing more for Hale," said Macklay, as he looked at the clock on the office wall, "but there's one thing more you might do. Tell Williams to make arrangements for horses for Si. Tell him to have two in Elko and two at the fifteen-mile house. We will arrange from here to have fresh ones at the half-way house, and we can have two more at Jake's ranch. Hale will look out for the relays between the ranch and Elko. It's moonlight and Hale will have no trouble following tracks; he should be at the mine by midnight or thereabouts. Si will make Elko in the forenoon; with changes of horses that will be waiting for him, he can make the half-way house by afternoon. He should rest there, and leave so's to get here next morning. Then he should rest. I suppose he'll come uptown between eleven o'clock and noon."

Macklay and Ralph found Sim down at the corral looking over the hearse and getting it in condition for use.

"A coroner's jury will meet this afternoon at three o'clock," he said, "and after that they'll take Randt and plant him, without grief or ceremony. Ike's friends are making arrangements for his funeral. We calculate to have it day after tomorrow, if Si gets here by that time. He will, all right. He'll come a-dustin' when he gets the news. Well, anyway, we got plenty of ice, and can wait a day or two longer if necessary. Beats hell what got into that Dutchman; just can't figger it out," he added reflectively, as he waved a feather duster he had been using in dusting off the hearse.

"That's one reason we've come down here, Sim, to tell you the story," said Macklay. "Let's go in the office and sit down, where we can be quiet and undisturbed."

"Set down," said Sim, waving his visitors to chairs in his living room, and biting off a huge chew of tobacco after first offering the plug to the two men. Ralph shook his head, and Macklay fished out a pipe from his pocket, which he proceeded to fill and light.

"This is what we've come to see you about, Sim," he said after one or two contemplative puffs. Then he rapidly told the story of Shorty's discovery and what had come of it. The tale was punctuated, now and then, by exclamations from Sim. By turns he excitedly walked the floor or sat on the edge of the chair with hands on knees, every now and then giving his leg a slap to emphasize his sentiments.

The story having been told, for a moment there was complete silence, broken by a long-drawn sigh from Sim, who said, "Well, I swan. Say, this thing ain't over yet, not by a long shot. Godamighty, what a rip-roaring romance it is.

Heard about the strike, of course, like everybody else in town, but none of us was onto any of the rest of the game. Kinder looks to me, Mr. Macklay, like there's goin' to be some more shootin' round this town afore we're much older."

"Don't you think you could stop it, Sim?"

Sim shook his head. "Not a chance, Mr. Macklay. Si wouldn't listen to nothing of the sort, and them cowboys over at the Circle R would make it their business if Si didn't. And anyway, I have a sort of feelin' that it ain't my job to interfere, any more'n to see that Si gets a square deal. I'll sort of post a few friends of mine around town, to see there's no shennanigan attempted. And beyond that I reckon it's up to Si and Patrick to settle their own difficulties. And," he added as an afterthought, "I reckon that's the opinion of the town, or leastways will be when the town gets the facts."

"Of course, you're right, Sim," replied Macklay. "I hadn't had any idea that there was much chance of stopping this affair now, but I wanted you to confirm my opinion. I had thought of urging Patrick to leave town, but I've hesitated to do that because—well, because I've a notion that Si can take care of himself."

A broad grin spread over the face of the peace officer as he said, "Well, Mr. Macklay, we both feel the same way about it, and all we got to do is to see that everything's on the square and then let 'em fight it out. And under those circumstances I ain't a-worryin' over the outcome. I know several fellers in town I'll run in tomorrow 'n' keep in the calaboose until things blow over. Ain't got nothin' particular agin 'em just now, but I have a suspicion it won't do Si no harm to have them fellers out of the way for a few days.

I've got a notion I won't have to keep 'em there more'n an hour or two after Si lands in town. In fact, I reckon they can go to the funeral, if they want to. Anyway," he added, with a droll expression, "they can come to the funeral next day, and it won't be Si's, neither, nor Ike's."

"I'm afraid," said Ralph, "that Si won't wait for funeral or anything else, but will make a bee-line for Patrick, wherever he may be, and have it out at once."

"Well," said Sim, "the undertaking establishment is only a little way up the street from here, and he has to pass it on his way uptown. He'll stop there long enough to see his brother's remains, and maybe tell him what he's goin' to do. But outside of that, he just naturally ain't goin' to stop more'n long enough to leave his horse here, and maybe he won't stop that long."

"In any event, Sim," said Ralph, "we must stop him here and talk with him or ride out of town to meet him. We can't let him go uptown without full knowledge of what conditions are."

"Guess we'd better do both," said Macklay. "You ride out and meet him, Ralph, and I'll wait here at the corral until you return."

"That brings up another thought," added Macklay. "I'll go to the telegraph office again and see that no messages to or from Patrick on the subject are sent out until after Si arrives. I don't think there's anything more now, Sim, so we'll get on uptown and find out what's goin' on there."

"All right," said Sim. "If you see anything of Sage or Turnbull, them two deputies of mine, ask them what they know. I got them staked out round town to find out what's doing. Them fellows will be mighty handy to have around. Neither one of them gets excited. Sage is the best of the two, only he will get full once in a while. If he's sober, there ain't a better peace officer in all Nevada."

As they passed up the street they stopped at the undertaker's. Silently the two men gazed on the face of their friend, then turned regretfully away and walked up the street. Apparently nothing had happened since the tragedy. Gossip was rife, but none of it touched the truth. The town as yet was ignorant of the real reason back of the killing, and was, of course, unaware of the tragedy that waited only upon the coming of Si Proctor.

One piece of news did, however, interest them. On inquiring for Bill Williams, one of the cowpunchers who came in with Ike, they learned that he had departed in a "cloud of dust" in the direction of the Circle R.

"He went, of course, to tell the boys what happened and probably to bring them back," remarked Ralph, as they stood on the sidewalk in front of the telegraph office, where Macklay had just made arrangements with Gault to hold up any messages to or from Patrick that had to do with the tragedy. "I can't tell you the reason just yet," he had said to Will Gault, "but be assured, Will, my request is in behalf of justice."

"Well, Mr. Macklay," Gault had replied, "since your company owns the line, what you say goes with me."

But Patrick neither sent nor received any message.

"There'll be no holding those punchers when they once know the facts," said Ralph.

"No, there won't," replied Macklay, "but they won't know the real truth, probably, until it's all over. Of course, if Patrick should kill Si, he'd have to fight every man in the outfit afterwards. Any way you figure it out, Ralph, Patrick seems to be doomed.

Just then a messenger from the telegraph office interrupted the conversation to hand Macklay a telegram. "From the doctor in Eureka," he said. "It's in reply to the one I sent, telling him of the killing and warning him to keep it from Shorty. He says Shorty is in no danger and doing splendidly, and he'll see that the news is kept from him for the present. Well, that's one thing to be thankful for. Mother and Mary must know of this at once. They can wait over now until after the funeral before starting for Eureka."

"Meantime, Shorty'll think he's been deserted," remarked Ralph.

"Yes, I suppose he will," said Macklay, "but it can't be helped, and when he knows the truth he'll forgive us. I've only one more thing to do before going home. I must wire Williams in Elko, to telegraph me the arrival and departure of Si. Knowing that, we can figure out fairly well when to expect him. Si will get the news in less than twenty-four hours. Two days should see him here."

Macklay was gone but a moment, and on his return they started off in the direction of the cottage on the hill, where Mrs. Macklay and Mary were waiting anxiously.

Chapter XL

Bill Patrick sat long in deep reflection after Bartle left him.

"We never had a chance," he muttered, "not from the very first. That assayer up at the Con was in on the grub-stake, and Shorty was smart enough to fool the whole lot of us and get me to put up the money for him to start his operations on. What a damn fool I've been, but, by God, I'm Solomon compared to that crazy Dutchman. And I'm the residuary legatee," he added bitterly.

Going downstairs into the saloon, he said to Bartle, "Hank, I'm going to get shaved. If you see Swayne, tell him I want to see him upstairs in my room as soon as I come back."

There were always hangers-on around the saloon, men who were down and out, mostly from whisky. They did odd jobs—carrying wood, sweeping out, running errands and the like.

"Hey, you," Bartle called to one of them, "chase out of here and see if you can find Swayne, and if you find him tell him I want to see him right away."

The man shuffled off and Bartle turned to some customers.

"Ain't found him yet, boss," he said to Patrick when he returned from the barber shop some half-hour later. "I got a feller out lookin' for him, and I guess he'll find him pretty soon."

"Nothing being talked of on the street but the murder," remarked Patrick.

"Yeah, I know," answered Hank. "Nobody comes in here but talks about it, and everybody says it don't make no difference whether Ike got Randt or not, that Si would anyway. They don't just figger out what it's all about. Everybody's wondering what the schoolmarm has to say. When they tackled Macklay on the street he said they hadn't asked her nothin'; she was too upset, and they wanted her to rest."

'That's about what Macklay would say," answered Patrick. "They're not going to set the town on fire just yet."

The half-spoken reply of Bartle was cut short by the entrance of Pete Swayne.

"Somebody lookin' for me?" he asked. There was little about him to inspire confidence, much to cause repulsion. Thick-lipped, coarse-featured, furtive in expression, and unkempt, he was a typical "hard citizen."

"Yes, I sent for you," said Patrick. "You come up to my room as soon as I get there and when nobody is in the saloon. Fact is, I don't want you seen coming or going."

Patrick walked over to the door and disappeared and Swayne, after having a drink on the house, followed him. At the head of the landing a door was open, and walking in he found Patrick sitting by a table nervously biting off the end of a cigar. "Want to make a stake, Pete?" he asked abruptly.

Swayne looked at Patrick keenly for a moment, and answered, "You're damn right I do. What's the game?"

"How far will you go?" ventured Patrick.

"Well, that depends on the price."

"I've got a man I want to keep out of this town, and I want to know if you will undertake the job."

Eyeing Patrick intently, and weighing every word, Swayne answered, "There's only one way I know of to keep a man out of this town permanent, and that's an expensive way, Patrick."

"Well, I'm not finding the way nor discussing your plans, but what I want to know is, what's your price to guarantee to me that Si Proctor will not land in Sulphide?"

"Him?" asked Swayne incredulously, "brother of Ike that was killed this morning by that Dutch assayer?"

"Yes, that's him," said Patrick, as he nervously moistened his lips with his tongue.

"Huh! What's he done to you? That's a hell of a fine job you want me to undertake, and no mistake. The whole town's up in arms now about the killing of his brother, and if some one by mistake was to load Si up with lead and got found out—well, there's lots of telegraph poles in town and plenty of ropes handy! I don't think much of your job, Patrick. But I tell you what I'll do. You give me $1000 and your I.O.U. for $9000 more, and I'll take a chance. Only tell me where he is, can yuh?"

"He's over the other side of the railroad, towards Eureka, and will be getting into Sulphide on horseback day after tomorrow sometime, probably travelling alone."

"Well, you can bet your sweet life I won't tackle him if he ain't," was the reply.

"I won't give you any I.O.U.," said Patrick, "but I will give you the $1000 and my promise to see you get the balance in San Francisco. If you fail, you don't get any more than $1000. Now, you go on downstairs and I'll meet you there shortly and give you the first $1000. Then you make your arrangements to get out of town."

Meanwhile, on the sidewalk a few doors from the Miners Rest, Sim was engaged in conversation with Sage.

"Only thing I've seen," said Sage, "is Swayne comin' up the street and bustin' into the Miners Rest. I got a look at him through a crack in the door, and he met Patrick and followed him upstairs."

"Well, well," said Sim. "I seem to have an idea that Swayne will be the first local resident to land in the jug. You run him in, Sage, when he comes out, And don't give him no chance to draw a gun or get ugly or nothin'. Just bring him in, dead or alive," said the marshal with a twinkle in his eyes and a drawl in his voice.

"Bet I will," was the reply, as Sim drifted off down the street.

Before long Swayne emerged from the Miners Rest and started down the street. Sage fell in behind him, and as Swayne seemed to be going in the direction of the local jail, he made no effort to stop or arrest him, but allowed him to go down the street until they came to the crossroad on which, half a block away, stood the jail.

Coming up briskly behind the unsuspecting Swayne, Sage poked a gun into his midriff, and remarked as he dropped a hand on his collar, "Hands up, Pete, and just keep a-goin' up the side street to your hotel, where we calculate to take good care of you for a while."

Promptly, with the feel of the gun in his ribs, and a quick sideways glance to see who was behind him, Swayne's hands went up into the air and he started down the street, as directed, cursing roundly and wanting to know what the hell-'n'-damnation he was being run in for.

"Just keep your shirt on a little while, old hoss, and you'll know more about it than I do," was all the reply his captor vouchsafed.

It was but a few steps to the jail, and as they entered the jailer met them and led the way into the room that served as an office. Deftly Sage ran his hands over his captive, and somewhat to his surprise found him unarmed.

"Thought you might have a gun," said Sage, somewhat apologetically, "maybe we made a mistake, after all. But anyway, Sim said to bring you in, so I got to keep you here till I see him; and, of course, we got to search you."

This latter suggestion brought forth a torrent of objections and abuse and vehement demands to know what the hell it was all about.

"Keep your shirt on, old hoss, keep your shirt on," was the soothing rejoinder of Sage, "and put your hands up so's Andy here can see what you got in your pockets; 'cause if you don't" said Sage menacingly, "I'll bat you over the head with this gun and you're down for the count."

Seeing it was useless to object longer, Swayne raised his hands, still cursing roundly. Deftly Andy went through his pockets, with little success until he came to an inside coat pocket from which, to his amazement and the equal amazement of Sage, he extracted ten one-hundred dollar bills.

"Well, what's this cache?" asked Sage, as Andy counted them over. All that he got in reply from Swayne was a venomous glare.

"Oh, well, don't take it so hard, Pete. You'll probably get it back and be turned loose with apologies shortly. But meanwhile, Andy, lock him up." This, amid a volley of oaths and protests, Andy did.

Stuffing the money into the safe, Andy entered the prisoner's name, pausing to ask inquiringly, "What charge?"

"Don't know," grunted Sage. "Sim said to bring him in and I brung him."

"I'll hold it up till you find out," was the reply.

"All right, I'll come back and let you know." Sage started off up the street to report to Sim that the arrest had been made.

"And you say he had $1000 on him?" said Sim shortly, but with a hard stare in his eyes when Sage told him what had occurred.

"Bet your life he did."

"Well, I wasn't far wrong in my guess," opined Sim. "There's a few more you can take in when you meet 'em." Sim ticked off on his fingers several names. "And you can trot right back to that calaboose and tell Andy not to let on to any one who's in there. I don't want the town, or none of its citizens, to know we're collecting a rogue's gallery of our own. Leastways," he amended, "not until after Si Proctor and Bill Patrick have had a little personal interchange of compliments.

"And don't be in a hurry about runnin' them other fellers in. I don't feel like pervidin' too many free meals, and, anyway, if they all disappear at once people will begin to ask questions, and I don't want to excite no curiosity sooner than's necessary. Just kind of keep an eye on 'em, and if you see any of 'em leavin' town, or acting queer, why just wait a good chance and land 'em along with our distinguished friend you have so recently and unkindly deprived of his liberty.

"Reckon a lot of the sistern and brethren back East that's all the time talking about what an awful wild and woolly place the West is would be throwin' forty fits a minute if they knew what was a-doin' here in Sulphide. But," he added with a glare, "all the fool cranks in the United States ain't goin' to stop me from seein' that Si Proctor gets a square deal."

Chapter XLI

LATE that afternoon the coroner's jury heard the evidence of the witnesses to the tragedy. The hearing was held in the Masonic Hall, the one room of any size in the town. It was crowded to the doors. The overflow on the sidewalk outside and the crowd inside eagerly discussed the tragedy and speculated on what would develop at the hearing.

Mr. and Mrs. Macklay, with Mary, were seated close to the jury with several other witnesses, including Curnow, the foreman of the Con, Fleming, the mill foreman, and one or two others who had been close by when the attack was made. The star witness, of course, was Mary Clark. Macklay had arranged with the coroner that her testimony should be taken first, so that she might slip out. She was none too calm and the ordeal at best would be a trying one. They had talked it over before coming down from the mine, and it had been agreed that it would be unwise at this time to make public all the facts.

"Justice will not be served in any way, Mary," remarked Macklay, "and if you were to tell the whole story you would be adding fuel to the flames. In the frame of mind that the town is in at the present time, it wouldn't take much to arouse the mob spirit to a point where some one would suggest a rope, and how many innocent people might be killed in the ensuing mêlée is hard to say. Patrick, of course, would not surrender without a fight, and never alive. He has some followers who might stick with him, and barricaded in his rooms over the Miners Rest he could put up a desperate fight. Given provocation, there is no doubt that the mob would fire his saloon, with the result that all Sulphide might be in ashes when it was over.

"You must confine yourself to a statement of just what happened. They may ask questions, and undoubtedly will try to find out what the motive was behind it all. Those questions you will have to answer as best you can, but try to keep Patrick out of it. You will no doubt have to discuss the attempt to get you to sign a deed, but what was back of that you need not attempt to clarify. Remember, the fewer names you mention, the less likelihood there is of more trouble. Take all the time you like in answering the questions. The members of the jury will all be your friends, and, of course, will be anxious to cause you as little annoyance as possible."

At a large table at the end of the hall the coroner was seated, surrounded by several deputies and newspaper men. At a little distance the jury sat in chairs arranged in two rows of six each. It was a typical Western jury, somewhat self-conscious, and gathered by the deputies under the coroner's directions. It consisted of two stockmen from nearby ranches; the postmaster; the express company agent; the Episcopal clergyman; three miners, caught as they were going on shift, apparently much to their disgust, judging from the remarks they addressed to the deputy when he handed them the summons; and two teamsters, whose freight-wagons happened to be in town. Every available chair had been collected and placed in rows facing the jury; these had long since been occupied. The standing room around the walls and at the back of the room was filled long before the coroner rose and hammered on the table preparatory to opening the proceedings. Conversations terminated abruptly, the hum subsided, every one turned expectantly in the direction of the speaker.

"Fellow citizens," he began, "it is the duty of the jury here assembled to bring in a verdict after the testimony has been presented. It is the duty of the audience to keep still and not attempt to show approval or disapproval by stamping, hand-clapping, or verbal remarks. It ain't a question of what your sympathies may be, and I guess we all got our opinions, but it's a question of what the facts are, regardless of what we think about 'em. We all know something of what's happened. And we'll know more before we get through this afternoon. But whether we do or don't ain't the question. The question is—are you going to keep quiet, or are you going to be thrown out? Big Sim is here with some of his deputies and I got some here, too. The bunch of 'em has instructions from me to preserve order. So all you fellers has got to do if you want to sit it out is to shut up."

He turned in the direction of the witnesses and said, "The first witness will be Miss Mary Clark. I will ask you, Miss Clark, to take the stand, be sworn, and tell what you know of this shooting."

Mary rose and walked to the witness chair, held up her hand and took the oath, and then seated herself. There was little about her to show the ordeal through which she had passed, and save for the clasping and unclasping of her hands and an occasional nervous movement of the body, she might have been sitting in the chair at her desk in the schoolroom.

"Now, Miss Clark," began the coroner, who was one of the school trustees, "will you please state to us just what happened at the schoolhouse?"

Save for the rustle as the audience moved forward on the chairs the better to hear the testimony, there was absolute silence as Mary began her recital. Slowly and with a well-modulated voice she spoke of the morning at the schoolhouse and of the trustees' meeting, and how after it was over Randt came to her demanding that she sign over to him the ownership of the claims Shorty had located. She told of the grubstake, of the discovery, and of Shorty's desire that she hold title in case something happened to him. She spoke of the assaying by Randt as the means through which he had acquired information as to the claims and their value. She told of his coming to the schoolhouse, of his attempt to coerce her into signing the deed, and of her escape. Then she faltered, and her voice became tremulous and tears filled her eyes as she spoke of her flight. "If you don't mind," she said, "I should like to stop now; there is nothing more I can add about what happened after that, beyond what other witnesses know, and I hope you will let them finish the story."

There were nods of approval and a shuffling of feet as a murmur of sympathy ran over the room when the girl buried her face in her hands and sobbed. Mrs. Macklay came forward and at a nod from the coroner took the girl by the hand and with an arm around her waist led her from the room through the closely packed spectators, who crowded back to make way for the two women as they left the hall.

Ralph Lee was the next witness, and taking up the story where Mary left off, he related how he had raced down the hill, stopped to speak to Mary, and then gone on in the direction of the cabin, only to find his friend Ike dying and Randt already dead. He could add nothing to what she had said about the events prior to the shooting, other than to amplify her statement about the claims, their ownership, and the general plan for their operation. He spoke of their desire to keep things quiet until they had some work done and the surveys made and the title generally perfect, so that if there were any trouble they would be in the strongest possible position.

Then John Macklay, Curnow, the mine foreman, and others gave their testimony. Before viewing the bodies, the coroner rose and summed up the case for the benefit of the jury and the audience.

"It is the duty of this jury," he said, "to bring in a verdict. As both of the men who took part in the shooting are dead, and as the facts have been vouched for by a number of reputable witnesses, there ain't much for this jury to do other than take a look at the remains and come to a verdict. That ain't difficult, under the circumstances. It's been proved that Randt knew about this prospect quite a while back, and that he made up some fool plan to grab it himself. God knows what he figured he'd do with it after he got it. I reckon it wouldn't have taken this town long to put him right about it, when once they got the facts of the case. Well, anyway, he done it; and he got what was a-comin' to him; only it don't seem on the square for a man like Ike Proctor to have to sacrifice his own life in squaring things with a skunk. I ain't, of course, a-tellin' this jury what kind of a verdict they should render, but I am calling their attention to some of the facts in the case, so they won't overlook nothing. We don't seem to have dug up any pardners of the late deceased, and there ain't any one who seems to have known whether he had any or not. If there's anybody here who has any information on that point, I wish he would step forward and advise the jury so the aforesaid pardners can be rounded up and held as parties to the conspiracy."

As he spoke he glanced around the hall, but no one came forward to add to the testimony already given. Sim afterwards said to Macklay, "Gosh, I wanted to holler right out and tell that crowd what you told me about Patrick, but in the frame of mind them fellers in that room was in, why, say, Patrick wouldn't have lasted ten minutes. I didn't want to start no riot, and I kind of had a notion that Bill Patrick would be cared for in due time and in a manner most satisfactory to everybody except Patrick; so I just remembered what the coroner had said about keepin' still, and I kept my mouth shut and let it go at that."

No one coming forward, the coroner resumed, "The jury will now view the deceased. You folks can sit here till we come back, or you can all go home. Anyway, it won't take us long."

He rose, and motioning to the jury, led them out of the hall and down the street to the building used as a morgue, where all that was mortal of Hans Randt lay in a simple redwood box. One by one the jury passed in front of it and looked upon his features. Most of them had known him well. He was not unpopular with them. His foreign accent and brusque manner were taken more as a joke than anything else, and as they passed some of them shook their heads as if it were a mystery that had something back of it which they did not know, which perhaps they would never know. Then at the undertaking parlor they viewed the remains of Ike Proctor, The formalities over, the coroner suggested that one of them act as foreman and come to a verdict. This brought forth a reply from one of the cowmen, "Hell, Bill, what's the use of goin' to all that trouble? We all know our minds, and the verdict don't need no studyin' over. Ike Proctor came to his death by a pistol bullet fired by Hans Randt, and Ike killed Randt—and it's a damn shame that Ike didn't fire a little quicker."

For a moment the coroner looked at the jury with a quizzical expression, and then a broad smile overspread his face as he asked, "Is that your verdict, gentlemen?"

"Good as any other," remarked one of the miners; but the clergyman protested.

"I don't at all approve of the language used, but heartily approve of the sentiment; and if you will permit me, I suggest that the verdict be changed to make two sentences; the first to stop with the word 'Randt,' the second to read, 'We regret that Proctor did not fire sooner.'"

With some demur, this verdict was finally agreed upon and the jury started back to the hall.

When Big Sim heard of it afterwards, he remarked to Macklay, "That sky pilot knows his business; he knowed he just couldn't get the crowd to withdraw their expression of regret that Ike was slow on the draw, so he toned it down to fit the occasion. I wonder what some of his ministerial friends back East would say about it, if it ever came to their ears? Most likely they'd want to throw him out of the church—and that's about all they know of how things is done here in the West."

Slowly the jury filed back into the hall, and again the coroner rapped for order as he turned and asked, "Gentlemen of the jury, have you agreed upon a verdict?"

Stepping forward, the cattleman replied, "We have," and read the verdict already agreed upon.

The coroner thanked them, and the meeting adjourned to the street, where it was discussed from every angle, especially from that of whether there had been any partners in on the venture. On this subject the town rather unanimously agreed that Randt was not alone in the scheme.

Attending coroner's inquests was dry work, so the crowd adjourned to the neighboring saloons and over their drinks discussed the pros and cons of the case. Hank Bartle was all eyes and ears, and with a few well-directed questions soon had the facts. Later in the day he joined Patrick in his room and related the gossip he had gathered.

"And you can bet your life, Bill, that crowd would string you up in a minute if they got wind of the real facts. I don't know why they done it, but Macklay and the whole outfit kept your name out of it from first to last. Nobody's the wiser for that inquest, and nobody's got hurt except the preacher and he only got his feelin's hurt because they wanted to swear and he wouldn't stand for it."

"But they're getting pretty close, Hank, and a few words from Macklay or Lee or the school teacher, and the town would know the truth."

"You bet I know that, Bill, and I got to say I think you're all kinds of a damn fool for not getting out of town. I think they all got the idea that this is Si Proctor's party, not the town's, and they are just naturally layin' back and waitin' for Si to come here. And when he comes, Bill, you ought to be in California."

Patrick shook his head in the negative, and puffed his cigar for a moment before replying.

"No, Hank, I've dealt the hand and now I'm going to

play it out. I don't amount to much, after all. There isn't a damn soul in the world that would care one way or another. In six months they would even forget Bill Patrick's name. And as for Bill Patrick," he added bitterly, "why he is just damn fool enough to think he couldn't live with himself if he turned tail and took to the tall timber. So you see, Hank, there ain't anything else to do but stay and see it through."

"Well, Bill, I can't help admir'n' your nerve—it's grand. But as for me, I'd rather be a live coward than a dead hero, any day. You're in for a hell of a time, Bill, and I want to go on record that I did all I could to get you out of town."

"Yes, I'll testify to that, Hank, but it's no use, so you go back and take care of the bar and keep your eyes and ears open, and if you get anything of real interest, let me know."

Slowly Bartle left the room, with many a shake of the head and backward look, and went downstairs to his bar, where he again began to polish and arrange the glasses.

On his way home after the inquest Macklay met Sim coming out of the postoffice.

"When is Si due?" asked Sim.

"Two days from today. You don't expect to stop him, do you, Sim?"

A smile gradually spread over Sim's face, as he replied, "Not exactly, but I got to have an alibi as to myself. I want to testify I warned him."

"And then post men all over town to see fair play?" said Macklay.

"Well, they'll be posted to keep the peace. Of course," he added hastily, "if anything was to happen, all of a sudden, maybe the men wouldn't be quick enough to stop it."

And he solemnly winked one eye. "Fact is, Mr. Macklay, this here feud is going to be fought out in spite of all the peace officers in Nevada, and I'm betting on Si; but I got to make some kind of a showin' as a peace officer.

"Another thing, Mr. Macklay," he went on, "this here town is going to get the idea before it's much older that there's something doing—or, leastways will be when Si arrives. Lot's of 'em have plenty time to spare for speculating what it's all about, and somebody who knows something is going to drop a word or two, and pretty soon Patrick's name'll be mentioned, and then it's all off. By the time Si gets here the whole town'll be settin' on the edge of the sidewalks just a-waitin' for things to happen—and you can bet your life things won't lose importance by being talked about, neither."

Chapter XLII

WILL HALE left Elko promptly and rode through to the Hale ranch. There he arranged with his father for the relay horses for the return trip, and after a hasty meal mounted a fresh horse and started for the camp that was yet miles away. The moon afforded ample light and he easily followed the main wagon road until he thought he was far enough along to turn off and head across country to the road that would lead him to the camp. He cut across through the sagebrush and struck the road leading to the mine. Following it, he finally saw the white canvas of the tents shining in the moonlight and the stream of water rushing down the mountainside.

It was after midnight as he rode up to the camp. A corral with several animals in it attracted his attention, and, removing saddle and bridle, he turned his horse into the enclosure. He then went to the largest tent, where the canvas flap that served as a door was fastened back. He saw in the dim light of the interior a number of sleeping men.

"Hey, you fellers," he called, as he entered the tent, "which one of you is Si Proctor?"

The men started up, one of them saying as he did so, "I'm Si Proctor."

"Wish you'd come outside for a few minutes; I got something to say to you. I'm Will Hale, of the Bar Z ranch."

As Hale spoke, he backed out of the tent into the moonlight and waited for Proctor, who quickly followed him. Walking a little distance from the tent and out of hearing of the men, Hale waited for Si's coming.

"Williams, the agent for the Sulphide Con at Elko, asked me to ride out here and find you. I'm mighty sorry, Proctor, to have to bring you bad news—your brother was shot and killed, in Sulphide yesterday. Hans Randt did it; but before he died your brother killed Randt. Here's the note to you from Mr. Macklay."

For a moment Si stood as though carved out of stone, and then reached for the envelope Hale held out to him.

"Just excuse me for a few minutes, will you, Hale?" he said, as he turned and walked into the mess tent, where he lit a candle and read the message.

"Poor old Ike," he murmured, "just like him to open that door and rush in; he never was afraid of nothing, and to think that that Dutchman who don't know a six-shooter from a Bowie knife should have got the drop on him."

Meanwhile, the other men clustered about Hale as he stood outside in the moonlight. To their questions he replied by relating the news of the tragedy.

"I reckon," said the sheriff, who was one of the group, "Si'll be startin' for Sulphide pretty pronto now. He'll want to see his brother and be at the funeral."

They talked among themselves until Si came up.

"Boys," he said, "I reckon Hale has told you what's happened. I ain't got nothin' to add to it, only I'm pulling out for Sulphide. You boys got to stay here and keep working while I'm gone. Got to rely on you, too, Sheriff. Want to ask you if you won't stay here and keep an eye on the claims for me for a few days."

"You bet I will, Si," was the reply. "I'll just naturally take charge for you while you're gone; and you can rely on one thing, Si," he added, "there ain't a-goin' to be no claim-jumpin' round here, if I have to swear in half of Eureka county to keep the peace.

"And, of course, Si," the sheriff continued, "the whole business is irregular. I ain't really got no right to turn you loose this way, but I'm just relying on your word that you'll come back here and surrender pretty pronto."

"Reckon you wouldn't let me go, Sheriff, unless you knowed I was coming back," said Si. "And I'm mighty obliged to you for letting me go."

"Just as well," remarked the sheriff, as he watched Si's retreating figure, "that that assayer is dead. If he wasn't, he wouldn't last long after Proctor got to Sulphide. Wonder if the Dutchman had any pardners. Maybe he had, and maybe Si knows who they be. Well, they got to have a first-class alibi when he gets there, if they don't want to get into trouble."

Si soon returned, leading his horse. "Just want to thank you, Hale, for what you done for me," he said simply.

"That's all right, Proctor," was the reply. "You'd do as much for me any day. There's a horse waiting for you at the ranch, and Williams has fixed things for you in Elko, and you'll have changes ready all along the road; all you got to do is to tell 'em who you are. My old man'll be on the lookout for you and so will all the others."

Si dropped the bridle rein and entered the tent. He came out in a minute holding a coat under one arm and strapping a six-shooter around his waist with his free hand. As he picked up the bridle rein and threw it over his horse's head, the men began to express their sympathy for him and to wish him a safe trip and speedy return.

"All right, fellers," he said, as he settled himself in the saddle. "Keep the old camp goin' while I'm gone. Get out plenty of ore and get it shipped. Sheriff'll look after any ambitious citizens trying to grab something that don't belong to 'em, won't you, Sheriff?"

"Bet I will, Si, and here's wishin' you a quick and safe return."

"I'll be back in a few days, boys, all right," said Si, as he started his horse into a gallop and disappeared in the moonlight.

It was five o'clock when Si rode up to the Hale ranch and dismounted. Hale was beside him as he swung down from his horse.

"You get into the house, Proctor," he said, "and get some grub; Mrs. Hale has got it waiting for you. I'll take care of your horse, and saddle a fresh one for you and have it ready before you finish breakfast."

"Thank you, Mr. Hale. You folks are sure good to me, and I aim not to forget it. Can't think of much else but my brother just now, and I ain't much of a hand at expressing my feelings, anyhow, but I won't forget your kindness."

Si turned and walked toward the house, and Hale began unsaddling Si's horse. He turned the horse into the corral and roped a fresh animal, which he saddled and bridled. He led the animal to the hitching post, tied him there, and went into the house.

Mrs. Hale had taken Si to the basin and pail of water on the back porch, and while he washed she had placed the coffee, bacon and eggs, and biscuits on the table.

"You go right ahead and eat, son," she said when Si came into the kitchen. "Reckon you won't want to do much talking, so sit right down."

"I don't feel much like talkin', ma'am," Si answered as he sat down. "Just can't seem to realize what's happened. Me and my brother was awful close to each other; always figured on having a ranch somewheres of our own. Thought it was all worked out for us when we got our interest in Shorty Peterson's claims. You see, Ike was comin' over to work with me when it happened; and now I got to go on alone. It's mighty tough."

Mrs. Hale put an arm across his shoulders and patted his head, as she replied, "Don't think about it, son. Just go on and eat what you want. I understand." And she walked out to the front door to meet her husband.

"Let the boy alone, Paw, he ain't in no frame of mind to talk to any one; he just wants to be alone to himself." They walked out onto the front porch and stood there talking until Si came out and joined them.

"Mighty obliged to you, Mrs. Hale, and to you, Mr. Hale, for what you've done for me. I got to get agoin', now."

Both of the older people protested that they had done nothing, and shook hands with Si and wished him Godspeed. He turned and went down the steps, tightened the cinch on the horse, untied the hitch-rope, mounted, and with a wave of his hand was off in the direction of Elko.

Hard riding brought Si in sight of the town shortly after nine o'clock. His coming had been expected; from the roof of the stable a lookout had seen the lone horseman coming from the direction of the Hale ranch. A horse had been brought out, and when Si dismounted all was in readiness to change the saddle to the fresh animal. Williams, the agent of the Sulphide Con, had been summoned and was at the corral when Si arrived.

"Got things all fixed for you, Proctor," he said. "Got

fresh horses every twenty miles. Mr. Macklay says to tell you that Ralph Lee'll meet you at Jake's ranch and ride in from there with you. The funeral is set for tomorrow afternoon at three o'clock. Mr. Macklay thinks you better hang up at the halfway house for the night and ride in from there in the early morning; you can make it by dark tonight, and if you get started early you'll be in Sulphide before eight o'clock."

Good wishes were quickly spoken, and with a wave of his hand Si was on the road again headed for Sulphide. All day he rode, changing horses at the various stations, as arranged by Williams.

Chapter XLIII

The Macklays had no means of knowing just what time Si might arrive. "Not before daylight, anyway," said Mr. Macklay in reply to a question from Mary before they retired. None of them slept well, Mary least of all. For hours she turned and tossed in a vain effort to find forgetfulness. Occasionally she would drop into a doze, only to dream of what had happened or what she felt might happen, and then awake with a start. Once she screamed in her sleep, and Mrs. Macklay came hastily into her room to soothe and quiet her. She finally fell into a restless sleep an hour or so before dawn, but with the first light of morning she awakened.

Mrs. Macklay and Mary prepared some breakfast, but none of them ate with any relish. Little was said at the breakfast table.

Ralph Lee had left the afternoon before for Jake's ranch. He had led an extra horse for Si to ride on the return trip. From the porch of the house Mary had seen him leave Sim's Corral, jog down the Elko road, ascend the slight grade, and disappear over the top.

At eight o'clock, Mrs. Macklay and Mary, having finished their household duties, sat down on the front porch with their eyes fixed on the Elko road. John Macklay, in the meantime, had gone up to the mine office, where he took up his daily routine. But he was unable to keep himself from dwelling on the occurrences of the last few days.

He stirred uneasily in his chair, as he thought of coming events, and kept glancing at the clock. "It's no use," he murmured, "I'm fit for nothing and shan't be until the day is over. I might as well saddle up and go down to Sim's corral and pass the time there with him as be sitting here wasting my time doing nothing."

He rose as he spoke, left the office and went over to the stable, where he ordered his horse and stood idly conversing with the stableman as he saddled it.

As he rode past the house Mrs. Macklay called, "Where are you going, John?"

He drew rein by the gate as he answered, "I'm going to go down to Sim's to wait there until Si comes. He ought to be along some time within an hour. I want to meet him there and talk to him before he goes uptown. I haven't any idea I'll make any headway, but I shall at least have an easy conscience, knowing that I did all I could to prevent trouble."

"Do you think I could do anything if I went down to the corral?" interposed Mary.

"Not a thing in the world, my dear. You would simply create an embarrassing situation. It is important that Si should not be disturbed or crossed in any way at this time. He needs all the steadiness of nerve that he can command, and the fewer of us that see him until this affair is over, the better it will be for all of us. This is no time or place for women to be in evidence. The two of you stay here, just where you are on the porch, or, better still, go in the house."

"Well, we certainly shan't go in the house," said Mrs. Macklay. "If we can't come downtown, we can at least sit here on the porch."

With a shrug of the shoulders John Macklay rode down

the hill. He saw nothing unusual; as he rode along the street, he saw no evidence of any tension in the community. Several pedestrians waved greetings to him. Will Gault was standing in the doorway. Macklay called, "Any messages for me this morning?"

"Not a one, Mr. Macklay," said Gault.

"Nothing from Williams?"

Gault shook his head and Macklay rode on.

At the corral he found Sim sitting on the shady side of the house tipped back against the wall, with his eyes closed.

Sim opened one eye and said, "Hello, Mr. Macklay."

Dismounting, Macklay dropped his reins to the ground. He brought a chair out of the office and seated himself facing Sim with his feet against the wall of the house. "What's new this morning, Sim?"

"Not much. I got about all the tough citizens in the calaboose, cooling their heels, and I got some sharp-shooters staked out on the tops of some of the houses. Two or three fellers is ready to kind of see that there ain't no advantage taken of a lone citizen peacefully strolling up the main street."

"What time do you expect they'll get here, Sim?"

"Ought to be soon now, I reckon. I'm going to try to persuade him to go in my shack and lay down for an hour or so," he continued, "so's to kind of rest up before he starts uptown."

"Think he'll do it, Sim?"

"Oh, I reckon he will. Patrick ain't a-goin' to be around much before noon, and after Si has seen his brother and come back here and sort of got ready to take a little rest, I reckon it won't be more than nine-thirty, say.

"Well, anyway, I done everything I could to get him a

square deal, and after I make a kind of formal protest, just for the sake of appearances, I figger that I've about done all that I'm called on to do. I'll just kind of walk up the street before he does and see that the boys are all set, and take a sort of general look around, so's when he comes he won't be thinking much about anything except the feller that's in front of him. We can take care of the rear all right."

"Seen anything of Patrick?"

"Yes, I saw him yesterday for a spell, in his saloon. He didn't have anything to say, kind of looked as though he'd like to cut my heart out if he had the chance. Some of the boys must have told him about his friends that I run in. Whole town knows about it now, gossiping from one end of the street to the other what it's all about. Sage tells me that some of them have begun to hook up Si and Patrick because some of Patrick's friends have been locked up. Town's a-buzzing all right, and when they see Si Proctor walking up the centre of the street and a few curious citizens with guns a-peerin' down from the tops of some of the houses, I reckon it won't take 'em long to be sure of something they suspect already.

"Reckon that's them, a-comin' right now," went on Sim as he got up with sudden animation, straightened his six-feet-four, and gazed intently down the Elko road. Two horsemen had just come into sight over the brow of the hill.

Macklay sprang up and gazed at them. The riders were coming at a gallop now in a cloud of dust, side by side.

"That's them," said Sim.

As they looked the horsemen swept on up the road. Ralph pulled up close to the two men and called to them, "Si's going up to see his brother and will be right back."

He spurred his horse forward until he was again abreast of Proctor.

Side by side they dismounted, allowing their bridle reins to drag on the ground, and went into the coroner's office.

"I want to see my brother, Ike Proctor," said Si to the undertaker.

The man rose to his feet. "Well, just come along this way with me, son," he said, opening a door and motioning Si into an adjoining room.

There, in a plain coffin, Si found his brother. There were no marks on the face, and the dead boy lay almost as though asleep. Si had taken off his hat as he came into the room, and holding it in one hand he stood beside the coffin, while he placed his other hand over that of his brother.

"I just wanted to tell you, Ike," he said, "that I come to town to see Bill Patrick. He can't get away with anything like this and live. I'm going uptown to find him, and when I find him, Ike, I'm going to think of you."

Tears welled into his eyes and trickled down his dust-stained face. Ralph Lee stood reverently in the background. It might have been five minutes, it might have been ten, when Si turned away from the coffin. Then he looked back, dropped his hat, and placing both hands upon those of his brother, said, "Good-bye, Ike. I was fixing up such a wonderful time for you and me in the future, and now I got to go on all alone."

He turned as he spoke, picked up his hat from the floor and walked out of the building, looking neither to the right nor the left. A crowd had collected upon the sidewalk. They fell back to give him passage. He turned to Ralph and said, "I reckon we better go back to the corral now."

They mounted their horses and rode back down the street to Sim's corral.

"Hey, Joe," called Sim to one of the hostlers, "take these two hosses and put 'em in the corral."

"You come on with me, son," he said to Si as he hooked his arm into Si's and led him in the direction of the house. Entering with Macklay and Ralph, he shut the door and motioned Si to a dilapidated couch that was in one corner of the room. "Better lie down on that for a few minutes, Si," he said, "just want to have a little talk with you, son. You see, I'm the town marshal of this here Sulphide and it's my duty to kind of call upon everybody to keep the peace."

Si threw himself down on the couch with his head buried in his arms. He made no sound.

"I reckon I know, son, what you got in your mind," Sim continued, "and, unofficially, I ain't got nothin' to say, but officially and without any idea that you're goin' to take it seriously, I just kind of want to warn you that this is supposed to be a peaceable community."

Still there was no sound from the recumbent figure.

"Well, goldarn it, what *are* you goin' to do next, any way?"

"Reckon you know, Sim," said Si at last, without moving, "what I came here from the mine for. Ralph told me this morning out at Jake's ranch all about what happened and we talked some more about it as we rode in, and he told me about the fellers you had run into the calaboose and how you said that you reckoned you was goin' to see that I got a square deal. Well, I'm much obliged to you for that, Sim. I ain't got a pleasant job on my hands, but I ain't got no compunctions about killing Bill Patrick when I see him, and I reckon he can't shoot quick enough not to get killed."

"So you've made up your mind, have you, Si, that you're going uptown and tackle Patrick?"

"You know durn well I have, Sim."

"Yes, I reckon I knowed about as soon as it happened what was a-coming, and I been kind of consultin' with Mr. Macklay here and a few others to kind of keep a vigilante committee in line just so none of them skunks around town would try any rough stuff. We're all ready for you, Si. The town's pretty well policed. I'll be walking uptown ahead of you, and Sage behind you; and you'll see some of the boys on the roofs of the houses as you go up the street, but don't get skeered 'bout them cause they're all your friends. What I want you to do now, son, is to just lay still and rest for a hour or two, and don't think 'bout nothin' at all. Just take it easy for a couple of hours. Don't suppose you could snooze, but if you could, it would be a good thing. But anyway, we're going out and goin' to shut the door, and Ralph'll sit here and kind of keep you company."

Alone with Ralph, Si lay upon the couch, his head buried in his arms. Ralph sat still.

Half an hour passed this way. Then Si rolled over and said, "You know, I'd kind of like to wash up, Ralph; got a lot of dust on my face and in my hair, and I believe I'd feel better if I'd wash some of it off."

He went into the adjoining kitchen, found a basin and some warm water, and washed with an abundance of soap. Then he threw himself on the couch full length on his back with his arms under his head. With closed eyes he remained thus for the better part of an hour, quiet and passive.

Then Si began to talk. "You know, Ralph, I'd just kind of like to talk with you now about the future. So far as Patrick is concerned, you needn't be at all alarmed about what's going to happen. I don't like to talk about Ike, so let's talk about the mine." And so for half an hour Si talked of the grubstake and the mine and its future development.

"By the way, Ralph," he said, "just kind of wish you'd get me a piece of paper, will you, and something to write with. I'm just going to write a line or two saying that if by any chance things don't go right, my interest in that mine is for you and Mary. Shorty's got enough anyway, and he ain't got any family, and I know from what he said to me that things will be all right with him. I'll just write out something short, before we get any further along in the day's arrangements."

He got up as he spoke, and seated himself at the table. Ralph found some paper, pen and ink, and Si wrote out and signed the following:

> When I die, I give everything that belongs to me to my friends Ralph Lee and Mary Clark, for them to divide equally between themselves.

"I reckon that will do," he said. "I'll just give this to Mr. Macklay." He folded it up and went back to the couch. "I wish you'd ask Macklay to come here a minute, will you, Ralph?"

When Macklay entered, Si handed him the paper, saying, "I'd just like to have you keep this for me, Mr. Macklay, until I ask for it."

"All right, son," Macklay said, "I'll hang onto it. By the way, Si, Mrs. Macklay and Mary wanted to come down here this morning, but I stopped them. They told me to wish you all the good luck in the world."

"Why, that's mighty kind of them, but it's just as well they didn't come, I reckon. I'm kind of all stirred up over seeing Ike, and I reckon this ain't no time for women-folks to be around, anyway. But you give them my very best, will you, Mr. Macklay?"

"Yes, indeed I will, but I don't see any need of that, because you can speak for yourself, Si."

"Well, I reckon I can, a little later in the day. Must be 'round noon, ain't it, Ralph?" inquired Si.

Ralph looked at his watch and said, "It's about half past eleven now."

"Well, Bill Patrick ought to be 'round by this time, I reckon. It's about time for me to be going on up the street. I'd like to speak to Sim afore I start," he added.

"Don't you think it would be a good thing, Sim, to kind of send word to Patrick that I'm a-lookin' for him?"

"I done that already, while you was lying on that bunk," said Sim. "I sent Sage uptown, and he walked right into Patrick's room and told him that you was in town and was a-lookin' for him and calculated to come up the street somewhere about half-past eleven or twelve o'clock. He said Patrick kind of studied the situation and said, 'All right, he needn't come up here looking for me, I'll meet him down the street.' So it seems things is just kind of fixed and waitin' for you to walk uptown."

"Well, I reckon then it's about time I was leavin'," said Si, as he got up from the couch and stretched himself, picked up his cartridge belt and holster, which he had taken off when he lay down, strapped them on, made a few movements of his arms and legs to limber himself up, experimented several times in drawing his six-shooter, and finally said, "Well, boys, let's go."

He walked out the door with Ralph by his side and met Mr. Macklay, Sage, and Sim in the corral office.

"I'm going to walk up the street alone," he said. I don't want anybody within a hundred feet of me. I'll get out in the centre of the street, and I reckon you and Sage, Sim, better walk along the edge of the sidewalk. Ralph can walk on the sidewalk behind me, and I kind of wish, Mr. Macklay, that you would go along up the other side of the street. I just got one request to make, and that is that if Patrick draws enough quicker than I can that that will end the matter and you'll let him go his way. It's just a quarrel, after all, between me and him, and if he wins I don't want any one else to pick up the quarrel. I wish you'd tell them this in town, too—what I say about it. I kind of feel I got a right to ask that of them."

"Well, I'll do my best to hold 'em," said Sim, "but if so be you don't come through, Si, I reckon it will take more than me or Ralph or Mr. Macklay to hold this town. But, of course, we'll do all we can. Another thing I want to say to you before you start, boy—you keep your eyes on the cross-streets. I got a kind of a notion that Patrick will be dodgin' out of one of them side streets, rather than meet you fair and square half-way between corners."

Si only grinned.

Chapter XLIV

"PARDNER," Si said just as they were starting to walk up the street, "I wish you and your wife all the success in the world and all the happiness that you're entitled to. I reckon we'll go on as pardners for a long time yet, but I kind o' thought this was an appropriate time to give you the good wishes that I intend to repeat at your wedding. And Mrs. Macklay, too, Mr. Macklay; I wish you'd give her my best respects and good wishes."

Ralph and Mr. Macklay nodded their heads, and with a wave of the hand Si went on ahead.

As they left Sim's office, Ralph had noticed that the clock marked a quarter to twelve. "It's curious," he used to remark in after years, "how little things will leave such a lasting impression. Whenever I see a clock marking a quarter to twelve the whole picture of that day in Sulphide comes vividly back to me."

The long, dusty street stretched ahead of them. Overhead the sun in an absolutely clear sky beat down fiercely. Heat waves shimmered in the distance. Two mongrel dogs were fighting. A stray child here and there was suddenly swept up in its mother's arms at the sight of the approaching men. As they walked they could see startled faces of men and women in doorways, some scurrying hurriedly back into the house, others dashing up the street ahead of them to spread the news.

As they approached the centre of the town, Si noticed

several men sitting carelessly on top of the wooden awnings, while others had perched themselves on housetops. Every one of them, Si saw, held a rifle in his hands. Ceaselessly his eyes roamed from side to side. More people had appeared on the sidewalks. Men stood in doorways intently watching the men who walked so silently up the street, McGurn was standing in front of his store entrance, conspicuous in his white apron. Will Gault was in front of the stage office. Other persons stood near openings into which they might beat hasty retreats. No one spoke or even nodded his head.

Ahead of the slowly moving men a hurried whisper had gone from mouth to mouth, "Si Proctor's huntin' Bill Patrick." With incredible speed it passed from man to man until the whole street was alive with the whisper: "Si Proctor's huntin' Bill Patrick."

Men seemed to be turned to stone almost, so motionless they stood as they gazed at Si and the two men walking along the sidewalk and the two others in the street. Si was abreast of the postoffice now; not more than 200 feet away on the corner stood the Miners Rest. There was utter silence. Not a single man was standing within a hundred feet of the entrance of the saloon. On the opposite side of the street there was also a bare stretch of sidewalk.

As he passed the postoffice, Si saw the bullet-hole in the side of the building that marked the spot where Jim Douglas had been killed on the Fourth of July. He saw that McGurn had apples piled invitingly in his store window, and involuntarily he thought he'd like to eat one. It was strange how his mind wandered to other things, to Jim Langford, for whom he had swamped on the sixteen-animal team; to Shorty, over there in Eureka, recovering from his wound;

to the mine and his partner, Ralph Lee; to Mrs. Macklay and the school-teacher; to the Circle R ranch, where he had been a cowboy; to Texas, where he had been born; and then to his brother, Ike, lying there down the street in his coffin.

They had passed McGurn's now, and were opposite Gillig's hardware store. It was not more than a hundred feet from the street corner, and Si speculated as he walked whether Patrick would come out of the saloon, or around the corner. He wondered whether Patrick would come from the side of the street that the Miners Rest was on, whether he would try a surprise attack from the other side, or whether he would come at all. "If he don't," Si thought grimly, "I'll walk into his saloon and march right up them stairs to where he lives, if necessary, to get him; but I'll get him."

His gun rested loosely in the holster, his hand barely touching it, ready in the twinkling of an eye to draw and fire. Suddenly he halted; his right hand with lightning-like rapidity drew his six-shooter. From behind the wall of the Miners Rest a man had emerged swiftly, gun in hand. He stopped and raised his gun. Si fired, apparently without aim, with crooked arm held half-way between waist and chest. The man staggered, his gun exploding harmlessly as he fell.

With six-shooter in hand, Si waited to see if there was to be any hostile demonstration. For a moment there was utter silence, then pandemonium broke loose. Cheers, questions, hysteric laughter, all mingled in a jumble, as the townspeople rushed forward, those who knew Si to congratulate him, others to pick up the body of Bill Patrick and carry it to the sidewalk.

Ralph Lee was the first man to reach Si. Making no concealment of his delight, he threw his arms around Si's shoulders and hugged him enthusiastically. John Macklay, a trifle more sedate, grasped Si's hand and wrung it hard. Sim, coming up on the run, stopped momentarily to slap Si on the back and say, "I knowed you'd do it, Si!" and moved on rapidly to where Patrick's body lay, while Sage and others in turn offered their congratulations.

At the firing of the shots, Hank Bartle had rushed out of the Miners Rest and knelt beside Patrick. Hank was in tears. Looking up, he said, "He was my friend, Sim, I've followed him for years. I'll see he is buried. He told me this morning that if he cashed in I could put on his tombstone, 'Here lies William Patrick—A Square Sport.'"

Sim knelt down beside Bartle, and after a momentary examination rose and held up his hand for silence. "Bill Patrick is dead," Sim said. "Hank Bartle is going to take care of the remains. Si Proctor is my prisoner, and I turn him loose without bail. There'll be a coroner's inquest here this afternoon, after Si's brother, Ike, is buried, and I reckon the jury will just naturally bring in a verdict 'death from some unknown cause' or 'justifiable homicide.' The coroner's goin' to call some of you fellers on that jury, and I reckon you know what the verdict is goin' to be," and he grinned at the assembled crowd. In reply they cheered for both Sim and Si and grinned their approval.

"Reckon I'll be goin' back down the street for a spell now," said Si to Mr. Macklay."

"No, Si, you're not going down the street," said Macklay. "You're coming with me up to the house. You're going to rest and talk with the women folks. It's their job now."

"Why, thank you, Mr. Macklay, I reckon that would be a

good idea," Si said gratefully. "I'd just sort of like to sit down with Mrs. Macklay and you and the schoolma'am and kind of talk about the mine. My work's done here. Reckon there ain't no use broodin' over what's happened. We got a sight of work ahead of us yet. There's goin' to be a big mining camp over there at Peterson—that's what we've named it. They're goin' in by the hundreds, staking out ground, putting up buildings. Before long it'll be as big a town as Sulphide. And we'll all be right in the middle of it—all except Ike."

He turned and, walking between Mr. Macklay and Ralph Lee, passed on along the street and up the hill.

Glossary of Mining Terms

Grubstake: In a "grubstake" the prospector puts in his time against a stipulated amount of grub for a given time and an interest. The law of the grubstake is well defined.

Sump: The shaft below the lowest level; used as a reservoir to hold mine water before it is pumped to the surface.

Ore Shoot: That part of a ledge or vein that carries pay values. These shoots are of irregular size and shape, often very erratic in occurrence. A vein is by no means all pay ore; much of it may be barren quartz carrying only a few cents a ton in precious metals.

Crosscut: A tunnel across the formation. Run to cut the vein as a rule.

Stope: The opening made in extracting the ore along the vein extending upward from one level to the next.

Winze: Small shaft sunk to connect levels or to prospect ahead, sometimes used for ventilation.

Comstock Lode: The greatest gold and silver camp in Nevada. Total recorded production about $420,000,000.

Moil: A kind of chisel or gad used in cutting or chipping rock.

Mucking: Shovelling and pushing cars underground.

Grizzly: Iron bars set three inches more or less apart, over which the ore is screened.

Extra-lateral rights: The right to follow a vein in its downward course beyond the side-lines of the claim.

Cage: The elevator used for hoisting and lowering men, supplies and rock.

Glossary of Mining Terms

Grubstake: In a "grubstake" the prospector puts in his time against a stipulated amount of grub for a given time and an interest. The law of the grubstake is well defined.
Sump: The shaft below the lowest level, used as a reservoir to hold mine water before it is pumped to the surface.
Ore Shoot: That part of a ledge or vein that carries pay values. These shoots are of irregular size and shape, often very erratic in occurrence. A vein is by no means all ore; much of it may be barren quartz carrying only a few cents a ton in precious metals.
Crosscut: A tunnel across the formation. Run to cut the vein as a rule.
Stope: The opening made in extracting the ore along the vein extending upward from one level to the next.
Winze: Small shaft sunk to connect levels or to prospect [illegible] workings used for ventilation.
Comstock Lode: The greatest gold and silver camp in Nevada. Total recorded production about $400,000,000.
Muck: A kind of [illegible] used in cutting or chipping rock.
Mucking: Shoveling and pushing cars underground.
Grizzly: Iron bars set three inches more or less apart over which the ore is screened.
Extralateral Rights: The right to follow a vein in its downward course beyond the side lines of the claim.
Cage: The elevator used for hoisting and lowering men, supplies and rock.